Also by Piers Anthony
and Robert E. Margroff
published by Tor Books

Dragon's Gold
The E.S.P. Worm
The Ring

PIERS ANTHONY AND ROBERT E. MARGROFF

SERPENT'S SILVER

A TOM DOHERTY ASSOCIATES BOOK
NEW YORK

This is a work of fiction. All the characters and events portrayed in this book are fictitious, and any resemblance to real people or events is purely coincidental.

SERPENT'S SILVER

A TOR BOOK
Published by Tom Doherty Associates, Inc.
49 West 24 Street
New York, NY 10010

Library of Congress Cataloging-in-Publication Data

Anthony, Piers.
Serpent's silver / Piers Anthony and Robert E. Margroff.—1st
 ed.
 p.   cm.
 ISBN 0-312-93103-4 : $17.95
 I. Margroff, Robert E., II. Title.
PS3551.N73S47 1988
813'.54—dc19   88-29163
                                                          CIP

First edition: December 1988
0 9 8 7 6 5 4 3 2 1

Contents

Prologue

HELN KNIGHT HACKLEBERRY LAY back against the pillows. Her brown eyes were closed, and her bosom heaved shallowly. Her shiny black hair framed her lovely oval face. She was as beautiful as she had been on their wedding day, seven months ago, Kelvin thought.

He lay beside her, squeezing her calloused yet very feminine hand. They were on their new bed in their new home, but they were not alone, and this was no pleasant interlude.

He glanced up at his sister, Jon, who was unusually silent. Then his gaze passed Jon's normally smiling husband, Lester, who was quite serious now. He wished again that he hadn't let them talk him into this.

She has to! It's your father and your brother! Jon had insisted. *They've been missing four months!* When had Kelvin Knight Hackleberry ever been able to argue his manly little

1

sister out of anything? She was correct, of course, but that did not make him feel any more comfortable at the moment.

Heln's hand was growing cold now, as if she were dying. Oh, it was so like death, this astral traveling—death from poisoning. Indeed, dragonberries did kill pointears; only roundears like Heln could survive them, suffering just the partial death of soul-separation. They were never sure of the safe limit, and he hated the risk. If she died, he would go with her into death, he thought, if that was the only way to be with her always.

His hand tightened on hers, but she did not stir. It was fortunate that he could experience some of her thoughts and share her experiences, he thought, while she was in this state. He could even communicate with her while her spirit traveled, freed by the magic that had once been the secret of the golden dragons. So he knew she wasn't really dead—not as long as her mind touched his.

Now he started receiving her thoughts. "I'm back at the underground river now," Kelvin said for her. He had become like a thing his father had once told him about: a radio receiver. He tuned in on the words and repeated them without conscious volition. In this manner she shared her experience with those standing by her body.

Kelvin became aware of her sensations: the cold cave walls drifting by, the passages twisting, splitting, merging. The dim glow of lichen on the walls, somehow distinguishable from the lamplight in the room the four of them occupied. Images in her mind and his, overlapping yet distinct. He remembered another device his father had talked about: the receiver of words and pictures known as television. Perhaps he was becoming like that, too. But he could not show the pictures to the others.

"The Flaw! The Flaw! I see it now!" He was speaking for her, but he saw it, too: the water falling, falling into a darkness filled with stars.

He willed her away from that dread void, thrilling to its menace. "The other room! The other room!" he cried.

Then she was taking him, through her awareness and his, through the round, solid door. Perfectly round: rounder than round ears! They floated into the metallic chamber that only roundears such as the two of them could enter without causing its destruction. That was what the parchment there claimed; they had read it only partially during her prior visit here, but he believed it.

They hovered together above an open book on a table, and a box the size of a closet. The walls of the box were lined with dials and what appeared to be clocks. Kelvin recognized the sort of instruments his father had talked about: they were gauges and controls that somehow ordered things to be done.

"He left here," Kelvin/Heln said. "Into the other frame. He stepped in here to follow the path of your father. It will still work for us. We can cross the astral bridge through Mouvar's magic. To where Kian and your father are."

For Kian was Kelvin's half brother. They had been on opposite sides, and had fought. Though they were friends now, Kian's guilt had led him to go on the risky tour through the dread Flaw, searching for his lost parents. He had not returned.

Heln and Kelvin entered the box. The vision became a blackness so deep it shimmered. There was something like a crash of soundless thunder; then a streak of fire that split their existence. Stars appeared, shining all around and through and into them. Existence whirled, collapsed, and expanded. Time and place ceased to have meaning. Then they were . . .

Moved. Into a hazy chamber closet like the one they had entered. The closet wall with its clocks reappeared, forming out of the confusion. The image needed tuning; it seemed to be far away. But even as Kelvin thought of that, the sights and sounds and smells of the new location came into clear focus. They had arrived—where?

Two sets of footprints crossed from the closet to a rock wall, where a large round metal door stood ajar. It might have been the same door they had just entered—but that one was closed. The footprints might have been their own—but they were going in the opposite direction, and in any event, Kelvin and Heln were not here physically. So these could be John Knight's and Kian's prints.

They began moving, bodiless but with direction. Kelvin smelled grass, and heard the songs for birds and the tinkling of what might be metallic chimes. This was an intelligible world, then.

They paused, Heln sensing the way. There was a metal rope ladder anchored to a solid ring in the cliffside. The ladder descended into a large tree that seemed similar to the beenut tree where Kelvin had found his magic gauntlet. That was a good sign! They swooped down to the roots of the tree and along the ground.

Heln in her astral state seemed to be drawn to a location or person of her choice. In this she was like the magnetic compass his father had described—or the magic needle that pointed always to The Flaw.

As Heln followed the pull of the brother Kelvin had first met on a battlefield and tried to kill nine months before, he looked around to the extent this form allowed. He saw or sensed displayed in a tall oaple tree the source of the chiming. Three silver spirals hung from a branch and produced the sound when the breeze twirled them. They looked like snakeskins, he thought uneasily: silver serpent hides that were stiff and dry yet also shiny and bright.

Now they were traveling across a wide valley, mountains, and rolling farmland similar to that of Rud. On and on interminably—but then swooping abruptly, hawk-fashion, to a palace on a river bluff. They entered the palace and drifted through spectacular halls filled with art objects, some of which seemed familiar. On down carpeted hallways, polished corridors, and banistered stairs. To—

A dank, dark, foul-smelling place that seemed made for fear. Kelvin jerked with shock.

"What is it, Kel?" his sister asked, hovering over his body. He had stopped talking, alarming her.

"Dungeon," he said. Indeed it was, exactly such a dungeon as Kian's mother, the evil Queen Zoanna, had used to confine Kelvin and his father and Rufurt, the good king of Rud.

Now he could see in the dim light that came through the high barred windows. There was his father, John Knight, haggard and dirty. There was his brother, Kian, in no better shape. And a third man, battered, blood-spattered, lying on the floor, propping his head with his arm, evidently too weak from loss of blood to do more.

Standing between them and a barred door was a wide man wearing a silver crown. Kelvin focused on the man's face.

"Rufurt!" Kelvin whispered.

But no, this Rufurt had round ears, as did the prisoners, while their Rud counterparts had ears as pointed as Jon's and Lester's. The Rud king's face, even after years of imprisonment, had a jovial appearance around the jowls that nothing could quite erase. This nearly identical face was taut and grim by comparison.

Yet a part of his mind shrieked: *It's Rufurt!*

At the king's gesture a man in uniform unlocked the cell, entered, and bent over the wounded man. John Knight grabbed the bars, seeming about to speak. Undeterred, the torturer pushed the unfortunate man's head down on the floor and twisted it sideways. Then he brought out a silver tube, held it above the prisoner's ear, unstoppered it, and tilted it carefully. Something silvery oozed out and flowed, undulating, into the man's ear.

The guard paused only long enough to make sure the vial was empty. Then he let go of the prisoner and stepped quickly away. He got out of the cell as if afraid of something.

The prisoner pulled his face from the grime of the floor. His hand came up to touch his ear, as if it itched. It seemed that he was not sure why the guard had departed without beating him again. Or that he was afraid to think about it.

Then his look of perplexity darkened into something else. He clawed at his ear as if trying to wrench it out of his head.

His eyeballs rolled back until only the whites showed. He screamed. It was a horrible sound, signifying something infinitely worse than pain.

The king made a ghastly smile that was all the more horrible for being on King Rufurt's face. "Silver's not so nice, now, is it, Smith? Now that the little beastie's chewing in you?"

Little beastie? Kelvin hoped he misunderstood.

The man shook all over, from head to foot. His eyes stared wildly, seeming ready to pop out of his face. His arms and legs spasmed. He screamed again, as if trying to vomit out his tongue, while the other prisoners looked on with drawn faces. The screaming continued, diminished, because the man could not take enough of a breath to make it loud.

"We must go back. We are going back," Heln said with Kelvin's mouth. With that the dungeon faded and slipped sideways. They were pulled, as though by elastic, back to the chamber, into the closet, through darkness and stars. It happened so swiftly as to be instant; their minds seemed to shatter.

Then they were home. They were on their bed in their room, with their closest friends looking down at them. Where their bodies had been all along.

Kelvin sat up, turning to his wife. That horror—

Heln's eyelids flickered. Her big, soft brown eyes opened to stare into his blue ones.

"Oh, Kelvin, we must help them! We must!"

"But—" He thought desperately, an enormous fear threatening to swallow what passed for his courage. "I have things to do here. There's the prophecy."

"And you will fulfill it, dear, you will. But you are a hero and a roundear. Only a roundear can journey to the chamber as Kian did. Only a roundear can make the trip we just did."

"You can't go," he said, being firm. Immediately he knew in his most cowardly secret self that he had misspoken. He should have said "we," including himself as well as her.

"Oh, Kelvin, you're so brave! I knew you'd want to go to

that other world and rescue your father and your brother! I knew you just couldn't do anything else!"

Yes, he thought glumly. Yes—but what had he done to deserve this hero mantle? He had never wanted to be a hero. Jon had wanted to and he had not. Now, because he had lucked out on one step of a prophecy, they thought he couldn't fail at anything.

"Don't worry, we'll take good care of her," Lester said, his boyish smile broadening.

Kelvin knew that Lester and his sister would do that. He had no decent excuse to get out of another mission of foolish attempted heroism. He wished that he had never agreed to let Heln take that astral trip.

Yet that prisoner, with the appalling silver beastie in his ear—was that the fate awaiting John Knight and Kian, if someone didn't get them out of the dungeon? Kelvin was sickly certain that it was, and that he was the only one who could do anything about it. He was a coward, but he had to act.

CHAPTER 1

Sacrifice

KIAN REACHED THE BOTTOM rung of the metallic rope ladder and looked down. From the chamber entrance the ladder had appeared to disappear into the top of a very large beenut tree. It still did. The rope was of a material different from any he had seen before, and it seemed to grow out of the trunk where the spreading branches formed the crown.

Well, he had been a tree climber as a boy. He was twenty-one now, and it had been some time since he had practiced, but he remembered. What fun it had been, peering in the windows of the palace from his secret perch and watching the comings and goings of the sycophants and courtiers!

This was a different world—but perhaps not too different, he thought as he clambered easily down the close-set branches of the beenut tree. The vegetation of this frame seemed exactly like that of his own. His half brother had climbed a similar tree in the park in Franklin and discovered a gauntlet with remarkable properties. Kian now wore an identical pair.

The armored gloves made climbing easier, but he could hardly say how. Well, yes, he could: he found that he could easily hang on to a branch by just a couple of fingertips, feeling no strain. It was as though there were muscles in the gauntlets aiding every move his hands made. Because he was a roundear, he knew, they worked just as well for him as for Kelvin.

He let go of a branch and dropped the remaining distance to the base of the tree. Catching his breath, he looked up but could not see the ladder or the cliff face with its open metal door. The secret was well hidden; he realized that he should mark the spot well in his mind, in case he ever wished to return to his own world.

The birds sang just as they did at home. There was no difference, so far, in anything. He found himself surprised, even though he knew this was the nature of the frame worlds. His grandfather Zatanas had tried instructing him on the nature of reality and what he called the magic art: worlds might differ, but not the fundamentals of nature and magic.

More recently Kian had read the parchment book he had found in the chamber before taking the gauntlets and the alien weapon, and launching his own adventure. Each overlapping world, he had learned, was almost like the ones touching it, but with small, subtle differences. "You may even meet yourself, or someone like yourself," Lester Crumb had said.

Kian shook his head. That didn't seem unreasonable for others, but he knew that his father would not be duplicated here. John Knight, after all, had come from a distant frame where they called the world "Earth." He had never figured out quite how his father had crossed over; it seemed to have involved war magic of a sort not understood in Rud. But John Knight was unique—and therefore so were his sons.

Kian had gone only a short distance along the stream,

admiring its blue water and leaping fish, when another sound reached him: a tinkling, musical note.

He paused, trying to locate the source. It seemed to come from a large oaple. He walked that way, staring hard into the branches where three long silver belts or spirals hung and twisted in the river breeze. Twirling, they touched each other to produce the sounds.

When he reached the tree he discovered that the belts were indeed spirals. Each had the apparent fragility of snakeskin, but was metallic except for an underlay of leather. They were silver, too: real silver, in a pattern like that of overlapping scales. He removed a gauntlet, fitted a thumbnail under a scale, and tried to pull the scale loose. It remained fast: the organic and inorganic were seemingly one.

Kian considered. Could he still find the large beenut tree and the ladder? Yes, he had marked the fact of the river making a sharp bend, and certainly such a large tree—one big enough to laugh at floods, if trees could laugh—was readily found. The chimes, whatever they were, might be to mark the upcoming bend.

He tested the scale of one of the skins with the point of his knife. It came away silver. Silver like that had to be very pure!

Could snakes here have scales of silver, in the same way that dragons back home had scales of gold? No, that hardly made sense. Dragons were virtually immortal beasts with powerful gizzards. The gizzards ground up weighty stones that the dragons swallowed in the course of centuries to pulverize their food internally. The food was rough, because dragons hardly chewed anything that no longer struggled, and even those big stones got worn away. They contained gold, and that gold migrated in due course to the brightly shining scales. Thus the gizzard was the key to the dragon's gold. But snakes—who could imagine them with gizzards? They swallowed their prey whole and let their digestive juices handle it. No stones in them!

He went on. When he judged it was noonday, he stopped to

rest and eat the lunch Jon had packed for him. "Don't tell Les," she had whispered. "He complains that I'm not feeding him well. I don't want him to grow a paunch like his father's! He just might be jealous." Kian had smiled and teased her in the manner Kelvin was always doing. She was easy to tease and to be with—this boyish, pretty girl whose ears were pointed, though she was Kelvin's sister.

Thought of his ears caused him to pull down the light-weight stockelcap. He wore it for concealment. Only a fool would choose to wear such a thing on such a warm day! Yet he might meet someone, and if this frame was not totally unlike home, his round ears would set him apart. Pointed ears had always been considered natural, and round years unnatural. Best that he wear the cap despite the discomfort.

He checked himself with the little mirror Heln had slipped into his travelsack, first adjusting the stockelcap, then smoothing his light blond mustache. It was essential to pay attention to appearances regardless of what frame he was in! He knew, and had known since near infancy, that he had a striking figure and a reasonably handsome face. There had been a time when that was important to him, and perhaps someday such a time would come again.

He resumed his journey along the road. At home this path would have taken him through the mountainous region near Franklin. Not far from dragon country. He smiled. Well, he wasn't about to venture into dragon country, if that existed here! Unless, of course, his father and mother existed in this world, in such a region.

Soon he would have to swallow one of the dragonberries in his pack and see if they worked. Not even Heln knew about these. If the berry made him sick, as it did most people, he would take no more. But roundears could eat them and not be poisoned, not fatally, anyway. The berries enabled Heln to take flight astrally, her spirit homing in on some distant person or place while her body slept. Because she was a roundear—and Kian was a roundear, too. He, his half brother, Kelvin, their father, and Heln were the only folk he had ever encountered with ears of this unnatural shape. What an advantage, if the berries worked for him!

The road forked. Impulsively he followed the side branch into the mountains. He felt more comfortable this way, though he could not have said why; after all, at home it would have taken him into the domain of the dangerous wild things. Maybe he was just trying to be an adventurer, as his father was: someone who would choose the wild way.

A deoose crossed his path soon after lunch, and a bit later a fleet-footed meer bounced out of the bushes and then across the path in sprightly leaps. Red moss was on every tree; it was really still much like home. Possibly there were dangers similar to those in his own frame. At this stage he preferred familiar dangers!

As if in response to his thought, a bearver reared up from some appleberry bushes and greeted him with a loud woof. Then, perceiving that he stood his ground, it came out on the road and began a stalking advance.

Kian started to draw his sword, which was a properly polished blade his mother had chosen. But bearvers were large and unreasoning beasts, dangerous at all times. He knew he might be able to kill it, but he also knew that the chance of that was slight. One swipe from that huge paw could disarm him, gauntlets or no, and then—why hadn't he fled the moment he saw the predator?

Even as he foolishly drew the blade, another thought occurred. What about the alien weapon he carried? That might scare the beast so that it would think better of charging him. No known opposition could cow a bearver, but the unknown might.

Kian drew the weapon from its soft, curved alien scabbard. He pointed it, letting the gauntlet on his hand control his action. Then he tried to tell the glove to aim ahead of the beast, rather than trying to destroy it. This was partly because if the weapon were only partially effective, the effort would enrage the beast, making things worse, and partly because he preferred merely to scare it away if he could, and partly to see whether he had this kind of control over the gauntlets. He was in trouble, granted, but if he got out of this he might learn something that would help him the next time.

He—or the gauntlet—aimed the weapon. His—or its—finger squeezed. From the bell-shaped muzzle there came a series of sparks and a low hissing. The bearver gave a bark and charged.

Kian didn't have time to consider. The gauntlet straightened the weapon, this time taking dead aim, and pressed the trigger. And again the result was a few sparks and hissing. There was no evident damage to the bearver.

What was this, a toy?

Disgusted and now thoroughly scared, Kian dropped the weapon and leveled the sword. But the bearver, unpredictable as always, now swerved in its charge. Kicking its big heels back in a frolicsome manner, it made an ungainly leap over to the side of the road and plowed into the fringing bushes. It paused to look back, seeming almost to grin; then it woofed comically and disappeared.

"Bearvers will be bearvers," Kian remarked, weak with relief. It was a common saying at home. A bearver might decide to eat a person, or it might simply amuse itself by scaring a victim into loosening his bowels. He was thankful that his bowels had only twitched as the monster charged, and that his pantaloons were not in need of washing. He had escaped both death and shame, this time.

Now the road was descending into a valley, a lush region that should have held farms. There was nothing of the sort. In another oaple tree hung another of the spiral chimes. Parchment-thin yet curled into stiffness.

He stared at the silver and listened to its tinkle while he ate a few appleberries. A chill ran up and down his back; he had a feeling that something was wrong. Through the mists far below in the valley, among rocks that had rolled down over the centuries, he could see a movement. People—maybe a crowd. From this distance they seemed short and broad, reminding him of Queeto, his grandfather's dwarf apprentice. In the midst of the crowd, a little to the front and grasped by either hand, was a taller, slimmer person. It was hard for Kian to see, but this could be a woman or a girl of normal stature.

He strained his eyes, wishing that he could make things out better. The dwarfs gathered with the prisoner—for so she seemed—at a spot between two upright rocks the size of horses. Two of the dwarfs did something that produced a flash of silver. Then all the small people withdrew, leaving the woman or girl apparently shackled between the two stones. The small ones disappeared the way they had come.

What was this—a human sacrifice? It had that aspect! Was the woman a criminal? The dwarfs magical creatures? Just what had he come upon? It was probably a bad idea to interfere—but for all he knew, the woman could be his mother. Surely not—yet how could he be certain?

Half running, wishing he had a horse, he descended the slope in as fast a fashion as he could manage. He did not know how long the woman would be there, or what sort of danger he might face. He just had to *know,* lest he forever regret it.

When he broke through the bushes and faced her at close range, he was startled by her beauty. Her slim arms were stretched on either side, tethered by chains of silver. She had long blond hair, and deep blue eyes, and a figure that—

"Leave! Oh, leave!" she begged. He had no difficulty understanding her, because she used the language of home. Her head bobbed in the direction of a perfectly round hole in the side of the cliff. "Before it comes! Before it slithers out and devours us! Please!"

"You need help," he said, drawing his sword. Her lips were lying to him, he thought, while her eyes were speaking truth. She did not want him leaving her to some terrible fate.

"No! No! It will come soon! The appointed one! The one that always comes!"

"You're intended as a sacrifice?" He went closer, sword in hand.

She tossed her head, her hair flipping from her left ear and exposing it for the first time. Now he understood: *she was round-eared!* Round, not pointed! As it was back home, so it must be here! Roundears either hated for being different or at best barely tolerated.

"It's coming!" she cried. "I hear it!"

Indeed, there was a strange slithery sound coming from that hole. The whisper of it sent the hairs on the back of his neck tingling.

"I'm not afraid of it, whatever it is," he lied. This was surely worse than what he had faced before! And what was it, anyway? A burrower the size of a bearver? A tunneler through solid rock? Whatever it was, the size of that hole made him shudder. He fixed his eyes on the dread aperture and waited, knowing that whatever appeared was not going to run or tease.

So suddenly as to be startling, a large silvery snout thrust from the hole, just in time to catch a ray of sunshine that lighted the cliff's face. Then a flat silvery head emerged, followed by a long, long, undulating silver body. It was a serpent as large around as a war-horse!

A serpent covered all over with silver scales—surely real silver! Just as at home a dragon's scales were real gold. This serpent must be the overgrown version of the snakes from which the silver skins had come. It was as large as the legendary anaconda John Knight had told about. Kian had thought that to be a mere story. Some story! This thing could swallow a man and his war-horse together!

Kian doubted it could help, but he reached for the alien weapon he carried. His hand slapped only the holster; the weapon itself was gone! He had neglected to pick it up after his encounter with the bearver. The weapon, worthless though it might be, was back there on the road.

"Run! Run!" The girl was shaking with terror, and whimpering, but still she tried to warn him away.

Not a chance! His legs wouldn't work for him now. His gauntlets and his sword had to work together to save them. With the gauntlets, he had to believe, there was at least a chance of accomplishing something.

The serpent emerged sinuously all the way from the hole, lifted its head, and reared back. The eyes swayed above his own. A long, drawn-out hiss like that of a salivating dragon came from the mouth. Then that dread mouth opened, revealing dagger-length crystalline fangs. Drops of clear liquid fell to the ground, spattering and hissing and emitting little puffs of steam. Where the drops struck grass, the grass writhed, turned black, and crumbled into ash.

What a beast! What a monster! At least as formidable as the dragons! Wait till Kelvin heard about this—if Kelvin ever did hear about it. If Kian survived to tell him! If!

The beady black eyes looked into his. They held him as the body writhed behind the head, getting into better position for attack. The head and fangs moved closer. The body coiled around under that elevated head as if independent of it, the tail section undulating in unnerving fashion.

Kian found himself staring into bottomless pits. Beady eyes? Now they were windows into some kind of hell! He saw, peripherally, the open nostrils and the bright spots reflecting from the flashing scales. He felt overwhelmed!

He shook his head, trying to clear it. This was magic! The magic a snake used to immobilize its prey. All the prey had to do was break that gaze and flee, and the snake would not be able to catch it, but somehow that seldom happened. Now Kian understood why. He *couldn't* break the gaze!

The snout darted suddenly, along with the long, flat, enormous head. The mouth opened wide, the fangs dripping their corrosive poison. The girl screamed.

He tried to snap out of it. He tried to raise the sword. The gauntlets, unaffected by the serpent's spell, raised his unresisting arms and his sword-hand for him.

The left gauntlet grasped the lower jaw of the serpent. The right gauntlet swung the sword hard at the serpent's eye. The blade rebounded from silver scales, leaving a barely detectable groove. His arm felt the jolt, and pain lanced through his shoulder.

The serpent's head went back again. It was not hurt, but now it seemed more cautious. Perhaps it distrusted anything that resisted the power of its mesmeric gaze.

His brother, Kelvin, had slain dragons by driving a sharpened pole and a heavy lance through their eyes and into their tiny brains. This serpent's eyes were smaller than a dragon's and no easy target, despite their hypnotic power. He had no lance, no pole. His sword was worthless against any part of the serpent except the eyes, and he couldn't get a clear shot at them!

Now something else happened. His left hand, within the gauntlet, began suddenly and severely to hurt. It was as if he had thrust his armored hand into a fire! His hand—and the gauntlet—were being injured by the serpent's venom!

The left gauntlet dropped from his hand and landed on the grass. His hand continued to hurt, still burning. His right hand still held the sword—but what could he do with it? The angle was wrong; he could not get at that eye with a side slash, and he could not orient properly for a stab with the point.

Hissing the hiss of a thousand lesser serpents, the monster bared his fangs again and prepared for the final strike.

As if in a dream, Kian heard the drumming of a war-horse's hooves. He heard a voice, a man's, screaming something that sounded like: "Back! Back! Into your hole, you worm!"

He would gladly retreat, if he only could!

A whistling sound filled his ears, and that, too, was coming from outside the range of his trapped vision. His eyes remained locked by the serpent's; only his ears were free.

Belatedly he realized that it was to the serpent the man was yelling, not to Kian.

Help of some sort had arrived. But was it soon enough, or strong enough? Could it break the spell that held him, and give him even a slight chance to survive?

CHAPTER 2
In-law

THERE WAS AN ABRUPT knock on the cottage door. Heln gave Kelvin a startled look, then put down the dough for the exotic dish she was making: an appleberry pie whose recipe had been in both their families. "Who?"

Kelvin shrugged. He was putting things together in a travelsack for the journey he didn't want to make. Yet it was expected of him, and he did feel obliged to rescue his father and half brother. It wasn't as though he wouldn't have the laser and the gauntlets that had saved his life numerous times. Kian should have taken the laser, the only operating laser in the Seven Kingdoms. Instead Kian had chosen the unfamiliar and alien weapon found in the hidden chamber. Possibly he had also taken along the levitation belt the chamber still held. But Kian had almost been killed while using a flying device from his father's world. Of course, that was partly because Jon had felled him with a stone from her sling. Still, it showed the hazards of flight! So if the term "levitation" meant what they thought it meant, neither he nor Kian wanted any part of it.

"I expect Jon to come over," Kelvin said as Heln wiped off her hands and started for the door. "She and Lester won't let me start out alone, or with just you and my horse." He added to himself: *But I wish all of you could come along. All of you all the way to wherever Kian and our father and our terrible former queen have gone.* Because all of them had more actual courage than he did, though no one ever spoke that truth openly. Especially Jon, whose nature at times seemed more like that of a big brother than a little sister. That had changed substantially when she got together with Lester. Still—

Heln made a face at him for joining wife and horse in the same breath, though in truth the two were of similar value in many Rud families. She often made faces like that, and despite her worst effort she remained as pretty as ever. Tongue out in a mock spell of insult, she went to the door and heaved at the heavy latch. It released with unaccustomed ease and the door jerked open—leaving her making a face at the visitor.

"Heln Hackleberry?"

She jammed her tongue back in her mouth and put her face straight, too late. She would have blushed, but instead she paled. The stranger at the door was a formidable sight.

He was a big, rawboned man with a stockelcap pulled down around his ears despite the heat of the summer day. He was approximately Hal Hackleberry's age, with a big ugly nose and black beard, dirty clothing, and a travelsack on his back. He wore a formidable sword.

"Yes, I'm Heln Hackleberry," she said, stepping back. Kelvin, fearful of robbery or worse, positioned himself for a quick rising and charge. "Mrs. Hackleberry."

"You won't recognize me," the stranger said with considerable understatement. "You never laid eyes on me before. Adult eyes, that is."

Heln frowned. Kelvin held his position. This didn't sound like robbery, but . . .

Abruptly the man reached up and pulled off his stockelcap. His ears popped into view. They were large and red—and round. As unpointed as her own and Kelvin's.

"I'm Sean Reilly, nicknamed St. Helens," he said.

"St. Helens!" she gasped. "You—"

"Right, girl. I'm your father." His dark eyes swept past her to Kelvin. "And you be the Roundear of Prophecy, son?"

Kelvin and Heln looked at each other. Kelvin felt as though the floor had vanished.

"A Roundear there Shall Surely be," the man said. "Born to be Strong, Raised to be Free."

"Fighting Dragons in his Youth," Heln continued faintly. "Leading Armies, Nothing Loth."

"Ridding his Country of a Sore," the man said, reciting the prophecy of Mouvar. "Joining Two, then uniting Four." He looked directly at Kelvin.

"Until from Seven there be one," Kelvin said reluctantly. He had been thrilled by the prophecy as a child when his mother had told him about it, but as an adult, he had been wary of it. "Only then will his Task be Done."

"Honored by Many, cursed by Few," the man concluded. "All will know what Roundear can Do."

Kelvin experienced the old embarrassment. "I've heard it all my life, but I'm not sure that it applies."

"Hmpth. I'm not sure either, son. But you did slay dragons in your recent youth, and you did, to your great credit, rid Rud of the sore that was her queen."

He had indeed—but the accomplishment had been far less heroic than the prophecy made it seem. Kelvin was afraid that any further testing of the prophecy would get him killed. So he changed the subject. "You're really Heln's father?"

"You doubt my word?" the man demanded gruffly.

"I don't know you," Kelvin said with some asperity. Ordinarily he would not speak this way to such a formidable stranger, but the man's attitude and round ears had shaken him. "How can I know whether your word is good?"

"Maybe I should go elsewhere!"

"No, no, come inside," Heln said quickly.

Kelvin could hardly protest. If Heln believed in this man, there must be something to it. Certainly there were few roundears in Rud!

St. Helens entered, and Heln closed the door. He looked around the cottage, as if evaluating it.

Now Kelvin began to see certain trace similarities between St. Helens and Heln. Nothing tangible, just hints in the lines of the face and the manner of gesture. This, he fought to realize, really was Heln's father: the last male survivor of John Knight's twelve-man squad from unlikely round-eared Earth.

"I've come from the kingdom of Aratex," the man said. "I've come to visit my daughter and my famous son-in-law. But I've come for a purpose."

"You have?" Certainly it was easier to accept this formidable man than to doubt him. St. Helens and Mor Crumb were about the same size, Kelvin decided, though Mor's girth was greater and St. Helens seemed all chest and muscular arms. There was a wildness about this giant's appearance and manner that reminded Kelvin too much of men he had only pretended to command in the war.

"I'm here to lend you my age and experience. 'Joining Two' might as well mean Aratex and Rud. You agree?"

"It might," Kelvin agreed. But it might also mean any one of the other kingdoms. Or, as was the way with prophecy, the words might mean something else entirely. He had speculated once that they might refer to his marriage with Heln, or the marriage of his sister to his friend Lester.

"Things are right in Aratex. The dissatisfaction is great. Together we can do it, son."

"You mean annex Aratex?" Kelvin asked numbly.

"Annex is a good word. So is invade."

Kelvin shivered. The thought of going to war again, of risking everything he had so narrowly gained, and in an unnecessary war at that, was just more than he cared to contemplate. He feared that his face gave him away.

"You know about Blastmore, of course?" St. Helens inquired. "Rotten excuse for a king. Good chess player, but otherwise rotten. In his way he's as bad or worse than your former queen."

"I, uh, heard reports," Kelvin agreed. "He has a witch to keep people in line."

"Old Melbah. Ghastly hag! She goes up to Conjurer's Rock, waves her fingers and shouts gibberish, and everybody faints. People there are real cowed—afraid to do anything on their own. With help, well, that's a different matter."

"I've heard she controls the elements through magic. Wind, water, fire, and earth. That she can make the wind blow, the water rise, the fire burn, and the earth tremble."

"Superstitious nonsense!" St. Helens flared. "Are you really my commander's boy? John was a skeptic."

Kelvin found it difficult not to flinch. Indeed, his father had been a skeptic! John Knight had maintained that all magic was superstition. But that had changed after Zatanas the sorcerer had demonstrated his power. No one would have disbelieved, after seeing what Zatanas could do! But this attitude of St. Helens was exactly what was to be expected in a member of John Knight's crew, and went far to confirm the man's authenticity.

"I, uh, haven't made any plans to invade Aratex," Kelvin said after a moment. "I have something else to do that may take time. My father and half brother are in another frame, and in trouble. I have to try to help them before—"

"Yes, yes, I reckon they'll come in handy. Is it true that the queen escaped?"

"I'm not sure. Kian thinks she's alive—or he did before he left. Heln couldn't find her astrally, so maybe she's dead."

"Or at least out of action. As far as this frame's concerned."

"I—suppose." Kelvin still wasn't comfortable with the

concept of multiple frames, though he certainly couldn't doubt them. The implications—

"Well, we'll just have to go together. You'll need my help, and later we'll make plans together for Aratex."

"Go? You mean with me?" Kelvin felt new alarm. "Into that other frame? That other existence? Only roundears can enter the chamber and make the trip."

"I know." St. Helens smiled and tweaked one of his own very prominent ears. "I've got the tickets on either side of my thick Irish head. Don't worry, you and I will do just fine."

CHAPTER 3
Outlaw

As the serpent twisted around in the direction of the disturbance, a rope with a large loop at its end sailed neatly over the wide, flat head. A gigantic black war-horse with a large dark-featured man in the saddle made an abrupt turn in front of Kian. The noose tightened, yanking the head to the side.

The serpent swayed but did not fall. It darted at the horse just as the rope reached its limit. Obviously the serpent found the noose no more than a nuisance—an irritation that would quickly be dealt with.

The man in black brought down a sword on the serpent's snout. The horse leaped with instinctive dread, barely escaping the dripping fangs. The two actions were beautifully coordinated, so that instead of sinking its fangs in flesh, the monster received a smart rap on the nose.

Kian felt the spell relax as the serpent's eyes pulled away

from him. He was standing there, wearing one of the magic gauntlets, holding his sword. Meanwhile, a total stranger was doing the fighting. This wouldn't do. Kian had to act while he had the chance.

The girl screamed again, apparently in fear for the horse and the heroic rider. But both were safe. The flank of the horse swept on by, and the great head struck the grass just in front of Kian.

Now the rider was circling a tree, the rope still attached to the serpent. The slack went out of the rope and the horse backed as the rider jumped down and ran on foot, charging the serpent with a long spear. It was no dragon lance, but it was a far more effective weapon than a sword in this instance.

Kian's right gauntlet dropped the sword, pulled his arm to the left gauntlet on the ground, and replaced it on his hand. The poison was still in it, and the pain resumed in his left fingers. Yet he knew he had to endure it. *Good gauntlet! Good gauntlet! Make me brave as Kelvin! Make me brave!*

Kian did not know what he could do, if anything. But he had to try. He ran to the side of the serpent, waving his sword and shouting something unintelligible even to himself. The notion of frightening the monster this way seemed ludicrous, but it was all he could think of. If he could distract it so that the other man could attack it more effectively—

Now the spear was flying through the air, right toward one of the serpent's eyes. It struck near the lid of the eye and bounced off. With a clatter it alighted almost at Kian's running feet.

The gauntlets acted. They had the spear by its shaft and his sword stuck in the ground before Kian had quite stopped.

A forked tongue darted from the great serpent's mouth. Then the head snapped upright. The rope that held it snapped like a thread. The head swiveled to orient on the dark stranger, who was retreating after casting his spear.

Galvanized by the gloves, Kian's arm moved. The spear flew upward. This time it struck true, right in the center of the serpent's dark eye. The razor-sharp point and balanced heft of the weapon had effect; the specially forged spearhead plunged deeply in. The serpent jerked all along the length of its body, and gyrated, moving its head violently, but the spear remained in place.

The gauntlets hauled Kian forward. With no wasted motion they reached for the moving silver wall. Then, to his complete surprise, they propelled him into a handspring that landed him on the monster itself! They prevented him from pitching off the rounded hill that was the serpent's back and tugged with astonishing insistence at his arms.

Kian found himself running along a slowly moving and abruptly sharply jerking surface. *He was riding the serpent!* The scales were slippery, and threatened to cause him to slide off at any moment, but he never slackened his pace. The gauntlets wouldn't let him! On and on, ascending the slope of the thrashing monster.

Now he was on the huge, tossing head! How had he gotten here? He was at a dizzying height, and slippery blood was spattered across the silver, making his footing even more treacherous. Indeed, he skidded, unable to handle the violence of the head's motions.

His feet went out from under him. But the gauntlets were straining to reach the spear's haft. The left glove, overriding the pain of his hand, grabbed the edge of the eye. The right glove captured the shaft of the spear.

The serpent vented a deafening hiss of anguish and threw back its head. The left gauntlet shifted its grip as Kian's body slid entirely off the snake's head. He found himself pulling on the spear with both hands, hanging in midair. But the spearhead was barbed; it would not come out without inflicting far worse damage than it had on entry. The serpent's head twisted, rotating sidewise—and the spear angled straight up. Still the gauntlets clung, and now the weight of Kian's body bore down on the spear and rocked it back and forth, so that it dug yet deeper into the socket.

Scarlet blood spurted, some of it onto him. But he could not let go. Acid drops flew from the bared fangs, hissing where they struck. One drop of it struck Kian's face on the left cheekbone. It burned like fire. Still he clung, unable to do anything else. Relentlessly the gauntlets forced the spear inward, rocking it, questing for the serpent's brain.

The head snapped about with such violence that even the blood-soaked gauntlets could no longer hold. Kian screamed as he was hurled through the air. The ground came up to smash him. He grabbed at it, and the gauntlets helped him. Pain seared him as he somersaulted and lit somehow on his feet.

A weaving silver hill nudged against him. Another shoved him out. He was still among the coils of the serpent! He scrambled awkwardly to his feet and ran away, heedless of direction, trying to get clear of the body of the serpent before he was crushed by it.

A loop of rope landed on him and tightened. Kian was hauled in a new direction, helplessly. In a moment he found himself up against the horse. The stranger was there, slapping something cold against his face.

The pain abated. Kian raised his left arm with its gauntlet, and the stranger put the medicine on its burn; instantly the brown spot disappeared, and so did the burning in Kian's hand.

Now at last he could orient on his surroundings. He saw by the scuff marks that the stranger had used the rope to haul him away from the thrashing serpent; he might otherwise have been crushed, as he had had no idea where he was going. He owed the stranger his health or his life!

"You are one brave warrior!" the man exclaimed. "First you scored on the eye after I missed; then you ran right up the thing's neck and drove it in for the finale! I never saw nerve like that!"

"I—" Kian said, trying to protest. It had hardly been bravery!

"But you got disoriented by the venom, so I lassoed you out. I knew you couldn't see well anymore. The stuff gets in your eyes and your brain, so that even when you win, you lose. That's a bad burn! But we got the salve on in time; you should be fine now."

"The gauntlets did it," Kian said. "I—I only followed where they led."

"Gauntlets! They're magic, aren't they? No wonder! Must have come from Mouvar."

"Mouvar? You've heard of him?"

"Hasn't everybody? Where've you been?" The stranger took his hand. "Not that it matters. The name's Jac. Smoothy Jac, they call me. Best skin thief in the Seven Kingdoms. And you?"

"Kian. I'm—a stranger." He was looking at the admitted outlaw's round ears. Round ears—could they be common here?

"Native to Hud? Or from one of the other six?"

"N-no." Rud at home; Hud here. Still seven kingdoms.

"You know the girl?"

He started to shake his head; the pain was not nearly as bad now, and the burning had become more of a freezing sensation. Then he realized that he did know her. Or almost did. Back home that face, that beautiful face, and the curvaceous form with the definitely jutting breasts had belonged to a girl his mother had wanted him to marry: Lenore Barley.

"You look as though you do."

"Eh, someone. Almost the same." But Lenore had pointed ears, he remembered, and this one's ears were as round as his or Kelvin's or John Knight's, if he still lived in this land, or the outlaw's. Truly, it seemed that round ears belonged here.

Then Jac surprised him. "Damned flopears," he said. "Sacrificing a slave girl any rich man would pay a fortune for!"

Oops! "You deal in slaves?"

"No! I *was* one! I deal only in releasing them. King Rowforth, cursed be his imperial name, is the reason there's still slavery. His wife, good woman that she be, would like to end it. But I suspect you know that as well as I."

"No, I didn't. I'm really a complete stranger." He managed

to sit upright on the grass, turning to watch the weaving coils of the dying serpent. He was still recovering from the horror just past, and adjusting to the newness of this situation.

"We wouldn't dare try to take the skin before sundown, and by that time the flopears will be here," Jac said. "Besides, no war-horse foaled could ever carry a skin weighing as much as that one. It's a shame; there'd be a fortune. Release a lot of slaves with what that'd bring."

"The girl," Kian said. "We'd better release her." That should have been the first thing he did, but he had needed time just to get himself together.

"If we do, the flopears will try to follow us."

"After facing that," Kian said, nodding at the huge serpent, "I'm not much scared." Who were the flopears? Was there really a third kind of ear?

Jac went to fetch his horse, which had wandered during their dialogue, and Kian retrieved his sword and ran back to the girl. Up close she looked even more like Lenore Barley. She always had been a pretty girl, but he hadn't wanted to marry her. It had been his mother's idea. At home he had always thought Lenore aristocratic and vain, not at all like the friendly kitchen women and serving maids. But now, as he looked into this sweet face, he wondered if he should not have married Lenore despite her upbringing.

With one easy swing of the sword the gauntlets cleaved through the chain, first on the left, then on the right. The chain came away clean and bright: genuine silver. "Oh, thank you! Thank you," the round-eared girl exclaimed, her bosom heaving in maidenly excitement.

"I'm, eh, a stranger," Kian said, trying not to be too obvious about what he was noticing. "From out of this world, you might say. You?"

"Lonny Burk, originally from Fairview. I'm afraid the tax collector took me directly to the flopears. They want a sacrifice each year and they want her to be a stranger, comely, blond, and"—she hesitated momentarily, blushing—"virginal."

"Then you've never actually"—he hesitated, then went bravely on—"been a slave?" Slave boys were routinely beaten, to break their spirits; slave girls were routinely raped until they stopped resisting. He tried to tell himself that this was irrelevant to his assessment of her, but his inner self didn't see it that way.

"I told you. I was never taken to the Mart. To please the flopears and collect the most silver, the agent kept me safe. Even so, he made me an offer—to take me out of the line if I agreed to—you know—and not let on. But I knew he was married, and he was so ugly and smelled so bad I knew I'd prefer the serpent."

"Perhaps you made a fortunate choice." Because, he thought, if she had chosen otherwise, they would never have met, and then he would never have realized that Lenore Barley was the girl he should marry. Lenore—Lonny's near counterpart. "You mentioned flopears. Were those the short people I saw here before—"

"You don't know about the flopears?" she asked, amazed.

"As I said, I—"

"They can freeze a mortal person in his tracks just by looking at him! That's why we can't resist them."

"A mortal person?" he asked, surprised at this term. "But all of us are mortal!"

"Yes," she agreed unhelpfully.

He was rubbing her wrists where the circulation had been restricted by the shackles when Jac appeared, leading his horse. "I'm heading back to the Barrens before the flopears come back. You two want to come?"

"If—we can ride," Kian said.

"Oh, don't worry about Betts," Jac said, patting the war-horse. "She can carry all of us. Only no skin, blast it, and I'm afraid not even that chain. Enough weight is enough for her."

"These Barrens—"

"Blank, worthless land inhabited solely by outlaws and other dangerous creatures. Surely you've heard of it?"

"Yes." Back home it was the Sadlands; here it would, of course, be almost the same.

"Well, climb on. You, missy, ride in front of me. You— what was your name?"

"Kian. Kian Knight."

"That's right: Kian. You ride behind me and hang on to me or the side of the saddle."

It wasn't quite the arrangement Kian had envisioned, but he took Jac's hand and allowed himself to be pulled up on the back of the great horse.

"I've, eh, left something back on the road," Kian said. "It may be worthless, but then again, I can't say."

"You know where you left this, eh, thing?"

"Close. It's where I encountered a bearver."

"A bearver! Near the main road?"

"Not too far. There were appleberry bushes. I'll know the place."

"So will I," Jac said, turning Betts upslope. "There's that one stretch where the berries grow and the bearvers come. Good place for berries; bad place for bearvers."

Kian cocked his head to a now familiar sound. It came, musically, tinkling from the oaple tree he had noticed before.

"Jac, if you want skin—eh, silver—why don't you take the chimes?"

Jac looked back at him, astonished. "You daft?"

"No. I'm a stranger. If you want silver, why not—"

"Because," Jac explained patiently, "the flopears treat the chimes with their curse. You don't take a chime or even a part of one. If you do, you'll die before night."

"Really?" This might be the outlaw's notion of a joke.

"Really."

Kian thought of that as they rode nearer to where he had left the weapon. "Jac, if you don't mind my asking, why the chimes?"

Jac laughed. "You certainly don't know much of the world, do you!"

"N-no. Not this world, at least."

"It's to mark boundaries," Lonny said, turning her sweet face. "At least that's what's always said. Something to do with where the serpents are and where there are ancient secrets much better kept by flopears. No one in his right mind goes near a chime. You must be—you must be from another world."

"I am," Kian said.

"That doesn't surprise me," she said. "Anyone who would come wandering into Serpent Valley on foot has to be from a really distant place."

Considering that he had come into it in order to rescue her, this remark seemed ungracious. "Actually, in my frame, it's—"

"That's it?" Jac demanded, pointing at something that gave off reflections in their path.

"That's it," Kian said, relieved to have the subject changed. He eased himself down from the horse as Betts came to a halt. He was facing the others at close range as he did so. Lonny had nice legs, he thought, looking at the portion that emerged from her gauzy gown. Then he made his mind shut up, and turned to fetch the device.

"Weapon, isn't it?" Jac said as Kian put it in his scabbard. "Any good?"

"No. At least I don't think it is. I tried it on the bearver. First time."

"May I see it?"

Kian drew the weapon and handed it to him butt-first. Jac took it, reversed it, and looked into the bell. "No bow?"

"It's not a crossbow."

"So I see. It's something of Mouvar's, I'll bet."

"It is."

"And it doesn't work?"

"Didn't for me."

"Hold on to it. Could be valuable. You ready to ride? Really ride?"

Kian climbed up and got a good grip on the saddle. "I am now."

Jac dug his heels into Betts' sides. "Get, Betts!"

They rode like the wind through forested, mountainous country that would have been near dragon country had Hud been Rud. They rode past towering cliffs and stunted trees for what seemed miles, then onto a side path that took them through brambles and brush. After numerous slaps from branches and scratches from vines they were in bleak, semi-desert country known in the world of silver serpents as the Barrens. To Kian, contemplating the bleakness, the Sadlands seemed a much better name.

CHAPTER 4

Relative Pain

KELVIN WASN'T AT ALL happy about having to leave Heln and
Jon and his friends the Crumbs, but he was even less happy
about St. Helens' offer to accompany him. He thought around
it all day long while they visited and caught up on family
matters that neither had learned before. There was just no
way out of it, he concluded. Every time he attempted to say
that it was his responsibility and his alone, St. Helens was
certain to turn it about.

"Yes, yes, I agree, Hackleberry! Very important that we get
your father here if he lives. He can train the troops and make
the plans better'n me. Not that you're not round-eared, of
course. But then remember, so are St. Helens and your old
man." It was evident that St. Helens had pretty well assessed
Kelvin's incapacity as a leader and was moving to fill the
void. That was a significant part of what bothered him.

Kelvin tried to explain it reasonably. "I really don't know about Aratex yet. I feel Rud shouldn't interfere unless we're urged to by Aratex's people. Beside King Rufurt—"

"Rufurt, that old fraud!"

"He's a good man. A good king."

"Hmpth. Good for nothing, if you ask me. Who let the bitch-queen take over? Who sat around while your father— no offense, lad—bedded her and made a son?"

"By then the king was in the dungeon, and—"

"And your old man was weak. He wasn't like that in the old days! Or maybe her old man, Zatanas, cast a few spells. A little tampering with the wine, and any man . . . " He faded out, evidently understanding that kind of temptation all too well.

"It could have been," Kelvin agreed, a bit jealous that he had no basis to understand the temptation. "Zatanas was a powerful magician."

"Destroyed by a boy! No offense, lad, but that's what you were. So now, a few months later, you're a man, or think you are. Doesn't matter. The point is, you're right. That old man of yours was my commander, and from what I hear, he's come to his senses. We need him for Aratex and for what comes after."

"I really don't know yet." If only he had some of that competence and certainty his father must have had!

"Of course you don't! How could you? Roundear of Prophecy or not, you're still the boy."

"Mr. Reilly," Heln put in.

"St. Helens, lass. It's St. Helens or Father."

Heln reddened. "I'd rather not call you Father. To me, my father is—"

"Flambeau. Yes, yes, good man. I know how you feel. I don't insist on it, though it is my due. St. Helens will do just fine."

"St. Helens," Heln said with a spot on either cheek that was now intense. "What do you mean by coming here and insulting my husband and his father? We didn't even know you were alive before you knocked on our door. Why should you—"

"Hey, hey! A chip off the old block, hah, Hackleberry? My own daughter, sure enough!" Reaching out a brawny arm, he gave her an obviously unwanted hug, pressing her soft cheek to his rough beard. "Well, I didn't insult them. I'm not insulting the best commander I ever had in the Normerican Army and his son! No, ma'am, not me. Not the old saint! They didn't call me Truthful Reilly for nothing before I tired of it! When I spout off, I spout the truth. Always have and am always gonna."

She was unmollified. "St. Helens, I really think that's enough!"

"Yes, it is, lass. 'Deed it is. Hackleberry, don't you think those red spots on her cheeks are cute? Her mother used to get those. Once when I came home late with a load—potent stuff, that local brew!—she got 'em real fierce. Gave me the tongue-lashing of my life, and I stood there and took it because I had it coming. She made me sleep in the barn that night, and me a big, randy buck in those days who lived mostly for lovemaking and fights."

"Mr.—eh, St. Helens," Kelvin forced himself to say. "We're grateful for your visit, but my wife and I aren't used to, eh, visitors. We've just gotten back from visiting my mother and her parents—her mother and foster father, I mean—the Flambeaus. We've just gotten this house built and the furniture moved in and then Heln checks up on my missing brother—"

"Yes, you told me. Nothing to do but go there and rescue them, I agree. Fools shouldn't have gotten themselves in a mess, but things happen. Me, I want to see that other frame so bad it's tormenting me, but from what I'm told, it will probably be almost the same as here. I'm not sure of that myself. It just could be that other frame is Earth, where your father and I came from."

"It can't be Earth. Heln and I saw."

"Yes, the vision bit. Guys in my army outfit used to inhale an herbal smoke and claim they had visions where they could see all over the earth. Maybe they did, but me, I doubted it."

"That's very interesting, St. Helens, but with dragonberries you don't just see visions, you move away from your body at the speed of thought. You go anywhere you want to, and—"

"Yes, yes, and I'm ready to take your word for it. My old commander's son doesn't lie."

Kelvin tried to control his reaction. Why did that statement make him feel so defensive? "No, sir. He doesn't."

"So when do we go? We've been wasting time talking here when all the time you say the commander's in trouble—in a jailhouse, no less."

"Dungeon. Apparently the dungeon of the local king."

"Then we'd better get moving, hadn't we? You ready to go now? I'm ready if you're ready."

"Now?" Kelvin couldn't believe this was happening. St. Helens was like a force of nature resembling a great wind. "But you've been traveling by foot and the day's far gone. I thought—"

"An early morning start. Most sensible. The commander would approve. Can't fight if you're exhausted. That reminds me: Heln, you got any more of that appleberry pie? And how about some of the local grog before we sleep—a little wine?"

Kelvin gave Heln a look of helplessness, looking over his father-in-law's shoulder. Possibly he could resolve the matter in the morning. Certainly he did not feel that St. Helens was anyone he would wish to have constantly at his side, but how could he convey this without setting off the man's volcanic temper? Subtlety just didn't seem to exist in St. Helens' universe!

"I'll get the wine, eh, Father," he said. The sarcasm was heavy, but he suspected the man would not detect it.

"Fine! Fine, lad. Nothing too expensive, though from what I hear the king settled on you, you can afford it. Take no heed, son. I know the pride you'll take in serving your daddy-in-law the best."

Kelvin left the house for the local wine shop, hoping his formidable irritation wasn't showing. He wasn't sure whether St. Helens really was Heln's father, and wasn't sure whether he would prefer the man as an impostor. An impostor could in due course be unmasked and kicked out! But those round ears made it all too likely that the man was genuine. What a mill-stone!

He reached the shop and made his selection by the nearness of the bottle. He was counting out the rudnas from his coin-bag when he looked up and saw a large man with the point of one ear missing. Mor Crumb, Lester's father and Jon's father-in-law. This was the day for in-laws, he thought, but was still glad to see his old companion-in-arms.

"Kelvin, you rogue!" Crumb exclaimed. "You and the little girl celebrating a Hackleberry-to-be already?"

"Eh, no. Not yet, I'm afraid. May be just as well. Things keep coming up besides those you know about. We have problems."

"Your marriage?" Mor was concerned.

"No, no. Nothing like that." In a moment he was telling Mor about Heln's visiting relative.

"And you're really going into The Flaw with him?" Mor demanded.

"Not if I can help it. But he's a little hard to discourage."

"Tell you what, Kelvin," Mor said, putting a friendly arm around his shoulders. "Lester and I will just sort of casually drop by in the morning. It's a long way to the old palace and that river chamber. Least we can do is tag along. If you want your St. Helens to stay, we'll see that he does. Call it payment for the times you've saved my life and my boy's life."

"If he doesn't talk you into thinking it's a good idea!"

"Huh," Mor said. "That windbag you describe couldn't talk Mor and Lester Crumb into a free fight!"

Kelvin didn't answer. That "windbag" seemed to be having no trouble talking Kelvin himself into anything.

* * *

Heln busied herself in the kitchen while St. Helens ate the pie. As she scrubbed away at a pan that had held the pie and didn't really need that much scrubbing, she tried hard to control the temper she knew she had inherited.

That man my father? I can't stand him! I can't stand him!

The center of the pan became mirror-shiny as she scrubbed it too hard with the grit she was using. She could see her face. At the moment she did not like her face: there was too much of St. Helens in it.

The man was twisting Kelvin around his fingers! He really was! St. Helens obviously wanted to use Kelvin for his own plans. Poor Kelvin wouldn't stand up to him because he thought he was doing her, Heln, a favor. Kelvin thought that just because she derived from the man in name and in blood, she was a devoted daughter. Some father! She wished he had never showed up. She wished he were back in Aratex. She wished he were dead.

She froze, appalled, staring into her reflection in the pan. How could she even think such a thing? Yet she knew she did.

In the Hackleberry dining room St. Helens was savoring the last bites of the pie. Appleberries baked in a pie had the tartness and texture of raspberries combined with the flavor and aroma of a Jonathan apple. How the memories of Earth food and drink lingered! He could still recall the smell and taste of fresh brewed coffee and of at least a thousand foods and beverages. Yet there was nothing wrong with local fruits and vegetables and local cooking. True, both he and John Knight had had to teach the baking of pies, but then the local fruit tarts were quite tasty and satisfying. Still, man did not live by dessert alone.

The little girl was angry with him. He could see why. He'd have to work on that, hide the old basic nature and bring out the winning charm. After all, it would be only for a short time, and then he'd be no more charming than he felt like being. Once he had control he'd be in charge, and they would know it as well as he.

"Heln," he said, raising his voice slightly. "Does Kelvin still have the laser the commander gave him? You know, the Earth weapon he used in the war?"

"He has it, St. Helens. His father said to get rid of it, but he held on to it. As long as he has it he doesn't have to worry about any danger he might face."

"Father, I said." She was coming around, maybe.

"Father." Her tone suggested that she'd like to call him something else. His daughter, all right! Poor Kelvin. Pity him if he ever got to be a bad husband. She'd put him in his place right enough.

"He's taking it with him into the other frame?"

"Of course!"

"And the gauntlets—he's taking them also?"

"Certainly."

"That's fine, just fine," St. Helens said. He smiled, thinking how very fine it would be even if the boy didn't come around for him. Not that he wouldn't; he was a smart enough boy. But if need be, St. Helens could take the laser *and* the gauntlets, and then let old Melbah try to stop him! Just let her try, and he'd fry her and prove to the Aratexians just how vincible the invincible crown actually was. If need be, he knew he could do it all, entirely by himself. If he had the weapons.

Jon finished polishing the last of her throwing stones and dropped it into her ammunition pouch by her sling. She had been fiddling with these preparations since before dawn, and now soon it would be time to go. She turned from the table as Lester strode in, and seeing he was alone, she voiced her thought.

"Les, I think we should talk him out of it."

"What?" Lester was incredulous, as she had known he would be. "Talk Kelvin out of going for his father and his brother?"

"There's also the queen," she said, just as she had planned

to. "We can't be certain she's not there alive in that other frame. Would you want her back in Rud?"

"No, but that's ridiculous. The war's over. She ruled only with the help of Zatanas' sorcery. Even if she were to come back here alive, she'd be powerless."

"She's Zatanas' daughter. That could mean something."

"Very little. Now that Kelvin's fulfilled the line of prophecy."

Jon sighed, knowing that what she most wanted to say would be misunderstood. She knew that Kelvin wasn't brave; he was just—just Kelvin. Without her and her sling, and Lester and his father, and the gauntlets and laser—without those he would be just another man.

But since there was no avoiding it, she forced a smile and said what had to be said, even to her husband. "You're right, dear. He's slain dragons and he's won Rud citizens their freedom, and he's saved my life and yours. He's a hero born and there's never been his equal in all of history. Kelvin, my brother, is the Roundear of Prophecy."

But she knew how much that hero needed proper buttressing. Prophecy was fine, but it took little note of human weakness.

CHAPTER 5
New Familiar Faces

THE OUTLAW'S CAMP WAS nothing more than a small collection of tents, several of them ragged and flapping with great holes. The land was as barren as most desert, but a few prickly plants of assorted sizes grew, and a fence of sorts had been made around the camp by dragging in some of the larger specimens and forming them into a line. There was no material here for proper shacks of the type used in the mountains.

A man with a broad chest came forth to meet them. He was a startling sight. He was the very image of the opposition leader in Rud who had supported Kelvin: Morton Crumb. Except for his whole, round ears.

"This is Matthew Biscuit," Jac said, making the introduction. "Matt, this is Kian Knight from a far and distant land." Jac dropped off the horse and assisted Lonny down; Kian dropped down by himself.

"This'un's Lonny Burk from Fairview. She was going to be the sacrifice. Between us, Kian and I slew a really big serpent. You should have seen him fight!"

"Silver?" Matt asked, interested.

"What else? Of course silver. But far too big. We'd need a dozen good horses just to drag it here. Besides, you know the flopears will be out."

"No doubt." Matt frowned. "What's he doing here?" He jerked his thumb to indicate Kian.

"What are you doing here, lad?" Jac demanded.

Kian took a deep breath. "My father and mother came to this frame from a world almost like it. We haven't any silver serpents, but we have golden dragons there."

"Dragons?" Biscuit sounded offended. "Them's legendary beasts! Story-book stuff."

"So are serpents big enough to swallow war-horses. Back home, I mean. In the frame I come from."

"Frame? What're you talking about?"

Kian swallowed. "If you don't know—you may think I'm making this up. There are worlds made up of tiny specks my father calls atoms, and much space between these atoms, just as there is between stars. Most everything is space, considered this way. So worlds and universes lie side by side, interpenetrating, sometimes overlapping, touching slightly here and there. Each universe, each world connecting in adjoining universes, only a little different from each other. Our world's people have pointed ears, while another world's people have round ears. One world has silver serpents, while another has golden dragons."

"Bosh! Superstitious junk!" Matt declared. He seemed quite angry. "The rulers want us to believe that nonsense so's they can keep us repressed."

"But it's so! I know it is, because my father originated on a world where they have horseless carriages and moving pictures and talking boxes and all sorts of strange things. Then there's the alien Mouvar, who left a chamber from which roundears could travel to other worlds. Mouvar the Magnificent, we called him. He lived long, long before my time, and he left my home frame after a battle with a local sorcerer. The sorcerer was later destroyed by my brother."

"By your brother?" Matt sounded even more skeptical.

"Yes. The roundear Mouvar predicted would, well, he predicted a lot for him in my home frame. He slew dragons in his youth, as the prophecy says, and he rid his country, Rud, of its sore—a tyrannous government." He did not think it necessary to add that for all purposes his own mother had been that government.

"It sounds as if you had very much the same setup as here," Jac said. "We too have a tyranny. Our leader, King Rowforth, has to be overthrown someday. You don't suppose you could give us some tips?"

"I'm afraid not. I was—" Kian hesitated, knowing that he must not say that he had been on the wrong side. "Not really part of it. My brother could help you, or my father, if we can find him."

"You think he's here? In our world?"

"I hope so. I read the instructions carefully, and I know the setting on the machine hasn't been changed for centuries. I feel this is where my parents went. Certainly this must be where Mouvar went. You have legends about him?"

"We have Mouvar," Jac said. "Or at least we had. Strange old man, it's said. He performed some miracles and then sort of vanished. Some say he's still around, but no one knows."

Kian felt a thrill of hope. Mouvar—the original Mouvar? —here? With Mouvar's help anything should be possible. But then according to legend Mouvar had been defeated by Zatanas, and if that was so, Mouvar was less powerful than Kelvin!

"Of course there's our local magician, who claims him as an ally," Matt put in. "He's prattled about him for years. He's shut up about him lately, though—ever since Rowforth took his daughter to wed. If you ask me, all his talk was just a scheme to make that happen. The one opposition leader in the land—and his daughter just happens to have beauty that kings would trade their thrones for. He makes out fine now, old Zotanas does, but he's not conjuring much. Word is that he's a permanent guest at the palace and King Rowforth's main helper."

Zotanas here; Zatanas at home. Zotanas alive; Zatanas destroyed by Kelvin. Kian shook his head; there were just too many angles. It was getting harder and harder not to be confused.

"Well, I certainly don't believe in your almost identical worlds," Lonny Burk said. As comely as he had first thought her, Kian also found her a bit annoying at times. "I heard those stories when I was a child, but until now nothing has ever shown up to confirm them."

"Mouvar. Mouvar showed up," Kian pointed out. Why did pretty women seem to have an innate ability to irritate him?

"Maybe he did, and maybe he's just a story." She looked at him quizzically, and he had the feeling that she knew something, despite being a woman and a recently intended sacrifice. Why did she choose to disbelieve him? He had come to rescue her, after all!

Glancing around the camp, frustrated, he was surprised at the faces he almost recognized. Men whose aspects he had seen around the palace during his youth. Some of them he identified with guardsmen. They had been loyal to his mother the queen, but enemies of his father and Kelvin. Could all of this similarity be mere chance? He shuddered, thinking about it. He wished he were elsewhere—at least until he had figured out more about this situation. He would just have to watch his step.

A very small man running on the short legs of a dwarf came from a nearby tent and up to them. Quickly this person took the reins of the war-horse, and led it to a spot near the fence where he tethered it to a ring set in a large rock. He clambered up on the rock and moved the horse around while he wiped it down with a rag. Then, rushing to the tent, his legs blurring with the speed, he turned quickly and called, "Happy return, Master!" just as he plunged inside. A moment later he returned, carrying a sack of grain for the horse on his bent but adequate back.

"Queeto!" Kian said. Queeto—the dwarf apprentice to the magician Zatanas! Destroyed, along with his evil master, by Kelvin and a great cleansing fire!

"What's that?" Jac asked.

"Queeto. The dwarf."

"Heeto, here," Jac said. "You knew him well?"

"Not very." He did not care to elaborate. Queeto had been a most misshapen creature in both body and mind, as evil and fearsome as his magician master.

Jac called his attention to the way the dwarf was patting the horse's muzzle and feeding it by hand. "That one's a saint. Kindest person I ever saw. Hardest-working person I ever knew. Cheerfulest, best-natured person ever. Was he in your world as well?"

"Not exactly a saint," Kian said, thankful that he did not have to tell the embarrassing truth.

"How do you plan on finding them?" Jac asked.

Kian jerked his attention away from the dwarf and back to his host. "What? Oh, my parents. I have a plan. Unless, of course, you can help me."

"What's your plan?"

Kian told him about the dragonberries and showed them. "You have anything like these in Hud?"

Jac shook his head. "Never heard of 'em. But they sound like something that might eliminate the need for a lot of spy work."

"They did." He proceeded to tell about Heln's spying on the evil queen and magician during the war. Carefully he avoided mentioning that they were his mother and grandfather, and that he himself had fought on their side.

"When you going to take one?"

"I thought—" He swallowed, made uncomfortable by the thought. "Maybe when I had somebody to watch me. My heart will stop beating. My breathing will stop. I'll look as if I'm dead."

"I'll watch," Jac said. "Come along to my tent."

Kian followed him. In a few moments he was stretched out on a bearver hide on the floor of the tent, holding one of the small dark berries up to the lamplight. Nothing much to do now but to go through with it, though he dreaded the prospect. Not giving himself a chance to think, he popped the berry into his mouth.

He tasted a taste that made him want to retch. He fought off the urge, then swallowed.

There was nothing for a moment. Wasn't it working? He felt a guilty relief. But if it didn't work, then how would he search for his father?

Then he noticed that the top of the tent was nearer than it had been. Had a supporting pole broken? He turned his head and looked down.

There was his body below, lying deathly still. The bandit stood peering down at it, frowning. The berry had worked! He was out of his body! He had felt no pain at all! In fact, it had happened so readily that he felt wonderful!

But he had a job to do. He thought of moving outside— and abruptly he floated through the tent wall without making contact, and emerged at the front.

There was the fire—and there was Lonny, looking back at the tent with a scared and anxious expression. Evidently she was concerned about him, and that gratified him. Not that he had any personal interest in her, despite her beauty. Or did he? She had tried to warn him away from the serpent, and that struck him as a pretty selfless attitude. Maybe—

He brought himself back to business. How did Heln do this? Oh, yes: concentrate on a person. On a face.

A face came to mind: a woman's oblong visage, of clear complexion, framed by hair as red as the sheen of a dragon, with eyes the color of green feline magic.

Instantly he was transported, moving past hills and villages as if flying, to a palace high on a river bluff. The palace was almost like the one in which he had grown up, though the Rud structure had been on low ground, with an underground river almost beneath it. Then he was inside, moving from room to room so blurringly swiftly that he was unable to note their details.

He stopped.

There was the face: his mother's beautiful face. She was seated on a divan. Beside her, holding her hand, was a tall, straight, elderly man with dark gray hair. His grandfather!

Both were gone from his home frame, one departed, the other dead—yet here they were alive and unhurt. His mother and his grandfather, oblivious of his presence. He was shaken, despite having no body to shake.

He could hear them speaking. His mother—or was it really she?—had been crying. Zatanas—or was it he?—had evidently been comforting her.

"Please, please, my child. Remember who you are. You are Zotanas' daughter, and the queen."

"But—but he—how can you permit him, Father? How?"

The old man sighed. "I told you, my magic is only for little, good things. I can help keep him controlled, but I'm powerless to destroy him."

"Oh, Father. Father, if only you could stop him!"

"Hush, dearest, you are speaking of your husband the king."

"But he's so—so evil!"

"I know, and he's getting more so all the time. Bringing flopears here was bad enough, but offering to share his rule with them if they would help him conquer is worse. I have nothing, I fear, to combat it."

Hearing the words, Kian was finally able to realize that the woman and man were not his mother and grandfather. Both had round ears, while his relatives had ears as pointed as anyone in Rud. But this was Hud, he had to remember, and here things were different. Yet they did have the faces.

How long would the berry last? He had wanted to find his mother, but he had zeroed in only on her face. Did that mean that she wasn't in this frame? Or did it mean that the berries worked only on natives? He could not decide, and he knew there was little time.

His father. Think of his father.

He visualized John Knight's face as well as he could. The walls of the palace disappeared and he was above hills and rivers and farmlands, moving with that unreal velocity of thought. Then he was back in the valley where he had killed the serpent. He moved along the ground, everything blurring, and then through a rock wall and into an area where flopears abounded. Their ears—but he was already past them. Along and through a rock doorway in a cliffside. He halted.

There, on a bed, pale and unshaven, was John Knight.

"Father!" Kian cried. "Father, you're alive!"

The man's eyes flicked back and forth, but he did not open his mouth.

"Who's that? Who spoke?"

Astonished, Kian saw the other person in the room: a young flopear female. Yes, those ears really were flopped over! What a sight!

The woman moved over to the bed. She raised a straw broom in her hands and looked around the room threateningly. "You leave, bad spirit!" she cried. "You leave!"

She had heard him! He had no body, he was present only in spirit form, he could make no physical sound, yet there was no doubt that this odd woman had heard!

Should he speak again? Should he try to let her know that he was visiting his father? She seemed protective. Could she mean John Knight harm?

Kelvin's wife, Heln, had discovered that dragons were sensitive to the astral state and could hear her when she spoke in the astral state. The odd-eared folk here must be similarly sensitive!

"Go away!" the girl insisted. "Leave here! Leave before I get help! Herzig can capture you, you know! He can imprison you, put you in tree or serpent! You want that, spirit?"

"No. No," Kian said. Her manner was so fierce he thought

it best to placate her. Yet he still felt he would like to tell her
who he was, and that he meant no harm.

"Then go instantly!"

He went. It seemed the politic thing to do. Obviously she
could hear him, and so her threat might have substance, too.

Besides, he had the feeling that his astral time was about
used up. There was a feeling of waning, of diminishing, that
gave him warning.

But he made himself pause to look at the huge cauldron
where the flopears were melting down silver. Even as he
looked, one came bringing an armload of what seemed like
featherlight serpentskin. The flopear mounted the wooden
steps of the scaffold and dumped the armload into the silver
soup. There was a puff of steam. Another flopear stirred the
broth with a huge ladle.

"Boo!" Kian cried impulsively.

The flopear almost dropped the ladle. He teetered for a
moment at the edge of the soup, in danger of falling in. He
recovered his balance and looked frantically around. "Who
spoke? Who said?"

Kian willed himself back, away from the connected valleys.
Back to where he had started.

In a moment he was in the camp again. He zoomed from
face to face, trying to see how many he almost recognized.
There were several that would have been a previous part of
his life, with pointed ears.

Then he was back at Jac's tent and inside and lying on the
bearver hide. He struggled to sit up, to open his eyes. He
managed.

"Gods," Jac said, looking at him somewhat wild-eyed. "I
thought you were dead for certain."

"Not dead, just near," Kian said. As rapidly as he could, he
told the bandit leader what had happened.

"And you're certain he said Rowforth is making a pact
with the flopears?"

"I told you what I heard."

"If that's true, there isn't much time. Zotanas could be

mistaken, and I hope he is. But if he makes a pact, Lord, old Rowforth will end up bossing all the Seven Kingdoms with them!"

Kian wondered whether Rowforth could be that bad. Then he considered that this man had been the one ultimately responsible for sending beautiful maidens to the flopears for sacrifice. Could any ruler possibly be worse?

"If we can rescue my father, perhaps he can help. I'm not sure how, or maybe he can go back to Earth and get Earth weapons. Lasers, flying devices—they might help."

"I'm not sure what you're talking about. But if you think your father can help us defeat Rowforth, then we'll rescue him. Only that won't be easy. The serpent people aren't like ordinary mortals. They have magic—the ability to stop a fighting man in his tracks with just a glance. That's only one of their talents."

So Kian had discovered! "But there has to be a way!"

"I'll grant you that. And with your ability to spy, just maybe we'll find it. To start with, we can't actually face flopears. If we try it, they stare at us and we're helpless sticks. That means we'll have to steal your father from them some way, and that won't be easy. From what you say, they can even detect you in the astral state."

"Yes, but only when I spoke, I think. When I was silent they didn't know I was there."

"But you didn't keep your mouth shut! Thanks to that, they may now know what to watch for."

Kian was chagrined. Jac could be right. *Damn!* he thought. *If only my brother Kelvin were here! He's the hero of prophecy, while I'm just an accident!*

It occurred to him that he had never felt less confidence in himself in his life.

CHAPTER 6
Going, Going . . .

KING PHILLIP BLASTMORE OF Aratex chuckled happily with his own cleverness, and moved the black queen across the board. "Check."

Melbah, pudgy and squat and so wrinkled of face that it resembled a badly cured animal pelt, looked up. Her rheumy eyes seemed to focus not on the board but on his artificially darkened little mustache. It was as though she did not even have to glance at the board.

"Well?" Blastmore demanded. He felt like jumping up and down. "You concede?"

"Oh, King," the witch inquired in her creaky, wispy voice, "do you wish to win this game, or do you prefer for Melbah to demonstrate her strategy?"

"Demonstrate your strategy," he said challengingly. But it was a bluff. He had a feeling that he knew what she was going to do, and he didn't like it. Melbah was Melbah, and she had been surprising him for all of his fifteen years.

"Then this is what I will do." Leaning over the board, eyes still focused on him, she puffed up her cheeks so that the wrinkles faded to mere patinas and blew out a stream of breath so foul that it staggered him. He heard a thump, and when he finished blinking his eyes he saw his black queen on the carpet.

"I'm afraid that's not permitted, Melbah," he said. "You can't touch a piece except to move it in the designated way."

"You say this is an ancient game of war. In war all things are fair."

"Well, yes. But—"

"I did not touch your queen. I only sent air to remove her from the battle."

"It's still not permitted." He sighed. Melbah had such a one-track mind. Yet who else was there for him to teach this game to?

"Then perhaps another strategy," Melbah said. She pointed a finger so knobby it most resembled a dead twig from an appleberry tree, and the black queen burst into flame. Within a couple of sharply drawn breaths it was only a charred piece of wood on the carpet.

Blastmore blinked. "Really, Melbah, you should not have done that. Now that the roundear has left, who will duplicate it for me?"

"No problem." Melbah snapped her fingers and the piece on the floor became uncharred painted wood. "This time illusion. In battle to save your kingdom, real."

"That certainly does make an impression," Blastmore said. The old hag had to be insane, but her magic was formidable. It had been a whim to teach her St. Helens' game—a whim whose price turned out to be endless frustration.

"Or," Melbah continued, "if the markers you call men were really men and threatened the kingdom . . ." She picked up a vase of flowers and tossed them on the carpet next to the

queen. Just as he was wondering what she was up to, she
sloshed water on his side of the board. As he hastily left his
chair the water spilled across and dripped on the floor,
carrying with it a wash of black pawns.

Blastmore stood over the board and contemplated the
prevalence of white chess pieces. He picked at a pimple on his
right cheek and pondered what to say.

"I agree," he finally said. "That would win a battle. But this
is a game."

"Yes, game." Melbah moved her hands in a circle above the
board and the board began to shake. One by one, the black
pieces were jolted off while the white pieces remained. When
all of his pieces except the king were gone, and he was
surrounded by white chessmen, the shaking stopped.

"Game finished now," Melbah said.

"Yes, finished." In fact, he wished it had never started. He
should have known how she would act. But he exercised
kingly discretion, and complimented her. "You did well. So
well that we will not have to play again."

"Good! Game pieces not needed here. Melbah can direct
forces without."

"I'm sure you can, and have." Poor Melbah must think
chess an aid to magic warfare. Not that her magic was of the
sympathetic kind. Or maybe it was. He had seen her cheeks
puff out and a great wind rise. He had seen her eyes glow like
coals before there was a fire. Perhaps if one understood it
correctly, all magic used similar principles.

Melbah stood up. "I go now to my quarters. Your general is
coming."

"He is? How do you know that?"

Melbah laughed. It was an awful sound; "cackle" was not
adequate to the description. He watched her swirl of dark
skirts as she seemed to drift rather than walk across the floor.
By the time he had blinked and reblinked she was gone,
apparently vanished from the room and possibly the palace.
It was the way she always exited. He never had quite pinned
down the exact nature of it. Certainly it awed others; he had

almost no palace staff, because ordinary servants tended to be too frightened of the witch to function properly. Fortunately he didn't need many, by the same token: Melbah could do almost anything that needed doing.

He sat there for a moment, rearranging the chess pieces as if for a game. The black ones were scattered across the floor, forcing him to reach and collect tediously. He wished that he had not had that falling out with St. Helens. He had really enjoyed the roundear's companionship, especially his wonderful stories about an unlikely world called Earth. He thought again about the way the big man had shown up asking for something called sanctuary, and the way he had paid for it by making himself a friend. In all his life, St. Helens the roundear had been his only friend.

True, when he was a child he had had playmates. But when he became angry with them, as he concluded in retrospect he too frequently did, Melbah had arranged for things to happen to them. By the time he cooled off, it was too late; they were gone. Then there were his parents and his sisters and brothers and all his relatives. Things had happened to them, one by one, and not by his design. The kingdom of Aratex just seemed to be experiencing a wave of misfortune that never became overwhelming. He would have been more inclined to wonder about this, if it had not coincidentally worked to his advantage.

So there had been servants and courtiers and soldiers in diminishing number—and Melbah. Mainly there had been Melbah. She was bad company, but there was something about her; she was always there when he needed someone. As with the attempted chess game just now: he had wanted someone with whom to play, and she had played—in her fashion. At least it hadn't been boring!

But in the past, when he had somehow been unhappiest despite his improving material position, St. Helens had shown up. The big gruff man had seemed to like the young prince for himself, and they had gotten along fine. Sometimes when misunderstanding threatened, Melbah had assisted;

nothing had happened to the roundear. Blastmore had suspected that she was responsible for the roundear's existence. Then he had decided that St. Helens was too complex to be her creation, but that she tolerated the friendship for her own reasons. He did not question this, because he valued the man's company too much. St. Helens might be big and rough and crude, but he was real; no need to worry about him being involved in any conspiracy. St. Helens always said exactly what he thought, and his remarks about the, as he put it, "ass-kissing" courtiers were delightfully on target. If Blastmore wanted a candid opinion, St. Helens would give it, not worrying or even caring much about possible offense. Even about Melbah herself—though there the man had had the caution to lower his voice before calling her a "bag of excrement." The actual term had been unfamiliar, but the context had clarified it.

Now St. Helens was gone, and depression had returned. Blastmore's one hope was that soon he would be of an age to marry. He was viewing some of the young ladies of the court with increasing interest. Melbah never let him get really close to any of them alone, but once he got to marry one, it could get really interesting. At least he would have good company again.

The chessboard whirled before him as he sat staring at it, waiting for the general Melbah had promised. Sometimes he got these dizzy spells when he thought of St. Helens and how much the big man had meant to him. They had gotten along so well! If he had asked the man about women, he was sure to have had a crude but pertinent answer—exactly the kind he craved. St. Helens had given so much and asked for so little: just food and sleep and safety. "I know what it is to be lonely, lad. I know," he had said.

But then the roundear had started paying attention to what Blastmore did and what Melbah did and to all who came and went about the palace. He began asking questions. Suddenly, unexpectedly, St. Helens had become angry with him.

"It's not right, the condition of your people, lad. It's all that old bag's influence! You've got to stand up to her! You've got to rule on your own!"

"But how, St. Helens? How?" He had been genuinely baffled, for this was the first time anyone had said anything like this to him.

"I'll tell you how, lad!" St. Helens' big fist had smacked into his own palm. "First of all, you've got to realize that she's just a person. She might know some good conjurer's tricks, but let me tell you, I've seen some pretty clever performances back on Earth. She's got the people scared of her, and for good reason. You've got to undo some of that! Let people bring you gifts because you're their monarch and they love you. Don't force them to bring tribute or face ruin at the hands of your witch! A good king can rule wisely and well and have everything. A wise king doesn't have to worry about enemies. Tell your tax collectors to ease up on people. Sometimes a man can't pay and sometimes he doesn't want to pay. If he really can't pay, you have to try treating him so that he can."

Blastmore shook his head. It hadn't surprised him that when he did nothing about the tax collectors or Melbah, his friend had disappeared. He remembered seemingly unconnected episodes of the past, when there had been murmurings among relatives about policy and taxes, and then those relatives had suffered misfortune. Getting a glimmering of the way of it, he had been smarter with St. Helens. He had had the man followed and watched. He had forbidden Melbah to harm him. "Let him alone and things will be as before," he promised her. "He can't harm us. He doesn't have your power."

"That is true," the witch had replied. "But still, roundears do bear watching."

"I'm having him watched," he reminded her. "If he tries to do harm I will learn of it, and then I will give you instructions."

"You will give *me* instructions?" She seemed amused, and not as displeased as he might have imagined. "Very well, when he causes trouble, you give me instructions."

Blastmore knew he was young, but he was not as young as he once had been, and he had taken the trouble to learn as much of the way of things as he could. He knew that he was the last of the royal line; if anything happened to him, there would be no help for it but revolution, because the people were incapable of selecting a new monarchy without violence. Melbah would be their first target. So it was in her interest to keep him safe. After all, he hadn't countermanded her tax policy; he knew the value of wealth, and the advantage of keeping the peasants poor. He wished St. Helens hadn't chosen that particular case to argue. The man had assumed that Blastmore was ignorant of the ways of the tax collectors, and it would have been awkward to disabuse him. But now it was time to begin asserting himself with Melbah, knowing that they were in agreement anyway. He needed to prepare for the time when they might not be in agreement.

Now, raising his eyes from the chessboard, he found General Ashcroft standing in front of him. A tall man with heavy eyebrows, he had always appeared as if conjured by Melbah's magic. The general was her man, Blastmore knew. He was making it a point to know the identities of all her men, just in case.

"Your Majesty," General Ashcroft said. "Following your specific orders, I have kept track of the roundear known as St. Helens. As you know, he tried to stir up sedition and create rebellion in various parts of the realm. Each time, following orders, Melbah has thrown the fear of magic into those he appointed leaders. A tornado, a fire, a groundquake, a flood—and rebellion dies before it's born. All who foolishly still opposed your policies have died, with the exception of St. Helens, who was allowed each time to escape."

"That is well," Blastmore said. How clever of him to have thought this out! It hadn't even been Melbah's suggestion, though he knew she gladly dealt the punishments. It was like a chess game, leaving an avenue for the opponent to escape a trap—an avenue that led to a worse trap. "And now?"

"Now, Your Majesty, the Roundear has left Aratex's borders."

"What?" Blastmore could hardly believe his ears.

"He has recrossed the river into Rud. He has heard reports that his daughter is now married to the Roundear there. It is believed by my agents that he has gone to this Roundear of Prophecy to get his aid and perhaps also help from the king of Rud."

"Against me? Against Melbah?"

"Do you wish to send assassins?"

Hmm. Assassinate the Roundear of Prophecy, and that would stop St. Helens from seeking his help. But possibly St. Helens wasn't bent on mischief, and besides, Blastmore had so enjoyed his stories and his chess. He had hoped that after some experience with the degenerate rebel elements of the kingdom, St. Helens would recognize the need to keep them down, and would have a change of heart. That might still occur. Suddenly he had an inspiration.

"I want him followed in Rud. When this is practical I want him captured, taken across the river into Aratex, arrested, and brought here in chains."

The general nodded, saluted, and departed.

There, he thought with a satisfied smile. This was going to fix everything.

Kelvin regretted having the Crumbs and his sister along, long before they reached the capital and the site of the old palace. St. Helens was like a lizard that changed its coloration to suit its background. Not only did he soothe them with his rough charms, he also won their respect. When he wasn't talking to Mor about the battles that had been fought on Earth, he was imparting knowledge to Lester of what Earth was like. If he wasn't reciting bits of Earth poetry to Heln—

who seemed to like it in spite of herself—he was delighting
Jon with accounts of something called Women's Liberation.
"We need that here," Jon said at one point. Trust her to
pick up on this! As roughnecked as ever, despite her late-
found femininity, she had just demonstrated her prowess by
downing a distant game bird. As she put her sling away Lester
rode for the bird. Kelvin stayed and listened, trapped here
regardless of his preference. "I never did see why men should
have all the fun."

"Bite your tongue, Brother Wart!" Kelvin said in the
manner of their so-recent youth. "You walked with me into
dragon country, you helped fight Rud's war, you reached the
palace ahead of the troops, you rescued me from the magician, and you got yourself almost drained of your last drop of
blood. What more could a man enjoy!"

"I did all that disguised as a boy," she reminded him. "And
when you treat me as an equal you always call me Brother
Wart! What kind of equality is that?"

"All right. *Sister* Wart."

St. Helens slapped his meaty thigh where it bulged from the
borrowed saddle. He laughed, making it almost a roar.
"Brothers and sisters are the same on Earth! Mabel, my sister,
and I used to tease each other all the time. She talked
Women's Liberation, too, and I always made fun of it. It's not
that I don't think women should be equal to men, it's just that
most aren't."

"Oh, is that so!" Jon said, clearly enjoying this. "Well, I tell
you, St. Volcano, it isn't easy being female!" She had learned
that his name derived from that of a volcano back on his
home world of Earth, and made much of it. She did not seem
to share the dislike Kelvin and Heln had for the man. "I
wanted to be a boy until I met Lester! Do you think I would
have gone around disguised as a boy if I hadn't had to?"

"Hah, hah," said St. Helens, turning red in the face. "Hah,
hah, hah."

"Well, it's the truth!"

Lester was returning with the blue-and-green ducphant swinging from his saddle. "Good news—we eat! Jon, Heln, get the fire started and the bird plucked. Your menfolk want a feast!"

"Chauvinist!" Jon spat, but the edge was gone. She and Heln did as they were bidden, and the bird, even in minute portions, was delicious, as only the food cooked outdoors could be.

The next day of travel St. Helens got on his political horse, lecturing one and all on and on about one world and the necessity of having one. "Now, Aratex just isn't right! It's too much the way Rud was before the revolution. Oh, they don't have slavery or the Boy Mart and Girl Mart, but they've got tax collectors who are just as bad as Rud's used to be, and soldiers as uncouth and discourteous. People aren't satisfied with their boy king, nor should they be. The truth is that it's that old witch Melbah who rules! It's time for a change. Once the witch is out and the country has a good, strong man in charge, Aratex can unite with Rud just as it says in the prophecy."

The astonishing thing to Kelvin was that the others seemed increasingly to buy it. True, he had always known the prophecy would get him into additional trouble sometime, but he had hoped to put it off, just as he had hoped to put off this rescue. Just listening to St. Helens' enthusiasm was getting to the others even if not to him. Thus the sight of the burned-out ruins of the old palace in the morning mist was in every way a relief.

"You say we'll need a boat?" St. Helens asked. "Well, seems to me there's a river above ground and people have boats along it. Why not get one ready-made instead of making one?"

"Those stairs aren't in good repair," Kelvin reminded them. "It might be easier to carry down the material for a raft and then—"

"Nonsense!" St. Helens insisted. "You're the Roundear of Prophecy and I'm your good right-hand man! No raft for us—it wouldn't be fitting."

And so it was that Jon again spoke to the river man who was Tommy Yokes' grandfather. He had been the one to row her across the river and help her with her disguise before she rescued Tommy and went on to the palace to rescue her brother. The old man smiled to see her and they embraced as though they were long-lost kin.

"My, you don't look like a boy any longer!"

"Nor do I want to! But thank you for helping me before, and now in renting us your boat."

"No rental! Glad to lend it to you. You did a mighty good turn for Tommy, and your brother ended slavery permanently. Things are better now for everyone, even old duffers who live by fishing and feeding a few goats. But I know some people who are going to want to see you just to shake your hand. Don't worry about getting the boat down those stairs—there are plenty who will be proud to help."

Thus did they spend an enjoyable day chatting until finally, assisted by a dozen pairs of willing hands, Kelvin and St. Helens were at last properly launched and on their way on the river. The water was aglow with the lichen's eerie luminescence. Kelvin only hoped that this strangeness did not foreshadow the nature of their mission.

CHAPTER 7
Flopear Magic

"I UNDERSTAND," KIAN SAID over lunch with his host and the girl who so resembled the girl he now longed to wed. Funny that it had taken this otherworld twin with round ears to make him realize this!

"You understand flopears," Jac said, chewing thoughtfully on a leg bone of a desert fowl. "But do you really? From what you say, there is nothing like them in your world."

"Only legends," Kian said. "Old legends—stories, really. We heard them as children. The small immortal people who once lived in the mountains and invented gold smelting. They were supposed to have gathered up the scales the dragons shed. No one really believed it, but they were nice stories for children. We all got those tales along with stories of knights and dragons and magicians and castles. Some of those last were true."

"Hmm. But here we have the serpents. Acid flows in their

mouths. Their teeth crush rocks. They tunnel constantly, only coming to the surface to shed their skins and collect their yearly sacrifice. Flopears collect the skins, and have from time immemorial. Our government has always traded with them, though they live as a race apart."

"Intermarriages?" Kian mused.

"Unheard of. It may be possible, but then again it may not. The flopears seem much like the serpents in that they're somehow of a different, more magical nature. I can't imagine any normal human wanting to unite with a flopear. But the objects they make from the silver are beautiful. They never do art objects picturing themselves. Another name we have for them is serpent people."

"The ear flaps keep little serpents out," Matt Biscuit said. "If there's one death more horrible than being devoured by a giant serpent, it's having one of those little ones tunneling away, little by little, into your head. A man with one of them in his brain lives for a long time, but he doesn't live sane."

"Little ones? I've never heard of little dragons. I mean, of course when they first hatch they're smaller, but even so they wouldn't tunnel into a head, they would snap the head up entire."

"Well, the serpents may be different. It's believed they take many centuries to grow big and that if the big ones keep growing they will eventually be the size of hills."

Kian shuddered. "Has anyone—"

"In legend, of course. But that one you described is as big as is known. That was gigantic, and I don't see how you survived."

"It was—" Kian hesitated, not wanting to reveal too much about the gauntlets. "Luck."

"More than that, I'd say," Jac said. "You should have seen this man! He ran right up the serpent's back and grabbed the spear and worked it in deep into the eye! Blood and poison spat all over, but he jammed the point right on into the brain before he let go. Then I pulled him out before the dying convulsions crushed him. We outlaws have slain serpents from time to time; we rope them and drive our spears in both eyes. But we never tackled anything even half the size of that one. It was big!"

The others were gazing on Kian with new respect. This embarrassed him. "Will the flopears follow us into the Barrens?" he asked, trying to divert their interest.

"They never have. Probably they can't take the sun. Once we're in the Barrens we're safe."

"Don't the soldiers of the king come after you?"

"Not often. The Barrens, as you may have noticed, isn't a particularly inviting place."

Heeto, the misshapen dwarf, ran to the fire carrying a bright silver vase. Unasked, he carried it to Kian and held it out to him.

Kian looked at his host. "What?"

"Flopear work," said Jac. "But flopear art of a special kind. He wants you to look at the figures."

Kian took the vase and held it to the firelight. Rotating it, he made out the figures of a knight in armor and a woman who might have been a princess. The road and the castle were in the background, and the knight and the lady appeared to have come from there.

"I don't see—"

"Look close," Jac advised. "At the people."

He did, and saw nothing other than perfect execution. Real artists had made this; the figures appeared almost alive.

"Here," Jac said in exasperation. His finger reached out and stroked—and immediately knight and lady turned, arm in arm, and strode back to the castle, disappearing at last through the gate.

Kian blinked.

"Now to make them come out, do this." Jac's finger pressed the gate. Immediately it opened and the two strolled arm in arm to their former place.

Kian drew up his fallen jaw. "I've never—never—"

"It's flopear art. We don't understand it, so we say it's magic. From what you say, there are few objects in your world as strange."

"Very few," Kian agreed weakly. "But in my father's world—"

"The match of this?"

Kian told of the box his father had described, with the pictures of real people moving and speaking inside. Now he was finding that less unbelievable!

"Amazing," Jac said. "So his world has magic even more wondrous!"

"He always said it was science," Kian said. "He always said science has cause and effect, while magic just happens."

"To me they seem the same."

"And to me also. After all, magic does have cause and effect if you understand it. Flopears caused this vase to have a magic effect. How and why, I have no way of knowing."

"Nor I!" Jac agreed.

"Perhaps," Heeto said suddenly in a piping voice at Kian's elbow, "it's to remind. Flopears can and do command magic."

"Of that," Kian said, turning the vase around in his hands, "there can be no doubt."

Morning, and Jac woke him with a gentle shake.

"Well, Kian, you ready for another trip?"

Kian looked up at Jac looming over him and tried to decide. He could plead that it was too soon, that he might die if he tried another astral trip. But then he thought of his father lying there in that bed, and shame for his hesitancy overwhelmed him. He had, after all, eaten and slept. Heln might not have taken journeys so close together, but that didn't mean he couldn't. He did, however, feel excessively weak.

He got up, dressed, and meekly followed Jac to his own tent. At the flap he looked back and saw Lonny. She was staring after him with achingly blue eyes, fingers to her lips, her face pale. The foolish girl probably didn't even know what was going on, and yet she sensed that he was endangering himself. She had listened to everything Jac had said, to everything Kian had said, and she had made no comment. Possibly she was starting to realize that many of the things she had rejected as nonsense were actually fact.

In the tent he lay down again on the bearver hide. He took out a berry from the pouch, held it between thumb and forefinger, and popped it into his mouth. This time it slid down easily, and though a taste rose to fill his mouth, he did not feel quite the same need to retch. Could he be acquiring a taste for this?

He lay back, looked up at Jac, then focused on the ceiling of the tent. When that grew closer, as it had before, he would be out of his body and into his astral state.

He started counting his heartbeats. One, two . . . three . . . four . . .

That was the sky overhead. He had drifted up through the tent ceiling without realizing it. Definitely the astral state. He felt relaxed to an extent he had never experienced in the body. He really could get to enjoy this! Possibly he should have taken two dragonberries, so as not to be rushed. But his supply was limited, and he didn't know his tolerance for them, so one at a time seemed best.

A bird flew by, and he realized it was far below him, as were the distant objects that must be the tents. He had to will himself down or he'd be leaving the planet and would drift above the moon and around the stars. At another time he might do that, just to satisfy his curiosity, but now was no time to drift.

He concentrated on his father's face and the room he had been in. Then he was down near the Barrens, above the hills, above the mountains, moving across and then into and then through the connected valleys. He watched the bright flashes as the serpents in the serpent valley squirmed about and shed their skins. There were several large serpents, though none as big as the one he had slain. Among them were two boys. Two flopear boys armed only with pink and blue flowers in their hands. These boys ran to the serpents, spoke to them, patted them, and picked up their cast-off skins.

Kian felt distracted. What he was seeing was new and strange, though evidently routine in this frame. He needed to hear what was being said. He willed himself close.

"Hissta, sizzletack," one of the boys was saying. "Nice serpent, nice giver of silver. Thank you for your gifts, revered ancestors. Someday we will join you and be one with you and live forever and be great."

He shouldn't have snooped, Kian thought. But somehow he just had to hear it. This was, after all, something few if any humans had witnessed.

The great serpents, easily of a size to swallow the boys, allowed their snouts to be petted and their nostrils to be touched with the blossoms. They did not purr in the manner of houcats, but he could readily imagine it from their actions. Obviously the boys and serpents had no natural fear or distrust of each other. It was as though the serpents were pets—or actually the boys' ancestors. That was a disturbing notion!

Well, enough of this. He didn't have all day, much as he might like to. He kicked himself, mentally, for swallowing only the one berry. The risk entailed seemed slight, compared with what he might gain by making a full study of the interaction between the flopears and the silver serpents.

He had to think of his father and go to him while there was time. He had to discover something worthwhile on this trip that might enable Jac and his band to rescue John Knight.

He thought of his father, wanting to be where his father was. Without any obvious transition, he was back in the room where he had seen his father stretched out in a bed.

The bed was still there. So was his father. The flopear girl was there, too, now feeding John Knight from a bowl.

The flopear girl dipped a spoon into the bowl and brought out what appeared to be a chunk of well-soaked bread. There were pieces of vegetables and bits of what might be meat in the bowl. This was obviously broth.

"Here, nourishment," the girl said. With tender care she positioned the spoon before John Knight's lax mouth.

Slowly, as though controlled by forces outside himself, John Knight took in the spoon and the broth-soaked bread. He chewed, swallowed, and waited for more. He gave little other indication that he was alive.

"Good, good, Mortal! Soon you be well! Soon your mind and body whole again. Gerta cure. Gerta would like to keep always, but Gerta not boss. Herzig want to trade you to mortal king of Hud. Make Gerta sad, but Gerta not say. Gerta like mortals too much. That why Gerta not really serpent person. Gerta's mother lay with mortal father, and that why Gerta not all good."

Lord, Kian thought. *What I'm overhearing!* But aside from Gerta's belief that she had a mortal father, there was information here. Kian's father was to be made well and traded to the king of Hud. If the king had any sense, he would not simply kill him. The flopears might know he was from another world or they might not. Having magic, they probably would.

Gerta fed John Knight until the bowl was empty, then blotted his mouth with a cloth. Kian watched his father close his now lusterless eyes and ease back onto the pillow. Gerta left the bedside and carried the bowl into another room.

Kian considered. Gerta believed herself to be part mortal and she was as tender a nurse as he had ever witnessed. Perhaps while he was here he might risk speaking to her again. This time not accidentally, and not just to placate her. He'd try to tell her what he had wanted to tell her before. If she knew he was a disembodied spirit and was not evil, then perhaps the mortal strain in her would be required to help. If his father was to be traded, there might not be any problem anyway, but he trusted the king of Hud less than he would care to trust a serpent.

He willed himself into the kitchen, where the flopear girl

was washing the bowl. "Gerta, please don't be frightened," he said.

Her eyes widened and she looked frantically around the room. "Spirit! You returned! That not wise! That not good!"

"I mean you no harm, Gerta. I mean none of your people harm. I'm here because of my father—the mortal for whom you are caring."

"He not well!"

"I know. But you are making him well, aren't you, Gerta?"

"Y-yes." A little hesitantly.

"Then listen to me, Gerta, because I may not have much time. I'm here because I swallowed a dragonberry. My body lies back in the Barrens, and I will need to return to it. I'm mortal, like your father and like mine."

"Like my father?"

"Yes, just like your own father. And I've learned something, Gerta. I've learned that the Hud king wants to involve your people in wars with other mortals. Your people must not agree to it, Gerta. It would mean disaster for the mortal people, and for the serpent people as well."

"Spirit," Gerta said craftily, "I can help you."

"You can?" Hope filled him as it hadn't for some time. "How?"

"I show you." Opening a cabinet, she reached in and brought out one of the silver serpentskin chimes. She held it by its top and ran a finger along the inside of the spiral. The spiral vibrated to her touch and gave off a clear, musical note.

Kian listened to the note of the chime. He felt himself moved by it, and he vibrated as it did. He was part of the note. He was the chime!

"Now, spirit, are you there?"

"Yes, Gerta," Kian said, and the words vibrated out of him, out of the silver. The note was silver, purest silver, and he was the chime.

"Now," Gerta said, "you prisoner. You not go back to Barrens. You told me what you are. You evil being, evil mortal, like Gerta's father."

Lord, Kian thought. *What did I say?* "Please," he chimed. "I only want to leave now. I only want to go back."

"No!" Gerta said sternly. "You should not have come where it is forbidden mortals come. Herzig will decide. He may leave you as you are and hang you in a tree to guard against our enemies. Or he may put you in a serpent."

A serpent! Kian thought, and shuddered so hard he chimed.

CHAPTER 8

Gone

As the boat moved slowly around the bend, propelled by the current and St. Helens' expert rowing, Kelvin reflected that he had previously seen all this through Heln's eyes. But did spirits have eyes? Rather, did a disembodied mind have eyes? If a mind could separate from the body, how was that different from the spirit?

Well, perhaps the distinction wasn't essential. He *had* seen, and this remained eerily familiar. But this time he was in his physical body and would not be able to float free of any danger in the manner her astral self could.

He watched the softly glowing walls and continued to muse in a way totally unlike himself.

"Houcat got your tongue?" St. Helens asked.

"Sort of." The man used the same Earth expressions as his father. All his life Kelvin had been familiar with houcats, but had never seen one with anyone's tongue. He had concluded that the expression was intended as alien-frame humor, so naturally it didn't make much sense here.

"You thinking about what I was telling you? About what we'll do about Aratex?"

Kelvin had to reorient his thoughts. He had been mainly watching for the turn into the side passage and the chamber, letting his thoughts muse on about Heln and their out-of-body trips. "You mean the Aratex affair? Their boy king and the witch Melbah and the troops you want to recruit?"

"I mean the Aratex revolution! Haven't you been listening to me? Don't you want to displace that kid dictator, get rid of the witch, and unite Aratex with Rud? Aren't you a little bit enthused?"

"I'm afraid I don't like it, St. Helens."

"Why not? You'll be running things. You with your dad's help, and my help, too."

"I don't like war. The glory of slaughtering people is lost on me. I don't feel that when I fight it's fair. I'm not a natural warrior, but as long as I have the gauntlets there's not a champion anywhere in the Seven Kingdoms who can win against me."

"That's bad?" St. Helens was incredulous. "Seems to me you should be glad the gauntlets exist."

"Sometimes I feel as though everything is an accident. I never wanted a prophecy and I certainly didn't want round ears. My sister, Jon, was always more battle-minded than I."

"Quite the little Viking, isn't she?"

"She always had the spirit," Kelvin admitted. He had heard of Vikings from his father: some sort of warrior who had lived back on Earth. He wondered if St. Helens had been one.

"She and Mor Crumb seemed enthusiastic. Lester sounded as if he'd come around. But it's your choice. It's not for me to talk the Roundear of Prophecy into anything."

Then what was the man trying to do now? Talk him out of it? Ha! "I've never been comfortable with that title."

"It's you. You slew dragons and you rid your country of a

sore. Now that the queen isn't oppressing Rud, it's time to move on to another line of that prophecy. Next line: 'Joining Two.' Only two words, but clear enough."

"My mother used to say, 'It's as true as prophecy.'"

"That's it, lad. As true as prophecy. It's your destiny, like it or not. Manifest destiny, I say."

Something was bothering Kelvin, in addition to the man and his attitude. Suddenly he put his finger on it. "I thought you were like my father."

"Lot like him, lad, in what counts," St. Helens agreed. "Different in what doesn't count."

"He never believed in magic."

"And right he was! It's all just sleight of hand and smoke and mirrors and illusion. But the credulous folk believe, and that gives it its power."

"But prophecy is magic. So why do you accept that?"

"I *don't* accept it, lad! Except to the extent that it influences people. What they call self-fulfilling prophecy."

"Then how can I have any manifest destiny?"

"Because the people believe," St. Helens said earnestly. "Because they accept it. So we have to make it come true. You're the one they think will do it, so they'll follow you. It won't just happen on its own—you have to *make* it happen. Otherwise you'll ruin their belief in the prophecy, and the whole thing goes down the tubes, and our one best chance for making things better is gone. That's why you have to do it."

Kelvin was dismayed. He had thought he had caught the man in an inconsistency, and instead St. Helens had made the case stronger yet. He trailed a hand in the water and watched silvery bubbles form off his fingertips. The air smelled damp and green here, probably from the lichen. As damp as his hopes of reprieve!

"You know you'll come to it," St. Helens prodded. "You've got to. It's our, eh, your manifest destiny, just as I said."

"Perhaps." Kelvin felt even further out of sorts than usual. "But really, one step at a time. Once Father and Kian are back in this frame, then—" He paused, took a deep breath, not liking where his father-in-law was leading him.

"Yes, son, yes?" How eager he seemed!

"Then I will think about it."

"You'll *think* about it? Is that all you're going to say? Can't you at least say that I'm right?"

Kelvin shook his head. "Not until I have thought."

St. Helens eased up on the oars. His face got very red as he stared into Kelvin's. Anger pulsed just below the surface.

"Am I to understand, Hackleberry, that you might not go with me into Aratex?"

"I might not," Kelvin agreed. It was only his honesty speaking, not his good sense.

St. Helens' eyes grew hard and his expression harder. When he spoke it was with a threatening lowered tone. "How would you like it, sonny, if I were to abandon *you?* I could row the boat back and leave you to go on to the other frame alone. Leave you to search all by yourself for your relatives. How about that?"

Kelvin's heart leaped. *Oh, thank you, Gods! At last something is going right!*

"St. Helens, that would be wonderful!" *Just what I hoped for! That you would go back!*

St. Helens erupted. He swore fearsome Earth oaths that John Knight had sometimes used, and some he had never used. He banged a fist repeatedly against the air, seemingly trying to hammer a nonexistent spike. He swore on and on for what felt like a very long, uncomfortable time. No wonder he was named after a volcano!

Unfortunately, he did not row back the way they had come. Apparently that threat had been a bluff.

"There's The Flaw!" Kelvin exclaimed. It had appeared just in time. "Bear to the left, St. Helens. We have to keep away from it. That's our passage over there." He pointed to where the water branched from the main channel. The spot was unmistakable.

St. Helens sat at the oars. His lips firmed. He folded his arms on his chest and rested his beard.

The man was stubborn and dangerous, Kelvin thought. St. Helens would try to force a promise from him by waiting as the terrible roaring falls loomed closer and closer. He could see stars shining up from the dark anomaly like cold, hard eyes: the occasional bright spark streaking through the blackness that waited to swallow them.

"Row, St. Helens!"

St. Helens took no heed. His expression was that of a statue carved from ice.

The danger was real. The gauntlets, propelled by his knowing, acted. With a swiftness that startled both St. Helens and himself, his hands grabbed the oars. It was awkward rowing from the bow, but the gauntlets were expert.

"LET GO OF THOSE!" St. Helens roared, grabbing for the oars. He caught them below the gauntlets, but his resistance was like nothing to them; the gauntlets just kept pulling, moving Kelvin's arms and shoulders and torso as required. St. Helens, heaving back with all his strength, was yanked forward to the extreme limit of his arms. He paled noticeably, as though his blood had drained.

Guided by the gloves, the oars bit into the water, turning the boat around, so that now Kelvin was in position to row it effectively. He did so.

"You surprise me," St. Helens gasped. He struggled for a moment, his face reddening again, and then again white. "I—I see now that you're the true, the one, the only Roundear of Prophecy. You, not I."

"Do you, St. Helens?" Kelvin asked, surprising himself with his own level voice. "Considering that you don't believe in magic?"

The boat was now crawling into the passage. Just ahead was Kian's tethered boat on a small ledge. The gauntlets pulled their boat up beside it and tethered it to a waiting ring.

St. Helens seemed to have recovered from his surprise. "Look, lad, you've no call to get smart-mouthed about—"

Quite independent of Kelvin and what he might have done had he been making the decision, the right gauntlet swung wide and whacked his father-in-law on the side of the head, interrupting his statement.

"OW!" St. Helens cried. He held his cheek, looking startled as well as pained. Then a cloud of renewed anger crossed his face. "Why, you young snot!"

As St. Helens started to rise from his seat, the gauntlet slapped the top of his head, crushing his stockelcap flat, and pushed him back down. The boat rocked; water lapped the top of the gunwales.

"You stay here, St. Helens," Kelvin said. He now fully appreciated the enormous advantage the gauntlets gave him. They were making a man of him—a man of prophecy that did not exist without them. "I'll go on alone. You go back and tell the others what happened."

"No, sonny, no!" St. Helens gasped. "I was foolish to have doubted you. I was going by appearances. To me you look and act like a boy."

Kelvin's gauntlets were already exerting the small amount of strength required to move the lever on the round door. With no squeak whatever, the huge metallic thing rotated, revealing, as in a vision, the sphere's interior. Lights of an alien magic lit up the chamber as brightly as day. In the center of a table waited the parchment. Beside it lay the levitation belt Kian had scorned to take. Next to them, the closet with what to Kelvin appeared to be clocks.

Kelvin found that he was actually feeling heroic. Getting the upper hand over his father-in-law accounted for it.

He began reading the parchment. He skipped over the sections concerning the chamber and its other contents as well as the message he had read through Heln's eyes. What he wanted to learn about, and quickly, was the transporter to other worlds.

"Wait, son!" St. Helens cried from beyond. "We're kin—remember?"

Kelvin glanced up from his reading, annoyed. "We're not—"

"I'm Heln's father, at least. If you don't want me along, that's your right. But let me inside with you, please."

"You can stay where you are."

"No, I want to see the chamber. I'm from Earth, remember. I might be able to tell things you can't."

What harm would it do? St. Helens was no worse than many of the men Kelvin had commanded during the fighting for the kingdom of Rud. And St. Helens was his wife's sire. He might hate the thought, but he couldn't deny it.

"All right. Come on in." He took off his laser, perhaps unnecessarily, and placed it on the table next to the parchment. Now just let St. Helens try something as foolish as he had in the boat! One wrong word from that coarse smoothie mouth and he'd point the laser at him and order him home. No way to treat decent kin, perhaps, but this was St. Helens.

Obediently, even meekly, St. Helens climbed from the boat and joined him in the chamber. Possibly, just possibly, he had learned. At least the chamber didn't object to the man's entrance; he was a legitimate roundear. At times Kelvin had wondered; after all, surgery on pointed ears could make them look round.

"You've got your nerve, St. Helens."

St. Helens looked around, wide-eyed, at the chamber's few contents. "Always have had, son. Nerve is why I'm here. Your old man knew."

Kelvin decided to ignore him. His gauntlets were bothering him now by feeling warm. Since there was nothing to fear from his father-in-law, he bared his hands and dropped the hero-savers beside the levitation belt.

He went back to studying the parchment. The instructions were simple in the extreme: "Set the dials, then walk into the transporter. A living presence within the transporter will activate it."

"Hmm, maybe so," Kelvin said, looking at the closet. How long since the dials on the outside of the closet had been moved? He took a step away from the table, thinking to examine them.

A sudden movement by St. Helens startled him. He started to turn, but in that moment St. Helens acted. A ham of a fist struck the side of his face. Stars exploded. He reached out, took a wobbly step, stumbled, and collapsed forward. Falling, part of him realized, into the waiting transporter.

Into—

Purple flashed inside the closet. It was deep and bright, yet almost black. St. Helens blinked as the color vanished, and with it Kelvin.

"Gods!" St. Helens said, awed more than he had even been before in his life. "Gods!"

He shivered from head to toe. *I shouldn't have done that! I shouldn't have! But dammit, the kid needed a lesson! Better him than me. Better get out!*

He glanced at the parchment, written in those hen-scratchings that he had never bothered to learn to read. Then down at the levitation belt and the gauntlets.

"At least I can take the laser. At least that!" he said.

His hand shook as he picked up the familiar weapon, checking its setting and safety. It would do. Do for old Melbah and, if necessary, for the brat king and an entire army.

He felt a little better now. The weapon put him in command.

He would like the levitation belt. He could work out how to use it, he was certain. Take that with him into Aratex, levitate above Conjurer's Rock, and scorch the old crone's feathers. That would end things fast!

The gauntlets lay like severed hands on the belt. If he was to take one, he might as well take all.

Reaching down, not letting himself think about it, he grabbed up the gauntlets and quickly slipped them on. He stood for a few moments trying to feel something, anything, but his hands felt just like his hands. Interestingly, the gauntlets had stretched over his hands for a perfect fit: hands twice the size of Hackleberry's.

"Damn," he said. "Damn!" He flexed and unflexed his fingers, feeling stronger second by second. They would work for him, these fancy gloves; he knew they'd work for him! He would succeed now; he'd have to. With a levitation belt, a laser, and the gauntlets, he had to be very nearly invincible.

Placing the laser under his shirt and stuffing the levitation belt down beside it, he reflected that he was now as well equipped as he could imagine. Unless the old witch had an atomic rocket hidden, she was finished.

Feeling good about his suddenly improved prospects, St. Helens left the chamber, closed the door, and climbed back into the boat.

CHAPTER 9
Lonny

THE MORNING SUN WAS partway up, its warming rays lighting the sparsely spaced rocks and plants of the Barrens. Facing the rays, feeling their warmth, Lonny Burk tried to lose her thoughts in the physical sensations of the sunshine, the very light breeze, and the sand she was trickling between her fingers. None of it worked. She was still thinking about him: about Kian Knight and what he was doing for them. She knew he had consumed one or more of the berries, and she knew why.

A scorpiocrab the size of two of Kian's hands darted from behind a pile of horse droppings, snapped its pincers, moved its eyes in and out on their stalks, and then disappeared behind Jac's tent. They had been in there for an unusual length of time and it worried her. She hated to think of him lying there, his perfect body unmoving and lifeless while his inner self went out to the flopears. It was so much like death, this astral traveling.

Jac wanted her. She had no doubt of that! Why couldn't she desire him instead of the stranger? She knew Jac was a good man, a fine thief, and a true patriot who wanted to overthrow their king. Such a man should be a logical catch for a girl from Fairview. He had even been in the serpent valley to save her, and of course he had done that, with Kian's help. She had seen him looking at her, appraising her, as the tax collector led her out of town on what had been her father's favorite horse. It could have been the horse that interested him, but she knew it wasn't. Thus Jac had gone alone to try to rescue her, to steal her as he stole the skins. Then Kian had come, Jac had rescued Kian, and Kian had behaved madly or heroically or both and rescued them all. Then they had come here, and now things were proceeding much too quickly. She had hoped to love Kian once, just once, before his leaving.

But Kian hardly seemed aware of her. When he had charged down to rescue her, she had assumed, naturally enough, that he was somehow smitten with love for her, for why else would he have taken such a terrible risk? He was handsome and evidently from a far realm, and that fitted so nicely with her notions of the ideal man that she had responded instantly. Of course she had urged him away, crying to him, "Leave! Oh, leave!" without really meaning it, and of course he had seen right through that and become more determined than ever to rescue her. Somehow she had known that he would be brave and kind and gentle, each when it counted, and then when he had acted with such total mad bravery, actually running up the serpent's neck and ramming in the spear—well, there had been no doubt in her mind or heart.

Then Jac and Kian had talked, each not wanting to rush to free her in the presence of the other. Men were like that; they considered it a weakness to get openly emotional about women, so they pretended they didn't care. Finally Kian had come to chop away her chains, and she had thanked him effusively and told him she was a virgin—that was another thing about men, their interest in this detail—and he had rubbed her wrists while she thrilled to his touch. She had been about to find a pretext to embrace him, perhaps arranging to fall so he would catch her, and then their lips would meet—but Jac had come up too soon. Jac had acted indifferent, and so had Kian, as if neither had had anything to do with saving her life (there was that man syndrome again), but they *had* saved it, and that was what counted. She really had nothing to regret, considering that she had almost been eaten by the serpent, yet somehow she wished that the timing had been just a shade different, so that she could have gotten close enough to Kian to break down his masculine reserve and make her preference known.

She thought back to when she was three years old. Her parents had been working in the field, powerless to avoid this service, and she had been left playing in the yard. In front of her was a stand of trees, screening off their view and hers. Thus she had stumbled while running, the way she had done off and on since as long as she could remember. She fell hard, and was helped to her feet, crying. Her helper, she saw, hovered in midair, and had a very large head and a greenish skin. The fingers of his hands where he held her were webbed.

"I am Mouvar," the being had said, "and you have a destiny." Then he had flown with her secure in his arms above the fields and the farms. From above she had watched her parents toiling, and the wild creatures moving at the edge of the forest. He had taken her over Serpent Valley, and she had looked down to see a flopear approaching a large serpent. "Someday you will be brought here, but that will not be the end. You will meet someone here and you will love him and then he will leave you and return to a distant world. Remember this when you are grown, for that, too, need not be the end if you do what you can."

Then the being, so different from anyone she had known, took her back to her backyard and put her down. He rose into the air and up into the clouds. It was a hot day, and when she told her story her parents had believed she had been sun-struck. For years she had tried to dismiss the memory as a dream, and had stoutly denied the prediction. People spoke of other worlds from time to time, and of Mouvar, and always she pretended she did not believe. If Mouvar did not exist, the man she was to love could not return to another world. (She ignored the corollary that the man might never come at all.) For too long a time she had lived with this persistent memory, and tried to abolish it.

Indeed, it *could* have been a dream! She could have been struck by the sun, or by the shock of her fall, and suffered a vision concocted from wisps of stories she had heard. What little girl didn't dream of becoming the object of distant love? So probably her parents were right, and the persistence of the memory was simply because of her secret longing for just that sort of thing.

But when she had been chained out as sacrifice for the serpent, that memory had blazed forth again, undimmed by time or reason. Now she *had* to believe, because it was her only hope of rescue! She had been brought here, and it must not be the end. It was the place of the vision, and Kian had come, and he could be the man! She remembered now that the vision had not said she would lose him, just that he would leave her but that it need not be the end. Now she had a better notion of what she should do, for she knew herself to be a pretty woman, and men liked that. So if she could just capture Kian's heart before he went far away, then maybe he would change his mind and stay. It certainly seemed worth the try, and even if it wasn't the vision, it was worth doing. Because the dream might not be real, but her love was, however foolishly based. It wouldn't be foolish anymore if she could only—

Jac stuck his head through the tent flap and called for the dwarf. Heeto came running, his short legs blurring in the way they had as they carried him from the horse he had been grooming to his master's tent.

"Heeto, bring a shovel!" Jac said.

"Master, is he—"

"He must be. It's been far too long."

"NO!" It burst from her involuntarily. "No, he can't be dead!"

Jac looked at her with a stricken face. "I don't want him to be, but facts are facts. If he was going to come alive he'd start breathing. It's been too long. He took one berry, same as before, so we know how long it takes."

"Wait! Wait, because he will come around!"

"You seem certain."

"I am!" she said, hoping that her vehemence made up for her uncertainty.

He studied her, perhaps coming to understand the secret of her heart. If Kian died, there would be no one for her but Jac. But not if Kian died because Jac had buried him too soon. "You want me to wait until he deteriorates?"

"Yes! Yes, wait that long!" For that would happen long before her love died.

"The ants will be coming. And the flies."

"I'll watch! I'll keep them off him."

Jac shook his head. "That won't be pleasant. Perhaps Heeto—"

She pushed by him into the tent. Kian lay there on a bearver hide, apparently quite dead. She sat down, crossed her legs and arms, and waited. Jac, accepting the way of it, silently squeezed her shoulder once and then left.

As time passed and no life returned to the body before her, she reached over and took up his pouch. She tipped it up and four of the berries rolled out into her palm.

She gazed at them, appreciating their nature. These were otherworld berries, and they caused a round-eared person to do an astral separation. Apparently roundears were rare in Kian's world. They were common here; did that change things? Would the berries work for a local roundear as well as they did for him?

She had to do something, according to the vision. She had thought it was to make him love her, so he would return, but maybe it was more than that. Maybe she had to *bring him back*. From whatever realm his spirit had gone to. Suppose, just suppose . . .

Quickly, not thinking further about what she did, lest she reconsider, she pushed the berries into her mouth. The taste was strange, though not unpleasant. She hesitated only a moment, then swallowed.

In mere heartbeats she began to feel that she was in fact leaving her body. She saw the top of the tent much too close. Then she was outdoors, and the sky was as blue overhead as her own eyes in a mirror. There were soft, wispy clouds.

If this was another vision, it was a fine one! But she was gambling that it wasn't. "Kian, Kian—I am coming for you," she said voicelessly. "Whether this be death or astral separation, I am doing what you have done. I am coming to where you are, Kian. We'll be together, maybe for always."

The world drifted by, and Serpent Valley. She shuddered, again with no body, knowing what had almost happened in that valley. She had guessed that Jac would come to save her, but had not been sure whether he would come in time, or whether he would choose to free her before the serpent arrived. If the flopears were watching, and saw him do that, they would kill him. Once the serpent came, they would not watch, because they honored the serpent's privacy during special moments such as feeding. So what had been her chances, really? She had had to believe in her private prophecy, because it couldn't happen if she got eaten first. She had had to believe that she would somehow survive—and indeed she had. But she had doubted, too, and now she understood how deeply she had doubted. Jac had not come in time; Kian had. There was the key to her emotion.

Then she passed another, connecting valley and went right through cottages, rock walls, and deep through the ground.

She was in a room. It was an ordinary enough room with a bed. There was a man in the bed, but he was not Kian. Could this be Kian's father, whom Kian had sought? Did this mean that Kian, the man she loved, was after all dead?

There was something in the room that seemed to her not to belong. It was a spiral serpentskin chime such as Kian had asked about. She felt drawn to it, but could not fathom why. It seemed to her that she hovered beside the object, seeing its silver brightness and scaly beauty. Why was she here? Why, when it was Kian she wanted?

She heard footsteps outside. Two flopears entered: a girl and a man. "Here he is, Herzig," the girl said, indicating the chime.

The male flopear stared at the chime, not touching it. "You're certain?"

"Yes. He's in there. He can tell you himself."

"You in there, mortal?" Herzig said to the chime.

"He's sulking," the girl said. "Spirits sulk when trapped. Maybe he think if he be silent you not think he there."

"You would know, Gerta. I wish I did. I can't talk to spirits the way you can."

"That no matter. I do it for both. You take out?"

"Might as well. The ancestor needs a tenant."

A spirit trapped in the chime? Lonny hardly needed to guess whose spirit that might be! But how had it happened, and how could Kian be released?

She followed the male Herzig as he carried the silent chime out of the stone house, with Gerta coming along. They crossed a yard and entered a shed. Here lay the long body of a serpent, its head and one eye covered with a heavy greenish glop.

"Almost healed, not yet activated," Herzig said. "Better a flopear spirit, but mortal spirits also need rest."

"Not get rest," Gerta said with a smile. "Not in ancestor."

"No, perhaps not. Not if they don't like being there. But given time—several hundred or a thousand years—a mortal spirit will be the same as a flopear ancestor. It can take that long to become, though usually much faster."

"Yes. Tunneling, bringing silver, enjoying sacrifice. In time mortal spirit and ancestor be one."

What were they talking about? Lonny had the feeling that

the body of the serpent Kian had slain was going to be brought back to life. By—a mortal spirit? Just what was going on?

Herzig climbed some steps to a platform. Here he held the chime over the serpent's head. He looked to Gerta.

"Have you something to say, spirit?" Gerta asked.

The chime spoke, musically chiming each word. "Let me go! Let me go! Let me go!"

"Kian?" Lonny said, excited. "Kian, is that you?"

"Lonny? Lonny, Lonny—go! Go, go, go!"

Just the way she had begged him to go before the serpent came, not meaning it! Now she had to try to rescue him from the same serpent, dead though it was. "Kian, I am here! Let me touch you, bring you back—"

"No, Lonny, no! Get out, get away, before they trap you!"

Gerta looked about. "There's another one!" she said. "He spoke to it."

"Can you get it, too?"

"Maybe. Activate ancestor."

Herzig shook the chime. The chime vibrated with a sweet musical note. Then the serpent raised its massive head.

Lonny knew she had to act. She dived for the chime, reaching out to Kian. She caught hold of him, somehow, astrally, and tried to pull him out, but he was securely anchored.

"Lonny, let go!" he cried. "You'll only trap yourself!"

She let go reluctantly, aware of the truth of his warning. But as she did, she saw something move from the chime to the nose of the serpent. Kian was being drawn to the monster!

Now Gerta took the chime and swung it toward Lonny. "Go in chime!" she ordered.

Lonny jumped away—but in so doing, she came up against the serpent. She felt a strange sensation. Could the serpent that had come to devour her body be ready to devour her spirit? Kian had killed it, but now it seemed that his spirit was being used to reanimate it. If it took in her spirit, too, she would be with him. Alive with the man she loved!

"Go, Lonny!" Kian cried. "She'll capture you as she did me. Go tell the others back at camp!"

It made sense, but she hesitated. To return and give warning, or to be with him? What was the meaning of her vision? To leave him—or join him?

Then she saw Gerta extend the chime again with a crafty expression on her face. Gerta would have her in the chime instead of Kian!

It was not right! She would not stand for it! She would be with Kian! Now!

She was abruptly in the serpent's body, looking through its single eye. With her, she sensed, was Kian.

"Lonny, why, why?"

"To be with you," she said.

"It will be for eternity. Or until we both forget."

"Not eternity, Kian. Mouvar said you'd leave for another world."

"This *is* another world—the astral realm. But—"

"Mouvar said it need not be the end if I did right. So I joined you."

"Lonny, what are you talking about? Mouvar? Have you seen him?"

"Once, long ago. He said what would be. He told me and then I forgot. Or tried to."

"Lonny, are you mad? You're not making sense."

"You have part of an eternity to decide that. During that time all that must be said will be said."

"But you are young and beautiful! You have a good life to live! It is crazy to throw it away like this!"

"It would be an empty life without you, Kian. I want only to be with you. Now I am."

"They're both in the ancestor," Herzig said. "Good work, Gerta. That is as good as having one in the chime. The ancestor has been much weakened, and two spirits will help it recover better than one would." Climbing down from the platform, he put his head out the door and called: "Tripsic, Synplax, Uternaynie—come!"

Three flopears came running from a stone wall they had been constructing. They stood obediently before Herzig, awaiting his instructions.

"Ancestor ready," Herzig said. "Clear way."

Tripsic, Synplax, and Uternaynie ran out, waving their arms and shouting to busily working flopears to clear a path. Gerta stepped outside the door and back inside carrying a freshly picked blue-and-pink blossom. She touched the blossom lightly to the tip of the serpent's snout.

Lonny had the sensation of a lovely perfume in her nostrils, but they weren't really her nostrils or Kian's. They belonged to the serpent, and the smell was rousing it.

The great body began to undulate. It flexed along its length. Then it crawled from the shed, following Gerta, sniffing the blossom she held.

"Kian, are you doing this? Are you moving us?"

"No, I have no control," Kian said. There was no sound from the serpent; it was a mental signal that came across as speech. "I'm here. You're here. I don't think either of us can do more than we can in our spirit bodies. Worse than that, we're trapped. We're in this thing forever."

"No, not forever, I told you."

Neat stone cottages, stone walls, and patches of carefully tended ground slipped by. She was seeing it through the serpent's one good eye. She saw it but could not affect it; she had no control over the serpent's motions.

"Oh, Kian, isn't this fun!"

"FUN!" he responded indignantly.

"Yes, the thrill of being a part of this! Oh, my goodness, I never thought of this, never dreamed of it!"

"Yes, it's a nightmare."

"But look at how beautiful everything is! We're a part of this creature, and we're conscious. We're alive, both of us!"

"I wonder for how long."

"For hundreds of years, they were saying! Much longer than our regular bodies would last!"

"How long as *us*," he clarified darkly.

How depressing, she thought. She wanted to snap him out of it. Just being alive, just being with someone you truly cared about, that was after all what life was mainly about. She did not quite dare express this. Kian didn't know that she loved him. She was able to read this in him now, and it did not cause her grief, because she saw his side of it. He had come to rescue her because he believed it was the right thing to do. He—he did not think that he had any future with a woman of this world, when he was only going to leave it soon. So he—he liked her, he found her beautiful, but he did not think more of it than that. He did not understand that she had loved him the moment he came to her rescue, because of the prophecy. He did not understand how important it was to her, just being alive, just being with the person she truly cared about, fulfilling the prophecy. But there would be time, plenty of time! She would at the proper moment acquaint him with her love, and she was sure that then he would love her back. It would be wonderful. It was already wonderful, for her; then it would be wonderful for him, too.

They followed Gerta through the flopears' valley and on into Serpent Valley. Here there were a few serpents shedding their skins in the bright morning sunshine. They wriggled on, into the higher hills and then into the mountain.

Here Gerta stopped. She stroked the monster's snout with the flower, talking to it, telling it what a beautiful ancestor it was. Then she said, "Return, Ancestor. Return, live, thrive."

Lonny noticed that Gerta was gone from the serpent's sight. Going back home, she suspected. That left the two of them alone in the serpent, as it were.

Light from the eye ceased and all seemed black. The serpent was tunneling, its teeth crushing rock, boring into the mountain. "Oh, Kian!" Lonny cried out. "Isn't this exciting!"

"Isn't it, though." He did not seem pleased with her. She would have to curb her enthusiasm until he understood.

"We're together now!" she continued, though she knew she should wait for him to get better adjusted. But in her spirit form, or her serpent-residency form, she lacked the controls

that her natural body had. She tended just to express herself
without thinking. "We're together, and—"

She began tasting what the serpent was tasting: a rich, sharp
tang that her—its—instincts knew was silver. The serpent
was dissolving the metal ore, digesting it with its acid. And
she and Kian could taste it!

"Oh, Kian, oh—"

"It won't last forever," Kian said. It was grim the way he
saw it; she felt the aura of his concept. "Even this enormous
body can only hold so much."

Behind them, the serpent's digestive processes functioned,
and wastes squirted. They had killed this creature, and now
they had brought it back to life, their spirits replacing the one
it had lost when it died. This notion would have horrified her
before, but now she was part of the serpent's new life, and it
was all quite natural and even grand.

Oh, but she enjoyed the taste of silver! She loved the
shivery feel of the scales sliding along the forming tunnel, the
mighty body undulating, even the casting of wastes. She knew
that Kian didn't. Was it that all men were unappreciative, or
was it just him? Yet she loved him just as she had when he had
first come to her rescue. Her ignorance was being displaced
by knowledge, but her emotion remained intact. Someday,
when it was right, he would know and share.

"Gods, I hate that taste!"

Lonny sighed, nonphysically. Being with Kian in the
interim might not be quite as much joy as she had imagined.
It was said that those who got married soon enough discovered things in each other they didn't like. She did not believe
that, but she was beginning to wonder. Still, this was far
better than having him leave her for another world.

But suppose, she thought uncomfortably, he somehow left
her *here*. All alone in the serpent, shut away from all human
contact, becoming daily more and more serpent, less and less
human. She had come here to be eternally with him; without
him, it might not be fun at all. She shivered, and it seemed to
her that her shiver went out through the body they were in.

Unheeding, the great serpent tunneled on in the dark. It seemed that though their spirits might lend it strength for its recovery, it was not aware of their presence. It was an animal, however remarkable it might be.

Heeto stepped into the tent and looked down without surprise at their bodies. The girl had taken the berries, he feared, and now both of them were dead. Unless, of course, through some means he could not know about, they could wake again and live.

A fly buzzed. He swatted at it with his hand. He touched their faces: cold.

How long should he wait? A body would deteriorate if not alive. They would start to spoil and stink and then they would have to be buried. But until then, he'd wait.

Sighing regretfully, Heeto sank down by the bodies and prepared to wait out the entire day.

CHAPTER 10
Taken

JON HAD BROUGHT DOWN a goouck with what she knew was a lucky stone but what she pretended was only the skill that had saved her brother and the king from the evil sorcerer. Lester, shaking his head admiringly, had ridden across the river and fetched the big bird back. Mor had stood stroking his chin and pulling at his one-half ear and his full ear alternately, saying over and over, "I don't believe it! Nobody's that good with a sling! Nobody! A girl especially!" Now, somewhat later, the bird was a mouth-watering brown on the spit and the chauvinists and heroine alike watched as Heln, so unexpectedly expert at culinary skills, turned it, pausing now and then to savor the aroma.

Mor was there first with the big knife he had carried into war. He cut off a generous slice of the bread Yokes had brought them. He took a big sniff through his big nose, tried to bite into his repast, and burned his tongue. He moved back a way with his meal, and took up the bottle of rasple wine he had hidden from St. Helens. He took a swig, made a face, and then passed the bottle on to his son. Lester followed suit, though waiting just a bit on the bird. Jon sawed off another two hunks of bread from the generous-size loaf and joined Heln.

"He really should have waited," Heln said, watching the juices trickle into the fire and make loud spats and tiny curls of steam. "It was bound to be hot."

"Men!" Jon said, as though not a dedicated liberationist. "All they think about is their bellies and their—"

"JON!"

"Eh, horses."

"Yes, horses." Heln smiled. Jon was going to be a tomboy until she became a mother. Considering the way Lester and she doted on each other, that might not be such a long time. It was hard to think of Jon ever being a mother to anyone, but then she had proved herself to be an unusually gentle and caring nurse, a fact that must have gone a long way to winning a grateful Lester.

"Well, I'm going to try a slice."

"Just don't put it in your mouth too fast."

"I won't."

Jon cut a slice of the white leg meat, preferring that to the dark meat of the breast. In that preference, at least, she was typically female.

Heln watched her march away to join the men where they were laughing over some joke and passing the wine back and forth. It was such a warm night that no one actually needed the fire to keep warm.

Heln fixed her own meal, scooped a few ashes onto the fire with the board she had for that purpose, and looked toward the rest of her party. They were laughing it up now, and Mor's heehaw competed with his son's more gentle laughter and Jon's unfeminine thigh-slapping accompanied by giggles. Why couldn't she enjoy this sort of camaraderie? Heln wondered. Somehow she couldn't. Perhaps it had something to do with that Female Liberation her natural father had explained. Too many of the jokes people laughed at seemed to her to be demeaning rather than amusing. Sometimes she thought people laughed out of nervousness and embarrassment. Certainly she could never see humor in a supposed joke that centered on someone's debasement. She suspected that having been brutally raped in the notorious Franklin Girl Mart and almost destroyed as a consequence affected her outlook.

Musing on how Kelvin had saved her in more than just a physical sense, Heln took her sandwich, dripping with hot goouck grease, along to the bank of the river. Such a nice night! So good to get out and just breathe. She appreciated the spicy smell of the pinruse trees and the water roslies growing pink and beautiful in the backwaters. There was the splashing of a raccossum in the shallows searching for crasters and other succulent water creatures. A fish popped out of the water with a splash, and a small wolok splashed eagerly after it. Night birds sang away in the woods, putting the calls and whistles of their daytime cousins to shame with their natural symphonies.

As she walked now, danger was the farthest thing from her mind. The war was over, unless of course her natural father could persuade enough Rudians to start it up with Aratex. In her heart Heln believed he would not prevail; people had had enough of war. Even Kelvin's old comrades-in-arms, the Crumbs included, would not want to go through again what they had suffered for their homeland. Jon possibly, but then Jon seemed to have put all the agony of her torment by the sorcerer and the dwarf out of her mind. Jon, to hear her tell it, had spent the entire war rescuing her clumsy brother and insisting that he be brave and fulfill the prophecy. Jon was really something, and Heln quite understood when Kelvin, sometimes exasperated, would say with the hint of a sour growl, "But so what?"

Perhaps it was thinking about Jon and her boyish ways that made Heln assume that the stealthy footfalls were hers. It would be just like Jon to sneak up on her, she thought, though Jon knew Heln didn't enjoy that sort of thing. Any moment there would be a bloodcurdling screech and Jon would leap out of concealment and grab her.

But there were two sets of footfalls. Two people behind? Something moved in the bushes ahead. Bearver? At night? Possibly, and if so, she should not just walk up to it.

Heln slowed her feet. Should she go back? Should she call out, hoping to scare the animal and alert her stalkers? And how could there be two, anyway? Lester wouldn't participate in his wife's foolishness, and neither would Mor. Besides, Mor was much too big and clumsy to sneak.

A shiver started at the base of Heln's spine and traveled all the way up her back. Bandits? Within hiking distance of the capital?

A sudden hand around her mouth cut off her thought. She twisted half around and saw a face covered with a dark hood. The hood resembled a torturer's in that it covered all but the eyes. Another arm was around her waist. Breath, redolent of onlic, puffed into her face.

"Be quiet and nothing will happen to you!"

She tried to believe this, but all she could think of was the physical and mental agony of rape. She had to scream out, she had to.

But there was no chance.

Back in the bushes, out of sight of the camp, a light appeared in the form of a shaded candle. Another dark figure stared into her face, again breathing onlic.

"Where is he?" the face demanded.

"Where's—who?"

"St. Helens."

"St. Helens? You want my father?" Heln was bewildered. She would not have imagined them after him.

The man looked close at her, moving the candle. "It *is* his daughter! Look at those ears!"

Someone moved nearer, looked, and nodded a hooded head.

"He left with my husband for—" Something warned her. "Some place."

"Ah. And St. Helens will listen to reason if we have you."

"No!" Had she made a mistake? Perhaps she shouldn't have said that.

"Corry! Bemode! We're taking her with us back to Aratex!"

The two men moved near. Both wore the dark hoods and dark clothing. Corry was tall; Bemode, wide. Corry took her by her left arm, Bemode by the right. The other man, the one who gave orders, walked ahead carrying the shaded candle.

They walked through the woods on a path probably pounded out by meer. The night birds still sang, as they did in nearly every forest. The moon and stars shone down through overlaps in the branches. As the trees thinned out along the path, the man walking ahead paused, raised the lantern, lifted its shade, and blew out the candle. Now it was only the natural light that showed their path.

"It's not much farther now," Corry whispered to her. "We'll cross the river and then we'll be in Aratex."

"Shut up, Corry!" Bemode snapped.

They walked on in silence, except for the crunch of their footsteps and the sounds of the birds. They came out of the forest and paused long enough for the men to sweep the moonlighted banks with their eyes. No one was in sight as they stepped down into the water, and it swirled up cold around her ankles. She wished now that she had her boots. There was already a thorn in her right foot, picked up on the path.

The man carrying the dark lantern splashed ahead. Water rose up around his knees and then his waist. Still he splashed on, confident that he knew the river here and that no unseen ledge was about to trap him. Moving just behind him, propelled partially by the hands of the men on either side, Heln was thankful that she wore greenbriar pantaloons instead of skirts.

The man at the head of their procession reached the opposite shore and climbed up on the bank. As Heln started to follow she tripped and almost fell. Corry let go of her left hand, and she planted a knee and hand firmly in the mud before Bemode yanked her back to her feet. Well, at least she had left a sign, she thought, not bothering to comment.

The man with the lantern pushed back his hood, revealing dark hair and eyes in a stern face. Corry and Bemode pushed theirs back as well. Each of them seemed to be just a man. That was a certain relief, though not a great one; men were not as bad as supernatural creatures, but men were more apt to rape a woman. How well she knew!

Still unspeaking, the leader led the way up a bank and to four horses tethered in a small clearing. He made motions, and Corry and Bemode saddled and bridled the mounts while he stood watching her. She thought to run, but knew it would do no good. Even if she could outrun the men, she could never outrun a horse. If they had to chase her down and catch her, they would surely bind her and perhaps do much worse. Her best course for the moment was grudging cooperation.

Corry finished his work and led her to a mare. He helped her up and into the saddle, retaining his hold on the reins. The others joined them. All mounted. All rode.

They followed a road, well lighted by the moonlight, through towering cliffs that loomed up like tall bright sentinels. Past a huge rock with a road winding to its top. On through the night, no one speaking, and then they were approaching a palace with high gates. The gates were opened by guards wearing armor and swords, looking horribly formidable. Heln knew that her chance for escape was gone.

They rode to a stable and stopped while liveried attendants took charge of the horses and led the people inside.

"Well, Major?"

The tall man with the dark eyebrows had appeared so suddenly as to startle her despite her worn, frightened state. He looked her up and down. "This is his daughter?"

"Yes, General Ashcroft." The major saluted; so did Corry and Bemode.

"Very well. At ease. I'll take over now." The general

motioned for Heln to walk ahead of him, into the palace. She obeyed him, not certain whether this was normal procedure for the handling of prisoners. The sun was just coming up, lighting the palace and its grounds with the first pearly rays of day. They had traveled all night.

Inside, an aged servant escorted them across carpets and down a hall and into a bedchamber. There, sitting upright, eyes very wide, was the dark young man with the pimply face she knew to be His Royal Majesty King Phillip Blastmore.

"Your Majesty," the general said. "Pardon the intrusion so early in the day. This is the daughter of your former companion, St. Helens of the round ears. She is also the wife of the upstart who destroyed Rud's sorcerer and defeated Rud's queen and ended her reign. He is known as Kelvin, the Roundear of Prophecy."

The young king drew in a long, shaky breath. "Thank you, General Ashcroft. You have done well to bring her to me."

Heln could feel Phillip's eyes on her, and she did not like the feeling or his rosy blush. He was not a man grown, but he was of an age where his glands were telling him things. She distrusted this young monarch's sly, almost timid expression, and the way his hands whitened where they gripped the bedclothing.

"Perhaps you would like me to leave her alone with you?"

"No! No, General Ashcroft." Now the boy's face was as red as a sunrise. "That won't be necessary. Yet."

"But you like her?"

"Yes."

Heln knew herself to be a complete mess. Her legs were steeped in drying mud, her hair was in tangled disorder, and she was sure there was dirt all over her face. But she also knew that any man could see through such superficialities when he wanted to, and recognize her beauty. If the king liked her now, that meant real trouble the moment she got cleaned up—or before.

"Perhaps she would make a nice toy," the general said. "A man your age needs toys, Your Majesty."

"P-perhaps a queen? I need a queen."

"Perhaps, Your Majesty."

Heln jerked. She had been listening to their soft voices, watching their strange eyes, and now there could be no doubt of what they were discussing.

"But I'm married!" she exclaimed. "I have my husband!" Which was one way of reminding them that she was no virgin, though she feared that would not turn off this stripling king. Men cared a lot about virginity when they chose to, and not at all when they chose not.

"Husbands die," Ashcroft purred. "Girls are widowed."

So much for that feeble ploy. She knew already that she would do far better to pretend to forget all about her husband, no matter what that entailed. But she couldn't.

She looked from one face to the other. She took a step back from the bed and then another step. She tried to move a third step, but General Ashcroft fixed her with his deep yellow eyes, and it was as if she were shackled to the floor.

"I suggest putting her in the guest chamber for now, Your Majesty. She can be watched there, and if you wish to visit her and play—"

"No, no. Not until after the royal wedding."

Ashcroft's heavy eyebrows drew down. It was evident that he thought of Heln as a hostage and a potential plaything for the king, not as a potential bride. "As Your Majesty wishes. And, of course, Melbah can prepare her some wine. She can forget the roundear in Rud, and even her father."

Enchanted drink! That would ruin any chance at all for her to escape, assuming any existed. "No! No!" she shrieked, terrified.

"Yes, that will be fine, General. For now, she is my guest."

"I don't want to be your guest! I want to go home! I'm a roundear, can't you understand? A *roundear!*" She yanked back her hair and showed her ears, making her status quite plain. Her ears had made her almost valueless at the Girl Mart.

"His Majesty is not prejudiced," Ashcroft said. "Though

perhaps those ears would tend to disqualify you for queenly status."

Heln shut her mouth, as it was just getting her into deeper trouble. A potential queen would be treated better than a potential plaything, and perhaps spared the enchanted drink if she seemed to cooperate. It gagged her to think of it, but she might do best to play up to the stripling king.

"This way, please." The general indicated the hall beyond the king's chamber. The king did not protest, though his eyes were doing their best to strip away her tattered clothing. All too soon his boyish reticence would become fumbling boyish eagerness, and she wanted to postpone that as long as possible.

She found her feet moving, though she hardly knew how. Silently she went down the hall and up some stairs with a long polished banister on either side. Then another landing and some more stairs. A third set of stairs, and then a wearying fourth. Finally, near the roof, General Ashcroft opened an isolated door.

She went in. It was a beautiful room with a window giving a view of the grounds. The window was not barred, but the drop to the cobblestones below would surely kill her. Best she think about that.

The general faced her, blocking the exit. "I must ensure that you do nothing foolish."

She glanced out the window again, and shuddered. "Have no concern, General. I won't jump." Because that would certainly end her chance to escape. She had endured rape before, and tried to kill herself. Having survived both, she concluded that another rape would not be as bad as successful suicide. Then she had had no one else; now she had Kelvin. She had to live, whatever the cost.

"Strip," Ashcroft said.

"Oh, not you, too!" she exclaimed, almost beyond outrage. She had been bracing herself for the king's gropings; this was too much!

"It is necessary that I verify that you carry no weapons,

before I leave you alone with King Blastmore. You will strip, and I will take your clothes; then you may clean yourself and don new clothing."

Oh. He had a point. It would surely have occurred to her soon enough to try to kill the king and get away while others assumed he was indulging himself romantically. She knew that if she did not cooperate now, the general would force the search.

She gritted her teeth and stripped. Ashcroft watched impassively. When she stood naked before him, the knife she wore strapped to her thigh was revealed. She removed it and its holster and dropped them on her pile of sodden clothing.

Ashcroft gathered up the bundle and walked toward the door. "You will find appropriate clothing in the closet," he said, nodding toward it. "I will lock you in, but if you ring the bell, a servant will come." He indicated a pull-cord that evidently operated the bell. "I repeat, it is best if you do not do anything foolish."

Dully, she nodded. He had more than made his point.

The general stepped back and started to close the door. He moved so silently, even burdened by her clothing, so almost floatingly, that it was eerie.

"Wait! Wait!" she cried. "What about my husband? What about Kelvin, the prophesied hero of Rud?"

Ashcroft's eyebrows drew down. "He will be remembered there. You may be remembered also. Only you yourself will not remember."

Because they intended to dose her with a potion to make her forget. How was she to avoid that? "You mean he will be—" She swallowed. "Killed?" She hoped that threat had been empty, or only to force her cooperation.

"Of course. The sooner the better. Unfortunately, His Majesty needs a bit of prodding."

Sudden realization washed over her. The general's odd ways, his evident disinterest in her naked body. "You're not—you're not—"

"Yes, my pretty?"

"You're not a man."

"I'm not? Then what am I?"

"A witch. The witch Melbah."

"Very astute of you, my dear." With that the tall figure vanished, and with him his uniform. In his place was a squat, ugly old crone, still with the armful of clothing.

Heln shivered. "You control him! You run the boy king!"

"Obviously, my dear. But I do try to provide him with suitable entertainments."

Heln refused to be distracted by that implication. "And you want Kelvin destroyed so that he can't destroy *you*. And you want my father—"

"The king will decide about your father, once he is in chains as he commanded."

"That's why I was brought here, so that my father and my husband will come to rescue me."

"Why, of course. That's very, very good reasoning. You just may live to make a shrewd queen of Aratex."

"But you don't want me as queen! You only want me as a distraction for the king!"

"Perhaps I have changed my mind. You just might become both. Suitably prepared, you could become a genuine asset to our cause."

"*Your* cause! If the king should—should fall in love with me, you would have an even better lever to control him!"

The witch nodded. "Yes, I believe you will serve very well, my dear. Those round ears will prevent the populace from ever supporting you, so you will have no base for power in your own right. Only I will be able to make the people accept you—so long as the king wishes."

With that the large door swung shut without being touched by the witch. There was a loud click from a lock, and the sound of a heavy bar falling in place across the door.

She had known she was in trouble. Now she realized how much worse that trouble was than she had imagined!

Heln looked at the bed and the dresser and then back at the window. If only she had some dragonberries! How she would like to fly home and see what the others were doing. Then maybe, just maybe, on into that other frame world to Kelvin and St. Helens. And if she could somehow find a way to communicate with her husband, to warn him—

But then reality returned. She had no chance to do any of that. She flung herself on the bed and sobbed.

CHAPTER 11
Resolute

THE LASER AND THE levitation belt were concealed beneath his brownberry shirt and the gauntlets hidden in a deep pocket of his greenbriar pantaloons when St. Helens reached the top of the flight of steps. It wouldn't do to let them see too soon. Time enough when his plans were made.

They were still camped near the ruins of the old palace. Jon and Lester and Mor, all with worried expressions. St. Helens studied their unsmiling faces in the early morning light. Something was definitely wrong. Where was Heln?

"Where's Kelvin?" Jon asked.

"Why, he, ah, went on alone. We decided it would be best."

"He went and you stayed?"

Was this sharp-eared girl accusing him of something? St. Helens felt an uncomfortable squirming sensation, though it was not fear. They couldn't know what had happened.

"Never mind," Mor said. "The fact is it's morning and

106

your daughter hasn't come in yet. She's been missing all night. We were just about to go in search."

"Missing?" St. Helens chewed on the thought. "You think she wandered off, got lost?"

"No. More likely kidnapped. And by somebody you may know, St. Helens."

"I assure you, if Heln is missing, I don't know what could have happened." An agent from Aratex, trailing him, not finding him, finding instead his daughter? The thought chilled him. St. Helens did not care a lot about these people personally, but his daughter was something else. He had always known that eventually he would be reunited with his baby girl. Her name derived from his, from the time when she had first tried to say his name and garbled it into a single syllable: Hel'n. It had been so cute they had kept it. She was a big girl now, but still his to protect. For sure, he wouldn't let the minions of Aratex get her! If that boy king ever laid eyes on her—

"Well, let's not waste time!" Lester said. "We knew she went along the river. We could see her footprints even in the dark. Kelvin said she liked to wander off by herself sometimes—almost the same as he does. Just to look at the stars, listen to the birds, breathe the clean river air, and think."

"That would be my daughter," St. Helens said. He had done that himself when she was a little girl. Her mother hadn't always been too pleased, either, thinking he would run into one of the queen's agents. Now, over a dozen years later, Heln was following the practice she had learned from him, just as Kelvin must have learned it from John. To be restless seemed to be a roundear's nature. No television or radio or bars here, so what else should be done when the night was around and the need was for solitude?

"St. Helens, come!" Mor ordered, and started with the others in the direction of the river.

They weren't even giving him time to catch his breath! He was resentful of anyone who commanded him, even a man who reminded him of a top sergeant. But he stifled that, and followed; he could not afford to arouse any suspicion.

There was a burned-out fire with bones of a fowl around it, the bones now being chewed by chipoffers and gomunks. The furry little rascals always seemed to be there when food was dropped. He wished he had some of that fowl; it appeared to have been a goouck or an incredibly large ducoose. Good eating birds in this existence, even though he sometimes remembered stuffed turkey and fried chicken. You can take the roundear away from Earth but you can't take Earth away from the roundear, he thought. John Knight had said that to the men he commanded one stormy night when there had been much grousing about unfamiliar foods and unfamiliar ways. He had been right, the commander had, about that and a lot more. Too bad he hadn't thought of those words when the bitch-queen had worked her wiles!

"Here's her footprints," Jon said. She was pointing at the very clear prints in the mud at the river's edge. Heln had been barefoot again. She liked taking off the heavy leather boots they all wore and walking in the mud. But that could be dangerous. She could cut her toe, or get stung by something.

St. Helens shook his head. He was starting, he realized with a shock, to feel like a father. Of course he had always been a father, but it had been mostly memory and dream, something removed in either the past or the future. He had told himself how great it had been or would be. Now it was the present, and it wasn't great, it was nervous. He was really worried about her! If she really had been kidnapped—

"She stubbed her toe on this rock," Lester commented. "See how the ball of her foot came down here and then here, and then she caught her balance and went on walking."

"Good tracking eye," St. Helens observed. That was another thing about the pointed-ear folks—many of them had the sharpshooter's eye and the tracking ability of legendary frontiersmen. He wished he had thought more about that before returning to Rud.

Lester was wasting no time. Like a hound St. Helens had

known in the American South, he was dashing along the bank checking for indents in the mud and signs that were far less obvious. Here she had stopped, half turned, obviously listening to something. Here—oh-oh, here were other signs. Boot signs, and not quite the heel marks of the boots made in Rud. They had come from the woods in the dark, stealthily: two men. They had come up behind, and here they had grabbed her, she had struggled, and they had dragged her into the woods. There the two men had been joined by a third.

Now, frantically as the light got better, Lester moved on ahead, checking the grasses and the bushes for signs of passage. His darting eyes found indications aplenty, and he did not pause to explain—if it was possible to explain—what to his eye was as clear as a map.

Over here, over here, and now over here. One of the men had stopped to relieve himself. Heln had stepped on a thorn with her bare foot, leaving a tiny speck of dried blood. They had gone straight through a thicket, thorns pulling threads from their clothes. A candle-lantern had been set on a bare spot of ground, drops of wax spattering on a rock as the candle had been extinguished. A meer trail had intervened and they had followed it, their own feet beating away more of the soil and crossing the hoofprints of the trailmakers. The trail led to a river and a fording spot, and beyond it, a marker on the other side proclaiming the kingdom of Aratex.

There was no doubt now. Agents of King Blastmore had indeed kidnapped St. Helens' daughter and spirited her into the adjoining land.

"Whoa, we can't go crossing borders. This border especially," Mor said.

"They did! And so can we!" Mor's son replied.

To that there could be no argument; they could not rescue Heln if they did not follow her trail. But somewhere ahead, St. Helens knew, there would be an ambush. They wanted him, after all, not his daughter. They wanted him to follow— which was why they had not bothered to obliterate her trail.

But what the agents did not know, what Mor and Les and

Jon could not realize, was that St. Helens was prepared. The agents were unwittingly playing right into his hands. With the laser and the gauntlets, he could defeat three or a dozen agents and rescue his daughter. Then he'd be the hero he needed to be, to enlist the aid of the Rudians in the battle for Aratex.

Yes, indeed, the campaign ahead would be triumphant. The very first skirmish, the histories would proclaim, in St. Helens' war of liberation.

Mor rode ahead with Lester at his side and Jon following. St. Helens was bringing up the rear. That was not the place he should occupy, he thought. As the horses splashed across the river, their feet sucking at a mud bottom, he thought hard on how best to deal with the ambush he knew would be ahead. The first thing would be to get the Crumbs out of danger; once that was accomplished, he could deal on his own.

Mor brought his horse to a stop on the opposite bank. "Here's her knee and palm prints," he said. "She must have stumbled, probably deliberately."

"Nice going, Heln!" Jon said.

Lester looked along the shore and the edge of the Aratex forest. "They may have an ambush."

"Exactly what I was thinking," St. Helens said. Now was the time for him to move, if ever. "I think it best if the three of you wait back in Rud, and I'll go on alone. I know this country, and I don't think the rest of you do. If I'm not back with her in a reasonable length of time, say by nightfall, bring help."

"You think you can rescue her all by yourself?" Mor asked.

"I think I should try. If I can't, then I'll call on the rest of you."

"You think you can just sneak in and fetch her out?" The man's incredulity was evident.

"I know people who can help. I know ways to avoid detection and get to the palace. But I'll need to leave the horses and go it on foot."

Lester jockeyed closer. "St. Helens, you really think you can avoid an army patrol?"

"I was a good soldier," St. Helens said.

Jon hefted her sling. "St. Helens, maybe—"

"No! Trust me, all of you. I think I can get Heln back. She's my daughter; I'm the one who should try first. If I can't do it, then I may need you to act."

The Crumbs looked at each other. St. Helens dismounted and handed his reins to Lester. "I'll be back," he promised. Then, before anyone could say another word, he turned his back and walked up the old horse path into a clearing where horses and Heln's captors had recently been. He avoided looking back, and started down a meer path that should take him out of the forest and away from the road. A few steps in, and he left the path for the thicket and let the thorns tear at his clothing until he had gone some way. He paused, looked back, and saw nothing but solid green. Time to prepare for action.

Removing the gauntlets from his pantaloons pockets, he drew them on. Now let a soldier attack him! Let three or a dozen try! He knew a trick or two with the sword, but mainly, he knew the laser. He drew it out and checked its setting. Better set it on wide sweep, just in case he did find an ambush. He set the laser, and aimed it, making a quick test. The beam touched nearby foliage, slicing it away as if by an invisible sword. Yes, it worked!

Next he drew out the levitation belt. Now this might be more difficult, but it was certain to enhance his power enormously. He carefully fastened it around his waist and looked at the controls. They seemed simple enough: a vertical and a horizontal motion lever that should control his flight, and a button that should activate the lift. He moved to a place where there were no tree limbs overhead. Really slow, now, so as not to get out of control and injure himself; unfamiliar equipment was dangerous! This was not only unfamiliar, it was alien. But time was passing, and he needed to test it.

Carefully he placed his thumbs on the large red button in the center of the buckle. He pressed. There was no hum, no flashing light, but he believed it had worked. All right, now slowly vertical up and then horizontal a few yards, and then vertical down on the ground. If it worked as it should, he would consider it to have been an adequate test. He didn't want to waste its power, because he didn't know how much remained.

He placed a forefinger on the lever that had to be for vertical and nudged it in the direction he judged would take him up. Immediately he found himself pulled down by the belt so hard that his pantaloons slipped, baring part of his rear. Oops! Evidently the up position of the lever did not mean that he went up, but that the ground went up relative to him. Alien logic, surely. He made a hasty grab at the control and nudged it in the other direction—too hard. He shot up above the treetops, his pantaloons raised back not only to their proper position but beyond it; he was hanging painfully on the crotch of them.

He nudged the lever to the neutral place. He now hovered above the forest. He worked his body around so that his crotch was more comfortable and looked around. He could see the Crumbs behind, moving across the river with their horses.

If they looked this way they would see him. That was no good. He lowered himself with an exceedingly careful nudge to the lever. He started down slow, then edged the lever back into neutral. He hovered near treetop level, out of sight of the party on the ground.

Now horizontal: another exceedingly delicate testing. Forward, and he moved smoothly forward; at least the alien logic had not reversed this! Backward, and he moved back, not liking the height or the sensation, but loving the feeling of power.

The lever would also move to the sides. He tried that, too, and it worked properly. Left, right, forward, back, up, down. He had it. He was master of the device!

He lowered himself to the ground, landing with barely a bump. He had completed his test, and the power was so sure and strong that there had to be plenty of reserve. Whoever had made this device was some craftsman! After decades or maybe even centuries, it still worked flawlessly. He could use this thing right now, and strike much faster than the enemy would believe possible.

He prepared to travel to his destination as rapidly and effortlessly as possible. He tightened the belt so that it would act on him rather than on his pantaloons—after all, he hoped to have some wenching yet to do in his life!—and turned it on again. Moving the controls with a featherlight touch, he rose to a comfortable height above the ground and maneuvered himself back to just above the meer path, staying clear of the thorns. Then he decided to take a chance and rise up so that he could get better visibility.

He floated just above the forest. Deadman's Pass was back that way, and over there was Conjurer's Rock. He knew his way around. If he could bring himself around to the west side of the palace and escape discovery, his old guest room would be right above him. Heln, he felt reasonably certain, would be there. He should be able to rescue her without great difficulty, providing he went undetected. Travel was so swift and easy with this belt that he could cover in minutes what would have required hours on foot.

He did the necessary maneuvering and was soon concealed in the woods, looking up at the west tower. He waited for someone to show, but no one did. Until, just about the time he was ready to give up hope, Heln's face appeared at the window. Confirmation!

Now was the time to act! But an instinct that had served him well in the past made him wait. The cunning witch Melbah could have set her trap right here.

On the roof he finally spied a soldier, undoubtedly armed with a crossbow, looking down. The soldier seemed to be making a routine scan of the nearby woods. Yes, that was where St. Helens himself would have stationed a watch, had the situation been reversed. He steeled himself to wait until the man's head had disappeared from his sight. Then he stepped quickly out of the woods, oriented on the window, and activated the belt.

He floated up, clicked the control into neutral, and looked in through the window at the woman he now thought of as his daughter. The cherished little-girl image was fading, and the adult version was taking its place in his heart. She had seemed like a stranger at first, there with her stripling husband, but now he knew she wasn't.

Heln looked back, turning to peer out the window just at that moment. Since the belt made no sound and he made no noise, it was either sheer coincidence or feminine instinct.

"Father!" she said. Not St. Helens, but Father. His heart leaped with pride.

Then pain lanced into his left hip with shocking impact, catching him totally by surprise.

CHAPTER 12
Flight

ALMOST, ST. HELENS HIT the control in panic. Almost. He twisted his head, fighting the pain, resisting any urge to cry out. There in his left hip was the bolt. Down on the cobblestones was the crossbowman, taking aim for another shot.

Quickly, almost reflexively, he snatched out the laser, thumbed off the safety, pointed it, and fired. But the bowman loosed his shaft first; it just missed as St. Helens touched his lever and jogged aside.

The bowman, having no inkling of the nature of the weapon he faced, took no evasive action—and indeed, it would have done no good. The laser scored—and the wide red beam made an ugly smoking hole where the crossbowman had been. Not a hole in the man, a hole in the ground. What power in this Earth weapon!

"Father! Father!" It was Heln at the window, all astonishment, all surprise, all anxiety.

115

"Help me in!" St. Helens ordered. His fingers moved the control infinitesimally and he floated through the frame. In the process he bumped his wounded leg; he winced and almost lost consciousness.

"Oh, Father, you're hurt!"

"Of course I'm hurt! Rip off a sleeve and get a tourniquet on that! Don't get fancy; we haven't time."

Shaking, she did as he bade. Meanwhile he gritted his teeth, grasped the shaft, and wrenched the bolt from his thigh. New pain seared through him, but he was braced for it. The bolt tore out, and he threw it away.

He had to balance on his right leg and watch the blood coursing down the wounded leg and puddling. Heln wasn't squeamish, he noted with peripheral satisfaction. She tugged at a sleeve of her silken dress—she was dressed like a princess, he saw with surprise—and when it wouldn't tear she quickly turned her back and took it off. She wore only panties beneath. Suddenly he realized that they must have taken away her original clothing, to make her dependent on what was at the palace. How could she flee, wearing a royal gown? She would stand out among the peasants like the royal prisoner she was!

"Hurry, lass! Hurry, there's no time!" For the report would be bringing guards clambering up the stairs to this suite; he expected to hear the pounding momentarily. If only he'd kept an eye on the ground as well as on the roof, and spotted that bowman! He had been such a fool to overlook the obvious. He'd been that way in the old days, too, which was why John Knight had been the commander. Old John had his points, good and bad, but he'd been a good leader in the crunch.

Heln turned, holding the bundled dress in front of her. She noted the size of St. Helens' thigh and stretched out the dress, making a kind of rope of it. She hesitated, obviously reluctant to give up the scant concealment the dress offered; then she decided that squeamishness was foolish here. She knelt to pass it around his leg and knot it in front. Having no stick handy, she reached to take his laser.

"Uh-uh. I'll hold it. Just knot it tight as you can and get on my back."

"Your back!" In her amazement she straightened up, showing her bare breasts for the first time. What a looker she had turned out to be!

"Remember when you were tiny? I used to carry you that way. But grab something else from that closet! I'm not going to have the whole frame gawking at the naked body of any daughter of mine! Not that it's a bad body, mind you—"

"Father!" she exclaimed in proper flattered outrage. But she hurried to the closet and grabbed another dress. Had she not been disoriented by his sudden appearance and his wound, she would have thought to grab a new dress as a tourniquet, instead of baring her body. She had missed the obvious—just as he tended to. She dived into the thing and jammed her feet into fancy slippers. Those would fly off the moment she tried to run, effectively hobbling her—but she wouldn't need to run.

He heard the pounding of boots on the stair. "Now get on me!" he ordered. "Arms around my neck. Here, I'll move to the bed." He made two hops, braced himself against the footboard, and motioned with the laser for her to get on.

"Where's Kel—?"

"Later, lass, later! Just get a hold!"

She climbed on, moving carefully. Her left leg barely touched his, but the pain was excruciating. But he'd taken injuries before; he could handle it, because he had to. He had to get her to safety before he passed out from loss of blood. He allowed no more than a gasp to escape as he fought to concentrate on her problem as well as on his own.

"Lock your arms! Get a good hold—I don't want you dropping off."

"I'm ready," she said bravely. "Ready to fly."

"Lock your legs around my middle."

She struggled to obey him, hurting his leg again. "I—I'm afraid I can't—"

"Yeah, too much gut on me. All right, just hold on." He touched the control as he bunched his good leg for a painful but necessary hop. He wanted to nudge the lever just slightly, just the right amount. There was more weight now, so he needed more lift than before.

The pounding reached the door. It was locked; there was a respite while someone fumbled for the key. Time to act!

He nudged the lever, released the headboard, and hopped, jumped, and fell at the window. Behind, the door burst open. Floating almost as if in a dream, he lowered his head and shoulders and felt Heln flatten herself against his back. Then he was out the window and bobbing in the air, trying to keep his balance when his body was off-balanced by hers.

There were soldiers below, and they all had crossbows. There was another at the window behind. He hit the control hard, and they shot off and away at roof height. Turning his head, he saw crossbow bolts cleaving the air behind them at the spot where they had exited.

"Father—you—you're rescuing me!"

"What else?" A bolt flew by his face, far too close. From the roof, or the window. He had to counter that, and fast. He pushed up the lever and they rose at a belly-lurching rate. When they were higher than he judged crossbow range to be, he neutralized the lever and looked down at the toy palace and its miniature grounds.

"Father! Fa—ther!"

"Just hang on! You'll get used to it." What a flying device was this flying device! It sure beat the jetpacks he had trained on. Not only more maneuverable, but no roar. Truly this Mouvar's people had a technology!

"Father, I can't hold on!"

This was the last news he wanted! "Yes, you can!" he replied gruffly.

"I—I can't! I'm going to—going to—"

"You aren't either! You aren't going to faint!" That was all he needed! It was all he could do, trying to hang on to his own consciousness!

But he felt her arms loosening around his neck. Frantically, still holding the laser with his right hand, he grabbed her left-handed. He missed her left hand and his leg protested, and then he was dropping the laser and grabbing her with the right. He caught her right wrist and held on.

They floated while the laser fell butt over muzzle, spinning around. He followed it down, but knew it was hopeless. There would be no getting that back again, and that was the only existing laser and what he considered his irresistible weapon. Down below it bounced from the cobblestones and bounced again. He knew it would be in no fit condition to fire.

"Fa-ther!"

He stood to lose more than the laser! "Here, get hold of me! Arms tight around my neck!"

She did as directed. What a relief! Her problem was evidently just the height; now that they were lower, she could handle it.

But without that laser, just what could he do? Well, he still had the gauntlets, and this belt. Conquering might be harder than intended, but then it always was.

The wind hit them out of nowhere. One moment all was calm, the next they were being pushed by this incredible blast. Hanging on to Heln, thankful that the gauntlets multiplied his strength and influenced his dexterity, St. Helens looked down and saw a small dark figure with arms stretched in their direction. Melbah! If only he still had the laser!

Now they were moving, really moving, and the belt was putting up no resistance. They had to push back against the wind, to resist it with all the power of the belt. He moved a gauntlet to the control and tried to concentrate. The wind took away his stockelcap and streamed out Heln's hair and dress. The gauntlet had to move the control to push them back. It touched the control as he concentrated, hard.

Now they were resisting the wind, and they were moving

back. But suddenly they were doing it very fast, as the wind ceased as abruptly as it had begun.

He hit the neutral position. Then, just as suddenly, they were moving again. Independently of what he wanted. They swept above the palace in a curve, the ground and flagstones blurring. They were curving more and more, spiraling. They were in a whirlwind!

Frantically he worked the control. They were moving horizontally but still losing altitude. The forest was below, and a great big tree directly ahead. He grasped Heln tightly to him as the tree limb whipped out in the wind like a scythe and the branches opened and closed like grasping, evil hands.

Something struck. Things whirled, faster, blurring. Then everything went black.

Heln felt the gauntlet holding her slipping on her hand. Then she was falling. She reached out, grabbing and grasping for anything. She caught hold of rough bark. She held on, and looked down to the ground so far away. She felt dizzy, dizzier than when they had been far higher. Her fingers hurt on the bark, and she realized suddenly that there were branches holding her, and that she wasn't about to fall after all.

She looked at St. Helens, held there with his belt. The belt was pushing hard against the trunk. St. Helens himself was out, head down, breathing but unconscious. The blood from his wound was leaking from her crude bandage, running down his leg and dripping through the leaves to land far below.

The first thing she had to do was stop that belt. St. Helens' face was right up against the trunk and it looked squashed, though she thought that was just from the pressure. She had to stop the belt from pushing—but how? He had moved that little lever, but if she moved it wrong, what might happen? St. Helens could shoot up into the sky and then that whirlwind could come and suck him down again. Yet she had to try.

The gauntlets—perhaps if she put them on? They were supposed to know what to do, weren't they? Kelvin had spoken as though they did. And where was Kelvin? Why did her natural father have her husband's gauntlets and why did he have his laser and this belt? There were many things she did not understand, and there was no time to think them out. Perhaps Kelvin needed her—but how could she know?

The blood on St. Helens' leg bothered her. The head of the bolt might not have lodged in the bone, but it had certainly torn up the flesh! The way he had yanked it out—she could never have done that! It might have been better to leave it until there was competent help. At any rate, she hoped it was merely a flesh wound. St. Helens had a lot of flesh, and that was his good fortune, maybe. But she had to stop that blood.

The dress was knotted as it had been, but it had slipped. Consequently it was pressing against the bolt and the wound was being pushed partially open. She wished she were less squeamish, and that she had Jon's touch for this sort of thing. But she had to do what she could.

She pushed the blood-sodden dress a bit higher on his thigh. She took St. Helens' sword from its sheath and cut a stick from a branch, then rested the sword in a crotch. Next she loosened the red-stained knot, pushed the stick through its center, and twisted a proper tourniquet. *There,* she thought, *maybe I'm not as helpless as I sometimes think.*

St. Helens did not thank her. He remained unconscious. He seemed to be breathing adequately, and his heart maintained a steady beat. But his face remained pressed to the trunk.

Well, maybe this will help. She stripped the gauntlets from his hands. The soft leather with the metal plates yielded readily to her touch. She slipped her own fingers into the gloves until her hands were all the way inside. To her amazement the huge gauntlets fitted her perfectly, and now seemed like an extension of her skin. It was apparent that any roundear could wear them, though the prophecy applied only to Kelvin.

Hesitantly she reached with her gauntleted hand for the control on the belt. This little lever must move forward and back. But which way should she move it now?

Use your own judgment, gauntlets, she thought.

Her fingers acted. She was not certain whether she controlled them or the gauntlet did. The lever moved, pressing back all the way. The belt changed its thrust, and St. Helens' body shot through the branches with a speed and motion she had not expected. She watched helplessly as it left their tree and was stopped by the trunk of another.

She had to get him down! She knew that—but the neighboring tree couldn't be reached from this one. Even worse, the tree St. Helens was now in was growing straight up and down, with no branches at the lower levels. How was she going to touch him, let alone get him safely to the ground? She had expected the gauntlets to help her, and instead they had only made things worse!

A movement at ground level took her attention. Two horsemen were there, astride their steeds, looking up.

"There he is, Corry. How're we going to get him down?"

"Don't ask me, Bemode. We're going to need some help. Look over there!"

"What?"

"His daughter. How'd she get over there?"

"I dunno. What's that shine?"

"A sword. Must be St. Helens'. You up there, girl, you hurt?"

"N-no," Heln said. "But my father—"

"You climb on down. Bring the sword."

She hesitated. But according to Kelvin, the gauntlets were good at climbing. Besides, she had done some tree climbing in the past. Still, there was the blade. If she tried to carry that down without its sheath, there was every chance she might cut herself. She started down without it.

"Bring the sword, I said!"

There was no helping it. She was largely helpless, with or without the sword, and would only make things worse if she tried to defy these rough men. She reached up with the left gauntlet and it took up the sword as if it belonged in that hand. As she drew it down to her lower level she saw that there was an inscription on the blade that she hadn't observed before. Her eyes read it without conscious effort. "Given in Eternal Friendship, From His Majesty Phillip Blastmore, King of Aratex." Now what did that mean? Had St. Helens stolen the sword, or had he and the king really been friends?

"Come on, hurry it up!"

That Bemode sounded ugly. Probably he was a mean man, given the chance. Better not anger him. She tried to shut off all other thoughts except getting down.

"Look at those legs!" Bemode exclaimed.

She had forgotten what she was wearing! This silken dress exposed everything from below. But what could she do? If she tried to stay up in the tree, they would fire a crossbow bolt into her. She gritted her teeth and continued climbing down, though she felt the gaze of the two men almost physically on her moving legs. It was as if slime were coating them.

Sooner than she had expected, the right gauntlet swung her out on a limb and dropped her the short remaining distance. The men stood as if mesmerized, their eyes round, their mouths open. Because of her legs? In other circumstances she would have taken that as a compliment. As it was, she was disgusted, but didn't dare say so.

"You see that, Corry? She must be part houcat! I thought she'd fall."

"That would've been a waste!" Corry said.

Bemode dismounted. "Bring me that sword, woman!"

Heln transferred the sword from her left gauntlet to her right. The gauntlets did not feel as if they wanted to relinquish it. According to Kelvin, they made the wearer a master swordsman. But could they do that even for a woman?

"Help my father," she said.

"We'll help him when we get help. We've got chains all ready for him. Haven't we, Corry?"

Heln saw that there was a length of heavy chain fastened to Bemode's saddle. As she watched he unfastened it and the chain dropped to the ground.

"You are going to chain my father?"

"Have to. King's orders. But maybe not the same for you, if you cooperate. Your sword."

Cooperate? She hardly needed to guess what that meant. She remembered the first time she had been raped.

Corry dismounted. "Don't be rough, Bemode. The king wouldn't like it. He doesn't want her badly marked. Worse yet, Melbah wouldn't like it."

"Melbah's not going to get it."

"Still—"

"Pity," Bemode said, evidently daunted by the thought of Melbah's ire. "Still, we can make her say it's all right. Then—"

The sword in the gauntlet lifted without Heln quite willing it. A sudden determination came to her. A determination that if she could not be in charge she would at least be on her way to get St. Helens some help. He was, after all, in his predicament because of her. As for what these two planned for her—she wanted no part of it.

Bemode reached out to take the sword. "Give me that!"

Whereupon she would be weaponless, and largely helpless to resist them. "No!" she said. The sword darted at Bemode's face, pulling back before touching it.

"Well, I'll be a cuckold!" Bemode said. He whipped out his own blade and made a swipe with it. As he did, the gauntlet feinted, twisted her wrist, and Bemode's blade rebounded. Not only rebounded, but flew away with great force. The sword lit in some bushes and left Bemode standing with open mouth.

Corry reached for the sword sheathed at his hip. He paused, eyeing the tip of Heln's blade that was suddenly at his throat. Suddenly his mind was no longer on the sight of bare legs, but on bare steel.

"You," Heln said to Bemode. "Get that chain and drag it to this tree!"

Bemode did as instructed, looking worriedly at Corry. His horse neighed: it was almost a laugh.

"All right, stand with your back against the tree!" she

snapped. "You, Corry, stand next to him." It was the way she thought a man would have talked.

The men obeyed. Keeping her eyes on them while they eyed her blade, she took the end of the chain and circled the tree several times. Bemode looked as though he wanted to make a sudden move, but always the gauntlet guided the point of the sword to bear on his left eye and he reconsidered. Now what? Oh, yes, there was a lock at one end. She drew the two ends together and locked the chain. Then she stepped out in front of them.

"I'm going for help now. If your help arrives before mine, my father is not to be chained. His wound is to be cared for and he is to be rested and fed. If this is not done, your king and your Melbah will answer to the Roundear of Prophecy himself!" What was she saying? This seemed crazy! It was almost as if the gauntlets were making her speak!

Corry and Bemode looked at each other. Bemode swallowed. They might disagree, but they were not in a position to argue.

"And one other thing." Her gloves stuck the sword point down into the ground. "When my father revives he will want his sword. Take good care of it; it's a gift from your king."

Amazed at what she was doing, Heln mounted Corry's horse and the all-knowing gauntlets took expert charge of the reins. She thought she would remember the way to the border, but she doubted that she would have to. With her wishes firmly in mind, the gauntlets could be relied upon to do the rest.

As she walked her horse past her onetime kidnappers, Corry said to Bemode: "You, you fly-blown idiot, you had to tell her to bring the sword!"

"Well, if you hadn't been so busy looking up her dress, you'd have told me not to!" Bemode retorted.

Heln almost smiled. Maybe that dress had done her some good, after all!

CHAPTER 13
Prisoners

JOHN KNIGHT LAY ON the straw-filled mattress and watched as Gerta, his flopear attendant, ladled his soup. Miraculously his injured hand and broken finger had healed perfectly, as though treated by Earth's best surgeons. It had to be partially magic, he thought ruefully. He who had always declared that there was no such thing, even in the face of mounting evidence to the contrary—he owed his recovery to magic!

That reminded him of Charlain, his pointear wife, now his widow of the other frame. Wonderful Charlain! She had believed in magic, and now he knew she had been correct. He had a fine son and daughter by her. If only he hadn't had to leave her! But her life would have been put in peril had he stayed longer, and he couldn't tolerate that, so he had left. He had done so with deep and continuing regret, but had never doubted the need for it. He could not return to her as long as the fate of Queen Zoanna was unknown, and as long as Charlain's second husband, Hal Hackleberry, lived. Hackleberry was a good man, and so John meant never to return to that frame.

Gerta handed him the beautifully wrought silver bowl and exquisitely designed spoon. He took them, marveling again at how well his hand worked. He also admired the moving picture on the bowl; when the spoon approached it, the face on the bowl smiled. This seemed to be an actual change in the image, not a mere illusion. What phenomenal artisans these folk were! He sipped at the broth, really appreciating its rich chicurk flavor.

Gerta smiled down at him. Such big ears, covering the sides of her face like the ears of a puppy. Such gentle eyes, such a sweet face, albeit with a large slash mouth. About three feet tall and a little bit too wide, she was his picture of a female gnome.

"You want bread?"

"Thank you, Gerta. Yes. Please."

He watched her cross the room, its walls of unbroken stone, its interior that of a neat, clean cottage. She sawed him a hunk of bread from a loaf, using a large toothed knife. The handle was decorated, he saw.

"Gerta, would you bring the knife?"

She brought it, handing it trustingly to him along with a thick piece of bread. He bit into the crust, enjoying its rough oat texture and caraway-seed taste with a hint of pizza crust. The handle of the knife was in the form of a silver serpent, the tail expanding into the blade. When he touched the end of the handle, the eyes of the serpent moved to follow his motion. He knew this was just the magic of the sculpture, but it was eerie. How did they manage to animate their carved figures?

"You call yourselves the serpent people, Gerta?"

"That is true, John Knight."

But others would call them flopears, inevitably. He considered his outstanding luck. Injured, floating down a river toward the great incredible falls that seemed to drop into blackest, star-filled space. It had been coming closer and closer, that falls, and he had been paddling to save his life. Then the water and the raft and himself falling, then floating, then . . . here. It was a different world, a different existence from either the Earth he had originated on or the world that was inhabited by pointed-ear people who considered round-eared people strange. He had found himself on the raft on a different river, singing birds all around. He had realized that something, some force, had taken him and brought him here. Some atomic force such as had been released by the artillery shell that had transported him and a few of his men into a near fairyland of pointy-eared people and magic. It had somehow, someway, happened. That hole, that flaw in reality, The Flaw, had somehow brought him here.

He thought again of Zoanna, the red-haired queen of Rud who had bewitched him with a magic well known on Earth: the magic of sex appeal. He thought of how evil she had been, how she had killed and destroyed good folk without conscience, and been in almost every way a terrible monster. But he had been slow to appreciate that side of her, being fascinated by the single facet she showed to him alone: her beauty and her desire for him. How foolishly flattered he had been, how possessed by lust for her body—a lust she encouraged and freely obliged. He had willfully blotted out the evidence of her true nature for an unconscionably long period; he was ashamed to remember it now.

He had tried to destroy her in the end, even as his remarkable son Kelvin, by lovely Charlain, was fighting to free the kingdom from her. He felt he had destroyed her, and yet he was not certain. At least he had tried! It did not make up for his long sojourn on the wrong side, but it was better than nothing. He still owed that frame, he felt, though he had no idea how he could ever make it up. It was all far away now, in another existence, and perhaps best forgotten.

He dipped the bread in the soup and sucked at it. "You know, Gerta, I'm nearly well now."

"Yes, your mind and body both healed."

"Mind?" What could she know of his tumultuous inner doubts?

"You were mad."

Had he been? He thought back. Images came to him erratically. As in pictures flickering on a television screen while his mind dozed fitfully, coming awake now and then. Could he make any sense of them? Maybe if he tried to put them into chronological order.

Falling into The Flaw, down, down, eternally. Then, somehow, he wasn't falling, he was floating, in a sea of stars. Drifting without direction, without orientation. That strangeness penetrating his mind, making it—mad? Stray thoughts: how foolish to travel through this maelstrom without a map! So he had conjured a map, or dreamed it up, and scratched a route on it. A route to Mouvar. That made so little sense, even in his madness, that he laughed and laughed—but nevertheless moved along that marked route, which now was a glowing band in the void ahead. The band became a stream of light or of darkness, and a current carried him along. Until it became too swift, and he spun out or fainted or dropped into another level of madness.

Crawling up a slippery bank. Realizing suddenly that it was actually the muddy shell of a turtle as large as the Galápagos kind. Or larger. But not the tortoise on which the world was supported—wrong mythology. Maybe.

Running, falling, again hurting his sickeningly injured right hand. That hand was mangled horribly, dripping blood, sending pain messages in increasing waves. Trees, brush, rocks. Run, run, run.

Falling, falling, falling. Pain.

Something silver, long. A rope? He reached out his left hand, his working hand.

A loud hissing sound and the rope undulating. Jaws of a serpent, opening wide. A drop of clear venom hanging on a fang and then dropping.

Pain, pain pain.

Screaming. His own.

Now a flower gently tapping the head of the serpent. A blue-and-pink blossom resembling a cross between a violet and a wild rose. A stubby-fingered hand, holding the stem.

The serpent's jaws closing. The serpent settling down, sliding away.

Now a face above the hand holding the blossom. Very blue eyes and very large ears like a puppy's. Gerta's. She looking down at him, her mouth making a moue and her eyes squeezing. A tear running down her face.

Flower petals touching his forehead, gently, gently stroking. A flower scent a little like a poppy's, soothing his tired mind, easing the long pain. A puppy with a poppy! Pained laughter. Oblivion, again.

He shook himself mentally. It had been so dreamlike, and yet so real. It was more than a hallucination, or else hallucination could return in memory with entirely too much reality.

This was really Gerta. This room that was lighted by large phosphorescent toadstools placed all about. Walls that were rock, and apparently solid rock. It was like a room in a cave or cavern, but the walls were smooth. Laser construction here? Or magic?

"You wish to eat?" Gerta asked.

"Please." The language was the same, at least. Strangely, it seemed like other things to vary only slightly from frame to frame. Perhaps not so strange, if it indicated that man had spread out from a common origin and colonized the several frames. Obviously there had been travel between them, because Mouvar had sown his legend among the pointears in Hud, and if those legends were to be believed, Mouvar hadn't been the first. How could he have predicted the uniting of kingdoms if there were no kingdoms to unite? Roundear and pointear could interbreed; he had proved that! That meant they were closely related species. But these flopears, now— how close were they?

She brought him a robe. It was white and smooth and

shiny, and on Earth he would have known it as satin. There were underdrawers of a less shiny material resembling cotton.

He hesitated, a holdover from his Earth life when the sexes were cautious about naked exposure, then rolled out of bed and quickly donned the garments. Gerta, after all, had been his gentle nurse for a length of time he couldn't begin to estimate. It might have been weeks, though he had only been aware of days. During that time he knew she had aided him in all that was necessary, or else the magic was of a kind that allowed him to heal while suspending all body functions. That seemed unlikely! So though his memories were blurred, he was sure that Gerta had seen all of him, and all his functions.

"I haven't been up before, have I, Gerta?"

"Yes, you have. With me walking you."

"I don't remember."

"No. The healing clouds as it soothes and rebuilds the mind."

He thought about that, and he also thought of how very capable he felt on his feet. Gerta handed him a pair of soft slippers with curled toes. As he sat down to put these on he marveled that both slippers were decorated with large buckles, and that the buckles were silver. The designs on the silver changed as his feet entered the slippers. He had given up wondering what the point of such magic was. Art did not need a point.

He stood up, looked around the room, and spotted a door. He was certain he had looked at it for hours on end, but now it was like seeing it for the first time. It, too, had decorated silver panels that changed in their own fashion in their own time.

"I will take you to the workplace, John. You are now quite well. The magic has finished its work."

He marveled as he followed her. She moved quite fast for someone with such short legs. He felt a kindness toward her, a feeling that he might have had for a younger sister.

They went under stone archways, through some rooms without windows, and finally came out in a large natural amphitheater. Here there were many flop-eared men, wearing pointed caps not unlike Rud stockelcaps, and leather aprons. They were working at individual anvils. The cauldron around which the work centered contained silver in the molten state. The fire burning so brightly beneath the cauldron must, he realized, be of a magical nature to melt silver.

As he watched, one of the flopears walked to the cauldron carrying an armload of silvery, scaly-patterned skin. He turned the skin around in his hands and tossed it into the cauldron. Another flopear on a scaffold stirred the cauldron with a long ladle.

"My God!" John said. He whistled, then could do no better than to repeat his exclamation: "My God!"

The skin was serpentskin, and was purest silver! Shades of dragons with golden scales! Was there nothing that couldn't be in different existences?

His mind went back, scrabbling frantically for a shred of sanity. High school, science teacher getting his attention: "This article tells how shellfish ingest heavy metal and how the metal migrates to their shells. The flesh of these shellfish is unfit to eat, and the coloration metallic. I suggest you read this and report on it for tomorrow's class." John had nodded, sorry that he had thrown the paper wad, and he wanted now to shout back through the years: "Yes, and immortal dragons live on and on for centuries!" Serpents that were as immortal as dragons, ingesting silver instead of gold, the silver migrating through centuries to those brightly shining scales?

A flopear who had been going from anvil to anvil, checking the work, came up to them. He was no taller than Gerta, but his head was larger and he had the facial expression of a harried foreman.

"He healed, Gerta?"

"Yes, healed."

"Good. He will trade well."

Gerta squirmed. "I don't like to think of that, Harlick."

"No matter. You know the way."

"Yes."

John stared at them. "Trade? Me? To others like your-selves?"

"To others like yourself, John."

"Like me? People like me but with pointed ears?"

"Ears, pointed? No, John. Ears like ears on you mortal folk. Tiny ears low on the sides of your head." She tried not to show her distaste for this abnormal configuration.

John thought of this as they left the workplace and ambled back the way they had come. On the return he saw that there were many cottages but that the rooms he had been in were in fact inside a cliff. There were other doorways in the cliff, and some round holes that might have been bored by lasers.

"What will happen to me, Gerta? Will I be a slave?"

"I don't know, John. The roundears have their ways and we have ours. Their king of Hud buys all mortals who are prisoners of flopears if they are healthy. They trade for their own kind. What they do with them, I do not know."

John Knight pondered that, and was not reassured. It was quite possible that he would be better off remaining with the flopears, if he had any choice in the matter.

Kian tried to concentrate on other things than their punishment. He had discovered that he could think for himself without Lonny knowing his thoughts, but if he thought in terms of speaking, she knew them immediately. This was nice to know if they were going to be spending an eternity together. But would they? Would their thoughts and those of the serpent gradually merge, becoming one? Maybe that was what would eventually happen, but maybe it could be slowed, if not stopped. What they had to do, he felt, was concentrate on thinking thoughts that were human. That might enable them to merge while retaining human nature and intellect, instead of descending to serpent level.

John Knight, his father, had talked about were-animals once. He said it was all superstition and invention, but that some people believed in them. On Earth anything might be possible. Wolves and cats and other Earth creatures holding the spirits of humans and changing with them from time to time. Perhaps these stories owed their existence to beings like the flopears. If spirits could exist, and he was inclined now to believe that they might, then why couldn't there be two apparent species that shared the same spirits? If the serpents were truly immortal ancestors of the flopears, then was it strange that the . . .

His thought faded out, distracted by the serpent's feeding. The rock had a peppery taste. Seasoned with silver. The bad aspect of it was that he was beginning to like it. The worst of it was that he thought of the ingesting and could not otherwise concentrate. The serpent nature was taking over!

"Kian?" Lonny asked.

"Yes, Lonny." He had to be careful. He wanted to merge with her, and he doubted that he should. Because their mergence would be but the prelude to mergence with the serpent, and that would be the end of their humanity. Somehow he must get out of this body and into his own and go back to his home frame and Rud and find the girl she resembled. Only—how long had it been?

"Kian, do you think we can ever return? Be in our own bodies again?"

"Of course! What a question." Yet it was only the echo of his own doubt. His belief in that return was diminishing, but he didn't want to discourage her. He thought of the words of a song and tried singing it to her: "Oh, bring back, bring back, bring back my body to meeeee." It was a parody he had sung as a child, but it would do.

"I'm afraid, Kian! I just want to taste the silver and feel our body working."

"Not *our* body, Lonny! Get that out of your head!" Of course she had no head of her own at the moment, but it was no time to quibble about terms. "You're human, not serpent! You're a beautiful girl!"

"Am I, Kian? Do you really think that?"

"Of course it's true! Of course! I'm going to marry someone who looks just like you. I'm going to—" He fought back a surge of doubt. "I'm going to—to return."

"You really think so, Kian?"

"Yes, we're both going to return." How, he had no idea, but he had to cling to the belief.

"I mean, that I'm beautiful?"

"Yes, yes, I told you."

"You really mean it?"

He laughed, the mental version even more natural than the physical one. How could she doubt that? Their possible escape might be hard to believe, but her beauty was certain! "Of course!"

She evidently picked up more of that thought than he had intended. "You find me beautiful," she said, believing. "And you would like to—to hold me and kiss me and—"

"I didn't say that!" he protested.

"But it's true, isn't it?"

He discovered to his surprise that it was. He wanted to do it all with her! "Yes, but—"

"Yet you will marry this other girl?" Now she was angry. He felt the surge of it, and he could not deny the justice of it.

"I have to, Lonny. I can't marry you. I'm from another frame. That just wouldn't be right."

"Not right?"

"My—my father came to our frame from another, and—" He tried to sort out the immense skein of complications that his father's consortion with two women of Rud had generated. Kian himself was one result, and Kelvin another. What mischief! Was he to spread it farther by doing the same thing?

"Kian, Kian, I love you!" she cried, and the emotion washed through him, demolishing his bastion of objectivity as a wave destroys a castle of sand.

"I love you, Lonny," he replied helplessly.

"I want to—to do those things with you. To hold you, and kiss you, and—"

"No!"

"And make love to you," she concluded. "And you feel the same."

It was as though they were blending, melding like silver. He knew he must not allow that. He tried to resist, but simply could not think. "We—we have no bodies," he said desperately. Was that a commitment to do it at such time as they did recover their bodies? Then how could he return to his own frame? He was lost either way.

"Oh, Kian!"

"Oh, Lonny, I did not mean to—"

"I think we can do it now, Kian. Let me try."

"Now? But—"

Then he felt her kiss on his lips. He might not have a mouth, but he had the awareness of his human anatomy, and so did she, and it was certainly a kiss.

He tried once more to resist. "We shouldn't—"

She embraced him. Her spirit within the serpent interacted with his, and the sensation was exactly like a physical embrace, only more so, because there was nothing to get in the way. In physical bodies there could be no complete understanding; people more or less pretended that they understood each other, but it could be deceptive, as it had been with his father and his mother. His father had hardly known his mother at all! But here there were no physical barriers. He knew Lonny was speaking truly, and she knew he was not. The act of sex, physically, was said to be knowledge, but it could be nothing like this!

He gave up the unequal struggle. "Oh, Lonny! Lonny, Lonny, Lonny!" In one sense he was speaking her name, but in another he was speaking her essence, in that repetition possessing her and being possessed by her.

"Kian, Kian, Kian!" And she of him, similarly.

They no longer fought it at all. They came together, more intimately than either had imagined possible, and—

With a slurping, sucking motion daylight broke into their one functioning eye. Jolted out of their incipient mergence, they raised their silver head to the setting sun and breathed in through their nostrils and the air passages covered by their scales. They undulated, crawled, and wriggled out of the rock tunnel they had made.

Boys with big floppy ears were there for them. They shivered all their length, anticipating gentle touches, the soothing strokes, the exhilarating yet calming scent.

The boys held out their blossoms and touched their nostrils with the pink and blue flowers. They sucked in the scent in great waves. It filled their being, taking away all doubt and hope and questions. Taking away, finally, all sense of duality, and of self. They were one with the serpent.

CHAPTER 14
The Cliffs

JAC HESITATED OUTSIDE THE tent flap, dreading to go inside. Death had always been upsetting, though he had seen enough of it in his time. He thought of Heeto and the girl sitting in there side by side watching the body. He wanted her badly, but there could be no mistaking where her heart was. He would try to comfort her, and then, if the stranger's body had deteriorated the least little bit, he would bury him himself. Steeling himself for an unpleasant sight, he pushed on into the tent.

The sight that met his eyes was shocking, even to him. The lovely, recently intended sacrifice was stretched out by the body of the stranger, and both were apparently dead. She had joined him in suicide!

Heeto sat cross-legged by their heads, a leather fan in his hands. There were no buzzing flies.

"Master, I could not stop her! She took the berries. She followed him."

Trembling, Jac wiped perspiration from his forehead. The bodies were so perfect! All day long and no bloat and no smell. That beautiful face, that perfectly formed body, that had to go into the ground before it began to rot. Burying the bodies was going to be the most unpleasant task he had performed in his life! Yet it had to be done, and quickly.

"When did she—?"

"This morning, Master. Just after you left."

He had had to choose this day to get supplies for the camp! He should have known that Lonny had something like this in mind, and taken those berries away before she got to them! Yet he had also had to get his mind off the problem, and work or activity helped.

"We'd better—" He choked on the word "bury" and simply motioned at them.

"Master, I do not believe that they are dead."

"They're not breathing. Have they any heartbeats?"

Heeto shook his head. "No breathing, no heartbeats, but also no stink and no bugs."

"I'm not sure that means anything, Heeto." Yet maybe, just possibly, it did!

"I've touched them, Master. I have taken their hands. It's strange, Master, but I felt something besides their cold flesh. I was floating, Master, or felt I was floating, though I did not leave this tent. I was somewhere dark. There were rocks about, and dirt, and I could feel them the length of my body. It was not her body and it was not his; it was a serpent's."

"A serpent's!"

"Yes, Master. I waited to tell you. I thought that perhaps—"

"Yes, yes, I want to try!"

"That is not what I mean, Master. I thought that perhaps you would know."

"I know only what the stranger Kian told me. But if a serpent has them—has their spirits—"

"Is that possible, Master?"

"I don't know." He sat down by the dwarf, took a good grip on his feelings, and reached for Lonny's hands.

They were cold, but there was no stiffness. Proof, perhaps, that this was not actually death. He gripped the hands and closed his eyes. "Is this the way you did it, Heeto?"

"Yes, Master, but that was this morning. I had not the courage to try it again. Perhaps it will not work now. Perhaps I only imagined it."

"No, no, something's happening! I sense black and roughness and—a taste."

"A taste, Master?"

"Dirt! Bah, ugh! Now a more peppery taste. Silver! Silver ore! She likes it; he doesn't. They're inside it, inside the serpent!"

"I told you, Master!"

"Now I'm seeing something. Something through an eye. One eye. The serpent's eye!"

"Only one eye, Master?"

"Yes, only one. Now she and he are talking—talking in the serpent. I don't know the words, I don't know what they are saying, but . . . they seem to be—" He swallowed, disliking this, but obliged to recognize the truth of it. "They are attracted to each other. They are kissing, and embracing, and—" He took a deep breath. "And they seem to be merging, mingling as one mind. It's like sex, only so strange, and—" How he wished he were the one experiencing that! "Now—oh! Light! Outside, ground. Boys with flowers, extending them toward the eye. The flowers touch the nostrils, it breathes in and—"

He pulled himself away, dropping her hands. It was an experience he had never imagined. He looked at Heeto and the bodies, and he trembled and shook in every part.

"Are you all right, Master?" Heeto's hands were on him, touching his face.

He continued to shake. "It's—it's—I think it's digesting them!"

"Then they will die?"

He tried to still his shaking hands. "I think they must! I think they must! And, Heeto, this is mad, but—I think the one-eyed serpent is the one he killed!"

"Killed, Master? With your spear? In the eye socket?"

"That's the one! The very one! I'd swear to it!"

"Calm down, Master! Calm down!"

"We can't bury them, Heeto. Not until, until—"

"Until morning?"

"Until we have to! Until we know they are gone for good and there is only the serpent left."

"Master, that's so, so sad."

"Very sad, Heeto," he agreed heavily. "Very, very sad." With difficulty he got his hands to stop shaking. It was such a monstrous thing to think of her there. To imagine her spirit, or "astral self," as Kian Knight had called it, becoming a part of that gigantic serpent.

"We will leave the bodies in the tent for as long as we can. For now, we'd better sleep outside."

"There's nothing we can do, Master? Nothing to save them?"

"Nothing I know of," he said, wishing it were otherwise.

That night there was no way he could sleep. He kept throwing off his blanket, getting up, pacing, and then lying down again. All he could think about was her, she of the beautiful eyes and long, flowing blond hair. If only there were some way to save her, to bring that splendid body of hers back to life.

At dawn he moved quietly about the camp so as not to awaken anyone. He got his best and biggest spear and tiptoed with it to his horse. He saddled and bridled the mare, rubbed her muzzle, and called her "Betts, my pet." He fastened the spear to the saddle with his best rope and walked the mare until they were clear of the camp. He hiked up his sword, mounted, and rode at an easy walk. He had gone only a short distance when he heard the other horse. Turning around, he was quite surprised to see Heeto riding after him. He waited. The dwarf pulled up.

"Master, I want to go with you. I brought this." He held up the weapon Kian Knight had brought with him from another world, lost, and then found again. The "worthless weapon" to its former owner, though he had not relinquished it. A Mouvar weapon was still a Mouvar weapon.

"What good do you think that will be?"

"I don't know, Master. I just brought it."

"Do you know that I do not expect to return?"

"If you do not, I will not."

They rode on for Serpent Valley and its great curve of surrounding cliffs.

There were holes in the cliffside that he had seen before, some large, some small, many in between. The mist was still heavy as they approached. Jac kept glancing back at Heeto, adjusting his spear.

The largest hole in solid rock might have been made by the serpent they were after. But if they rode down it, would they find the serpent? Did the serpents use the same tunnels? It was surprising how little they actually knew about the serpents or about the flopears who guarded them. Yet morning after morning he had slipped into the valley to collect discarded serpentskins before the flop-eared boys arrived to pick them up. Sooner or later he might have been caught, almost certainly would have been, but now he sought a confrontation. The outcome of that would mean his death and Heeto's as well, but it might also mean the extinction of the life force in the serpent.

A slithering sound came from one of the larger holes. He motioned for Heeto to follow him and rode his horse into one of the smaller holes facing the larger one. They waited as the sound grew nearer. Then a stir of darkness within the larger hole, and the serpent's head appeared. As he started and stared at it, he saw that one eye was damaged; he could still see the wounds the spearhead had made.

Not giving himself a chance to think, he spurred his horse and charged with spear poised to stab into that remaining orb.

The serpent's head came up. It hissed, long and low, disturbing the morning mists. The eye, that single strange eye, bored at him. In that dark mirror he saw her face, and on the instant of that seeing he was paralyzed.

The serpent wriggled out of its tunnel. Its great mouth opened. Drops of acid formed on its fangs and dripped to the ground, hissing.

Jac saw but could not comprehend what was happening. He was frozen in place, unwilling to move or to think of moving; his mare, being but mortal, was in similar shape. Together their eyes saw the huge head advancing, lifting back, the mouth opening wide. There was no will or thought left for avoiding the strike; still less for making an attack.

Back in the dark Heeto saw his master ride out with raised spear. He saw the serpent's head rise up, though the mist fogged the details. He saw the horse stop; both horse and rider were motionless. Both were awaiting death. He saw death emerge from the hole in front of them as the serpent drew the rest of its body out and made ready to strike. They did not move.

It must not happen! He had to help! Hardly thinking what he did, Heeto pulled out the weapon from another world and raised it until it pointed over Master's head at the gigantic head of the serpent. He pressed the trigger on the weapon, as if this would accomplish anything. He knew the weapon didn't work; the stranger had said so.

Bright light filled the tunnel and splashed outside. Heeto was blinded by it; he felt as if that light struck right through his head! There was a WHOOMPTH noise, loud and unexpected and somehow echoing on and on instead of ending. His fingers loosened on the weapon. It slid from his hand and dropped to the floor. Unheeding, he placed his hands over his eyes, and he screamed less from pain than from shock.

Stillness.

He put down his arms. He could see again, his vision clearing by the moment. He took up the horse's reins. In the mists that were rapidly dissipating he could see both Master and horse and the swaying form of the otherwise motionless serpent.

He rode out, hardly thinking, blinking his eyes against the mist.

The serpent remained frozen in striking position; it seemed almost a statue of itself. His master suddenly jerked, and his horse jumped, almost throwing him.

"Master, Master, kill it!"

His master got the mare controlled, raised his spear to the eye, and looked directly into the eye. "She's not there, Heeto! I can't see her now. She's gone back to camp!"

"Master!" Heeto cried, hardly believing.

"I don't know what happened. It's not moving. Maybe it's dead."

A great slithering sound came from the neighboring holes. Serpents coming out to them! Master looked as dazed as Heeto felt, perhaps even more so.

"Let's get out of here, Master! Now, while there's a chance!"

Master's mouth worked, as if his jaws were still partially paralyzed. Finally he nodded, and together they took off at as great a speed as their mounts could carry them.

Kian opened his eyes and stretched. Above him was the familiar roof of the tent; under him, the bearver hide. He turned his head to the right, expecting to see Jac, and instead saw Lonny's lifeless form.

Even as he sat up with a cry of horror, her breathing started and her color returned. She stared at him, then sat up as abruptly as he had.

"Kian!" Spots of red came to her cheeks. "Kian, we—"

He thought rapidly, trying to deny it to himself. Wishing

despite himself that it could be true, yet knowing it was not. "It must have been an illusion that we were together," he concluded. "How could we be alive, without bodies, in the serpent? But even if it wasn't a dream, it hardly matters. It wasn't as though we were lying here joined. Astral bodies are like bodies we dream. Whatever they are, they don't count."

"Don't they, Kian?" She sounded faintly disappointed.

"No, not really." But was that the truth? If any part of what he remembered so clearly were true—and it had *felt* so true!—what did it mean? "But what happened? The last I remember we were—" Now he felt himself blushing. "Together in the serpent." More than together! They had been making love! More than love!

"I remember after that," she said almost eagerly. "I remember seeing Jac. He was on his horse and he had a spear and . . . and then there was a light."

"I remember the light." And how sorry he had been to have that serpent break out into the light of day, distracting them from their mergence within it. He knew it meant oblivion, because once they merged with each other they would be ready to merge with the serpent. Yet it had been such a wonderful experience in the making!

He reached out and took her hand. It was as cold as his own. "Jac must have come for us and slain the serpent. Reslain it, I guess."

"Yes." Her eyes widened in internal pain. "Oh, Kian, I hate for it to be dead!"

"So do I," he confessed. For he had seen an entirely different side of the monster, and not an evil side. The serpent, he realized, had been brought back to life by the presence of their spirits, and perhaps could not survive well without them.

The two boys stayed hidden in the mouth of one of the smaller ancestor tunnels as the two mortals rode away from the cliffs. Both remained silent, watching. After the horsemen had vanished in the mists, they crept out and approached the ancestor with their blossoms. The ancestor was aware now, and pulled back at their approach.

"Hissta, sizzletack," a boy said, extending his blossom.

The silver snout came forward. There was a great sucking sniff. The ancestor was already forgetting. But should it be happening this soon?

"Herzig must know," the other boy said.

"Yes," the first agreed. "We must hurry back home and tell Herzig what happened. Mortals must not be allowed to torment our ancestors."

The ancestor snorted loud, enjoying the fragrance of the blossoms. It had seemed bemused, but now was recovering.

They were almost to the Barrens when Jac felt his head fully clear. Turning to Heeto riding beside him, he addressed the matter he had not quite understood. "That white light—what was it, and how did it happen?"

Heeto yanked his horse's reins so hard he almost tumbled from the saddle. His face was stricken, as was his voice. "Oh, Master, I forgot it! It worked, Master. I'm sure it worked! Only I'm not sure what it did or why! I pointed it, I pressed the trigger, and . . . and then there was the light."

"Lord!" Jac said. He tried to digest this. "The Mouvar weapon—where is it now?"

"Where we were, Master. At the cliffs. Inside the tunnel."

"Lord!" Jac repeated. He shook his head. "It had to have been that! Because after that flash, the serpent changed. Maybe that weapon didn't work on a bearver, but the serpents are different; they carry captive spirits." He shook his head, hardly believing what he was saying. Was he raving? "We're going to have to get it! It could be the answer to everything! If it works, we may have the answer to flopears and Rowforth!"

"We can't go back now, Master. The sun is up."

"Yes, it is, isn't it!" He let the fact infiltrate his consciousness. Day made things so much clearer—usually. But the revelations he was experiencing, assuming they made any sense at all . . . "If we go back now, they'll get us. So we won't do it now. We'll do it as soon as we safely can." Which meant evening or night.

They rode on toward the camp, following their faint trail through the Barrens. That was as familiar to both as though marked with signs, but anyone else would not find it at all.

When they arrived, there was confirmation: Kian and Lonny in front of his tent, standing hand in hand, without question alive.

There went perhaps his last hope to win Lonny. But somehow the pain was less now. He was glad to have her alive—and a new horizon was opening on his activity.

Even as Jac hailed them he was already making plans for the recovery of the weapon that had worked so strangely to rescue them.

CHAPTER 15
Ambush

JAC DREW LINES IN the sand with a stick and motioned everyone around. It was battle plan time, and all his men— all fifty-six, including Heeto and of course the newcomers, Kian and Lonny—were grouped outside his tent.

"We'll have to do it this way." His finger pointed out the spot on his crude map. "Right here on the main road where you lost your way, Kian. We'll hide behind the trees and wait. Smith," he said to the man behind him, "you're the best crossbowman, so we'll station you in a tree where you can take out the leader. Take the leader out as soon as they offer resistance, and we may have a chance. If the flopears don't get to us first."

Kian felt constrained to speak. He had been mentally counting their numbers since they came outside and guessing at the number of troops he had seen and the number of flopears nearby. "I can't be certain this is the route they will take. I only know what I heard in the palace. By the way, that was my last dragonberry. If we don't win and you haven't got dragonberries growing here, that's the end of astraling."

"Yes, you're right, it's our only chance," Jac agreed. "Then, when the fighting is heaviest—and there'll be fighting, make up your mind to it!—maybe Heeto and I can get back to that tunnel and get back your Mouvar weapon."

"Are you sure it will do any good if we have it?" Kian found it hard to believe it would. Even though he and Lonny had been rescued by its use, he didn't know what it had done. Whether it could be effective against the flopears themselves, let alone the armed soldiery of Rowforth's—that seemed too good to be true.

"We'll see," Jac said. "And, Lonny—"

"Yes?" She looked up at the leader with her blue eyes.

"We'll station you on high ground overlooking the valley. If you spot any flopears, you'll warn us."

"Will my voice carry that far?"

"No, you'll have to run back. If you shout from the high rock on this spot above the road, we'll hear."

She nodded. "I won't have a horse?"

"Can't spare one. It all depends on your legs. It's a distance of about twice around this camp."

"My legs are good," she said with unconscious understatement. "I'll look out for flopears."

"It's too bad there's not another good spot for an ambush. But then maybe the soldiers won't think to ride for flopear help, and maybe the flopears wouldn't help. There's a chance."

Kian considered how different Lonny was from Jon back home. Jon would have been protesting that she should have a horse and her sling and a supply of rocks. Jon would want in on the fighting, and Lonny would be conscious that she was female and that fighting was only for males. As for Lenore, whom Lonny so resembled in appearance, he really didn't know. All he could remember of Lenore was looking away with embarrassment whenever she was near. Yet her appearance was almost identical to Lonny's. How blind had he been?

Matt Biscuit moved through the men until he was beside Jac. "You'd better use him," he said, jerking his thumb at Kian. "Him and his gauntlets."

"Right. Kian, you'll be in the forefront of the charge. Assuming there is a charge, and there's sure to be one. Rowforth's men won't give up your father without a fight. So you and I and Biscuit here will be at the head of any charge. Biscuit's good with a sword, I'm good, and from what you say, your gauntlets will make you better."

"I, uh, really haven't had the practice," Kian confessed. Now that he was facing battle, he felt quite ill. Kelvin, the hero, would never feel like this!

"You want *me* to wear your gauntlets?" Biscuit demanded.

"No! I'll wear them, and I'm good! I wore them in one battle back in my home frame, and there was only one other warrior my equal."

"Your brother, Kelvin," Jac supplied.

"Yes, Kelvin." He did not add that Kelvin had worn the left gauntlet, he the right. Nor that they had fought each other to a draw. Some things these local patriot bandits could know, and some he didn't want to reveal even under torture.

"Then it's settled. We know from your last reconnaissance that they'll be coming at dawn. On their way home we'll stop them and take away your father. If we do, we have your word he'll help us against Rowforth and the flopears. That right, Knight?"

"You know it is." Jac seemed just a bit belligerent, but then they all did. It was probably battle nerves and the fact that so far he had been more of a source of problems than a solution to any.

When he got a look at the soldiers through his physical eyes, Kian marveled at how little he had noticed with his astral vision. They were ordinary men by Jac's reckoning, but they were obviously top fighting men. Sturdy, strong, well disciplined, and their quality showed. His mother's troops had looked nothing like these! They would not release his father without a fight, and studying them from concealment, Kian wondered if Jac's ragtag crew could possibly prevail. Then he remembered the gauntlets he wore, and he knew that they did have a chance. Assuming he could stay astride his horse and get into the fray where it would help.

He sighed. He knew he would soon be taking men's lives and he hated it. But the alternative was to leave his father, and possibly, though he had not seen her, his mother. He willed himself strong for the coming fight.

The few crossbow bolts struck the road directly in front of the marching men as Jac rode out of the trees and raised his hand. "We want your prisoner! Resistance or a refusal to turn him over means death!"

"By the Gods, we'll have none of it!" The ruddy-faced captain turned to his troops and commanded: "Shields ready! Prepare!"

A lucky crossbow bolt from Smith found its target. The captain clutched at the feathered barb piercing his throat above the mail. Gurgling horribly, he pitched over the head of his war-horse, spraying blood on his way to meet the ground.

"Charge!" Jac ordered his bandit army, and Kian hardly had time for it to register before he was charging the foremost men. In a moment more he was crossing swords, cutting down, stabbing and chopping expertly. His gauntlets knew, and did what was necessary. He saw his father through the dust that now covered everything, and after he had dispatched his fifth man, he felt fully that he was effecting a rescue.

"Flopears! Flopears!" It was Lonny calling from the rock. If it weren't for the dust he could have bent back, looked up, and seen her. The battle had hardly started, but she was there, calling down to them.

Obviously the flopears had not been far away. Had they known what would happen, through their magic? Had one of them been astral-spying here? Or was it simply that the valley and its flopear population were far too close to the bandit camp? Whatever the case, it was doubtful that a rider had gotten back to them to beg their assistance.

Flopears, it seemed, were now fully allied to Rowforth and did not necessarily wait to be asked. In the past, Jac had confided, things had been far different, and dealings with mortals had been restricted to the once-a-year sacrifice.

Faster than he would have believed possible, the fighting tide turned. Kian found his gauntlets taking complete control of his hands and arms and almost his mind. Blocking, stabbing, slashing—his sword was busy while his shield hid the faces of dying men. But their horrible screams cut through to his ears. Who had ever fancied that combat was glorious? He could not think now, even to marvel at the speed of his blade and the intricate motions of his arm. He was simply a killing machine.

Then his horse screamed, and he was flying from the saddle over its neck. Somehow the gauntlets flung sword and shield and forced his body into an acrobatic roll. He bounced to his feet, twisted out of the way of a sword slash, saw Biscuit run the man through, and retrieved his weapons almost under the horse's hooves. These gloves played it entirely too close for comfort!

"We have to retreat! Quick, before the flopears arrive!" It was Jac's voice in the dust. Biscuit reached down a hand to Kian, but the gauntlet with the sword in it motioned him away.

Thinking only that he must get Lonny, Kian scrambled up the hillside, out of the lake of dust. How nice to catch a breath of fresh air! Once a sword cut at him, but his shield deflected the blow without even jerking hard. Then he was above the horses and on his way to the high rock and to Lonny. It was much too steep going, but the gauntlets knew no defeat. Without giving him a chance to do more than fight for breath, they grabbed saplings and brush and pulled his errant feet constantly upward on a path that seemed impossible for a mountain goeep. How nice it would be to have enchanted boots that governed his feet the way the magic gauntlets governed his hands!

Now he was at the crest of the hill, coming up by the rock. Lonny was on the rock, her eyes fixed glassily on a flopear advancing on her with raised club. In a moment the flopear would bash in her head and send her lifeless body tumbling down to the battlefield below. No wonder the gauntlets had hauled him up here so rapidly; had he realized the reason for their urgency, he would have strained yet more to make it sooner. As it was—

He could not make it in time; the remaining distance was too great. But even as he realized this, his right glove whipped his sword down, slicing at the ground broadside. The point caught a stone and drove it out and up in what his father called a golf drive. The little stone sailed across and flew at the flopear's face. Then, as if its job were done, the gauntlet sheathed the sword.

The flopear, no slouch, saw the missile coming and ducked, and the stone missed. But this distracted him from the girl. He looked across and saw the new enemy cresting the hill. The flopear reoriented, bracing himself and taking a defensive posture with the club. Then, satisfied that he faced only one new enemy, he lifted the club for a smash. There was no point in bashing the helpless girl if he got his own head lopped off immediately after!

Kian's gauntlets got him to the top and on his feet and his shield up in front of his face before the flopear could fully turn and redirect his blow. But he no longer held his sword! He had foolishly sheathed it, and had no time to draw. Kian lurched on his feet as the club smashed against the shield. Despite the gauntlets, he almost fell. This flopear was a true warrior, balanced and ready despite his surprise, while Kian was a bumbling fool!

Then his right glove jumped forward to catch at the flopear's left knee, and his left glove shoved the shield back hard against the club and the attacker's face. The flopear tried to step back but could not, because of the caught knee. He had been caught by surprise by an unworthy foe. He cried out and flung away his club, trying to recover his balance, but he could not. He fell, and now the gauntlet let go of the knee with a shove, and the flopear stumbled back too violently. He lost his footing at the edge of the steeper slope and fell down, rolling over on the slope, tumbling head over boots. Thump, thump, thump, bash. Then, mercifully, a speck of silence.

Other flopears would be here momentarily. Kian had dealt with one, thanks again to the genius of the gauntlets, but there was no reason to think he could handle three or four. That one had been too apt, too quick and sure; only the surprise hold and push when Kian had seemed to be falling (seemed?) had caught him. Once a flopear eyed him, he would be done for, and the same for Lonny.

He grabbed her hand and yanked. "Come!"

He ran, hauling her along, his gauntlets helping him decide the route. But Lonny tried to hang back.

"Kian, we're going the wrong way! The serpents—"

With shock he realized that his hands were urging them past a pole holding a serpentskin chime. Turning his head, he could just barely see short-legged flopears toiling up the hillside. That way would be suicide or capture. Ahead— ahead was the bigger of the two valleys: the one Lonny's people called Serpent Valley.

Unhesitatingly the powerful gauntlets pulled them on, down the steep hillside where silver serpents lay basking lazily in the morning sun.

John Knight could hardly believe that they had arrived, but they had, and they looked just like the troops back home that Rufurt had maintained. Only here it was Rowforth, and if he didn't misinterpret Gerta's expression when she talked of him, he was not the ideal monarch for this familiar yet strange fairy-tale land.

"I'm sorry you go, John," Gerta said as she led him from her cottage. "You good man. Not like most mortals."

Blinking in the sunlight, John considered the good manly uprightness of the troops, the neatness of their green uniforms, and the shine of their highly polished mail. With troops like these, could Rowforth be bad? Possibly he had a wife such as Rufurt had had—Queen Zoanna, sinister mistress of men, certainly mistress of John Knight. Evil women, he was beginning to think, existed everywhere.

"Good-bye, Gerta," he said, directing a grateful look at her. The flopear girl had been kind to him. She was strange in the way she had talked to that chime as though it contained something living, but he had come to know her as a person rather than as a thing.

"Up on your horse, you!" a captain commanded.

He mounted. The saddle was a bit tight. Riding horses had been but an occasional recreation in his Earthly life. Flying with a jetpack or legging it over mountains was more in his experience. Of course, he had ridden bicycles as a boy and later driven cars and trucks.

The procession rode out. Turning, looking back, John marveled anew at the cottages and the round holes that had been turned into dwellings and buildings in the surrounding cliff. The roundness of the holes made him think of wormholes. Had he imagined the great size of the serpent he encountered? Gerta hadn't said, but he remembered vividly her holding out the pink and blue blossoms to that great, flat head.

He breathed in, savoring the delightful green smells of spring. It was spring here, he'd bet. You could mistake a lot of things, but you couldn't mistake the feel of seasons. Not when you were outside and a part of the natural scene.

They were leaving the valley now by a road he didn't recall but must once have traveled. He could see that it was a valley and that there was another valley connecting it. The hills, the mountains, were much like those in Rud. In a way it was like some areas of the Americas, if they had not been ground down by glaciers. But if there had been no glaciers here, should there be such valleys? Pondering this, he mentally shook his head. He was no geologist, so his conjectures were hardly definitive. Whatever made the valleys in these mountains, they ran big, and whatever made the mountains, they ran rough. Now, as in other things, he wished he were more the expert on the subject.

Ahead were wilds: trees and brush. He supposed he had run, crawled, or somehow moved through these parts. Yet he could hardly remember. The magic medicine Gerta had used on him had dimmed any memories of what otherwise might be coming back. It was plain that he had gotten here from the river, and he must have traveled this road. More he simply could not evoke.

They were stopping. The captain was talking to someone, and oh, how red his face appeared. Then the captain was falling, clutching at his throat. Horses neighed and danced. Swords leaped from scabbards. Shields were raised. In a moment a full-scale battle was on. It was like old times, thus abruptly: swords swishing and shields clanging and men crying out from wounds or giving their death rattles. Wild-looking men without uniforms were everywhere, attacking green uniforms.

A man screamed and fell from his horse, and another man and horse raced after a third. Dust billowed voluminously, like smoke. That was the thing about battles: they were never neat and choreographed; they were always messy and dusty and ugly in both sight and mind.

Briefly he glimpsed the face of a man not wearing a uniform: a young, now very grim face. *Kian!* he thought. *Kian! My son!*

Kian must have followed him to this frame. But who were these men he was with? Who were these rough, ill-clad, undisciplined folk? They looked like bandits from the Sadlands! And was it really Kian, or did it just look like him? With similar-looking people turning up in this frame, it was hard to be sure. He had to find out!

He dug his heels into his horse's sides and crouched low on the neck, trying to make a break. The horse leaped forward as it was supposed to do, and as he took off he shoved the soldiers on either side of him from their mounts—or tried to. His outflung arms did not accomplish much. Then he was past and there were other matters at hand.

The man he had thought to be Kian was in that battle ahead. John didn't have a sword himself, or any kind of weapon. Still—

The blow took him from behind and sent him out of the saddle and down to the dust. He threw up his arms to protect his face. The ground came up very, very fast.

The next thing he knew, someone was pulling him up by his arms. Who had him, and why, he did not know. It was all he could do to hang on to his dwindling consciousness.

CHAPTER 16
Serpent's Hole

KIAN FELT HER STIFFEN and the gauntlet jerked. He knew she had been pierced by the gaze of a serpent or a flopear. At least he hoped that was it, rather than an arrow! He felt himself swing around, pulled by the left gauntlet, and the jarring thud as shield struck hard against a flopear's face. The flopear went down in a heap, his raised club flying from his hands.

Kian gave Lonny a quick slap and saw her eyes unglaze. He could hear more flopears coming in the distance, uttering hoarse shouts. The only flopear in sight was the one he had knocked unconscious.

They had to hide! There was no fighting these flopears! If they didn't get out of sight, they were going to be killed or captured.

A hole showed there in the rocks. A cave? A den? What did it matter? It was a hiding place!

He jerked Lonny the distance and pushed her ahead of him

into the darkness of the hole. If they could just stay here until the flopears were past—until nightfall, perhaps.

Outside, the flopears were calling to one another in hoarse shouts. Yes, they'd have to stay hidden. They hadn't been seen or discovered yet. They had found the club-wielder and were trying to decide what had happened.

"Kian," Lonny whispered, moving close. "Kian—"

"Not now, Lonny." God, how he wanted her arms around him! But he didn't want her to feel his trembling. Heroes, after all, were supposed to be brave.

"Kian—I—I love you."

That was what he had been afraid she would say! He was so attracted to her—and this in the wrong frame!

"Kian, there's something you should know."

He was afraid he already knew it. That mergence in the serpent—that hadn't been just because they were both captive. It had been because they both wanted it. They both wanted it now, in their physical bodies, too.

His arms found her and held her. He could feel her heart beating under her light shirt. The trembling of his limbs now didn't seem to matter. In a moment, except for the danger, he might forget himself. Blessed be the peril, part of him thought. *Damn!* another part retorted.

But if they were in immediate danger of dying, why was he holding back? Why save himself for a woman of the other frame if there was to be no encounter with her? Wouldn't it be better simply to take advantage of that scant time remaining here?

"Kian, we're about to die."

"M-maybe not," he managed to say. Evidently her logic was paralleling his. She was such a precious armful, all sweet and soft and female. "I've still got my sword and my shield and the gauntlets. Even if they find us, they can't make eye contact in the dark. I can defend this cave for a long time." But was that what he really wanted to do? How much easier to abandon thoughts of combat and simply lose himself in her!

"Kian, this isn't a cave. This is the tunnel a big serpent makes."

He shuddered in spite of himself. A part of his mind had known where they were, but he had been suppressing it. Trust Lonny, troublesome as only a comely girl could be, to come out with it.

He moved his back up against the wall of the tunnel. He resheathed his sword and put his gauntleted palm against it. A thought screamed at his consciousness: *If we move back, back, back, maybe they won't come in here after us! Maybe they'll never find us!*

Lonny moved still closer to him, scaring him almost more than the darkness, in quite a different manner. He took her hand firmly in his and whispered low so as not to be overheard by any sharp-eared flopear. "If we retreat far enough back—"

"But, Kian, we can't know what's here! There might be a—a—"

"And there might not. Not all the holes are occupied." He hoped! "Come—"

He led her stumbling and cringing through the blackness, his gauntlet scraping the side of the tunnel. The gauntlets wouldn't lead him into unnecessary danger, would they? In any other place he would have found it easier to believe that.

There was no indication, but he felt that the tunnel was old. If it hadn't been used for a long time, just maybe they might follow it to a spot where the original tunneler had resurfaced. It was a possibility, though remote. After all, the one they had been in had eaten silver, then come to the surface. They did like to sun themselves after a meal.

"Kian, is that a glow?"

He paused. He had thought it wishful thinking, but yes, there was a lightness. Outdoors! They'd survive after all!

But no, he felt no breeze, no hint of fresh air. His nose, in fact, seemed clogged with dust. So if that wasn't daylight, what was it? There were no alternatives but to go on, or stay where they were, or return to the entrance. Even now the flopears could be tracking them down, entering the tunnel; the flopears had no fear of serpents!

His gauntlets were tugging at him, forcing him to move away from the wall and follow their lead, lest he be drawn off balance.

It could be daylight! he thought without any proper conviction. *It could be daylight!* he kept telling his doubting self. But his self knew it was a lie. The light was greenish, and that meant—

At home it would have meant moss of the luminous variety that had enabled him to row out on the underground river and travel through the rock walls to Mouvar's concealed chamber. Here—

Here it meant luminous moss on rock walls. There was a blaze of green light and then he stopped, grabbing Lonny's arm. They were right in the exiting mouth of a serpent tunnel that led from a wide, natural chamber! The chamber's walls were coated with the luminous lichen. Other serpent tunnels, not of this size, also entered it at irregular intervals.

Kian took a great breath. "Maybe we *can* find a way out! By taking another tunnel."

"Yes, Kian! Oh, yes!"

She was so quick, so positive! He liked that, knowing he had no business to react to it. He had aroused her hope, he thought, and now he would have to deliver. The gauntlets, he feared, really did not know more than he did which serpent tunnel might lead them to a reasonably safe exit. How *could* they know? They were not of this frame!

Holding Lonny's hand in his, feeling awed by the size of the chamber, he led her into it. There were outcroppings of rock and stalactites of great size above them, stalagmites rising up like raised spears from the floor. In the green radiance all was clear for a surprising distance. It was as though they had entered some mammoth building. There was little dust, and fresh air was coming in through serpent holes far overhead.

Lonny's face held the same awe Kian felt. The place they were in stretched as far as they could see, and there seemed no end to the radiance. Even if one of the serpent tunnels presented an immediate exit, the impulse to explore was overwhelming.

They walked hand in hand, admiring the beauty. Fear diminished; fear could not flourish in loveliness like this! There were crystal outcroppings, natural shelves and stairs and doorways. There were beads in some outcroppings that seemed bluish and yellowish and even reddish in the light. With some difficulty Kian realized that the beads were actual gems of a size that in his home frame would have been unheard of. Silver ore outcroppings here and there, like rivers and streams of shining mineral flowing frozenly through the rock. A crystal waterfall, greenish and sparkling, as high as any waterfall Kian had ever seen.

"Oh, Kian! Oh!" Lonny exclaimed.

Inadequate, but accurate, he thought. It was almost worth the danger to see this place, to know of its existence.

"It's as pretty as the flopears' silverwork," she continued.

He had to agree. The people of this region drew the beauty of their images from it, along with the horror of their serpent companions. Yet, after being inside a serpent, he realized that horror was mainly how a person saw it. There was beauty within the serpents, too.

They walked between the stalagmites and found themselves in a narrow chamber. Here there were luminous mushrooms such as flopears used for lighting, and beyond the mushrooms was an area that descended as if by means of man-made stairs to a lower level.

Kian took a deep breath, thankful again for the good air here—who would have thought he would appreciate serpent holes like this!—and led Lonny on. There seemed no end of wonder to this place; no physical end in sight.

Ahead, silver. Lots of silver! He stopped, staring. The silver was in long, thin belts and made of overlapping scales. The silver was discarded serpentskins, many of them from giants!

"Gods, Lonny," he said, "there's a fortune! They must

have been coming here for ages!" His eyes swept along the shining carpet. It stretched for as far as he could see and then was closed off by a bend in the cavern.

"If only Jac and his men could get down here! They'd never have to steal silver from the flopears again! They'd be rich as any king! They could go out and buy themselves an army or a kingdom!"

"Kian?" Lonny whispered. Her face was very pale; what was the matter with her, reacting so to such wealth?

"It's all right," he said.

"Kian," she gasped, "remember where we are!"

Yes, she would remind him, he thought. Remind him that they would in all probability never get back to Jac and his bandits. Still it was something, just knowing this was here. If an army needed to be raised, the means of raising it was here.

Listening, he heard a great, dry rustling. It grew louder and louder, and then silver appeared in one of the serpent tunnels. They stood frozen as a great serpent snout—larger even than the one they had been in—protruded from one of the holes. That could be why the tunnel they had entered was empty: it was too small for a serpent this size! It did not see them, and Kian pulled Lonny away, back into a natural alcove.

Other rustlings, other sounds. It was as though the cavern walls had come alive. Serpents of great and simply large size, serpents the size of ordinary snakes, and serpents the size of worms, squirming out of open tunnels and tunneling themselves out of rock. Bits of rock dust fell here and there as serpents broke free of the honeycombed rock. The slithering grew louder and louder and was accompanied by hisses as the serpents broke into the cavern.

"Oh, Kian, Kian, hold me! Hold me before it's too late!"

He did, trembling and shaking. Any moment a head might emerge at their backs. Any moment a serpent might set its freezing eyes on them. Once discovered, they would be gone. There was nothing to prevent their being snapped up, chewed, swallowed, digested, and made physically a part of these monsters. Magic gauntlets, sword, and shield were as little protection as their clothing. There was nothing to do but stay hidden and wait.

Plop! Plop! Plop! The sound of serpent bodies sliding, gliding, falling onto rock. This huge cavern that had seemed so much like salvation from pursuit had turned out to be the most dangerous place of all!

He held her tight, no longer daring to speak any word. It was amazing that the serpents didn't smell them, but perhaps the odor was too diffuse to alert them. But any sound now—

After a time he found her face turned to his. Silently, he kissed her, and it was very sweet. Perhaps they would soon be horribly dead, but at the moment they were wonderfully alive.

Herzig came as fast as his short legs could carry him. The flopear motioned to the body on the ground, and he pulled up by it and looked down. Danzar, he thought, staring into the wide features of the unconscious man. His club lay near his hand, but there was a bruise on his forehead.

"Herzig, do you think they have a way of deflecting the serpent eye?" Kaszar asked. Kaszar was bending over Danzar, his stubby fingers lifting his eyelids to reveal the whites.

Herzig snorted. "With a bruise like that? No, if they could resist the eye, they would have taken him with them. Look here in the dirt; tracks of two mortals."

"Then Danzar got careless?"

"Yes. Never underestimate a mortal. They are stupid, but some are less stupid than others."

"Like Rowforth?"

"Rowforth, their king of Hud, is too cruel to be entirely stupid. Not stupid but not wise, and not what mortals call good!"

Danzar groaned and looked out again through his eyes. "Ohhh," he said, his hand going to his bruise. "Two mortals. A man and a woman. I thought to club the woman dead, but he threw a stone to distract me and then swung without looking at me."

"He swung without looking?" This was very interesting. Suggestive of a power, if not actual magic.

"Yes, his shield. He swung around fast and the shield caught me so fast I didn't see it. And my knee—he grabbed my knee, so that I fell. I never expected such coordination when I thought him done for."

Herzig nodded. He didn't really like fighting mortals. They were so frail, for the most part, and few were worthy of joining in the cycle. It had been an act of kindness to put those two into the ancestor, just as it had been pity for a wretched creature that had driven Gerzah, Gerta's mother, to mate with one and bear it a child. But mortals by and large were untrustworthy, as that one had proved to be. Poor Gerzah had joined an ancestor early, and her daughter, Gerta, was without mate or child. That was what came ultimately of kindness to mortals. Still, as it had turned out, Gerta's mortal heritage enabled her to understand mortals better, and so she was good at helping them recover. That had been most useful in the case of the mortal John Knight.

Kaszar pointed to an opening in the rocks. It was an old ancestor tunnel rather than a natural opening. A pair of footprints were clearly in the dust in the tunnel's opening.

Herzig delivered himself of a long, painful sigh. Such stupidity just wasn't possible! But there it was—they had entered the domain of the ancestors. Deep in the ground the ancestors would find them and devour them, and then, just as food eventually became flesh, they would become part of the cycle.

"Should we go after them, Herzig?" The question, Herzig thought, was really quite rhetorical.

"Why? You know what will happen to them."

"But should it?" Kaszar's face flashed with anger. "These mortals, a part of our ancestors, joining in the cycle?"

"The cycle has seasons," Herzig replied. "We are none of us but ourselves, and yet making up ourselves are all our past ancestors. Mortals are the same way but don't realize it. On the next cycle it won't matter. Do you ever wake to remember tunneling, Kaszar? No, nor do I. The lives of ancient serpents are not a part of our daily existence."

"Uh," Kaszar said. He nodded, seemingly mollified. He reached out, grasping his leader's shoulder. His face smiled, widening his mouth. "I've heard it before, all my life, but I have to be reminded."

"We're none of us dirt, Kaszar, and all of us are dirt. Mortals as well as serpent people."

"Yes. That is true."

"What do you want to do about those mortals? Now that you have been reminded of what they are and what we are and of the endless cycle governing all?"

Kaszar took his hand off his leader's shoulder and walked to the tunnel's opening. He funneled his hands around his mouth and shouted in: "Mortals! We are coming to get you, Mortals! Run! Hide! Run until your hearts burst! We are coming, Mortals! We are coming!"

Herzig glanced at Danzar on the ground and found the big club-wielder smiling broadly in satisfaction. He helped him to his feet. Then all three left the tunnel to the ancestors and to the very temporary mortals therein.

Heeto watched from concealment in the rocks as the flopears left the vicinity of the tunnel. He had watched as Kian and Lonny ran into the tunnel to hide, and he had seen the three flopears talking and now leaving. They would be back, he thought, with help.

Should he go down there and try to get the two strange young people out of the tunnel? No, he knew he hadn't time. It was sheer chance that he had remained undiscovered as flopears had raced by his hiding place.

"Heeto!"

He turned to see Jac on his mare. Jac had ridden up behind him, knowing where he was, coming to him by way of the cutoff route that few actually knew about.

"Heeto, we're not winning," Jac said. "Too many flopears joined the soldiers. We can't get John Knight from them. We can't slip into Serpent Valley and get the weapon. We're beaten, Heeto, beaten!"

Heeto looked at the master with sorrow. He had been against the ambush all along, knowing as he did that flopears were too near and too numerous and far too magical. Against the soldiers alone Jac and his men and the magical gauntlets might have a chance, but once the flopears came, the fight was done.

"Master, Kian and Lonny are in that tunnel. Three flopears have just left."

"Then they are as good as dead," Jac said. His face showed his sorrow. The lady, Heeto understood, had been special to him.

"Kian knocked a flopear down with his shield, Master. Then the two others came. The two who did not see them, but I know they know they are there."

"Good man, that Kian. Young, but good. It was the gauntlets that did it, of course. They did the fighting and they struck the flopear."

"I know."

"The flopear was caught because he thought he was fighting a man. Had he known he was fighting magic, it might have been different."

"That must be," Heeto agreed. "But the serpents—the gauntlets can't overcome them! Not down in their own realm!"

"Come."

Reluctantly Heeto let his master take his hand and lift him up onto the front of the horse. He had always found riding uncomfortable. More so this way, half lying on the neck of the mare.

The horse walked at a slow pace back the way it had come. Soon they came out of the brush, and dead and dying men were everywhere. Some were like statues, frozen in place by some absent flopear's stare.

Jac called to Matt Biscuit, who was helping a man who had been wounded in the arm by an arrow. "Start rounding up the survivors! We're going back to the Barrens."

"We lost, didn't we?" Biscuit demanded. "All because we trusted that foreigner! Him and his magic gauntlets and his hero father and brother! I knew it was a mistake!"

"We had to try," Heeto's master said. "Now at least we know Rowforth *can* enlist flopear help. Knowing that, we know what we're up against and who we fight."

"We! How many do you think you have left? Maybe twenty men, and half of them wounded. You think you'll take over a kingdom with that?"

But the master simply kept riding, acting as if he saw no death and hadn't heard a word of Biscuit's.

CHAPTER 17
Exits

KIAN DREW LONNY BACK behind a rock outcropping and dared not peek out at the serpents. As near as he could tell, this was a gathering place where they sometimes shed their skins and where perhaps they mated. It could be that they had other things on their minds than feeding, so weren't alert for prey here. After all, how much thought did he himself have of food when he was guiltily kissing Lonny? So maybe the serpents were attuned to prey when on the surface, where living creatures ran, and to silver when tunneling below, and to shedding when in this cavern, and simply had a one-track-at-a-time mind-set. So they might smell the living intruders here but not be hungry, and would ignore them. If so, it was about as lucky a break for the two people as they could ever have hoped for!

His father had talked about an elephants' graveyard, where the beasts came to die, leaving their valuable ivory tusks.

But how could there be a serpents' graveyard if the creatures were immortal? Yet how was it known that they were immortal? That could be just another story. Also, what about the little ones? They would have no business coming to a graveyard—and there should be no young in an immortal society.

The hissing and slithering convinced him at last that he had been correct the first time: serpents of all ages gathered here, shed their skins, and mated. Maybe there was something very sexy, in serpent terms, about shedding, so mating naturally followed. Or maybe not—but certainly the shedding occurred here, and that was enough to account for what he saw. After all, if they died here, there should be skeletons, and there were none.

Lonny was trembling within his embrace. Neither of them dared make a sound. Yet eventually one of those sliding silver bodies would come close and discover them. Then his theory about their safety would be tested—and he had little faith in it. After all, even if a serpent wasn't interested in hunting at the moment, it would hardly pass up a couple of succulent morsels that turned up right under its nose.

If they could only get away! But how?

Feeling behind him in the dark, Kian felt no wall. Maybe a passage was behind them? A way to escape?

Or another serpent tunnel, along which might be coming their doom?

He tugged Lonny in that direction, his gauntlets helping him. He had to trust the gauntlets; their guess was at least as good as his!

The serpents were clicking on rocks, hissing, tumbling. What a dialogue they must be having! Maybe this was an annual or a seasonal thing, during which they could renew acquaintances. Well, the more distraction for the serpents, the better.

There was some chance that the two of them could fade back unseen into this unknown darkness. But there was no telling what the tunnel held. If not an oncoming serpent, perhaps a sheer drop-off to some unfathomable depth. Or possibly a dead end.

If he was hesitant, the gauntlets were not. They tugged at him, pulled him, and he followed their lead. The smoothness of the tunnel floor meant there was little to trip them, and the gauntlets apparently sensed in a way he could not the turnings and bends. There was no doubt now: this was a serpent hole. But evidently the gauntlets believed it was unoccupied.

It was terribly black; there was no phosphorescence here. He felt as if he were walking into a wall of black velvet, almost feeling the physical touch of the darkness. Why was there no dim green glow here? Because the monstrous body of the traveling serpent wiped the passage clean?

Gradually the sounds behind them faded, first to a steady spluttering, then to a softer, muted roar. Finally it seemed hardly audible. But this only let the darkness close in even more tightly, as though it was now so thick that not even sound could penetrate it.

They had been walking for what his father would have called miles. Lonny was gradually developing a whimper that tore at him and added to his own discomfort. Even though they were trying to flee death, he didn't want her hurting.

Then, ahead: greenish radiance!

Was it the cavern they had left? Did this winding tunnel simply double back to where they had been? That did not make much sense to him, but his opinion didn't count; what counted was what made sense to the serpents. The persistent gauntlets seemed to slow, perhaps not quite certain, but they did not stop.

Gradually the radiance grew stronger as they emerged from the total darkness. Suddenly there was a big gap in the floor. It cut off the tunnel, and beyond it the wall was blank; the other side of this fault had slid along, taking the rest of the tunnel with it. That must be why there were no serpents here: even they did not care to navigate a discontinuity of this size! It would be easier to use an unspoiled tunnel. Or perhaps they had redrilled it, only to have the fault slide again. Maybe this was a low-silver region, so they didn't bother to maintain the tunnels. The radiance came from the crack.

They stopped. Kian had no idea how to proceed, and Lonny seemed as if she would not dare even try to think of an idea. Were the gauntlets in similar doubt?

He examined the cleft more carefully. This seemed to be the same type of moss that lined the cavern walls. The rent in the stone was a fracture that might have been caused by a quake, or by the movement of a gigantic body. It had sundered the serpent tunnel, cutting it off, making it useless. Probably there were a number of tunnels spoiled by such cracks. Odd that the moss grew so freely here, and not at all in the tunnel. Perhaps there was a better supply of nutrients in the air that passed through here. For there was air; he felt its slight, cool motion along the crevice.

By the glow he could see Lonny's frightened, drawn face. "Kian, what—"

"Shhh," he said. It was all he trusted himself to say. The serpents might hear, true, but mainly it was that he needed to appear positive, and anything he said would soon dispel that impression.

There might be a use for this luxuriant moss if it could be carried. The radiance was an inferior light source, but it did permit a limited vision, and it was far, far better than nothing! He drew out his sword from its scabbard, thinking to scrape off a handful.

"Kian," Lonny whispered. "Down there, way down, see it?"

He placed his cheek next to hers, an act which would have been delightful in any other circumstance, and perhaps even in this one, and strained to see what she saw. There was something! Way, way down the narrow cleft he could see a softer, lighter glow. It seemed to come from a series of fist-sized knobs.

"Glowrooms," Lonny whispered. "Flopears use them for lighting. They have them in their cottages and carry them like lamps."

Kian remembered seeing them in the cottage where his father was kept. He knew nothing about them except for what Lonny had said. "I'll get one," he said.

"Be careful!"

"I will. You wait." Worming himself down into the cleft, he banged his head and scraped his back.

Slowly, painfully on hands and knees and sometimes on his stomach, he made his way toward the lighter glow. There they were, clustered about another crack from which came more greenish glow.

Kian sucked in his breath as he saw that the crack opened almost directly below him. Creeping slowly so as to avoid a sudden pitch downward, he was able to see moss-lighted water far below. Another underground river, and this one not of his world. But was the other any different? Did this, too, lead to a Flaw that went not only through this entire world but through many? He had used Mouvar's machine to come to this frame, but it might be that the rivers crossed between frames, too. Mouvar might simply have found a mechanical and reliable way to do what the rivers and The Flaw did randomly. He shivered uncontrollably as the mental vision became increasingly real. What a vast and complex thing might this system be!

"Kian, can you get it?"

"Y-yes." Her voice brought him back to sanity of a sort. He dared not think about what could happen if rock and dirt gave way almost beneath his face. The crack here was big enough to fall through, he felt, and might for all he knew to the contrary dramatically open up. The fall past glowing walls to the river so far below would surely kill him, and that would leave lovely Lonny with no further help.

Cautiously he cut off the thick toadstools and impaled three of them on his sword blade. Equipped now with a light, he twisted, turned, bruised himself some more, and got his head pointed the right way.

"Kian, I can see you well now! And, Kian, that hole, it goes way down!"

"I know. There's a river below us. Way below us!"

"Oh, Kian!"

"Better not talk! We can't be certain there's not a serpent about." But after seeing that eerie river, he had a notion why there were no serpents here. They must have the same awe of the environs of The Flaw as he did! The crevice had opened the tunnel to the dark river below, and the serpents did not trust that. Smart serpents!

"Y-yes."

He reached the edge of the moss-coated crack and raised the sword with its light. The tunnel continued ahead of the crack, after its jog to the side, he saw now; they had merely to squeeze through and across.

"We have to try going on, Lonny. This tunnel has to come out somewhere." His sword tip scraped the serpent's old roof. "We have breathable air, at least."

He helped Lonny with a gauntlet. They got into the next section of the tunnel, and soon left the crack behind. He was getting tired, physically, and he wondered about Lonny. He looked at her in the toadstool light and marveled at how very dirty she had become. He must be the same way. It was a dirty business, this scrabbling around inside a serpent hole. He wondered if the serpent who had once used this had been the one they had been part of for a time. This tunnel was evidently very old, but so was the serpent.

Something did not smell bad. He had gotten so used to the all-pervading earth smells of an abandoned serpent tunnel that he had difficulty with this concept at first. He sniffed hard. Then it came to him what the smell was—and he realized at the same time that he was starving. Bread!

Here? How could that be? In the light of the toadstool he saw the hole of a smaller serpent on either side. Apparently the lesser monster had cut through this one at some later date. He wasn't sure whether serpents had proprietary rights to their individual tunnels, so that intersecting one was forbidden, but that surely would not apply to a deserted one. The baking smell was coming from the hole on his left.

Motioning Lonny to silence, he tiptoed to the cross tunnel and sniffed again. Definitely bread! Looking at Lonny, he realized that she recognized it as well.

"A bakery," she whispered. "Down there?"

"Or a cottage. Flopears use old tunnels for rooms or for cottages."

"I know. We were there together."

"I wonder how far down the hole goes. If I go down there, I should at least be able to get us some bread."

"Kian, remember what happened when they had us!"

"But now we have our bodies. Maybe they'd just turn us over to Rowforth."

"Rowforth! He's worse than a serpent!"

"Perhaps." He divested himself of his shield and scabbard and handed her the sword. "You stay here and hold the light. I want to see just where this goes. If we have to just walk away, well, maybe we can."

"Kian, I'm afraid!"

He hesitated a moment and then took off the gauntlets and handed them to her. "You wear these for a while. If I'm not right back, they may have to get you out."

She drew the gauntlets on over her hands. "Why, they— they fit perfectly! How—?"

"Magic. Just think what you want them to do and they'll do it for you. Sometimes they do more than you'd think to do yourself."

"Be careful, Kian."

"I'll try to be."

He started crawling on his hands and knees and soon the light had disappeared and there was total darkness. His knees were soon punishing him, and he wondered whether he'd get to the end and find only a small hole just big enough to let the smell through. Turning around would be impossible if he didn't come out in a room. Of course he could always back out, but the thought was not one that he cared to contemplate. Just moving forward was hard enough.

Suddenly he put his right hand out and brought it down on

a point lower than he. The passage was sloping steeply downward. He put his left hand down by his right, and as he did a loud clatter came up and startled him, so that he forgot to brace himself. The next thing he knew, he was sliding, sprawled out at full length, trying desperately to stop. His face scraped and he tasted dust and the clatter got louder and a round light was below, and—

He dropped. There was a white room, and startled flopear faces.

He landed on something solid, and his face went into something soft that filled his nose and mouth before he had time to realize it. He was blind for the moment, his breath was knocked out, and his face, he realized, was down in a lump of dough.

"What's zat?" A flopear turned with a pan of bread just as Kian got dough out of his eyes. He saw four flopears, flour, and loaves of bread. He flung away bread dough that had clung to his face and breathed in the smell of a bakery. He looked around wildly, and then he saw the frying pan coming down at his head. There was no time to duck, no time to think about it.

He sank into oblivion.

When he next opened his eyes, painfully, it was to a familiar face.

Gerta's.

Lonny tried to see into the hole, but the light would only reach for a couple of body lengths. The source of the baking was farther than Kian had thought, as she had feared. It seemed to her that he had been gone for a long time. Should she follow? No; if Kian was captured by flopears he'd need help. It seemed unlikely that she could get him help, but she'd have to try. He should have kept the gauntlets; then he'd be all right. But then she wouldn't have them, and without them she couldn't even think of going for help.

From far down the hole there came a clatter. There were

crashing, banging, clanging sounds, pounding noises, and yelling. The voices of the flopears were surprisingly loud. "Get Gerta! Get Gerta! Get Gerta!"

They had him! She had feared they might catch him. She hadn't wanted him to go down there. But she was so hungry, and that smell of bread was so good! She should have made more of a protest; it was her fault.

But now that he was in the hands of the flopears, it was up to her. She would do whatever she could do. After all, he had saved her from the serpent when she had been set up as the sacrifice. She loved him, and even if he wasn't going to remain here, she wanted him safe.

"Gauntlets, help me find the way out!" she commanded. "Take me to the outdoors, Gauntlets!" She felt silly saying this, yet the gauntlets had seemed to pull Kian along in total darkness when it had been his wish simply to get away from the entrance. Now she wanted to get back to that entrance with all her heart, or at least to an exit. A *safe* exit! Even if she were captured by the flopears, that would be better than dying here. But she didn't want to get captured; she wanted to escape, and find help, and rescue Kian. Should she try to explain all that to the gauntlets?

The gauntlets tugged at her hands. She followed their direction, carrying the sword-light in her right hand, the shield in the left. The scabbard she had buckled around her waist, pushing it around to the side so it did not get between her legs. How did swordsmen manage these things? She was obviously not much of a warrior!

In a surprisingly short time, she found herself running, despite her fatigue, following the pull of the gauntlets. They seemed to lend strength to her entire body, though perhaps it was only their decisiveness that countered her confusion and made her seem stronger.

Great shadows danced and leaped on the walls, but they were shadows cast by her into the glowrooms' light. The gauntlets were more insistent than she had thought! She tried to make herself slow, knowing the danger of falling on a naked sword. Yet the gauntlets grew warmer, squeezing her hands and pulling her at a pace that terrified her. Kian had never told her of this, but then maybe he had not experienced it.

Her heart was pounding hard, painfully, and her breath was coming in gasps that felt as though they'd tear her lungs. She was no long-distance runner, she was only a poor soft girl! Yet the gauntlets would not let her rest. It was as if her life—or Kian's?—depended on her exerting herself to her limits.

Ahead shadows danced on the walls and the outrageous figure danced in a pool of wet. She tried to stop, at least to slow, but the gauntlets made her plunge on. Icy water grabbed at her ankles, splashed up on her legs, and even touched her face. She sped through the pool as though there could be no danger from it, her feet wanting to slow and the gauntlets pulling relentlessly. She stumbled, slipped—and it was as if the gauntlets gave a great yank on her hands and wrists, sending her head-down through the water and around a sudden bend. She negotiated the curve in the tunnel in a half-sprawling run that gave out at its limit and deposited her facedown on the rock. The sword with its glowrooms was stretched ahead at arm's length, and she did not touch the blade as the roof of the tunnel fell with a great and rumbling roar, dust belching up and over her, dirt and rock cascading just around the bend where she had been. She choked on the dust, gagged, closed her eyes, and felt dirt dropping on top of her. But in a moment the rumbling noise completed its course and the vibration came to a merciful halt.

Now she understood why the gauntlets had urged her on so mercilessly! Without them, she would have been killed!

She was buried, but not for long. The remarkable gloves let loose of the shield and sword and moved dirt away from her head and face. She sat up, fumbled for the glowing glowrooms and sword, and found these and the shield under the dirt.

She stood, shaking, gasping, her eyes tearing, bruised but alive. The broken glowrooms on the sword still gave forth their light, though the gauntlet quickly broke them all the way and put the seven separate pieces on the very tip of the sword. The tunnel behind was full, blocked solid with rock and dirt. Her grave—but for the gauntlets.

Kian, oh, Kian! she thought. *I must get help for you! I must!*

The gauntlet gently squeezed her hand and tugged. Now that the immediate danger was over, it would lead her at a more moderate rate.

She experienced a rush of feeling. *Thank you, Gauntlets!* she thought. *You are the best friends anyone ever had!*

Did the gauntlets give her hands a little squeeze in response? She couldn't be sure. But she felt so much better wearing them, now that she understood the manner in which they helped. She wondered what land they had come from, and whether there were many others of their kind, perhaps a whole society of gauntlets that used people only as mechanisms for moving around. When any two such people shook hands, it would be the gauntlets making contact with each other, not the people!

She smiled—and wondered again whether she felt their response, a trace quivering as of laughter. Maybe she was just imagining it, being alone and tired and frightened. But she lifted her right hand and kissed the back of the glove, just because.

The dust gradually settled as she walked. When she reached a spot where she could actually see the pieces of glowroom on the blade, she began to think it over. Up until this point she had visualized the entire tunnel collapsing. Yet she wasn't out of it yet and she didn't know if she ever would be. Her stomach growled its complaint of not being fed and her mouth protested its lack of moisture.

Bodies, she thought. *What a nuisance they are!* How much better not to have muscles that ached and bruises that hurt. Yet with only an astral form there had been limitations, too.

They had been dependent on the life-style of the serpent, and doomed to eventual absorption. Still, there had been rare delight in the prospect of mergence.

Would she and Kian ever join their physical bodies in the way that they had started with their astral selves? She hoped so. After this, Kian had to see. Whatever the qualities of the girl he had known, she was certain that girl would not do more for him than Lonny herself would. Yet if he truly wanted that other . . .

It seemed that she had been walking forever. Her calves ached and her ankles pained. How long ago had it been since Kian had gone down that smaller tunnel? Since that tunnel had collapsed? It felt like many hours, even days. She hadn't eaten, and she was so tired—

The gauntlets abruptly tugged her to the side. She followed their lead without resistance—and in due course came to a chamber that ended in a blank wall. "What?"

But the gauntlets drew her down. She felt along the wall, and found a hole at the base. She put her face down to peer into it, bringing the sword point close—and got a whiff of bread! The odor was wafting through the hole!

One gauntlet reached into the hole. It caught hold of something, and carefully tugged it out. It was a loaf of flopear bread. This must be a hole in the wall behind a flopear kitchen or pantry! She had just raided their food!

She stood, carrying the loaf. Now the gauntlets led her to another dark region, where a stream of fresh water flowed. She was thirsty; she put her lips to it and drank deeply. Then she sat down and gnawed into the loaf. The gauntlets had become quiescent, letting her rest and eat, so she did not worry about being discovered. What relief to eat at last, and to be off her weary feet!

She finished the loaf. She ought to get going, but it was so tempting to rest just a little more. The gauntlets would surely have her rushing forth soon enough.

She lay on the rock and cradled her head with her arms, making herself as comfortable as she could. She wished Kian were with her now; she could snuggle into him, and his arm would be protectively around her, and if there was anything she could do to make him realize what she offered, she would summon the energy for that before sleeping. It would be so nice . . .

She woke. It seemed just a moment, but her bladder was so full that she must have slept for many hours! She got up, found a place, and did what she needed to. But her legs were stiff from all the walking and running, so she lay down again for a little more rest—and in a moment was deeply asleep again.

Two more loaves and several sleeps later, she was rested and feeling much better. The gauntlets must have given her several days to recover. But what about Kian?

Abruptly guilty, she resumed action. "Gauntlets," she said severely, "you shouldn't have let me sleep so much! I've got to help Kian! You know that!"

The gauntlets gave a little squeeze on her hands. They seemed apologetic. Maybe they had needed to rest, too, after their labors! "I'm sorry—I wasn't thinking of your needs," she said contritely. "But maybe now—"

Immediately the gauntlets tugged at her, leading her on, resuming the route they had been following before she ate and slept. They were back in action! She only hoped the delay had not been disastrous for Kian.

There was still a long way to go. She tired more rapidly than she had before; evidently her strength had been more depleted than she had realized. All too soon she was trudging again, but this time she did not plead for any rest.

There was another serpentine bend. No more water seepage, at least. Every time she went around one of these bends she wondered whether there'd be a serpent or a pool of water waiting. Or maybe, incredible thought, a small, irregular opening to the outside.

The gauntlets teased at her hands. *They* knew the answer! They knew where they were going, and she trusted that. They were quite comfortable now, not making her run, letting her walk at a natural if decreasing pace. She did not want to go slow, but she was so tired! Kian needed her help; that was all that really kept her going.

She walked around the bend and almost fell. Here was a larger tunnel crossing this one as the much smaller tunnel had done. The gauntlets pulled her, not overly roughly or insistently, into the larger serpent tunnel on her left. It was just like a mess of interconnecting roads, she thought. This new tunnel appeared to be no more recently used than the other; this entire region seemed to have fallen into disuse by the serpents. She wondered whether she and Kian could have been through this one before. Probably not; there was too much dust here, and it really hadn't been that long. The serpent's body would certainly have wiped it clean if they had taken this particular route. Actually, she doubted that she had circled around to their starting place; her sense of direction was hopelessly confused, but it made more sense to her that the serpent tunnels should go more or less in lines than in circles. Why tunnel through rock just to return to your starting place? So this was most likely some distant place.

Ahead—could it be?—a round hole of daylight! Was she hallucinating?

And voices—the voices of people!

She stopped, though her gauntlets didn't direct a halt. Those could be flopears, and probably were! Maybe she should just wait until the voices went away?

The gauntlets tugged at her with a come-along-now urgency. She decided to trust them.

Shivering with a renewed fear despite her faith in the gauntlets, she took a step forward, then stopped. The glowrooms would be readily seen! Fearfully, yet with determination, she stripped them from the sword blade and tried to conceal their glow with handfuls of dust. When she had effectively buried them and was standing in the darkness, she turned her attention to the exit.

It was then that she saw the object lying on the floor of the tunnel. The incoming daylight made it shine. She blinked, but it remained. Unless Mouvar had been down in the tunnels, that was the weapon Heeto had left. This had to be that tunnel! Which meant that it could be Jac and Heeto outside! But if it turned out to be flopears—

She had to get that weapon. It could be the means of rescuing Kian and defeating Rowforth! She must not let it fall into the flopears' hands!

She crept closer, closer to the daylight. Now if she could just reach out and snatch it back into the dark—

A man appeared in the daylight. She waited, hoping to see who it was. She dared not approach, though he was right near the weapon. Maybe he wouldn't see it.

The man stooped down to pick up the weapon. As he did, a ray of sunlight lit up his thinnish, tall form, and then his face.

It was a man Lonny had never seen before.

CHAPTER 18
Late Arrival

KELVIN BECAME GRADUALLY AWARE of the chamber's soft blue radiance, and the throbbing pain in his temple.

St. Helens! The man had treacherously struck him, and he had fallen into the transporter. Then what had happened? He strained to remember, but it wouldn't come.

He checked what was on him. His laser was gone, left where he had foolishly set it down. The gauntlets were also missing, left by the laser. St. Helens must have possession of both.

He still had his shield and sword, as befitted a hero of Rud. Much good either would do him without the gauntlets! Without the magic gloves to fight for him, he was simply no champion, just an ordinary (and not too bright, it seemed) person. St. Helens had played him for the fool he was.

As he looked around he could detect small differences in this almost identical chamber. This had to be in another world than the one of the golden-scaled dragons. This had to be the world where somewhere a king who looked like King Rufurt held his father and half brother in a dungeon. It could also be a world that held Rud's former queen, just in case she wasn't dead.

His first practical thought was that he should go back. Without his gauntlets and his laser he would be better off home. But if St. Helens anticipated this, and was waiting, did he want to confront him? He was too apt to be a sitting target, and this time he might lose his life as well as his weapons.

On the other hand, if St. Helens had taken the boat and the levitation belt and the weapons, wouldn't he be stuck there in the chamber? Better to give this new world a chance, whatever world it might be.

He rose, stiff, sore, and a little dizzy. There were footprints in the dust that had not been in the other chamber. They led across the chamber to a bluish curtain of light and, not quite to his astonishment, to a large and glowing E X I T sign. Through the curtain he could see a rock ledge. Kian had gone this way, and so must Kelvin.

He stepped through the curtain and found himself outside. Not in a subterranean cavern or by a dark river, but all the way outside. Looking back, he saw no sign of a blue, shimmering curtain of light. There was only the rock wall of a nearly vertical bluff.

A rope ladder led down from the cliff into tree branches. He approached the edge cautiously, feeling weak and dizzy enough to pitch over. The very notion of how high he was made him almost lose his balance and fall.

Have to get hold of myself, he thought. *Have to be the hero.* He knew that he was trying to build his own confidence. Like most do-it-himself chores, it was an amateurish job. After all, there had to be a solid basis to build on.

He turned back to examine his place of emergence. It looked like blank rock, but when he put his hand out, it passed through. In a moment he was back in the station, by the glowing exit sign. From outside, the curtain was an illusion of rock, perfectly concealing its nature.

But what if some native climbed the rope to this spot and blundered into the station? Well, that curtain would probably seem just like real rock to any person or creature who was not a roundear. Certainly there had been no such intrusion in a long time, if ever; the dust proved that.

He stepped out again and went to the ladder. Now he saw that the rope was not hemp, but some metallic material that would surely last millennia longer. It was of a grayish color, of a very fine weave, if that was the appropriate term, and anchored fast to a metal ring set firmly into the rock. That gave him the confidence to use it. Maybe the metal was another form of what the transporter was made of. All this had been Mouvar's doing, of course, or one of Mouvar's race.

He grabbed the ladder, got his feet on the rungs, and did not look down. This descent probably had not bothered Kian, but the very notion of such height made Kelvin's palms sweat—the worst thing they could do at the moment! He rubbed each hand against his shirt between rungs, so that it would be fresh and dry for the next hold. He adjusted his sword belt—some hero, he thought sardonically, letting the scabbard get between his legs!—and trembling at what he was doing, started down.

He had never liked heights. Just climbing that beenut tree in Franklin had been a task. As for scaling and descending cliffs—that was not in this hero's line. Sister Jon might have relished this, but she had the nature to be a hero. He felt a little sick to his stomach, and tried to keep his mind off that as he slowly descended for fear he would become a *lot* sick. He pictured himself trying to explain to some anonymous bystander: "Why did I vomit on the ladder? Well—" That made him feel ashamed, but not better.

The branches reached up like hands, though it was just the breeze that made them seem to clutch. At least he was getting down to that level! His feet found the limb at the end of the final rung and then he held the ladder, trying to look down through branches to the still-distant ground. His head throbbed and the dizziness returned. *Why did I vomit on the tree branches? Well—*

He swayed, hung on, and then lowered himself from one branch to a lower one. After that it was almost like the ladder, except that he could not see as much. He had kept his eyes rigidly fixed on the cliff before his nose, so that hardly made a difference. All he could think of as he descended was how much more confident he would be if he were wearing the gauntlets. His palms never sweated in those! Finally he reached the ground, and stood for a moment, weak with relief.

But he still had no clear route to travel. The huge tree was rooted at the edge of a tangled forest that left no leeway for intruders. He had to scramble just to make progress.

The river purled along beside him as he stumbled along, looking for a path. Where had Kian gone? He saw one faint trail, perhaps made by meer or some other ruminants. He directed his steps that way, wanting to sit down, feeling he might fall, but willing himself to be brave and durable. Here he would be just another roundear, he thought—just another contemptible misfit who happened to have the wrong ears.

Midday and the sound of splashing. Fish jumping in the river. Jon would have been interested, and have wanted to fish. He wished she were here, with her optimism, her unfailing courage, and her sling. But she had pointed ears, so could not get through the transporter—and anyway, would he want her to suffer dangers that frightened him? Her bravery was the very thing that too often got her in trouble.

Bring! Brrring! Brrrringgg! A sweet metallic chiming from a big oaple. Those three silver spirals he had seen through Heln's eyes on their astral trip. The tree was close enough, and his time was not pressed; he could afford an inspection.

He walked over and found the chimes within reach. They did appear to be snakeskins with scale patterns, but the material was of a light metal. Silver in thin belts resembling the skins shed by snakes. Whatever the meaning of this, silver was precious where he came from. If this land was similar, as it should be, silver would buy things such as a horse, food, shelter, and a way to the dungeon, discreetly managed.

Yet the silver was not his, nor did he know its purpose. He pondered the matter until his stomach growled, reminding him it needed feeding. One chime might not be missed, and besides, he might be able to replace it on the way home. So he made up his mind: he would borrow one of these.

He drew his sword, cut through the leather thong holding a chime, and caught the silver trinket as it fell.

Bring! Brringg! BRRRINNGG!

It was as if the two remaining chimes were angry. Well, his need was great, so he would just have to endure their anger. He compressed the spiral flat and found it held its new shape. He slipped it into a back pocket of his pantaloons and walked on.

For a moment or two he felt great. Doing something on his own initiative always had that effect. For what it was worth.

A mountain path was ahead—a real one, not a mere animal trail. It seemed similar to a path he and Jon had once trod in dragon country. No dragons here, he hoped; if there were, it was going to take more than one silent silver chime to save his unheroic self. He noticed that he was growing weaker; he had been growing weaker since taking the chime. Could there be some magic connected with the things? This was a great time to think about it! But it hardly made any sense. Maybe he was having trouble adjusting to this new frame, since he hadn't traveled this way before.

He was only a little way up the path when dizziness and weakness overwhelmed him. At the same time he heard a drumming: horses.

His knees buckled as his legs turned limp and folded. His head buzzed like a nest of hornees.

The horses came around the bend and he got a look at a rough-looking, ill-clad man on a horse, followed by at least two others similarly clad. The horse was black, and the man had black hair; something about the combination bothered him.

Mists of memory rolled through his foggy head. Jon, screaming as she was carried away on horseback. Himself, staggering back from a blow delivered by the horseman. The horseman had been clad all in black, had black hair, and rode a coal-black horse. There had been a scar on that man's face that was probably an old sword wound.

The face looking down at him had a smooth cheek. Otherwise it was the same: exactly the same. Kelvin struggled to deny the thought that came immediately to mind, but could not.

Jack! Cheeky Jack! Outlaw villain of the Sadlands!

Kian felt the bump on his head with his fingers and winced as Gerta reached out a finger covered with ointment and motioned his hand away. Kindly people, these flopears, sometimes. He obeyed with mixed feelings as she touched the bump and made a circling motion. A coolness spread out from her fingertips and the pain and the headache vanished, as had the delicious smells of the bakery.

He sat up, realizing fully for the first time that he was in bed. It was, he guessed, the same bed his father had occupied, and his nurse was now Kian's. It was the room where he had come in astral form.

"Gerta!" he gasped, determined to use her name. "Gerta!"

"You know my name?" She did not sound as astonished as he had expected her to. "Explain."

"I was here before. I am Kian Knight. You put me in a—a serpent."

"That was my cousin Herzig who put you in a serpent ancestor. You may wish you had remained."

"I come from another world, Gerta, as does my father. That's why I'm here. I came to take him home."

"John Knight, your father?"

"Yes. You cared for him, maybe saved his life."

Gerta stared full in his face. He froze as though from the paralyzing stare of a serpent. Not for nothing were they called the serpent people, he remembered.

"Now, Kian Knight, we see if you lie to Gerta. Maybe you think Gerta dumb. Maybe you think all serpent people ignorant."

He wanted to respond, to give her some reassurance, but could not. He was unable to move.

Her hands cupped his face. Her pupilless eyes stared into his and melted into a blue sea. He felt her *coming in,* and knew that he was more truly naked than he had ever been before, even when merging with Lonny in astral form.

She pulled back, startling him. He felt a weakness that had spread all through him. Her gaze had done that, and still he was paralyzed.

Gerta went to the door of the cottage. She called outside, out of his sight. "Get Herzig! Hurry!"

She came back to him and looked again into his eyes, her eyes again melting. His eyes seemed to have become wide-open windows into his brain. "Herzig will have to see this. As leader of our people, he must decide what to do about it."

Do about what? he wanted to ask. But there was no moving his lips. Those deep, deep blue orbs—not like a serpent's, but somehow as powerful. It might be what his father had called hypnosis, and he had said that serpents did it to birds. Was he then just like a bird to Gerta's people? Were all of them mere birds, King Rowforth included?

Herzig came in and walked to the bed, his body rolling in the manner of a flopear. This had once seemed almost comical to Kian; it hardly seemed so now. Herzig stood on his short legs, staring at him. "You must see, Herzig," Gerta said.

The cousin leader held Kian's face. His eyes were black, and they seemed to sizzle as something happened in them. Kian was reminded of the void of The Flaw.

Then Herzig frowned, puzzled, turning to Gerta. "It is as he said. They are from the other place. They have no magic themselves but they use what magic comes: the dragonberries, the gauntlets, the Mouvar weapon that stopped but did no harm."

"The weapon lies in an ancestor tunnel, dropped there by the short-legged one."

"Yes. This one does not know which tunnel."

"You seem hesitant, Herzig."

"I am. I wonder what Rowforth will want to do when he learns of the place from this one's father. Will he want to go there as a conqueror?"

"You know Rowforth better than I."

Herzig looked back at Kian. "Can serpent people know mortals? Even such mortals as this? Perhaps with the gaze we can."

"You would gaze into Rowforth's murky mind?"

"I must. Only then can I learn what he truly intends. Only then can I know if we must break the alliance."

"If he wants to conquer this world and others—"

"Then we must withdraw ourselves. Serpent people cannot long leave these mountains, let alone this world."

"Will Mouvar interfere, Cousin?"

"He will if Rowforth conquers. We must not go against Mouvar. His race has magic even stronger than ours, and unlike ours, his is not bound to one world in one frame."

"Do you think Rowforth can be overthrown by his people? Replaced, as you replaced Dunzig as our leader?"

"Not if we give him all our help. But maybe we do not have to. You and I will take Rowforth a present."

"Kian?"

"Yes. He will have understood little, but it is best that he now forget. He will be our present to Rowforth, and he will remember nothing of what has been said."

Herzig snapped his fingers under Kian's nose. Kian realized on the instant that much had been said. But exactly what had been said he could not recover.

CHAPTER 19
Dead

"KIAN'S BROTHER," THE BANDIT face said. The words were directed to a large man whom Kelvin could not see clearly. It was alarming how suddenly weak he had become; before midday he had thought himself recovering from his father-in-law's blow. These bandits, if that was what they were, knew Kian by name. Not only did they know Kian, but they knew who Kelvin was as well.

"You ill?" the bandit asked him. "You appear unwell."

"Hit with fist," Kelvin gasped. "Walked far in sun. Dizzy."

"Hmm, yes. I know the feeling. They call me Smoothy Jac. Your brother told us about you. You don't look much like a hero."

"I'm not. Not here." *Not really anywhere. It was all luck. Luck and maybe a bit of magic, and a lot of belief by others.*

"In your own world you are."

"I had to be."

"Maybe here also." Jac moved his hand to his brow, pushing back a sweep of long hair. Naked ears were revealed as round as Kelvin's own.

"You—you're a—a roundear!"

"Most people are, in this world. Kian told us that in your world it's pointed ears that are the norm."

"Yes." He had known as much, or at least suspected it. His surprise had been a foolish reflex. That scene in the dungeon he had witnessed through Heln's astral eyes: the ruler who appeared to be Rufurt, their own beloved king. The prisoner. Not only faces that might be familiar, on totally different people, but also round ears.

Jac straightened up. "We'll take you to our camp in the Barrens, Kelvin. We have medicine there, and you can rest and recover. Can you ride?"

"I—I can try." He struggled to stand, felt dizzy, and gave up the effort.

"Biscuit," Jac said. "Get him on a horse. Tie him on."

"Ain't you had enough of foreigners?" Biscuit asked. "His brother got most of us killed. I say we leave him here."

What was this? The man addressed as Biscuit was the near image of Morton Crumb. Curse the dizziness, it was making things more and more unclear.

"Matt," Jac said, touching his sword hilt, "you and I have never fought each other. You have accepted me as leader and have done what I said."

"That's not changed," Matt said. "Just want you to know how I feel." He dismounted, picked Kelvin up, and slung him across the saddle. Kelvin felt himself being tied by his arms and legs. Then the big man mounted behind him, barely whispering, "Damned foreigners."

"Ready, Matt?"

"Ready, Chief."

"Friend. Companion. Jac."

"Yes, Chief." Not surly or disobediently, but not humorously. It was clear who was in charge.

"Let's ride." If there was tension, it did not sound in the voice. Jac spoke just as he had spoken at first.

After an infinite number of jolts, Kelvin realized that he was seeing sand passing beneath his eyes and that he had been regularly lapsing in and out of consciousness. Sometime after that he felt himself lifted from the horse. The big man's voice rumbled near his ear: "He does look pretty bad. I wonder why. That little bruise on his face can't account for it."

"Maybe poison."

"Maybe. Hey, fellow, you eat or drink anything since you arrived here?"

Kelvin struggled to think. "Nothing at all." He labored to deny the possibility that he was about to die. "Maybe that's why I'm so weak."

"You bitten or stung anywhere?"

"No. Nothing like that."

"We'll have Heeto check him," Jac said. "He knows more medicine than the rest of us."

"Hopeless," Biscuit said. "Some savior! Worse than the other!"

"Easy, Biscuit. It's not his fault."

Kelvin felt himself carried. Through blurring eyesight he caught the sight of faces: bandits, every one, judging from appearances.

A tent flap brushed his face, and then there was the rough texture of a bearver hide under him. He concentrated on seeing, and what he saw was a small man with a wide mouth. The face was familiar, hideously familiar. He screamed.

"Hey, hey, son!" Jac's tone was kind. "It's just Heeto! He's a dwarf, not a flopear."

Flopear? What was that? Not Queeto, but Heeto? Not the fiendish apprentice sorcerer? In his mind he saw again the crimson drops of Jon's blood falling slowly, drop by drop. He experienced again the tingle in his hands as the gauntlets he had worn then fastened like the jaws of a wild beast on the evil dwarf's neck and crushed it. He had killed the sorcerer's apprentice, or the gauntlets had. Later the body had burned, along with the body of the old sorcerer, and the terrible workplace in the wing of the old palace. It seemed to have happened in another life—actually in another world.

"Ahh, ahh, ahh," he said, his tongue swollen, his vocal cords strained so hard they were refusing to work. He needed to say something, but he didn't know what. The dwarf was staring in his face, making soothing motions.

"I'm Heeto," it piped. "You're Kelvin, Kian's brother."

"Y-yes," Kelvin managed.

"There's something the matter with you. Maybe I can help."

"No! No, no, nooo." He didn't want this creature touching him. Not after what he and Jon had endured by that parallel-dwarf's hands.

"He is hysterical and delirious," Jac said. "Dying, without a doubt."

"Yes," Heeto said. There was sadness in the voice, as though Kelvin's death meant something to him.

"Where's Kian?" Kelvin managed. It came out a croak. "Where's my brother?"

"He's dead," Biscuit said. "Swallowed by a serpent."

"We can't know that for certain," Jac said. "What do you think, Heeto? What's killing him?"

Kian, dead? Himself, dying? It couldn't be, it couldn't be!

"What hurts most, Kelvin? Tell us."

What hurt most? The something digging into his butt on the left side. The silver chime he had compressed into a spring, now trying to resume its former spiral.

"Ohh, ohh," he said, his voice loosened by the sudden pain. "Back pocket. Pantaloons."

"Let's see." Biscuit's big, rough hand lifted him and felt. "Something there, all right! I'll take it out and we'll have a look."

"Ohh," Kelvin groaned again. He felt as if the chime had grown a serpent mouth and sunk its fangs into him. Then he felt the fangs pulled away.

"Gods, look at this!" Biscuit exclaimed. He held the chime,

releasing it so that it made its sound, as if celebrating its release. "Talk about your lack of sense! Dumb foreigner!"

"He didn't know," Jac said.

"Poor man," Heeto soothed, stroking Kelvin's forehead. "Poor man, not to beware of magic."

"He'll die with the sun," Biscuit said. "Like a snake's tail at sundown. When the sun goes, so does he."

"Poor, poor man," Heeto mourned. The dwarf made a whispering sound that had the quality of whimpering.

"I've heard of something," Jac said. "I don't know if it's true, but I've heard that if the chime is taken back to its tree and properly hung there before nightfall, the victim lives."

"Old wives' tale," Biscuit offered.

"But maybe true. It does make sense, because the point of a curse is to prevent molestation of the thing it guards. That's no good if people steal chimes and then throw them away or sell them when they get sick. You've heard the legend, Heeto?"

"No, Master. I've never heard of a chime being taken."

"Nor I. But it could be. Since it's our only hope, we'd better try it. Kelvin, where did you get this?" He touched the chime, and it sent out peals that went round and round inside his head.

"I—I—" Kelvin struggled to recall. "I found it in a big oaple. Three together. I took only one. Near the river, before the mountain."

"Hmm, three chimes together. Big oaple. Mountain. I know that place. It's too far."

"Maybe not, Master. Maybe if I ride your horse—"

"You, Heeto? Alone?"

"I'm light, Master. Your horse can carry me faster than anybody."

"But, Heeto, to get there before night you'd have to start now and ride hard all the way."

"I will, Master. And I'll rest and feed the horse before starting back."

"I guess you have to try. I guess we all do. But it may not save him even if you get there in time."

"As you say, Master, we all have to try."

Biscuit snorted. "Huh! If the idea is to save him so he can save Hud from King Rowforth, I say don't ride. Save yourself, Heeto. For something important that can work out."

"You're a skeptic, Matt. But come along and help me get him started. That light saddle you had the other day . . ."

Rolling his eyes toward the tent flap, Kelvin saw that all three had exited. He closed his eyes, alone. It was hot in the tent; globules of sweat formed on his forehead. There was nobody to wipe it off for him, and he no longer had the strength to do it himself. A fly buzzed noisily and lit on his nose. *Heln, Heln!* he thought. *Oh, Heln!*

By and by he heard a horse's hooves pounding sand as it raced by the tent. Then silence as he fought with himself not to sleep—because he feared there would be no waking.

The sun was right at the top of the mountain as Heeto rode Betts down the ridge. He had spotted the two spirals in the big oaple from above, the sun glancing from the twin spirals in bright flashes.

"Please hold back, Sun. Please!" Heeto said. He spoke aloud, not bothered by the thought that it was insane. His thighs hurt from the saddle's chafe and he sympathized with Betts as she wheezed and blew back foam from her lathered mouth. Such a long ride, such a great effort for them both, and almost certainly for naught.

Bring, Brinnng, BRRRRRIIIIINNNNNGG! the chimes sang, urging him on with their companion. But the sun was already hiding, a dark shadow creeping relentlessly down the mountain at his back. "Please let me save him! Please let me save us all," Heeto prayed. He did not think of what he might be praying to, he only prayed.

The young man from another world was a hero. His brother had said that Kelvin had saved his own land, so similar to

Hud, and might save Hud as well. But the young man looked like a tall boy almost too slight to wield a sword. Yet he had come here just as his brother had, and if there was a way for him to live and to recover the Mouvar weapon—well, then all might not be in vain.

But first Kelvin had to be saved himself. He had to be saved by Heeto.

The sun was but a crescent at the top of the ridge, letting no more than a fingernail of light escape. The tree was almost shadowed, but stood where it caught the last of the rays. Urging Betts nearer with sharp jabs of his heels, Heeto continued to pray: "Sunlight stay! Sunlight stay!"

He stood up on the saddle, swaying, almost overbalancing, and grabbed the limb. Quickly with his free hand he wrapped the leather thong, tied it, and fell free of the limb and the horse.

Bring, Brinng, BRRRRIIIINNNG!

Had he succeeded? Had he done right? Had he done anything?

Bring, Brinng, BRRRRIIIINNNG!

The last glint of sunlight was gone.

CHAPTER 20

Pact

KIAN WAS SURPRISED WHEN Gerta and Herzig returned to him as soon as he had eaten. Somehow he had thought they intended to keep him in this small room indefinitely. Possibly (and the thought squeezed his guts) they had a hungry serpent.

"Kian, do you wish to be with your father?" Herzig asked.

He nodded. Silly question.

"Then the three of us will leave immediately for Hud's capital. Do you feel you can walk?"

He did. Their food and medicine were wonderfully restorative. The days (this was a sheer guess, falling between hours and months) he had spent in the serpent tunnels were as if they had never been. But what of Lonny? Was she still wandering around with the glowrooms, or, worse still, in the dark?

"You look troubled, Kian," Gerta said.

"There's someone else," he confessed. "Someone who was with me underground."

Gerta and Herzig looked at each other. He wished he could read the significance in that exchange!

"I wouldn't fear for her," Herzig said. "She will survive."

"But—"

"A little magic, Mortal. Magic spells can protect anyone we choose from the ancestors."

"The ancestors. You mean the serpents?"

"That is what we call them among ourselves. We believe that our people descended from serpents, while yours descended from apes."

Kian was startled. It was almost like his father talking! He had conjectured on the different lines of descent for roundears and pointears. But he had also said that the two were closely linked because they could interbreed. When Kian, then very young, had asked what that meant, John Knight had laughed and said, "You're the proof of it, son!"

Kian doubted that there could have been any physical descent from serpent to manlike creature. But his experience as an astral presence in the serpent suggested that there was indeed some kind of compatibility between them. Could the early flopears have taken astral residence in the early serpents, and could the minds of the serpents have come to the bodies of the flopears? Then the present flopears would indeed have serpent ancestry on the astral level, and the serpents would have flopear ancestry. It made a certain sense, especially considering the serpentlike power of the flopears' gaze, and the way the serpents cooperated with the flopears.

"We will go, then," Gerta said. "Walking, as is our way."

Walking to the capital? That, Kian thought, was going to take days! But once there he would be reunited with his father. Then perhaps he could find out about his mother and what kind of alliance the king had with the flopears. He was ready, and he felt quite excited about the prospects.

* * *

At the end of the second day they had left the mountains and were paralleling the river. The big oaple with the three silver chimes Kian remembered was somehow a welcome sight. He listened to their music for as long as he could. It was as though the chimes welcomed their approach and then bade them an affectionate farewell.

"You remember being in a chime?" Gerta asked him, seeing his attention.

"Well," he said, "I remember everything until after I was part of a serpent, and then my memories are blurred."

"That is because serpents have simple minds. You were becoming part of the mind you were in."

"But that serpent was dead—or had been! We killed it with the spear! How could it have a mind?"

"It was not dead, only badly hurt. We tended to its body, and healed it to the extent we were able. Then we put your mind in it, and the other, and you revived its mind as a new spark revives an old fire."

"What would have happened to me and—and Lonny?"

"You would have been absorbed. Generations from now you might have been part of a new intelligent serpent, or you might not. We serpent people have much magic, but we do not know all there is to know about the life force. There are mysteries even our wisest members have not penetrated."

"When I was in astral form I was me," Kian mused. "As alive and conscious of being alive as I had ever been. Yet in the serpent—"

"In the serpent you were changing, becoming more like the body you inhabited—but not entirely. This is why we put you there: we knew you would enhance the serpent after it had lost so much of its own mind. Whether you would pull it up beyond its natural level we could not judge, but certainly you would help it."

"Yet I felt as if I had a body when I was astral, and in the serpent, too, in different form. Nothing that hurt or could move objects, but a body. When Lonny and I—" But he did not care to discuss that merging, though probably the flopears already knew.

"That we think is mainly illusion. You are accustomed to a body, so you think of yourself as having a body. But then our spirits simply return to the serpent ancestors voluntarily and are absorbed into them. Your spirits—who can say?"

"Not I," Kian confessed. He plodded on, conscious that his feet hurt, and musing on the nature of things.

The capital, when they arrived, was just as he remembered. So was the palace. He would feel right at home here. But Herzig was speaking to a servitor, and then two palace guards were escorting him away from the flopears and toward—he recognized this route!—toward the dungeon.

For a moment he fought hard not to panic. Then he forced himself to relax, thinking: *Wily serpents! They do after all have a pact with Rowforth. They didn't bring me here just for my own good. Rowforth is a bad man here; I was told as much.*

Their footsteps rang hollowly down the long, twisting stair. Dank, dusty dungeon smells assailed his nostrils. Oh, this was going to be fun! Just as it had been back home, only here it was he and his father, rather than his father and brother imprisoned.

Light coming down from a high barred window revealed the ugly cells. In the first cell, a battered and obviously injured Smith, one of Jac's crossbowmen he recognized but did not know very well. In the second cell was a tall, haggard man who looked at him with wide-eyed recognition.

"Father!"

"Kian!"

The guard unlocked the door and pushed him inside the cell and into his father's arms.

Herzig watched with Gerta, his misgivings rampant, as the soldiers took a dazed Kian to join his father. They stood on the palace grounds, their firm legs supporting them with customary indifference. Soon they'd be ushered into the palace itself and have their audience with King Rowforth. For his part, Herzig was not looking forward to it.

"Cousin Herzig, will they put them together?"

"Almost certainly, Gerta. So they can talk and a guard can spy on them and listen. So that father can be tortured before son or son before father."

"Are they really that cruel, Cousin?"

"Rowforth has been in the past. Dunzig should have known, but Dunzig was cruel himself. If the king knew all our mind abilities, he'd want us to get the information. Only Rowforth is so cruel that he would probably torture them anyway."

"I am glad we are not mortals," Gerta said.

The servitor from the palace was approaching, his manner solemn and purposeful, as befitted his position. He stopped, inclined his head in a short half bow, and said, "You may come. His Majesty will see you now."

They followed the man as he strode off. A couple of guards joined them, one on either side, and a couple more marched in back. Rowforth took no chances with guests. Getting him alone and probing into his murky mind was going to take planning and luck. True, guards could be treated with the serpent-gaze at any time, but it was necessary that Rowforth not suspect.

Herzig stole a look at his cousin. She was looking askance at the inferior sculptures, tapestries, and paintings the palace held. The lowest of the serpent people artisans could greatly improve on the best of mortal work, Herzig thought, eyeing a broken-armed statue as they passed.

The great audience room was empty except for Rowforth on his throne. They approached him slowly, inclined their heads as was the custom, and waited.

"Welcome, friend serpent people," Rowforth said. It was about as sincere a welcome as anyone ever got from his mouth. "I am pleased at your gift of the stranger mortal, and now bid you welcome to Hud's royal palace."

"Thank you, Your Highness," Herzig said. "We are honored to be here in your presence."

The king nodded to Gerta. "And this is your wife?"

"Cousin. She nursed both the stranger mortals and restored them to health." *So that they may be tortured by you,* Herzig thought, thoroughly disgusted by the fact.

"Ah." His Majesty seemed interested. "And can she perhaps reveal things that they have said?"

"Your Majesty," Gerta said, "I spoke to them only as needed. What you would be interested in—military secrets and affairs of state—was not discussed."

"Pity," Rowforth said. His eyes moved back to the leader, seemingly evaluating him as he once must have evaluated his predecessor, Dunzig. "I suspect we shall need to make plans. Errotax, our neighboring kingdom, is becoming quite vexing to me. I plan on taking over that throne, and I believe you might occupy it for me."

"I'm afraid, Your Majesty, that serpent people have no wish to govern mortals. That, Your Majesty, is your responsibility."

"Hmm, yes. But surely you will want something. Dunzig did."

"Dunzig and I were not directly related," Herzig replied. "Nor did we always bask in the same light. He wished power over mortals for himself and for the serpent people. His wish for power drove him to make the alliance. One mortal sacrifice a year, he decreed, given freely by Your Majesty. In return we would freeze with the serpent-stare any enemy who opposed you."

"You are bound by Dunzig's word?"

"I am bound," Herzig agreed.

"But now you do not wish to rule mortals?"

"I never have wished that, nor have most of the serpent people."

"You would have wealth?"

"We have wealth already." *More than you dream of, Mortal!*

"Then, aside from the sacrifice and the goods delivered to your valley, only friendship?"

"That is sufficient," Herzig said. Rowforth hardly looked pleased; he did not trust those who weren't greedy.

"I, ah, see. But perhaps in the future?"

"Possibly. But for now, only friendship."

"Good." Rowforth seemed appeased. "When you want something, you will ask?"

"Yes."

Rowforth nodded sagely, as only a monarch can. "Tomorrow we will talk further of my plans. For now, you and your lovely cousin enjoy the palace grounds, the fruits of its orchards, the shade of its trees. When you get ready to leave, I will bestow on you a scrumptiously outfitted carriage, horse, and driver."

"Thank you, Your Majesty, but my people prefer to use only their own legs. We allow ourselves to be carried but seldom, and then only for pressing reason."

"I, ah, see." The distrust had returned. "Whatever you wish during your stay, simply ask it of a servant. Any special foods, drinks, entertainments, anything at all that you desire. The dungeon where the stranger mortals are now will be locked and guarded, but if you wish you may tour."

"No need, Your Majesty. One dungeon is like another, and the fate of the mortals does not concern the serpent people." He felt unclean, speaking like this!

"Enjoy your stay, then." The monarch made a gesture, and the servant and soldiers escorted them from his presence.

That night Herzig slipped from his bed, dressed, and rapped lightly on the adjoining door. Gerta joined him in a moment, looking to his eyes as though she had never slept.

"Be ready with the serpent-stare," he whispered. Outsiders thought that the stare was merely a function of looking, but this was hardly the case; it required a singular effort of will, and was best if prepared for. "Even this late at night there may be servitors, even guards."

She nodded, and together they left their room and climbed the stairs. They were almost to the king's chambers when, by a shaft of moonlight coming through a window, they saw a tall woman approaching in a filmy white gown. The woman had red hair and green eyes, and neither of them had encountered her before. Yet there could be no doubt who she was: the queen.

Herzig debated the matter only briefly. Then he used his stare to intercept the queen. They could not afford to have her spying on them! It would be a simple matter to cause her to forget that she had seen them.

She froze. Then it occurred to him that the queen could be a source of useful information. Should he take the time and energy to read her? He hesitated but a moment; then, standing on tiptoe, he cupped her chin in his hands, tipped her head forward, and probed deep, deep into her glassy eyes.

It was a shock. He had gotten much more information than expected! He withdrew, shaken. He turned to his cousin, controlling himself as well as he could.

"We will not need to go on to the king's chambers," he said. "He is asleep there with another woman. He taunts his virtuous queen constantly with his infidelities and the evil he does. He is the most evil of all evil mortals. There is no need to awaken him, for I have found what he intends."

"He intends to conquer?"

"Everything. Even our valley. Every land that he and his armies can reach. The stars themselves he would conquer. Only death or displacement will cause him to stop conquering. And the queen has a father—a father we must now go to see."

"The queen—?"

"As good a mortal as the king is bad. She will remember nothing of our meeting. Nightly she prowls these hallways clutching her agony inside. Come." He motioned Gerta back into a doorway and shadow, then snapped his fingers. Immediately the queen stirred, walking on; her mind, he knew, was in a quandary as she contemplated again the evil of her husband.

They walked down the stairs, and then, via another passage, to another set of stairs. They climbed the stairs in the dark, opened a door, and were in the tower chamber of Zotanas, aged sorcerer. A high window let in only a little moonlight and starlight, but a serpent person's eyesight was such that it required little in the way of luminescence.

Herzig walked to the big bed where the old magician lay sleeping. Gently, very gently, he awakened the man.

Zotanas' eyes opened. He saw Herzig bending over him, or at least his form. Not floundering in his thoughts as a normal aged person would be expected to do, he simply said: "Flopear?"

"Correct, Zotanas."

"Why?" Reedy voice, questioning everything with a single word.

"Because you may be able to help. You want to free your daughter of her marriage and your land of its tyrant. I know, I have looked into your daughter's mind, though she and the king must never know of this. There are mortals in the kingdom of Hud who would battle the soldiery and free the land, but they will need help. We serpent people, wily as serpents all, would break our alliance with your king."

"Why?" Zotanas repeated.

"I am the ruler of our people. I know that following your king would mean disaster for us. In other worlds nearly identical with ours, our people did not long coexist with mortals. Only separately can our people survive and prosper."

"What would you have me do?" Zotanas asked. Evidently this news came as no special surprise to him.

"Be ready to help the strangers to this world who will try to help other mortals overthrow your king. We serpent people are bound by an unwise covenant to aid your king, but it is a covenant I wish to have broken."

"But if you give aid, the king wins. Mortals can't fight your kind."

"No, they cannot. But neither must serpent people fight mortals."

"I'm not certain I understand."

"Nor is that necessary. You have been dreaming, but you will think on what you dreamed. When the time comes, you will use your strength and your magic. For now, sleep."

Obediently Zotanas closed his eyes. His shallow chest heaved and he began snoring.

Silently Herzig and Gerta stole down the stairs and tiptoed softly to their own rooms and beds.

For three days Herzig and Gerta remained at the palace, nominally enjoying the hospitality of the king, but actually studying every aspect of his government. They were aware when the king and his trusted brutish guard went to the dungeon to threaten the prisoners John Knight and Kian Knight by torturing their wounded companion, but did not interfere, because that would have revealed both their knowledge and their sentiments. But Gerta was shocked and furious.

"They have a baby ancestor!" she exclaimed. "How did that happen?"

Herzig was similarly angry. "One of the king's men must have found it strayed from its nest, and trapped it in the bottle. To force it to feed on mortal brains—this is shameful abuse of an ancestor! But we must not interfere. The serpent will have to fend for itself. Perhaps when it escapes, we can intercept it and try to ameliorate the bad food before it becomes too negative."

"We must keep alert," she agreed. "What an outrage!"

But the little serpent was slow to emerge, and two days later it was time for them to depart, without having had the chance to help it. Depressed, they departed the grim palace.

On the walk back they were to pass a big oaple with three chimes. But as they approached it Herzig saw that there were but two. *Brung, Brung, Brung!* they sounded angrily, out of tune.

"A mortal has been here and taken a sacred skin," Herzig said to Gerta. "It is another outrage! Whoever that mortal is, he will surely die."

"Yes, Cousin. But if that mortal is one who should live? Perhaps a stranger from another world who would not know of the curse?" For her experiences with the two prior strangers remained fresh in her mind. She knew she was too much influenced by the mortal part of her heritage, but she could not help it. This missing chime—she knew it was no routine matter.

He saw that she had a premonition, so he followed it up. Each member of their species had slightly different abilities, and she was excellent at perceiving and controlling astral spirits, whether within their hosts or separated from them. The magic of the chimes related to this, for it was to the astral portion of a mortal that they fastened, when disturbed. "Uncaution brings death. It has always been so. It would be an insane universe were it otherwise. But perhaps it needn't be."

"How?" By which she meant that this particular case was different, and deserved his attention.

"I will think, project my thought as well as I can. The talisman must be returned by the thief before night."

"But if the thief is already too weak, too far away?" She definitely knew something!

"I will project as well as I can. With the ancestors' help it may be possible. We must conceal ourselves and wait."

"That is good."

He began thinking, projecting outward the tale that no mortal had heard from another mortal for longer than any had lived, with the single exception of Zotanas. The way to avoid dying at sundown was to replace the talisman. He sent the thought out, following the faint astral spoor left by the thief. Out across the rough country and into the Barrens, where only the bandits and the true patriots went. Out too far for a dying man to return to. But a thought could be directed at more than one fading life; it could be directed to anyone near. Herzig projected at the main silver thief who had come time after time to their valley, the leader of the mortals who had attacked Rowforth's men. For a long, long time he projected, but though he knew the thought was received, the bandit leader did not come. The minds of mortals were so frustratingly limited! Still he waited, knowing that leaders sometimes sent others to do their bidding.

As the sun was creeping down below the ridge and out of sight below the far horizon of the Barrens, a rider appeared on horseback. It was the small mortal who in stature resembled the serpent people.

They waited until the talisman had been returned and the small mortal was rubbing down the sweaty horse. Then, and only then, did Herzig stretch out his hand. From his fingers an energy bolt of astral matter traveled as swiftly as only such energy could.

BRING! BRING! BRING! sang the talismans. They were back in tune. The small mortal turned to look, his face surprised by the sound coming without being evoked by a breeze. His broad features broke into a smile, for this was a song sweeter than any heard before.

"Thank you," the mortal mouthed, his eyes on the talismans. "Thank you for helping us. For helping all of us."

Concealed by the shadow on the mountain, Herzig had to wonder what if anything the small mortal had sensed. But more important, why had Gerta attuned to this particular mortal, the absent one who had thieved the chime? She might not be sure herself, but surely it was important.

CHAPTER 21
Stranger Coming

HELN RODE CORRY'S HORSE out of the brush and waved at the Crumbs and Jon on the opposite side of the river. They were probably thinking of going for help, she thought, as her hands inside the magic gauntlets urged the horse down the bank and into the stream. But this was the fording place where Corry and Bemode had crossed the stream with her. They had trailed her this far, and her father must have gone on alone. Even Kelvin's sister wasn't in Aratex, a fact that rather surprised her.

Jon was, as Heln had known she would be, the first to greet her on the proper side of the border. "You all right, Heln?"

"Couldn't be better!" That was a considerable overstatement, but it would do in this circumstance. Certainly she could have been worse! Had Jon really thought to use that sling against soldiers? Would Lester and Mor have let her?

"I didn't know you could ride like that!" Jon exclaimed. "And those gauntlets, and that dress!"

"I'll tell you about it on the way to the capital."

"The capital? Why? What for? And where's your old man? Where's St. Helens?"

"That's why we're going to the capital. I'll tell you while we ride." And she did, as they rode back the way they had all come and then on the main road for the capital and Rud's new palace.

"You're certain he's a prisoner?" Lester asked when she had finished her narrative.

"He has to be. I'm worried about him. He was still unconscious. And that Melbah is such a terrible person!"

"Terrible, all right," Mor agreed. "Best thing to do with a witch is to burn her. Once they're burned up they don't come back."

"Yet these gauntlets made me leave him there—and his sword," Heln said, bemused. "They almost seemed to put words in my mouth, making me sound like a warrior-woman!"

Everyone laughed, thinking she was joking. Who could imagine her as a warrior! She had to admit it was ludicrous, especially garbed as she was. She had not told them about the way the men had watched her climb down the tree, but probably they had guessed. Yet as it had turned out, that ugly business had helped her gain the upper hand. The gauntlets really did seem to know what they were doing, and could be quite devious on occasion.

"Why didn't we just ride on in and get him?" Jon demanded. "We're Rud citizens! We might even have gotten there before they got him down from the tree."

"No," Heln said. "Not a chance. We weren't that far from the Aratex palace. I don't think our being Rud citizens would bother Melbah, though Phillip might be a different matter." And there was another detail she had avoided mentioning: exactly how the boy king had considered using her, aside from as a hostage.

"King Rufurt may not want to send soldiers!" Mor protested. "He's cautious about starting a war, and not just because of Melbah."

"Have we any choice?" Heln asked heatedly. "They kidnapped me and now they hold my father! Rud can't allow its citizens to be kidnapped and taken to Aratex and imprisoned! They made the mistake, not we!"

"But could we win against them?" Lester asked. "From what you said about Melbah—"

"Yes, Melbah is powerful!" Heln agreed. "But we've got something Aratex doesn't have: we've got Kelvin!" As soon as she said it, Heln had to wonder. "Where is he, anyway?"

"He's not back."

"But Father's back! And he had that flying belt and the gauntlets and Kelvin's laser!"

"WHOA!" Mor cried, pulling his horse to a halt and signaling the others to do the same. Rud's shining new palace was in sight, complete with observation tower and newly planted orchards, but this was not why he stopped. "Excuse me, lasses and son, but old Mor smells a rodent on the dinner table and he think's it's St. Helens!"

"What? What do you mean?" Heln demanded. She was really angry with herself, because as soon as Mor spoke she had thought the same thing.

"He came back, your husband didn't. He had the weapons Kelvin was going to use to rescue his father and his brother and possibly another person I'm not about to mention. That sound right to you?"

"No," Heln admitted. "But—but he must have had a reason." She hoped! What could it be?

"Who had a reason—St. Helens or your husband?"

Immediately Heln was reminded of how badly her father had wanted a war between Rud and Aratex. Could he—would he have harmed Kelvin? Just how much did she know about him, anyway? He was brave and he could be charming and fascinating in a way that only a talkative adventurer could be, but he had been such a pain when visiting them. It was as though St. Helens had been struggling to make up for a first unfavorable impression. *Should they have trusted him?*

"Heln, you're losing your color!" Jon cried.

She did feel weak and dizzy. *I am not going to faint! I am not going to faint!* she thought.

"Grab her quick! She's going to fall!" That was Mor's voice.

Things were going gray. She felt herself sliding, and then, with no transition at all that she could detect, she was lying down and looking up into the face of a man she hadn't seen before. He was bearded, and it seemed to her that he was something in a thinking profession. Over his slight shoulder she saw Jon gazing anxiously at her, holding her gauntlets.

"Who—who are you?" Heln asked the beard.

"I'm Dr. Lunox Sterk, personal physician to His Royal Majesty King Rufurt of Rud. You shouldn't have ridden so far so hard, young lady. Not in your condition."

"What do you mean in my condition?" The way he spoke made her feel more than a little trace of alarm. She had not been wounded!

"You are with child."

She absorbed that, stifling a mixed cry of delight and protest. She had thought there might be a child, had hoped there would be, but now—now was hardly the time.

"I'll—I'll be all right. The baby, it wasn't hurt?"

"No, your baby should be fine. But that foolish dress and that collection of bruises on you indicate that you haven't been careful. You'll have to start eating right, and resting."

Resting? At this time? Incredible! "What I need," she said evenly, "is to swallow a couple of dragonberries."

The doctor looked horrified. Hastily she explained about the dragonberries' effect on her. "So you see," she concluded breathlessly, "I have to check on Kelvin! I have to know that he's all right!"

Dr. Sterk pulled at a pointed ear and cocked his head sideways; that made him look almost like a bearded bird. "I'm afraid, young lady, I can't allow that."

"You can't, but I can!" *Thank the Gods and my father I've learned of Female Liberation in time!*

"Heln," Jon said unexpectedly, "you'd better think about this. You know what a hero Kelvin is. Only roundears can follow him to where he is now, and that means either you or your father."

"Yes! Yes!" Heln agreed, suddenly reassured. "You're right, Jon, I *can* go *as I am,* without going astral. That's what I need to do! Oh, Jon, thank you! Thank you for telling me the way!"

"That's not what I mean at all!" Jon said. "Tell her, Doctor. Tell her she can't go into another world frame in either form!"

"Well said," the doctor agreed. "Young lady, if you'd keep your baby and want it born strong, you'll do what I say."

"But—but Kelvin—"

"Will have to take care of himself," Jon said. "He has before."

"But Father *left* him! He came back with the gauntlets only roundears can use, and the laser Kelvin had from his father and the war, and—and that belt!"

"We'll have to ask your father," Jon said, looking uncomfortable.

"Father! But he's in Aratex! Maybe in a dungeon!"

"Yes. Lester and Mor are taking steps. They're in audience with King Rufurt."

Heln sat up. On the instant she discovered she was lying in a big four-poster bed in a large bedroom with ornate statuary all around. They had brought her inside the palace!

"Jon, how long was I unconscious?"

"Hardly any time," Jon assured her. "Lester carried you right in the main entrance. I think the gauntlets kept up your strength until you got here, and then they did something to your nerves that made you faint. Heln, you *need* rest!"

"Piffle," Heln said.

"For the baby's sake." Jon looked over at the doctor, who nodded as though it was certainly true and obvious. Pregnant women should not gallop horses and run around interfering with affairs of state.

"Damn!" Heln said. It was an unladylike expression she felt justified in using as she had never felt justified before. Female Liberation at least permitted her that.

Someone knocked on the bedroom door. "Jon," Lester called.

"It's all right. Come in," Jon said.

Lester entered, looked at Heln in the bed, looked at the doctor, and looked at his wife. Evidently he had not received the news.

"With child," the doctor said, taking pity on him.

Lester's face cleared of momentary doubt and he clapped his hands and said, "Congratulations! Kelvin is going to be so happy!"

Heln permitted herself a frown. "Well, I'm not happy about it. Not now. I want to know about Kelvin and Kian and his father and my father in Aratex."

"Well, you certainly can't take any dragonberries now," Lester said. "They bring you too close to death—and what would they do to your child? Especially if your child happens to be a pointear, as it could be."

Heln hadn't thought of that. One of her parents and one of Kelvin's were pointears; it was certainly possible!

"So you can't go near those berries," he repeated. "Can she, Doctor?"

"No." Stern and positive.

"I'd take them for you if I could," Jon said. "But you roundears are the only ones who can take them. If I tried I'd get sick."

"You'd die," Dr. Sterk said. "Any normal point-eared person would. Apologies, Mrs. Hackleberry; it may be otherwise in other universes. All it means in ours is that here you roundears are in this way blessed."

"Blessed by Mouvar, I suspect," Lester said. "But even Heln gets weak after astro-trips. It takes a lot of energy from her."

"Then you won't do it, will you, Heln?"

Heln found herself glaring. But these were her friends, and

they wanted to help her, not keep her from Kelvin. She knew that they were right.

"What was King Rufurt's answer?" Jon asked, turning to Les.

"He's sending a delegation to Aratex. My father and I are going along."

"I suppose that means I have to stay?"

"Right. You and Heln. You two hold the palace until we return with St. Helens."

"*If*, you mean," Jon said, and Heln saw her bite her tongue.

"Right again, Wifey Dear," Lester replied with gentle irony. "There may not be a fight, you know. We just may get to King Phillip without difficulty."

CHAPTER 22
Border Crossing

MOR AND LESTER RODE at the head of the column of hand-picked troops with General Broughtner. It had been determined that a show of force would be best. They were to cross the border, ride on to the capital, and demand St. Helens' return. Since all were properly outfitted in Rud uniforms and the armor and weaponry polished until it shone, they did indeed make a magnificent spectacle to impress the imagination of the boyish king.

"What do you think, Dad?" Lester asked into his father's war-shortened ear. He had pulled his horse up close so that they were almost touching as they rode. The lusty lyrics of "Horsemanure! Horsemanure!" the obscene cavalry song (whose title was actually a bit more direct and less polite than the official representation), were just fading.

"Gods, son," Mor said, sounding almost angered. "How do I know? If that Phillip has the brains of a crawling loustick, he'll keep Melbah on leash. He can't really want war with us. Besides, he can't know that Kelvin isn't along."

Yes, Kelvin, Lester thought. Everyone believed he could do anything now, and the farther one went from Rud, the more exaggerated the stories. Mythic heroes were neither ignored nor challenged with impunity! Phillip might be a boy, but he was a boy king. Melbah might run things, but Phillip had the official final word and had to be aware that his commands were those of a king.

"You think we'll just ride in with no fighting and then out again with St. Helens?"

"Out again, anyway, I'd think. But I don't think it's fighting we need worry about."

"You mean Melbah and magic," Les said.

"Of course."

"What are you two talking about?" General Broughtner inquired, jockeying his horse near. It always made Lester smile to think of him as a general, though indeed he was the best; before Rud's War of Liberation he had been Franklin's ne'er-do-well, drinking himself into a ruddy complexion and a daily stupor.

"Just speculating on Melbah," Lester said. There, he had said it, and now must follow his unsoldierly doubts.

"It's wise to plan," Broughtner said. "If Phillip lets her at us, we'll demand her head."

"That'll stop her?" Lester wasn't quite certain he was joking.

"Gods, yes. She's not that powerful. If she turns on her big blow, we'll just squat down and wait it out. None of us will be flying like St. Helens. I could have advised him against that! Magic is bad enough, but when you pretend to understand it and call it science, it's worse."

"It is untrustworthy?"

"Right! Look at all the trouble it caused at the Rud palace."

"We don't know it was John Knight's laser that caused that destruction. But it probably helped."

"I just hope he burned up Rud's former queen with it. Personally, I doubt that she or the consort she was using survived."

"Kelvin thinks she fled," Lester said, not telling all that he knew: if Broughtner hadn't heard of Kian's trip and Kelvin's following after, he needn't enlighten him.

"Kelvin could be wrong. Remember, I rode with him, and you and I were there when you were downed and he got himself captured. That almost cost us the war."

"Only because no one but his little sister thought we could win against magic! We did win, eventually, though it took John's lasers and Kelvin's gauntlets. It was both magic and science that won."

"And the prophecy. Don't forget the prophecy!"

"Yes, maybe that helped most of all." They were approaching the side road that led to the river and Aratex. The general held up his hand, and the column that had been formed of four riders abreast now formed itself into a column of twos. They rode on, the general ahead on his big white horse, Mor on his black horse behind him, and Lester on his roan at the side of his father. They approached the stream and started to ford it. Lester raised his eyes and looked at the sky; clear, with only a few soft clouds. There was no wind, no breeze rippling the low waters.

The war-horses' hooves made a monotonous splashing. Now and then a few drops of muddy water lit on Lester's face. A glob of mud hit him in the eye: he knuckled it out, and again looked at the sky. The sky appeared darker now. Clouds were scudding overhead, possibly propelled by magic. A ray of sunlight fell full on the flat top of Conjurer's Rock, looming like a dark sentinel beyond Deadman's Pass. Was old Melbah up there? Or had she turned herself into a eagawk or more likely a buzvul? He could imagine that one of the dark birds circling was her. With such power as she was reputed to command, could the boy king possibly control her? Would Phillip the Weak even have the will to try? One did not start anywhere on just a whim. A delegation from one kingdom to the next, even if it was composed of armed cavalry in full armor, would hardly justify their attack.

Wind howled suddenly. Whitecapped waves formed on the water ahead of them and beneath their horses' bellies. Huge drops of rain began spattering them. Lightning cracked ominously in the sky.

General Broughtner raised high the standard of Rud: a flag displaying a large appear fruit crossed with a corbean stalk on a field of alternating brown and green stripes. Such a symbol raised in such a way at the head of a column meant peace, or at least nonhostile intent. It was the plan that they be accepted as a diplomatic mission from one sovereign to another, from one kingdom to another. Later, if this mission failed, as well it might, they could decide just what the show had accomplished. Back in Rud, King Rufurt had already cautiously dispatched a mission to Throod to arrange for mercenaries in case of war.

The wind blew stronger, stronger, much stronger. Head lowered against the blast, half suffocating in the water splashing from above and below, Lester wondered why General Broughtner did not order them back. Was it because it would not look right? Was it because if they succumbed to a bluff, he and his troops and all of Rud would be disgraced? But supposing it wasn't a bluff? Suppose old Melbah meant to attack and finish them?

The wind calmed, though the water continued to rise. Overhead flew a large dark bird. Was it the witch? Melbah?

"Ack! Ack! Go back! Go back!" the bird screamed.

So much for any doubt! Lester looked at Broughtner, then urged his horse up by the general's. "We'd better——"

"NO!" Broughtner said. He had made up his mind. He was not to be bluffed and turned away.

Mor rode closer. "I wish your Jon were here to clunk the witch with a rock, Les."

"Don't say that, Father! Jon would be sure to try!"

The general turned his face. "Archers, shoot down that detestable bird!"

Instantly a dozen arrows snickered from a dozen quivers, bows were lifted, strings drawn, and the arrows loosed. In the meantime the bird was climbing, seeing their intent. "You'll be sorry," it squawked.

Then the arrows caught up with it: four above, three below, two to each side, and one into its dark body. Blood and black feathers flew as an arrowhead lanced through the creature's heart. The bird plummeted, falling farther downstream. The current took it for a way and then bobbed it under. Blood stained the water where it had been.

The men gave a cheer. Lester found he was cheering as well. Good old Broughtner, he'd done exactly right! Thus would end the witch and her hold on the boy king of Aratex: end it forever and restore the kingdom to what it should be, a near duplicate of Rud.

As abruptly as a thunderclap, the sky was dark. The rain renewed itself, and the river seemed to rise all by itself to above its banks and above normal flood level. A hideous cackling laughter filled the air.

Their horses were now swimming, battling for their lives against a torrential current that had abruptly grown deadly. Large tree branches were swirling in it, and lesser debris.

"Don't leave your horse!" Mor advised. "Don't try, or your armor will sink you like a stone!"

Lester tried to answer, but a huge wave of muddy water splashed in his face, nearly drowning him upright. He was all but torn from the saddle, but hung on. Other horses, other men, were washing downstream, some free of their mounts. The river was bigger and uglier than any Lester had ever seen in what he thought fleetingly might be his short life. Banks went by and leaves and now the debris of whole trees. His roan swam for her life, as other horses were doing. There was no thought of reaching the other shore now, only of escaping.

If there were time. If only there were still time. They had really fallen into the witch's trap!

St. Helens opened his eyes and found himself looking down from a height. His face was pressed up against a tree trunk, his belt holding him there. His gauntlets were not on his hands and his sword was missing. Down below, two men were chained to trees—soldiers of Aratex, one of whom he was certain he recognized. Where was Heln? If they had her—but maybe she had fallen.

"Hey, up there!" the man called Bemode cried. "You, St. Helens, you awake?"

"What's it to you, child abuser?" This man St. Helens did not like. He had made up his mind definitely about Aratex and its need for Kelvin-style revolution after seeing what this man considered fun and within the rights of soldiery. St. Helens had ridden up on him one day when he was entertaining himself and a couple of friends with the small, sloe-eyed daughter of a peasant. The father had been begging him to desist, but the man had only laughed. Until St. Helens and the sword gifted to him by the boy king had put a stop to it. Had St. Helens had his way that day, Phillip would have hanged Bemode or at least demoted him and thrown him in the dungeon after a whipping.

"What's it to me? I'll tell you what. When our friends get here, we're going to chop you down. Then, after we break your arms and legs so you can't fly, and kick in your teeth so you can't sass us back, we'll turn you over to old Melbah for some real fun. Meanwhile, my friend Corry and I will ride after that girl of yours. We'll let her ride all the way to the border and then we'll grab her and use her in a way she's never been used before, and if she still lives we'll bring her on back so you can watch us do it some more."

"So that smart girl went to the border, did she?" St. Helens remarked. "Thanks. That's all I wanted from you; now you can shut up before all that dirt in your mouth poisons you."

"Big mouth!" Corry said to Bemode.

St. Helens pushed the lever on the belt, pushed himself back from the trunk, and let himself drift slowly down. There, stuck in the ground, was his sword! Apparently Heln had been so confident that he would wake before the soldiers got help that she had left his weapon for him to pick up.

He lifted the sword, eyeing the abruptly silent men chained to the tree. It would be so easy to run them both through right now! But much as he was tempted, he could not do it; they were helpless, and it would be no more than murder.

Instead he sheathed the sword, touched the belt, elevated, and locked himself on flight. He stayed low to the ground so as not to attract Melbah's attention. If another whirlwind came, he'd land.

"Get him! Get him!" Bemode cried.

Arrows zipped by, but they had been loosed from too far back. He twisted his head enough to see the soldiers riding hard through the forest, and then he zigzagged between trunks, finding a meer path and following it. He should have killed those chained soldiers when he had the chance! Then they would not have been able to give the alarm before he got clear.

If he could stay out of Melbah's sight and not catch an arrow, if he could catch up with Heln and get her across the border, all might yet be saved. But he did regret the loss of the laser; with that he'd have had few problems. Had Heln taken the gauntlets? Little, fainting Heln? It seemed doubtful, and yet he knew she must have. The gauntlets would have given her the courage and skill, and that Female Liberation crap he had spouted might have helped. She was one fainthearted little lady, and even with a warrior sister-in-law she hardly seemed his daughter. But now, if he was right, she was on the way to getting herself rescued. And maybe, just possibly, to bring her old daddy reinforcements. That gesture with the sword—the gauntlets might have thought of that, to let him know.

The thought of what he had just considered struck him: the war he had wanted could now get under way. But without the laser, what could be done? Well, if he could get the gauntlets back, and if Kelvin somehow survived . . . but he wasn't certain he wanted to think about Kelvin.

Conjurer's Rock was looming up there to his right, far above the treetops, like a giant guardian for the old witch of Aratex. He'd bypass that and Deadman's Pass again and just hope Heln was far ahead. His wound hurt abominably, now that the immediate threat had eased, and his head ached from its collision with the tree. He might have a cracked rib or three, too. But he looked on the bright side: he really hadn't lost much blood, thanks to Heln's tourniquet.

What he needed to do was get back, get healed, and then it would be St. Helens' wartime. He'd fix that old crone and he'd give young Phillip the long-delayed hiding of his life! Yes, sir, once St. Helens got into action the fight should be as good as won!

But what about the witch? Old Melbah could do a lot of damage with that wind of hers. What damage might she do with her other tricks?

He contemplated the situation as the ground slid on below. Grass, brush, rocks, meer, deese, squirbets, rabells, flowers, and weeds. Brown and green and gray. His head throbbed, but not nearly as much as his leg, and he wished he could make better time. Damn that crossbowman! If only the rest of him were as hard as his head!

Well, what about Melbah? He'd get her if he had to run her down. Sooner or later he'd catch up to her despite her tricks, and if he had the gauntlets on he'd grab her scrawny throat with them and they'd squeeze out her foul life the way another pair had strangled the dwarf for Kelvin. Yes, that's what he'd do eventually, just give him the chance!

Ahead the river flowed and sparkled through the trees. So peaceful, so pretty. For the sake of safety and in hope of spotting Heln, he'd have to stop. He aimed himself at a tall maysh tree and maneuvered himself carefully into its upper branches. Poised there, he could look down at the river from on high. There, starting from the opposite bank, were Rud cavalrymen. And at the head of the column, Kelvin's friends the Crumbs. There was no mistaking Mor on that big horse with that big girth. That was them all right, so Heln must have made it back.

Should he go out to meet them? No, he decided; that would mean a stop. If he stayed hidden and waited, the war would get started. Then he could come out, get a little medical help, get those gauntlets from Heln, and he'd be back on his way to victory. Yes, that was what he'd do.

Four very black buzvuls flew by his perch. One looked at him and seemed to wink. Funny, he didn't know they could do that! "Croak, croak," the bird said.

"No, *you* croak," St. Helens said, and almost lost his grip on the limb. The bird flew on by.

He watched the buzvul fly over the advancing party. It yelled something. Soldiers shot at it with arrows, and it was falling.

St. Helens mentally echoed the cheer given by the soldiers. One ugly bird down. Might it be Melbah!

But now something else was happening. The sky was in disorder. The clouds were gathering, the sky darkening. Big drops of rain were falling, and lightning flashed. Yet just a moment ago the sky had been clear!

"Damn!" St. Helens said, holding on to the limb for dear life. Could this be natural? No, it could not be natural! Nor could that bird have been!

Down below on the river, the soldiers were having problems. The river was rising with completely unnatural speed, making for unsteady going. Wind was lashing cold water and flinging it on the men.

Now the sky was darkening worse than it had before. Only momentarily did it clear. The rain was really coming, and the river rising yet more, and the wind whipping the tree, shaking it so hard that St. Helens thought his teeth must rattle.

Have to get down, he thought; *have to get down.* But there was no getting down with the levitation belt. With the wind blowing the way it was, he'd be smashed into one of the other trees. Melbah must be one of those birds, or have the eyes of one of them. He had heard that witches could do that— project their eyesight into the heads of birds and animals. He hadn't believed it before. Now he suspected that he had greatly underestimated the witch.

That first passing buzvul had been mocking him! The witch had seen him, and known he was about to be dashed down by the storm! The bird must have taunted the soldiers, too. They had gained nothing by shooting it down; in fact, they had allowed themselves to be distracted for precious seconds when they should have been scrambling quickly out of the water. The witch had tricked them all into deep trouble.

Now the tree shook so hard that it began to bend. Branches cracked off. Leaves sailed by. He hung on, unable even to see the river anymore, able to think only of himself and his predicament.

There was a roaring sound, not that of the wind. A roaring as of water. Of flood. He heard a horse neigh, a sound of pure horror. Men yelling, screaming. He began to fall.

He hit the button on the levitation belt just before he alighted. It cushioned his fall slightly and perhaps saved him from a broken back. Even so, the jolt was good and hard, and his wounded leg flared with pain.

He rolled over, gasping, choking, screaming inwardly from the agony. He hadn't broken anything, he was alive, but God, he'd landed with a smack!

It was calm now. The light was better. Looking below, he could see a river in flood and horses and men far downstream, struggling. Some mailed vests and other bits of armor seemed bright in the sun as the soldiers wearing them were tumbled over and over in the current.

Mor? he thought. *Lester?* Had they escaped? Was this pitiful handful of drowning men what was supposed to rescue Aratex?

"Curse you, old woman!" St. Helens screamed. Maybe she was around to hear!

"Yes?" a dark bird croaked. It had lighted on a branch over his head. It looked down at him with a scavenger's bright, merciless eye.

He got to his feet, staggering as the pain in his leg stabbed him. He wanted to grab that bird and choke the life out of it.

"Yes?" the bird asked again mockingly.

"Yes!" he said, throwing himself forward. Promptly his leg collapsed, the ground rose up, and try as he would, he could not protect his face.

"Come back, St. Helens," the bird advised as he spat out dirt. "Come back to the palace and your friend."

"Go to hell, witch!" he snapped.

The bird flapped its wings, issued a hoarse croak, and took off. It loosed a smelly dropping at him as it passed above him.

St. Helens was alone, looking out on a river and the destruction of his hopes. Far below, men struggled hard to save their lives.

Was it she? Or just her eyes and voice?

A chilling, cackling laughter sounded overhead. It went on and on while St. Helens lay on the ground and tried to think of something more sensible and productive than just cursing.

CHAPTER 23
Recovery

KELVIN OPENED HIS EYES and blinked. The interior of the bandit's tent had not changed, and the faces looking down at him were the same, with the exception of the dwarf's. Yet something *had* changed, and it took him a moment to figure it out: *he was no longer dying!*

"Well, Heeto made it," the bandit Jac said.

"He may still die," Biscuit said skeptically. It was almost as if he preferred that possibility.

"Look at those eyes. They're clear! He's about halfway recovered already. About all he's going to need to get his strength back are rest and food."

"The—dwarf?" Kelvin asked. He couldn't get out of his memory the way he had choked Heeto's counterpart to death. "I owe him my life?"

"You do unless you go ahead and die," Biscuit joked.

Kelvin considered that, not finding it funny. In his home

229

frame, Heeto's counterpart in appearance had been the most evil being imaginable, but here in this frame Heeto had undergone hardship and risked danger to save a stranger's life. What remarkable differences in such similar-seeming folk!

True, Heeto had round ears, as did Kelvin, while the evil Queeto had had pointed ears like those of the evil sorcerer Zatanas; indeed, like all who were not from Earth or descended from Earth immigrants. Here everything was similar and yet twisted around.

"Better get some sleep, Kelvin," Jac advised. "You can thank Heeto when he gets back, and then when you're strong we'll make plans."

When I'm strong, Kelvin thought. *Have I ever been strong?* He drifted into a dream in which Queeto awakened him to show him the pale corpse of Jon drained of her last drop of blood. There was blood on the dwarf's lips—surely hers. The dwarf gestured, and Jon was replaced by Heln, fastened to the table as Jon had been. Zatanas bent over her, preparing to take her blood.

"NOOOO!" He sat up, his hands reaching for the dwarf's throat. The throat was there, and he fastened on it and squeezed, hard.

"Stop him!" Jac ordered, and Biscuit grabbed Kelvin's wrists. He was back in the tent, and the throat he was attacking was that of Heeto, his benefactor.

"I—I—" Kelvin said. The enormity of what he had been trying to do was a shock.

"You dreamed," Jac said. "You dreamed Heeto was someone else."

"Y-yes." Kelvin looked into Heeto's wide-mouthed face, saw the finger marks on his throat, and the tears that had started in the dwarf's soft eyes. He was overwhelmed. "I'm sorry, Heeto. I didn't mean—"

"I know."

Suddenly he had his hands on Heeto's shoulders and was

pulling him near. His hands, almost of their own accord, reached around and patted the dwarf's hump. "Thank you, Heeto! Thank you for saving my life."

"It is a favor you may live to repay," Heeto said. "As your brother would repay."

"I'd like to try," Kelvin said, with no real idea of what he was saying. "You knew—know—Kian?"

"Yes," the dwarf said. "And with great good fortune he may still be alive. But it may take you to rescue him."

"That's why I'm here," Kelvin said. He stood up, astonished at how well and strong he felt, and looked down at his now foreshortened benefactor.

"We'll have to fill you in," Jac said. "About Kian and Lonny and the serpents, and—"

"Serpents? Did you say serpents?" Kelvin found himself shuddering. After his experience with what seemed to be a silver snake hide, he hadn't any desire to hear more of reptiles! But that might be what he most needed to learn about.

"We've got some big ones in our world, and they have silver scales on their hides. The flopears are an ancient people and wise, but once a year they make a sacrifice to what they feel are their living serpent ancestors, and—"

On and on, and at the end of Jac's explanation Kelvin felt he knew all that had happened to Kian since coming here. It sounded as though Kian and Lonny must have perished, but no one could be certain. Possibly they had been taken prisoner by the flopears. More likely they had been eaten by the monstrous serpents. But assuming the first, they might have been taken to Rowforth's palace. In fact—

Hastily he told Jac and the others about Heln's astral visit to this frame, and how they had found John Knight and Kian in what must be Hud's royal dungeon. There was the confirmation!

Biscuit swore. "That fiend! Putting a serpent in Smith's ear!"

"He was a good man," Heeto agreed. "A rough man, but good. No one deserves that treatment! Kelvin, you must help us free Hud from Rowforth!"

"I—I want to," Kelvin said. *But I'm not really a hero! I'm just a man who feels like a boy! The only thing that made me seem like a hero was the pair of magic gauntlets—and I don't have them now!*

"What's the matter, Kelvin? You look pale again." Jac looked really concerned, exactly the opposite of the way his unfeeling counterpart, Cheeky Jack, would be.

"I'm not sure that I can help. If I had the Mouvar weapon you had and that Heeto somehow used to rescue Kian's and Lonny's astral selves . . ."

"That's why we're so glad to see you now," Biscuit said with a grimace that belied his words. "You're going to recover the Mouvar weapon you had and show us what it is and how to use it to rescue our land."

Kelvin sighed. Now there was no help for it. They really thought he could do it, or wanted to believe that he could. He would just have to act as they wanted him to, and maybe, somewhere along the line, he'd find that he was able. It was a faintly comforting thought, and he tried recalling it frequently as the next few days passed, for what little it happened to be worth.

Then, one fine misty morning, they rode out: Kelvin, Jac, Biscuit, and Heeto. After crossing the Barrens they followed a road through mountain wilderness that reminded Kelvin of dragon country. That did not encourage him. Finally they reached the rim of one of two connected valleys.

"This is the one," Heeto said, pointing to the tunnel below them. "I dropped the Mouvar weapon after I triggered it. The shock was so great I never even thought of retrieving it until we were nearly back. And that tunnel way over to the far side of the valley is where Kian and Lonny entered."

Straining his eyes to see in the mist, Kelvin took the dwarf's word. But if he had been told correctly, and he felt certain he had been, they would face flopears or serpents down there. Was he really better off than he would have been facing golden dragons?

The mists thickened as they descended into the oblong valley, becoming what was very nearly rain. At least there would be no serpents sunning themselves today! But if they chose instead to let the rain wash the dirt off their scales . . .

Kelvin wanted to forget the Mouvar weapon and ride directly to the tunnel where sharp-eyed Heeto had last seen Kian and his friend (girlfriend?), but knew that would not be prudent. Once the Mouvar weapon was in his hands, he would feel a shade more capable.

While they were still trekking down, less than halfway to the valley's floor, a rumbling started. The vibrations seemed underground, and felt like a drumroll beneath their feet. Dust belched from three separate serpent tunnels to the left of their destination.

Kelvin swallowed and turned to Jac. "A serpent?"

Jac shrugged. This was evidently new to him.

"It could have been the Mouvar weapon," Biscuit remarked. "A serpent could have swallowed it, and the digestive acids destroyed the weapon and the serpent."

"I doubt it," Jac said, worried. "Let's wait for that dust to settle."

They waited, continuing their march. By the time it had settled, they were at the tunnel's mouth. There was no avoiding the matter of the weapon.

"I—I think I should go in alone," Kelvin said. He had decided on that far in advance. It was really only a gesture. If a human life had to be sacrificed, it should be his own life, on behalf of his rescuers. At least that might make him look like a hero!

"Suit yourself," Jac said.

"I'm agreeable," Biscuit remarked. Indeed, he looked quite agreeable, this time.

"The weapon should lie just beyond the entrance," Heeto said in his ear. The dwarf had stood up on his saddle and ridden up close in order to be at Kelvin's height.

Kelvin nodded, watching in wonder as Heeto resumed his saddle seat with a decided smack. The little man couldn't even use stirrups, he thought—at least not any made for an adult.

There was no stopping it now. Kelvin dismounted, handed the reins up to Heeto, and nerved himself to enter the tunnel of the serpent. By the size of the aperture, the reptile that used this hole must be big enough to swallow a war-horse!

The mist had vanished almost entirely during their short pause. The sun felt hot on his back. Did that mean that the serpents would be stirring momentarily? Delightful thought!

He stepped in. It was dark inside, but then his eyes adjusted. And there, lying just beyond the entrance, just as Heeto had said, was the Mouvar weapon. He could fetch it and get out of here with no trouble at all! What a relief!

He took another step, bent down, and picked it up. It hefted almost the same as the laser he had used to destroy so many golden dragons during Rud's war. Yet this weapon had been made by Mouvar's people, he knew, not by his father's people on Earth. That meant that this device was alien, and might not work in any familiar manner.

"Kelvin?"

He jumped. The voice had come from deeper inside the tunnel! But it was definitely human. "Huh?"

He saw her then as she stepped into the pool of incoming sunlight. She was covered with dirt and grime, and her hair was a tangled mess, and she looked hungry and tired—yet she was as pretty a girl as he could have imagined. But she looked like a girl he remembered hearing about in Rud. He hoped that if Kian loved this one, she was as different from her counterpart as Heeto was from Queeto.

"Lonny?" he asked, remembering the name they had told him.

She rushed toward him, dropping a sword. Suddenly, somehow, to his amazement, she was in his arms. "Oh, Kelvin, Kelvin, how I hoped you would come!"

"Where is Kian?" He felt embarrassed holding her like

this, because though she obviously needed comfort, she was such a lovely creature that anyone who saw them would be bound to misunderstand. What would Heln think?

"The flopears have him!"

She was wearing gauntlets that looked exactly like those Kian had taken from the Mouvar chamber. Magic gauntlets, he hoped! He touched the one on her right hand. "These are Kian's?"

"Yes." She withdrew from his embrace, to his relief, and slipped them off and handed them to him. "Yours now. Yours to use to rescue us. To rescue Kian."

And with these gauntlets he just might be able to do it! He could try to be the hero he was supposed to be! What a break!

He put down the weapon and drew on the gauntlets, saying nothing. The gloves felt right, adjusting immediately to his hands. But they tingled as soon as they were on.

That tingle meant danger. He had ignored that magical warning for the first and last time with St. Helens. He snatched up the weapon from the floor. He wondered as he did so whether he should instead have drawn his sword.

The ground rumbled. Outside, the horses whinnied and jumped and bucked with their riders. Kelvin whirled to look, Lonny clutching his elbow.

Very near, just outside the tunnel, a great silver head broke the ground. Huge serpent eyes bored at those who were out there, freezing them all: Jac, Heeto, Biscuit, and the four horses. All of them became as motionless as statues.

The stare penetrated past the group outside, and in to where Kelvin and Lonny stood. Something tingled in him and ran all the way from his brain stem down his spine.

This is it! he thought. *It's no wild story. I'm frozen! Just the way it happened to Kian!* But now the ones who had rescued Kian from the stare were frozen as well. Kelvin was helpless, and no help was possible. He could not shift his eyes to look at Lonny; he could not change any part of his position at all. What awful power in that serpent's gaze!

The silver body undulated and the great head passed under

the high entrance. The stench was something he had never smelled before. Standing there, paralyzed, as helpless as he had ever been in his life, he was reminded of the dragons.

The serpent reared its head. Behind it, its body undulated and coiled in a way no home-frame serpent could. Then it was in striking position, and the head was directly in line with Kelvin's face. The serpent had bypassed the men and horses and come directly for him. Somehow it knew! It could swallow him whole, and that might be preferable to being cut up by those fangs.

The gigantic serpent mouth opened.

For the second time since coming to this frame, Kelvin tried to accept the knowledge that he was about to die.

CHAPTER 24
Dungeon Daze

SMITH STIRRED ON THE straw, rolled over, groaned, and peered through the bars and into their adjoining cell. His face twisted with pain, and beads of sweat hung on his face. He lifted his filthy water jug from the even filthier floor and put it to his cracked lips. He rinsed his mouth and spat out the water he did not swallow. He fixed his yellow eyes on them, and a hint of recognition crossed his face.

"Kian? I thought I was alone. They catch you afterward? After the battle?"

"After the fight, yes." It was hardly a battle, Kian thought. He had been in battles, and the attack on his father's captors hardly qualified. "Lonny Burk and I ended up in Serpent Valley. She's still alive and free, I hope."

"Gutsy little girl. Make you a good wife. Ohh." He clutched his side where blood soaked his brownberry shirt.

Kian turned to his father. "Why separate cells? Why isn't he in with us?"

His father shrugged. Then he said what Kian had been waiting for. "Son, we've got a lot of catching up to do. You'll have to tell me everything right from the start. You came to this frame by a slightly different means than I did, didn't you? I blundered in on a raft. Went right into The Flaw on it, and then I was here."

"Mother?" Kian asked. He feared to know and yet he had to know.

His father's face looked strange, and he seemed to take the longest time with his answer. "She's gone, Kian. Lost from the raft. Drowned, almost certainly."

Kian hung his head and for the first time in years allowed himself to weep. Only after he felt partially recovered did he resume talking, and then there was no end to it. He went on and on, recalling every single detail of what he had witnessed and the adventures he had had. Now and then his father interrupted him, but only to ask questions. In the neighboring cell Smith seemed to be listening intently, but then the man's eyes closed and he slept.

The big guardsman with the craggy face brought them a tray. He motioned them to the rear of the cell and then pushed it through a slot in the door. There was moldy bread and a jug of dirty water and some unappetizing cheese. Smith received the same fare.

"Can't he have his wounds treated?" Kian asked, indicating Smith.

The guard shrugged indifferently. "What's the point?"

Kian shuddered as the guard left. What an attitude!

But Smith was wiser than he. "They may use me to try to get your agreement to cooperate," he said. "Torture's a game for Rowforth, isn't it, Guard?"

The guard took his keys and the empty tray and went back up the stairs. He had made no attempt to answer Smith's question. Smith made an obscene gesture in the guard's direction and lay back down.

But Kian was shaken more than Smith seemed to be. What were they in for? What would he do, in the face of torture? He had never anticipated having to face this!

Zanaan, queen of Hud, climbed the winding stairs to her father's quarters. She had been thinking about the two prisoners. Something needed to be done, but she was uncertain what she could do.

The big crested door at the top of the stairs was closed, so she opened it. Zotanas was up, as he normally was with the first morning light, and feeding his bird. "Eat your seeds, Precious," he was saying to the dovgen, and the bird was cooing and rubbing its head against his hand.

"Ah, daughter, what brings you to my quarters so early in the day?"

"You call yourself a magician, Father—don't you know what brings me?" she teased him.

"As it seems I never cease explaining, my precognitive abilities are, if anything, negative. I know nothing about what is going to happen at any one time."

She sighed. "The prisoners, Father. I think we should help them."

"I agree, my child." Zotanas fed his bird another seed. "Unfortunately, there is little that can be done at this time."

"We could release them. Save them from my husband's torturing."

"We could, perhaps, but would that be wise?"

"You're the one with wisdom!" She was becoming annoyed with him, as often happened.

"Age. I have not wisdom but age, and a little of the art."

She glared, wanting his help but recognizing the signs. When his back was turned and he was clucking to the fat bird, she edged across the room to his collection of powders and elixirs that were positioned handily but seldom used. It was but a moment's work to fill a tiny vial with a greenish liquid from a retort. Often he had given her the liquid when her cares became too great and burdensome. But this time the substance was not to help her sleep. This time she had a far different purpose in mind.

Thus it was that a bit later in the day she paused outside the royal dungeon and offered the king's man there, one Sergeant Broughtmar, a refreshing sip of wine. She pretended to have imbibed freely herself, thus making her unusual action a bit plausible.

"Come on, Broughtmar, old sourpuss, have a little drinkee on your one and only queen."

"On her, Your Highness?" Broughtmar asked with a straight face.

"Oh, you men!" She dug him familiarly in the ribs as she thought one of her husband's trollops might have done. It was difficult indeed to act this way, but she considered it to be a necessary evil. "You know what I mean. Just a little drink to beat the heat."

"I assure Your Highness, I meant no disrespect." Because even the hint of disrespect could cause a head to be loosened from the shoulders.

"None taken. Drink?" She sloshed the bottle around, waving it just within his reach.

"Your Highness, I am not permitted to drink while I am on duty." He did not even look tempted; he looked distinctly nervous.

"Oh, I know that! But the king isn't permitted to bed other women, is he? Yet we know . . ." She shrugged, not caring to speak what all knew. "Besides, I order you to drink."

"You order me, Your Highness?" He was having trouble assimilating this.

"Yes."

"In that case, I have no choice." He leaned his heavy pike against the wall, took the bottle in both hands, and lifted it to his lips. She watched as his throat worked and blue liquid streaked from his lips and got on his uniform. When he handed the bottle back, there was definitely some gone.

"Sergeant Broughtmar, aren't you sleepy?"

"I am, Your Highness." For of course there was more than wine in the bottle.

"Then sit down, for goodness' sake! Take a load off. Lean against the wall here. I won't tell."

"Your Majesty, it is forbidden to—"

"I order you."

Abruptly he leaned against the wall and slid down until he was sitting on the floor by his pike. A moment elapsed while he did eye tricks, opening and closing and then rolling them, and finally rolling them up. He snored.

She set the bottle down beside him, took his key-ring, and tiptoed past him and down the dungeon stairs.

No sooner had the queen vanished in the dark of the stairs than Broughtmar lifted his head, spat, and looked about for the king. The king, as he had anticipated, was only a few steps away. When he came around the corner of the castle, His Majesty had his finger to his lips and was winking conspiratorially.

"Did she guess you were faking it, Sergeant?"

"No, Your Majesty."

"You did just what I said? You swallowed none of the wine?"

"None, Your Highness. I did just what you said. I hate wine."

"Good. I myself prefer Hud's bleer. But you did right, Sergeant. You always follow my orders to the letter. That's why you're so efficient both as a dungeon guard and as a torturer. Come, now, we'll follow very softly and see what she's about."

Together they tiptoed after the queen.

John found himself looking into Kian's face and wondering again how such an incredibly evil person could have borne him. Kian was everything he wished he was: even-tempered and thoughtful to a degree that positively shamed Kelvin and

Jon. Of all people to share a dungeon cell with, his son had to be among the best.

Kian had now gotten through all his story and answered all his father's questions and was now starting to grieve for his mother. John wondered again if she was really dead—that beautiful, sensual creature who had bewitched him and reduced him to the depths. Thinking back now, he was convinced she had really enjoyed tormenting him. One by one, she had ordered the deaths of his men from Earth, not because they had done wrong but because he opposed her will. He remembered the way she had tossed back her red hair, smoldered his soul with her greenish stare, and said: "What, Dear Lover, you will not teach my loyal servants how to use the war toys of Earth? Then another roundear must die. And another tomorrow, and another the next day. Each and every day one must die, until there is only you left."

"What will you do then?" he had asked. "Will you kill me as well? Will you kill Kian, your own roundear baby son?"

Her eyes had grown if anything smokier, swirling greenly and catlike in their inner depths. "You wish to try me, Lover? To push my will that far?"

He did not, for he knew there was no bluffing her down. If he did not do her bidding, she might actually destroy all of them, himself and the infant Kian as well. After all, hadn't the sorceress Medea of Earthly lore brutally sacrificed her own children when the hero Jason left her? Queen Zoanna seemed to be cast from a similar mold.

"And so, Father," Kian was saying, startling him back to current awareness, "I really know now that I want to marry her. I hadn't realized it when it was what Mother wanted, but now, now that it can never be, I do. Mother was right all along. If I live to get back, I will marry her."

"If it is to be, it is to be," John said, wondering what he had missed. Charlain used to say that all the time, meaning it more literally than he did. Another saying of hers was "It's as true as prophecy." By that she meant that it was absolutely true, despite his considerable skepticism. After all, Charlain had married him, a ragged stranger, because of her confidence in prophecy. What a woman! Would he ever see her again? Would he ever hold her as he had so long ago? No, of course not, for she had remarried, believing him dead. Kelvin had told him that. It was as true as prophecy! Gods, how he wished for a prophecy that he would have her back!

"Father, do you think she's still alive?"

"Charlain?" Damn, why had he said that!

"My mother."

Again that Medea image! "You know it's unlikely, son. I was too weak to have helped her." If he would have helped her, he thought. Yet he had been bewitched by her, again, despite his break from her. He had tried to kill her, and had helped her escape instead, hating himself. "I'm sure I saw her drown. She was badly injured, hardly able to walk. She went in the water and bubbles came up and she never appeared again."

"She couldn't have swum away?"

"Not in that fast current." But it hadn't been that fast at that particular point. Yet if she had somehow gotten out, where could she have gone? No, it was most unlikely that she had done anything other than drown.

Better her than me, he thought. *Better her than me or you a thousand times over! Medea has to be dead!*

Kian nodded, his face solemn and wet with newly shed tears. "I guess you're right, Father. Only it's maddening, not knowing."

Yes, it was; how well John Knight knew! It was extremely frustrating. Now that he thought about it, he wondered: could she somehow have escaped? She had known about the river and the raft, as he had not; she had guided him there. He had come to kill her, and she had tried to kill him, yet somehow they had gone together to that underground river and set off. Could there have been some good in her, manifesting once the evil situation was destroyed? Could she have wanted to save him at the end? Or had she merely been using him to save herself, because she couldn't make it alone with her injury? Had she drowned—or had she known of some other route out, beneath the dark waters, and taken that, taking care to provide a witness to her "death" so that there would be no further search for her? In that case, could there be something yet to find, in that place that only he could locate precisely? Maybe, maybe . . . Oh, Lord!

Kian rose from the straw and looked toward the stairs. "Father, I think I hear someone coming."

Smith chose that moment to groan. He had rolled over suddenly, returning to what now passed for life. "If they torture me, don't agree to anything," he gasped. "I'm about to die anyway. They can't kill me more than once. Promise me you won't do anything Rowforth wants."

"I'll try," John said. But he was listening for the sound Kian had heard. It wasn't surprising that Kian now had the better hearing, but as always, it bothered him to remember that he had aged. What had he accomplished in his life, in his travels through the frames? Could the good outweigh the evil?

After a while he heard it: very faint footsteps on the stone steps. Light tread, cautious footsteps. Someone coming to rescue them? Who? Some of the bandit Jac's men? Perhaps Kelvin? Kelvin, his son by Charlain? No, how could Kelvin be here! Anyway, the tread was too light, almost childlike, or female. That made it baffling. No child or woman should be here!

He counted the steps. Three, four, five, six—how many had gone before? Now the person, whoever it might be, was at the very bottom of the stairs. It was dark there, even compared with the overall gloom of the dungeon, and he could not see.

Then the person stepped out into the single long ray of sunlight that was coming bravely down from high above them. The light from the barred window that was all the prisoners here ever saw of daylight. It was indeed a woman, in a gauzy night dress, finely formed. Almost like—

Her face turned toward him. Her hair was as red as the

sheen of a fiery dragon. Her eyes were the color of feline magic.

"ZOANNA!" he cried, unable to restrain himself.

For to all appearances it was Zoanna. Zoanna, his lost illicit love and enemy, Rud's terrible, evil queen! Zoanna, the mother Kian mourned.

CHAPTER 25
Royal Pain

YET HOW WAS IT possible? Even if Zoanna had survived, how could she be here in this frame?

She tossed back a lock of red hair. Her ears were revealed: round, not pointed. So it was Zanaan, the queen of Hud, and not Zoanna resurrected from the river and death. Kian had been talking about Zoanna, and suddenly there was her face! But it was the face of her double, the local queen—who would be good instead of evil, if the usual inversion held.

She carried a set of keys. She was coming to free them! There was the proof of the inversion!

To look so much like the woman he had foolishly loved, and to be good instead of evil—there was a dream he had not before dreamed! He had tried in his mind to resurrect the evil Zoanna, knowing it was futile, because even if she lived, she was not the type of person he could respect or even tolerate.

But a good version of that woman—that was a person he could love. Indeed, already in this instant—

She extended a key. But as she did so, two figures materialized behind her. "One moment, Your Highness," one said. It was the sergeant, the guardsman who had brought them their fare.

Zanaan jumped, startled. She turned slightly toward the stairs. She seemed stunned. The sergeant reached forward and took the ring of keys from her unresisting hand. There was no further chance for her to use them to free the prisoners. Even if she had thrown the keys into the cell, it would have been hopeless, for the guardsman was armed and strong and could have killed them all before they managed to open the gate.

"Your Highness, that was dumb," the guard said. It was hardly the tone or the words one should use on a queen.

But the graybeard behind him, in the blue-black robe, turned out to be the king himself, His Majesty King Rowforth of Hud. There was the authority behind the sergeant's insolence!

Now the queen's eyes blazed at the guard, as she realized how she had been tricked. They had known of her effort all along!

To John Knight, it was as though Queen Zoanna of Rud had been affronted. Lights seemed to explode in the greenish depths, and her mouth firmed. Did she resemble Zoanna in other ways? Only Zanaan's face was somehow softer than that of her double. Zoanna's complexion had been nearly white marble, while Zanaan's was that of very rich milk. The milk of human kindness? A foolish notion, yet perhaps true.

John looked at Kian to see whether he was seeing the difference. Kian was standing, staring, as if mesmerized. Yes, he appreciated the irony of this situation!

John looked back at the king. Rowforth certainly possessed Rufurt's big nose and tannish complexion. But this face was cruel in a way that Rufurt's had never been.

"So you sought to betray me," Rowforth said grimly.

"You talk to me of betrayal!" Zanaan snapped. "You, with strumpets in your bed every—"

The king struck the queen hard across the face. John winced, feeling as if the blow had struck his own face, and behind him Kian gasped. In the neighboring cell Smith emitted a groan, as though he too had felt that terrible hit.

The queen touched her right cheek. The king had struck carefully, calculatingly, John felt sure, with the back of his hand. A large gem on each finger of his hand had torn the lovely cheek, so that it dripped blood. The queen gave no other sign of the pain she must have felt.

"Yes, Zanaan, that was very dumb," the king said, echoing the insolence of the guard. "To think you could put something over on your lord and master. Was it your father who put you up to this?"

The queen did not speak.

"I should have you stripped and publicly whipped," he continued. "That would give the peasants something to enjoy! And your dear daddy I should have burned!"

The queen flipped drops of scarlet from her fingers, so that they lit on the front of Rowforth's robe. A single drop found his large nose. It was an oddly insulting gesture whose import was not lost on the king.

"You wish, then, to have me make good on my threats?"

"No." She was unrepentant, sad.

"I thought not." The king did not wipe away the single drop of his wife's blood. He turned to John and said: "You have had time to think over my proposition. What is it? Are we allies? Will you or this other one lead me to your crossing place?"

John had to think of what the king wanted: for them to agree to serve him and just incidentally show him how to cross frames. What mischief that would bring! "No, we won't," he said. "Never!" Actually, he hardly knew how he had crossed; the best he could do would be to lead the king to The Flaw, where the king might only get himself lost without return. But Kian had come here by design, using Mouvar's device, so it was best to keep the whole matter secret from the king.

"Never? That's a long time. Broughtmar, you may proceed with the demonstration."

Demonstration? For a moment John thought the king referred to his threat to strip the queen and have her whipped. But the guardsman went to the neighboring cell door, unlocking it. Then he was inside the cell, bending over Smith. The injured man groaned as the guard moved him, then spat carefully in Broughtmar's left eye.

"Last chance to reconsider," the king said. He spoke as if he didn't really care. In fact, as if he preferred to make the demonstration.

"You have my answer," John said. So it had already come to the test they had anticipated: the torture of their companion. He hated this, but knew he had to stand firm.

"Mine, too," Kian said.

The king signaled Broughtmar with a wave of his hand. The guard took a silver tube from under his shirt, held it close to Smith's face, and grinned.

Smith's sick eyes widened. "No! No, don't! Let me die clean, please! For the love of humanity, don't!"

"Very last chance," John," the king said. "Otherwise we demonstrate what will happen to your young companion, and you as well, if that should prove necessary."

"No!" the queen breathed, horrified.

What was so horrible about the vial? If it contained poison, then Smith's agony would soon be over. He felt the impulse to speak, even so, but knew that had to be overruled. If he could help Smith he would, but he would not sacrifice his adopted world for him. He would not ally himself with a king who might be as wicked as the queen of Rud had been. Nothing that could be done would ever force him to follow another Zoanna.

The portly king reached up and adjusted the silver crown on his head. "You two are wrong to defy me. Very wrong," he said with wicked satisfaction. "You have so much to lose. You'll see. Watch, now, what can happen to you."

At the king's gesture, Broughtmar pushed Smith's head down, twisted it sideways, and held the silver tube above Smith's left ear. He unstoppered it. Something silver oozed from the tube and flowed, undulating, into Smith's ear.

Smith's eyeballs rolled back until only the whites showed. He screamed.

The king formed a ghastly smile that was all the more horrible for being on King Rufurt's face. "Silver's not so nice, now, is it, Smith? Now that the little beastie's chewing in you?"

John Knight experienced a new and uglier chill. *Something alive had been put in Smith's ear!*

Smith shook from head to toe. His arms and legs spasmed. He screamed again and again while John shuddered.

"He's going to scream like that until his vocal cords quit," King Rowforth said. "Then for days and nights he'll feel that tickling, chewing sensation in his head. Into his brain, chew, chew, chew, tunnel, tunnel, tunnel. Not much pain, there in the brain. Just his mind. And he'll go mad."

"You put a—" John was too overcome by the horror to speak.

"Broughtmar put a tiny serpent in this man's ear. It's just like the big serpents but hasn't lived yet for centuries. It'll eat its way out, all the way out, and emerge from the farther ear. By then you'll be half mad yourselves, just watching your friend. Before then you'd better declare yourself my ally. We can begin making plans and you can move upstairs and be my honored guests. You will have anything you desire. Indeed, my lovely wife here will be directed to cater to your every whim, of any nature. That should be easy for her, since she evidently likes you."

John felt horror of another nature. Did the king know of his affair with the king's wife in the other frame? Did he know how phenomenally appealing John found the queen? That

Kian saw in her a better edition of his lost mother? Surely he suspected—and had abused the queen in John's presence deliberately. The queen herself was hostage to John's cooperation!

"As a symbol of your appreciation, you will lead me to your crossing place from the other world," Rowforth continued blithely. "I could ask the flopears, my allies, but they are conservative and reticent on ancient matters."

"I am, too," John said, though fundamentally shaken. How could he even think of unleashing this monster in another frame—any frame? He could see the king going back the way Kian had come, leading an army. He could see King Rufurt of Rud and Kelvin and the Crumbs fighting for their freedom all over again. He could see terrible carnage and misery for those he had tried to help.

No, he would not slacken! No way, ever, would he tell that monster anything. No way, ever, would he allow him to win!

But if the silver serpent was next to go into Kian's ear? He looked at Kian's shocked expression and felt himself shake. The king didn't know that Kian was the only one who truly knew the route between the frames. If he killed Kian, Rowforth would throw away his chance to cross the frames. But could that irony make up for the horror of Kian's demise? Could he, John Knight, stand by and allow that to happen? Or would the mere threat cause him to capitulate? He dreaded the answer.

"Suit yourself," Rowforth said. He faced the queen. "Move it, bitch. Your turn will come."

Yet again, John felt a surge of horror. What did the king mean by that? That there would be a serpent in the queen's ear, too, if John did not cooperate? He was very much afraid that this was exactly what the king meant.

Smith's screams continued without pause as Rowforth and Broughtmar ascended the stairs. Ahead of them walked the weeping, now hideously pale queen. Kian stood as if dead and cold on his feet, staring blankly.

The screaming went on and on and on.

Gods, as Mor Crumb would say in his own frame, would it ever truly end?

"Cousin Gerta," Herzig said to his companion. Both were in astral form at the moment. "It would seem that our appointed hero has found the weapon."

"Yes, Cousin. But can he use it?"

"He must, Cousin, if disaster is not to strike and the frames to fall."

"Disaster now?" Gerta referred to Kelvin, who was holding the weapon but remained frozen by the stare. The ancestor, unfrozen and unreasoning, was about to incorporate the man's substance. Nearby the girl was also motionless, as were the two mortals outside.

"Observe the gauntlets, Cousin Gerta. They helped make this mortal a hero in his home frame." He paused, then addressed the gloves:

Gauntlets, danger threatens! Use the weapon!

Who speaks? Not a mortal?

Correct. An immortal.

What weapon? The sword?

The weapon you hold. A Mouvar weapon.

The gauntlets were confused. *Mouvar programmed us to fight with swords and spears. This is of a different order. We can enable the mortal to aim it as he would a bow; the principle is the same. But we cannot use it ourselves. We only guide our wearer; that is our limit.*

Yes, the weapon is of a different order. But you can still act. You can stimulate the nerve of the finger resting on its trigger mechanism, causing that finger to convulse. Act now, Gauntlets, to save your host.

Still there was doubt. *We cannot fight immortals. We cannot fight magic. We cannot take the initiative in such a case. It is not in our program. We must have the directive of a mortal.*

The Mouvar weapon will fight magic. The Mouvar weapon will resist even immortals. You need not take the initiative; you need do only what you know the mortal must do to survive. To fail in this is to betray the trust Mouvar put in you.

Click-click, clack-clack. The gauntlets struggled with the concept. *We cannot. We cannot. We cannot.*

You must, you must, you must! Herzig directed them. *Now and henceforth. You must reinterpret your program to enable you to do this.*

A drop of digestive juice fell from the ancestor's open jaw as the reptilian head was poised ready for engulfing. The drop lit on a gauntlet, and the gauntlet screamed as its substance burned. The cousins shook from the force of the scream that permeated all the ether around them. He could almost feel the agony, but Herzig ignored the pain in his desperation.

You must, Gauntlets! You must! The destinies of not one but two frames depend on it!

The corrosive fluid ate through the gauntlet, adding urgency to the decision. The gauntlets had to decide: suffer destruction, or do what the immortal directed. To revise their program in a way they had never done before.

Click-click, clack-clack . . .

CHAPTER 26
Hero's Progress

SNAP!

Bright light filled the tunnel as Kelvin's gauntlet activated the weapon. WHOOMPTH! echoed and reechoed inside his head. His hand was hurting, and he was screaming, and above his face and head was an enormous open reptilian maw bordered by gaping reptilian jaws. The weapon was almost in the monster's throat, and the sword-length fangs were dripping acid drops all the way around.

He wasn't certain how it happened, but he was out from under the frozen reptile, and feeling the terrible burns on his arms and legs and shoulders where corrosive drops had hit. The girl, standing so close in the now darkened tunnel, was screaming, while outside in the sickly morning sunlight there was renewed activity. Heeto and Jac and Biscuit and the horses danced and jockeyed and moved with the unfreezing that coincided with the abrupt immobility of the serpent. *It* was frozen now, while *they* were free.

He grabbed Lonny's hand and pulled her outside. There, still screaming inside himself and starting to echo those screams with his voice, he pointed at his acid burns with the weapon, and waved at Jac's prancing horse.

Jac was down in a moment, applying the ointment that immediately soothed the skin and ameliorated the burn. There were four burns on his body, and the burn on the gauntlet, but all of them ceased to hurt the instant the balm was applied, and commenced rapid healing.

"Thank you, Gods, and thank you, Jac!" What a relief, what a relief! No longer to burn!

"We've got to get away," Jac said. "Before you-know-what happens."

"Right!"

In a moment he was in a saddle, the weapon stuck under his belt, Lonny in front of him on the war-horse. Then they were riding back the way they had come, out of Serpent Valley and its horror.

"You did it!" Biscuit exclaimed as they were clear of the tunnels. "You've gotten the weapon and you've rescued Lonny Burk! Now we can challenge Rowforth properly, and—"

"I didn't—" Kelvin started. But what could he say? That he had been frozen like the rest of them, but that the gauntlet had seemingly made his finger pull the trigger? That hardly made sense; the gauntlets had never done anything of themselves, they had only implemented the desire of their wearer. Sometimes they had been pretty devious about it, but that was what they had done.

Well, he had wanted to stop the serpent! So maybe he had done it. Maybe he had been physically frozen, but had willed the gauntlets to pull the trigger. Yes, that must have been it. So maybe he was a bit of the hero others thought him to be. He only wished he could be more certain of it.

"We'll need an army," Jac said. "Don't think that with one great hero and one great weapon—whatever it is—we've got the means! No matter how good Kelvin is, and I admit he's tremendous, we still need an army to pit against Rowforth's."

"You can have one." Lonny spoke up, surprising all of them. "Kian and I found treasure back there. With enough silver scales to buy all the weapons and men it will take! The only problems are that I'm not sure I can find the place again, and it's guarded by serpents in such numbers that there's no chance of getting in there, getting the treasure, and getting out alive."

"You did it," Kelvin said. "You got in there and out. You and Kian."

"Yes," she said. "But not with treasure. The silver skins were all over, piled head-deep. But the serpents—no way can I ever return there!"

"Not even to save Kian's life?" Kelvin asked.

She swallowed, looking into his face. "For that. Only for that."

The next day was spent in going over every detail of the time Lonny and Kian had spent in the tunnels. Lonny's memory wasn't perfect, but she recalled all the main events and the order in which they had occurred. Then they talked of going back, entering the tunnel she and Kian had found, and making their way to the treasure. With the treasure they could buy an army that was composed of hired soldiers. Here there was Shrood, a kingdom that dealt in mercenaries. All that was needed to buy an army was wealth: exactly as was the case back in the other frame.

"But the weakest part of all this is the weapon," Kelvin said amidst plans. "We don't know that it will always work. I have no idea what it does or how."

"You understand magic, Kelvin?" Biscuit growled.

Kelvin shook his head in negation.

"But you use it, right?"

"I—guess."

"Well, just say it's magic. Somehow it stops the critters. That's enough, isn't it?"

"I—I suppose." But would it *always* work? Would he always have time to point the weapon and activate it? He still could not remember pulling the trigger, or telling the gauntlets to. He must have done it, but . . .

"Your gauntlets know what to do," Lonny said. She seemed to be one of the nicest girls he had encountered, next to his wife, but like his sister, Jon, she was always speaking up.

"That seems true enough," Jac said, and Biscuit and Heeto both nodded enthusiastically.

"If only Kian had brought more dragonberries," Kelvin moaned.

"Well, he didn't," Biscuit said gruffly. "And I never heard of them before he appeared. I don't think they grow in our world at all."

"Maybe not," Kelvin said. "If you don't have dragons." What a crazy mixed-up world, that didn't have dragons!

"Who cares about dragons?" Biscuit demanded impatiently. "Or their berries? It's serpents we have to deal with!"

"Exactly," Kelvin said. "The dragonberries enable us to spy out the terrain before we go there. Without them—well, if we go in and let the gauntlets lead us to the chamber, and I carry the Mouvar weapon in my hand, what's to prevent a serpent coming up behind and—"

"Whatever that weapon is, it didn't seem to hurt us," Jac said. "It somehow released us from the motionless spell just as it froze the serpent."

"It's as if the spell is returned," Kelvin mused.

"Returned?" Biscuit asked.

"As if it bounces back. As if it returns somehow to affect the serpent instead of its prey."

"Good an explanation as any," Biscuit admitted.

Was it? Somehow Kelvin didn't think so, now that he had voiced it. Certainly his father would have wanted more of an explanation. But what after all was the difference? He couldn't come to any clear answer on that, either.

"You have how many men to carry out treasure, assuming we get there?" he asked Jac.

"There's eighteen of us," the bandit said.

Eighteen to carry out treasure. Eighteen to raise an army and fight a war. But at home it had been that way as well. He always seemed to be on the side that had to scramble just to make a decent showing, while the enemy always seemed to be dominant.

"What about the horses?"

"Heeto and Lonny can have them ready at the valley's rim. When they see us come out loaded with skins, they'll come."

"If they're not discovered!"

"They won't be. Heeto's very alert, and no flopear can run as fast as a horse."

"I want to come, too!" Lonny said, surprising all of them. She really looked determined.

"You said you wouldn't go back," Kelvin reminded her.

"I said I would, to save Kian."

"But you said Kian's a captive of the flopears, so he's not at the silver hoard."

"I changed my mind. I can help him best by helping you."

No one cared to argue with that.

"We'll need someone to handle the horses, and Heeto shouldn't have the burden alone." Jac spoke like a real leader then. "If you want to help Kian and your kingdom, you do what you're told."

"I—" Her face flushed. "I—will," she finally said.

"Good. Then it's settled. We'll leave the desert now, and camp in the mountains. First drizzly morning we get, we ride down into Serpent Valley as planned."

Thus it was much sooner than he had expected that Kelvin was leading a small army of bandits on foot down the winding road through a drizzly morning mist that was nearly rain. No one spoke on the walk down, and Kelvin felt the knot in his stomach hurting him as he walked. He was reminded of the trip he and Jon had made so long ago into dragon territory.

The dragon's gold had financed an army for them and made a revolution possible. Was serpent's silver going to do the same? All he could do was go along with events and hope; somehow it always came down to that when things were happening and a great deal was dependent on him.

But I never wanted to be a hero! he protested in his own mind. *Only the prophecy and a pair of gauntlets like these ever made me one! Only these, and in a different world than this!*

The mist was rising as they crossed the valley to the serpent hole that Kian and Lonny had originally entered. They would not be quite in the dark, because every third man would carry a large glowroom impaled on a sword blade. Coming back, if they came back, the blades with the fungus might reduce the amount of treasure they would carry, but light would be essential. Each man had a large basket strapped on his back, sufficient, it was thought, to carry a load of skins that would buy the mercenary services of a thousand good men. Even Kelvin had a basket, though he would rather have had his arms and shoulders entirely free. The thought of meeting even one gigantic serpent was chilling, but if Lonny had spoken true, and he feared she had, they might encounter a hundred. Would the gauntlets be able to move fast enough? Would the Mouvar weapon somehow magically cause all the serpents to freeze?

They reached the tunnel and entered it without mishap. They encountered not a single serpent or flopear. Somehow, that did not make Kelvin feel easy. The gauntlet on his right hand holding the Mouvar weapon led them on and on, and finally, just as he was beginning to lose hope, to the natural chamber with its eerily glowing moss.

Kelvin kept waiting for his gauntlets to grow warm and start tingling with the danger signal, but nothing happened. The party walked past the natural doorways and openings of serpent tunnels, seeing no serpents. They passed under stalactites hanging like gigantic teeth above them, and between stalagmites rising like gigantic teeth from below. They passed the crystal outcroppings, and there indeed were the

gems Lonny had mentioned. They came to the crystal waterfall, and Kelvin had to catch his breath in wonder.

Then the narrow chamber, which they entered single file
between two stalagmites, where the glowing mushrooms
grew, similar to those they carried. Now the natural stairs to
the deeper level, the good air coming in, the high-up serpent
holes, and the piles and piles of discarded serpentskins.

Yet still no serpents. None at all. The others were gratified,
but Kelvin was increasingly nervous. Where were those
monsters? How much better he would feel if he only knew!

Thankfully, they gathered up the skins and stuffed their
baskets. Then, loaded with several fortunes, they made their
way back. The serpents never made an appearance.

Lonny and Heeto brought the horses as soon as they were
outside. They loaded the baskets on the animals, and still
disaster did not strike. How strange!

The sun was out now, and it was a very bright day. There
should have been serpents sunning themselves, but there were
none. No serpents, no flopears.

They walked up the road, out of Serpent Valley, leading the
horses. Everyone was watchful, but no one dared to speak.
When they had at last reached the tree with the silver chimes,
Jac spoke to Kelvin: "I think that the Mouvar weapon scared
them so that they kept out of sight."

"That must be it," Kelvin said, but inside he very much
doubted it. There had to be more, some sound reason why
they had not been attacked and devoured by the serpents, or
killed or captured by their guardians. Somehow they had
been allowed to get away with it, and that bothered him even
more than if they had been attacked.

Kelvin had little time to contemplate the oddity of their
successful foray into the serpents' realm. Almost immediately
they were buying pack animals and replacement horses. Two
days later, slicked up and disguised as successful merchants,
they were on their way to Shrood.

For Kelvin, it was almost like a return trip to Throod. The

territory they passed through seemed almost the same. They ate the same fruits, saw nearly the same people and wildlife. Only one incident on the way seemed remarkably different. A large purple-and-cream-colored bird flew overhead, calling from its long beak: "Ca-thar-sis! Ca-thar-sis!"

Kelvin watched the bird fly over, and then asked Jac, who was riding next to him, "Primary bird?"

"Purgative bird," Jac said.

"Purgative? I thought it was excretory," said Biscuit, overhearing.

"It's called both," Jac said. "But primary? Where'd you get that, Kelvin?"

"From home," Kelvin said. "Another bird." He did not add that the bird was blue and white and called what sounded like "Cau-sal-i-ty! Cau-sal-i-ty!" Both frames, it seemed, had birds in this kingdom afflicted with philosophy. Somehow this seemed part of the natural order.

As on the first trip, or rather his almost identical journey back home, Kelvin noted that the bird had chosen to fly over just where the road ran downhill past a stone cairn. When he reached the cairn he was not at all surprised to be told that it was dedicated to the memory of Shrood's soldiers who had perished in the two-hundred-year-old war with Hud. Histories had paralleled closely, even to the length of apparent time that had elapsed.

"Recruitment House ahead," said Biscuit, wiping orange fruit juice from his mouth and pointing. Except that he was Biscuit instead of Crumb, and the fruit juice was of a different shade, it was the same as previously, when they had brought dragon scales for wealth.

"I suppose you have a Flaw?" Kelvin asked. It wasn't really a question. He knew they had to have one, because that was what linked the frames. What he really meant was whether they had a place where it showed at the surface, where they could go and look at it without boating a long way in the dark on some subterranean river. No matter where or how it showed, The Flaw was the primary mystery of the age.

"Of course!" Jac said. "You'll have to see it while we're in Shrood."

"I suppose I must," Kelvin agreed, though he felt he had already seen more than enough of the anomaly.

They dismounted in front of Recruitment House. Jac, Biscuit, and Kelvin entered to meet with Captain McFay. For Kelvin, it was almost like entering a familiar room. The furnishings were as sparse as they had been in Throod, and the soldiers hanging around drinking, playing card games, and swapping stories might have been what his father would have called a rerun. About the only difference he could see was that here the soldiers had round ears instead of pointed. Then he spotted the big, slightly balding man with one peg leg; except for his ears and his peg leg, he could have been Captain Mackay's twin. Captain Mackay had been gray-haired; Captain McFay was slightly balding but still had dark hair. Captain Mackay had been missing one arm; Captain McFay was missing one leg.

"You've received my letter?" Jac asked the captain.

McFay nodded. "If you've got the skins, we'll do business."

"Outside on the pack animals, and there's more that may be possible. Revolutions come high, I understand."

"They do," Captain McFay said. He was eyeing Kelvin with a puzzled expression, as though searching to recall.

"Oh, this is Kelvin Knight Hackleberry. He's the hero from the other world. The one they called the Roundear."

"His ears don't appear overly round."

"Here they aren't," Kelvin said. "In my own frame they were freakish."

"Hmm, really unusual, huh? But they're just like mine, only mine are bigger and redder." And his eyes were hazel, not gray, as were the home captain's eyes.

"That's because in my home frame most people have pointed ears."

"Pointed? I've never heard of that! I'd like to hear a little about your world, Kelvin." He motioned for them to sit down at a table, and then motioned for two grizzled officers to come join them.

And so, as at another time in another place, Kelvin was launched on his long, familiar story.

"Sorcerer's Spell!" cried a clean-shaven man with both ears intact and no scar on his cheek. "That was some story!"

Kelvin sighed. If only he could be certain that this one would come out as well. Different frame, different experiences, with possibly entirely different outcomes.

"Well, we've got to negotiate," Jac said. "We'll need an army of probably five thousand, and I'm afraid there won't be much help from the populace of Hud."

"There may be help," Kelvin corrected. "We may be able to get people to join us, if we ask them." He explained about the posters he had put up in the other kingdom before its revolution. "Some did join, but they were largely untrained farmers and villagers."

"We'll train them!" McFay promised. "If they respond to your posters."

"People did at home. Some."

"And you'll send a message to the king of Hud, Rowforth, giving him a chance to surrender?"

"Of course, once we're prepared to fight."

The talk went on and on, and for Kelvin, it really did seem to be a replay. Would the fighting also seem to be just a redone past experience? Possibly, he thought, but he couldn't escape the thought that at home there had not been flopears who had allied themselves to the enemy. Nor had the slovenly troops of the queen's been comparable to the well-disciplined, fully trained troops of Rowforth's. Would five thousand men be enough? How many would be killed or mangled under his leadership? How many would he personally kill before he was done?

"You look as though the heat's affecting you," McFay observed. "How about a mug of bleer?"

Kelvin nodded. Wine at home, bleer here. Whatever bleer was.

One of the company brought him a mug topped by foam. He took it, sipped bitterness, and wanted to spit it out.

"Your first bleer, Kelvin?"

Kelvin nodded again, miserable. Manly drinking seemed to him to be such a foolish means of escape. He downed more of the liquid and got an idea. "The Flaw—is it far?"

"No. It's very near, in fact. One of my men can show you. Why don't you go gaze at it while Jac and I conclude our business?"

Kelvin nodded and stood up. "I think I can find the way."

And thus it was that Kelvin again found himself gazing through a wooden barrier into the star-filled depths of the anomaly. Was it, as he had heard said, a crack through space-time that ran through countless worlds and countless nearly identical and some highly strange existences? His recent experience certainly seemed to confirm that!

On his first trip to The Flaw his sister, Jon, had tried to hit a star with a stone from her sling; it had been one of the few times he had seen her fail to hit anything. He smiled, thinking how annoyed and determined she had been. He wished that somehow then was now and that Jon and good friend Lester were there at his side looking into what felt like eternity.

Deep, deep in the blackest black something flashed brightly, streaked across an area where there were no stars, and vanished. Would they themselves vanish? Everyone at once in this foreign and yet so familiar world?

Kelvin decided he didn't need to drink bleer or wine in order to make his head swim. All he needed to do was gaze into this depth and let his thoughts dwell on its nature and the nature of all things.

Ahead, in only a few days' time, there would be a message sent to King Rowforth. After that, should history repeat itself, the killing and dying were as certain as prophecy to begin.

CHAPTER 27

Earth

St. Helens stepped out from behind some bushes and hailed the Rud army. General Broughtner and both Crumbs, Mor and Lester, were in the lead, as they had been before. St. Helens vented a sigh. He had assumed they would have survived, but as he had seen, many a brave man hadn't.

"Whoa! Halt!" the general addressed the troops.

The column obediently came to a stop. St. Helens spoke directly to the general: "They didn't release me, I escaped. There's bad business over there. You going to cross?"

"My orders—" Broughtner began.

"Hang your orders, man!" His leg gave a twinge of pain, but it was worth it. "Is Rud going to let Aratex get away with yesterday? How many men drowned? How many war-horses? How much good equipment washed away?"

Broughtner glared. "St. Helens, my orders are to cross the

265

river, march on the capital, and demand an apology and reparations.''

"Well, why didn't you say so!" St. Helens nodded at the Crumbs, glad they were alive. A thought hit him. "My girl, did she—"

"Why'd you think we came yesterday?"

"She wasn't hurt? She seemed to be getting weak—"

"Not hurt. Pregnant," Lester said.

"Pregnant? You mean—?" He started to smile then, in spite of himself. "You mean the Roundear—"

"Who else?" Mor thundered. "What'd you think, witchcraft? Don't you know your own daughter? She is with child."

Lord, and all that activity! The incredible flight he had taken her on! No wonder she had had trouble hanging on! It hadn't been weakness of spirit, but of body—because of her condition.

"That's, eh, good news." He got hold of himself, swiftly putting back the thoughts of being a grandfather and focused on the present.

"You look pretty beat," Broughtner remarked, eyeing him.

"My leg can use some attention. Maybe Heln told you; it got in the way of a crossbow bolt. A flesh wound, and she bound it up pretty well, but I am a bit worse for wear."

The general nodded and gave appropriate orders. A wagon pulled up; a young medic got out, took St. Helens aside, and worked on him. St. Helens gritted his teeth and went along with the disinfecting and bandaging without comment. When the medic was done, he had to admit to himself that the job was perfect.

"You had better rest now," the medic said. "You've lost blood."

"No time for that! There's a war to be fought!"

"But any other man with a wound like that—"

"I'm too old and tough to let a pinprick like that stop me," St. Helens said, proud of the effect he was making. The wound did hurt, and he did feel weak from loss of blood, and he'd like nothing better than to flop down on a soft bunk and sleep for a day or two, but he wouldn't let any of that show. He thanked the man and went back to the general, who was staring at the stream.

"General, how do you expect to get across? You don't want a repeat of yesterday."

"There won't be," General Broughtner said. "We'll make rafts and build a bridge. It's high time there was a bridge across this river."

"That's a good idea, General. But bridges wash out and rafts can be washed away. I say let me fly a couple of ropes across and then you make a suspension bridge: well above the water, see?"

The general scowled. "Strong enough to take the war-horses and the armor?"

"It can be."

Broughtner shook his head. "And if Melbah decides to blow up a wind?"

"She will. You can be certain of that. But with extra guy ropes holding the sides, the chances are better than in the water."

"I don't like it."

"The alternative, General?"

The former heavy drinker's frown intensified. "I didn't say you weren't right, St. Helens, just that I don't like it. If we construct the bridge so that it hangs just above where the highest waves might reach, then take a few men and a single war-horse across at a time, it'll work."

St. Helens found himself staring. He hadn't really expected Broughtner not to argue. But it seemed the man was competent after all. If they did things right, old Melbah might delay them but she wasn't going to stop them—he hoped.

"Right, General Broughtner, sir." He touched the control on his levitation belt and rose until he was a couple of feet off the ground. "Now if you'll just get me some rope, we'll get started."

The general turned and issued orders. An equipment wagon pulled forward and rolled almost to where uprooted trees and flood debris marked the limits of yesterday's water rise. Looking inside the wagon, St. Helens was surprised to see cut lumber and piles of heavy netting. General Broughtner had let him talk, but he had planned this all the time! Well, at least he could suggest a spot on a bend between two facing hills where the wind couldn't strike suddenly.

But Broughtner and the men in charge of the detail seemed to have planned well ahead of him. Quicker than he had thought possible, he was flying the end of a rope across and securing it to a tree. Then another rope for the other side of the bridge, then the netting sides, the guy ropes, and the plank floor. By noon they were finished and a secure bridge swayed in place.

Lester Crumb was the first across, and then his father, and then the general. The war-horses and pack horses were led across a few at a time, and then the wagons, and finally the men who had remained on Rud's side crossed by threes and fours. When the last man reached their side, the general looked across the bridge and beamed with obvious pride. "Good job, St. Helens."

"Very." What foolishness: the general was complimenting him for suggesting what the general had planned on all along. St. Helens knew this was merely an attempt to gain his favor and keep him in line—but it was working. He wasn't going to give Broughtner any trouble. A leader was a leader, and this was turning out to be a good one.

A black bird flew overhead. St. Helens half expected the bridge to burst into flames, or the river to rise. He had the unhappy feeling that they were doing just what Melbah intended.

"General, if we follow the road through Deadman's Pass, there may be an ambush."

"What's the alternative?"

St. Helens pondered. He didn't like having them pass under

the eyes of Conjurer's Rock, but to try slipping through the
forest might be even worse. Possibly if he were to scout on
ahead, he could find any traps and save the day. But then he
didn't like the thought of either flying low and getting hit with
another crossbow bolt or flying high and encountering another whirlwind. At least he could check the cliffs of Deadman's
Pass for archers and then come in behind Conjurer's Rock
and check for old Melbah. He twisted his mouth at the
thought of flying in behind her, unseen. Of Melbah watching
the troops in the pass, preparing some magical attack, and his
dropping on her suddenly like a hawk. With luck, it just might
work.

"I, eh, believe the road in is the only way, General. But I'd
like your permission to scout ahead. If you can agree to delay
your departure from here and reach the pass at about
sunset . . . ?"

"I can agree to that, St. Helens. But why?"

"The light will be less then." *And old eyes may have to
strain.*

"You have something in mind?"

"I have a witch in mind."

"You will need help. Some of the men to accompany you?"

"Better alone, General. Better just me and my levitation
belt and my sword, the personal gift of Aratex's King
Phillip."

"You have something definitely in mind. Some strategy I
should know about?"

"Only that it involves Conjurer's Rock. Buzvuls roost there
by the thousands. I just want to make certain there's not a
particular buzvul there. If she is there . . ." St. Helens
touched his sword hilt.

"I understand, St. Helens. But a party of archers, perhaps?"

"Alone," St. Helens said firmly. "It's the only chance I have
of reaching her undetected. If I pluck her magic, your archers
will no doubt have adequate targets between the pass and the

capital." Was that true? Would the Aratex army even be out? It was *she,* not King Phillip, who ruled. "If she's first with her magic, it's going to be at least a hard fight."

General Broughtner nodded. "Good luck, St. Helens. We'll time our march to be in the pass at twilight."

But as usual, his simple plan was complicated by random events. Thus it was that St. Helens, forced to walk partway because of flying buzvuls that could have been scouts, reached the edge of the forest under the surly lip of Conjurer's Rock later than he liked. He swore under his breath, but plowed on as his leg jabbed him with new pain. He paused in despair, because the shadow now lay like a great black blanket across the pass, and there, just within range of his sight, were the men and horses and wagons that he had hoped would be far back.

Then, even as he despaired, something happened that astounded him. The ground just beyond the rock's shadow shook as if from the tread of a giant. Ground that was occupied by horses and men and wagons cracked, gaped open, and swallowed troops and horses and wagons in huge, ugly closings. Rock from above cascaded downward, loosened by the trembling of the cliffs themselves. The rumbling sounds of an earthquake and of falling rock went on and on. With it were mingled the frightened screams of horses and the cries of dying men.

Just like that, the tide of battle had turned—before the battle even started. His worst fear had been not only confirmed but multiplied. He had assumed that all they had to handle were wind and water. What a misjudgment!

Melbah was up there, all right, and she was destroying them.

Heln sat up in her bed with a shrill cry. "Kelvin! Kelvin, oh, Kelvin!"

"Hush, it was only a dream," Jon told her. Heln's eyes were glassy; this was the worst nightmare she had had in the palace.

"Oh, Jon!" Heln's arms tightened around her neck. Jon found this both flattering and embarrassing, though she couldn't have said why. Heln had been so magnificently brave when she was wearing those gauntlets of Kelvin's, and now the gauntlets waited here for his return. Sometimes she wondered whether making Heln wear them would stop her nightmares.

"He was fighting again, in an army. And, and the faces— one of them looked like the guard in the Girl Mart who— who—"

"Hush. It's only a dream. That man is dead, slain by a brother of another of the girls. Lester saw it, and I know he wouldn't lie."

"But not in the dream, Jon. Not in the dream! He was alive. Alive and fighting."

"It's natural that you dream of Kelvin fighting him. After all, that evil man was the one who violated you."

"Not fighting against!" Heln's eyes were wide. "Fighting *with!* The two of them in identical uniforms fighting side by side. Fighting monsters, Jon, and about to die!"

CHAPTER 28
Battle

ROWFORTH, KING OF HUD, stood at the edge of the training field and unhappily inspected the twelve flopears in bright red uniforms. So squat, so broad, so ugly, and yet possibly of great value to him. They did not look like soldiers, and he hadn't anticipated that they would. What they did look like were flopears in especially made Hud uniforms.

"And now, oh, King," Herzig was saying, "you must see that they learn to ride."

Rowforth permitted himself a sigh. Herzig had proved unexpectedly difficult in insisting that his handpicked dozen fighters wear the Hud uniform. That had entailed special orders and individual tailoring to fit the odd contours of the flopear bodies. What needless delay! Now they had to learn to ride—these squat, seemingly awkward creatures! It would mean special saddles with special stirrups and a long, painful instructing time. He hoped that his cavalry master could do the job before the abominable green-clad troops swept all the way to the capital. This had originally not been his plan, but there was sense in it: a uniformed flopear cavalry should prove to be even more efficient than a few stationary flopears waiting for eye contact. On horseback these unlikely troops could ride up to the rebel leaders themselves, paralyze them with a stare, and strike them dead. There would be little need for executions after the war. The flopears could execute the entire armed force right from their saddles. When they went into action, no matter what occurred before, victory was assured.

Brownleaf, the cavalry master, stepped smartly forth from the stables, leading a mare. The mare bore a special small saddle on her broad back and towered well over the heads of her potential riders. As she was led near she began to whinny and skitter and jerk in the manner of an untrained horse.

King Rowforth eyed the cavalry master and the horse and the untrained troops, and wondered. Beside him, Herzig spoke: "Danzar, eye!"

One of the uniformed flopears stepped out of line, displaying all the soldierly style of his short-legged race, devoid of grace. The flopear eyed the mare, who was now trying for all she was worth to break free of her handler.

The horse froze. Danzar waddled close, climbed the rope ladder depending from the saddle, settled into the cupped depression, and took the reins.

"Danzar, release!" Herzig commanded.

Instantly the mare reared, came down on her forelegs, and bucked. Danzar flew clear of the saddle, letting go of the reins on his way up. In awe Rowforth watched the tiny body sail up to a height that bordered on the magical. Then down, down, like a stone. SPLAT!

To the king's astonishment, the dust had scarcely settled around the small body when it stood. The flopear was unhurt! It focused its large eyes on the mare—and the mare, turning her head, rolling her eyes, was caught as before.

Danzar waddled up again, climbed the short rope ladder, and resumed the saddle. And went flying.

"How long will this go on?" Rowforth asked Herzig rather than his cavalry master.

"Until Danzar controls."

"That will be—?"

"As long as it will take. Horses can be stubborn. That is why none of the serpent people now ride."

"So these will be the first? The first in history?"

"Yes, the first in history, for this species of animal. The first of the serpent people ever to conquer the equine." But Herzig's tone indicated that he did not consider this remarkable. Evidently he expected the flopears to succeed; it was just a matter of time. Herzig did not seem concerned about the rapidly diminishing time the king had left. Who would have thought those ragtag revolutionaries would be able to hire such a well-equipped and trained army! Where had they gotten the money?

Only twelve, King Rowforth thought. Only twelve, but a sufficient number considering their power. Yes, indeed, the flopears, even more than his fine army, would hold and expand his realm. Once the revolution was dispatched, he would torture its surviving leaders until they revealed the source of their mysterious wealth. Then he would make that source his own.

Out on the practice field Danzar was again clawing wildly with both hands as he climbed above their heads into the blue, cloud-flecked sky. It would have been comical, if not so serious.

As Kelvin had feared, it was one obscenity of a battle. Oh, his men fought hard enough and his gauntlets knew what to do, and there were volunteers aplenty, even in the midst of a fight. But war was war, and after he had spilled the blood of perhaps his twentieth man, Kelvin would have liked to give up the fray. Was it worth it? he wondered, watching the guts spill from his last opponent. Were even the lives of his father and his brother, and the freedom of this country, worth it? He saw the man topple with a stricken face and land under the hooves of the war-horses. Maybe that enemy soldier was somebody's father or somebody's brother; maybe he was just earning money to support his family! At what awful price was anything being accomplished? Yet really, what choice did he have? What choice did any of them have, other than to fight?

Day followed day, and the Shrood mercenaries fought for Hud as if it were their own land. Nobody liked a dictator bent on world conquest; even Rowforth's closest people seemed secretly to hate him. But people followed dictators, intent on the spoils that conquest brought. Whether such plunder was logical, considering that the opposing armies were apt to do the same to the families of the plunderers, Kelvin could not say; he just knew that he wished he were no part of it.

The soldiers of Hud's royal army were at least as good fighters as Hud's Freedom Army; in fact, the two sides were astonishingly well matched. Kelvin was glad that in this fight the Shrood-trained officers were in charge, not he. Yet they did ask his advice, and looked on him as a champion, as did all the troops. With luck and his magic gauntlets, he thought wearily, he could win against the toughest fighters.

Only one thing bothered him, and that was that the flopears did not appear. If they did show up as Rowforth's allies, he hoped that the weapon he carried sheathed on his hip would come to his aid as it had back in serpent territory. But until they did appear, if they did, the Mouvar weapon was only so much extra drag on his sword belt.

"When are they going to use them?" Biscuit demanded one evening, as if he knew.

Kelvin shook his head. "It bothers me as much as it does the rest of you. Maybe he's holding them in reserve."

"And maybe just knowing we have the weapon keeps them out," Smoothy Jac said. These days, in his green officer's uniform, he looked nothing at all like a bandit chief. Neither did he sound like a man whose main interest had been in stealing silver serpentskins from the magical flopears. All of them seemed to be changing, Kelvin thought. Considering what bandits were, that was for the best.

Shagmore came and went, and it was almost as big and potentially as disastrous a battle as the one for Skagmore had been in the home frame. Possibly Kelvin's recounting of the battle of Skagmore helped, as his recollections, suitably modified, of other battles had helped. He was watched carefully by Jac and his compatriots and did not get himself captured as he confessed he had at Skagmore. He had thought that here, surely, the flopears would appear, because this spot had been such a turning point in Rud's history and could be the same in Hud's history. Shagmore, like Skagmore in the home frame, was within a day's ride of the country's capital.

Thus it was that they were fighting a pitched battle outside the capital itself and winning, little by little, without having yet seen Rowforth's magical allies. It began to seem that the flopears were not going to appear, and that the palace itself would be taken by the Freedom Army. Kelvin fought on, trusting the gauntlets, and gradually as men died all around him he ceased to think of the flopears and of the Mouvar weapon he carried. In the back of his consciousness there was a cry of alarm, but that was hard to hear when the immediacies of battle preempted his attention.

Men with pitchforks and staves were in their midst, some riding plow horses and others traveling on foot. Peasants from neighboring farms were coming to help the Freedom Army take the palace. Kelvin winced to see those unarmored men and boys who had never before stood up now standing up. As a consquence too many of them were dying, often horribly. Better late than never, some had said, but as he watched them being mutilated and killed, he wondered. Yet peasant hands did pull the proud, red-uniformed Royalists from their saddles; knives, axes, and clubs did bring the Royalists death, as did the flashing swords and twanging bows of the Freedom Army. On and on they battled, the day becoming bloodier as it wore on.

At noon, when the sun was beating down most cruelly, and

fatigue was a smothering blanket weighing down the muscles that guided the horses and swung the swords, they arrived at the very gates of the palace. Still no flopears, Kelvin thought, that alarm sounding again in his mind. Victory almost in their grasp—

Suddenly the gates fell, crashing thunderously. They fell *outward,* pushed by men in red uniforms. A dozen war-horses charged from the palace grounds. Each horse carried a rider: squat and ugly, with great flopears. Flopears in uniform! Flopears on horses!

There was no time to react. Men in green uniforms froze before the flopears' stares. Men in red uniforms froze as well, but these were not the targets of the ferocious young flopears with swords. Those swords cut down only the men in green uniforms, and these toppled and died without resistance.

At the side of the action Kelvin fought to move close. Oddly, the gauntlets did not cooperate. They were warm on his hands, and he was reminded again that this meant danger. Well, danger there certainly was, but with luck he and the gauntlets would stop it. He reached for the Mouvar weapon holstered to his waist.

His gauntleted fingers encountered nothing where the weapon should have been. The holster had been cut away. He was without the critical weapon!

A flopear was standing up on a saddle, right in front of Kelvin, his oversized sword raised, his eyes glowing. Those eyes held Kelvin *and* his war-horse!

The flopear was going to split him all the way through, and he had no way to stop it!

On his hands his gauntlets were very, very warm. As if he couldn't see the danger for himself!

CHAPTER 29
Victory

Zotanas turned away from the high window where he had been watching the ongoing carnage. The king had mismanaged the war so badly that every last soldier and guard had had to be marshaled to defend the palace. The servants had fled—or, perhaps more likely, sneaked away to join the Freedom Fighters. The palace was virtually empty. If the flopears turned the tide, as the king believed they would, everyone would quickly return to serve as before; otherwise . . .

Something was happening that he should know about; his magic told him that much. Zotanas tiptoed down the winding stairs to the palace proper and slipped by slow degrees through the glittering array of objets d'art that took up so much space. If only the quality of the king were up to that of the artifacts he collected! He came to the statue of a former (and better) king and paused behind it, hidden for the moment. Just on the other side of the statue, King Rowforth was berating Zotanas' daughter, the queen.

"Trying to release the prisoners once was bad enough, but twice! And with those idiot soldiers losing the battle and the flopears refusing to help until the last moment! What was in your mind, woman?"

"You must not do what you swore to do, Husband!" she responded. "You must not destroy them! Your enemies are already at the palace gates!"

"Yes, Wifey, yes, but they will not destroy me, I will destroy them! The flopears have delayed participating, and I can't push them, but once they eye the enemy, it will be over. You know that; you always have. So why?"

Zanaan began sobbing like a little girl. "Oh, Husband, they are good and you are evil. If the Freedom Army loses, you will know no restraint. You will war on other kingdoms and take them with the help of your magic allies. You will conquer this world and you will attempt to conquer others. If the strangers live, you will make them take you to their own world, or show you the way to get there."

"Yes." The word was spoken grimly, through obviously gritted teeth. The king lived for power! "And you will be instrumental in making them cooperate, because the young one sees you as very much like his mother, and the older one sees you as very much like his mistress. When you promise them both fulfillment in return for their loyalty to me, they will capitulate."

"No!" she cried, appalled. "That cannot be true!"

"It *is* true! I had my minions listen from hiding as they conversed. I suspected something of the sort, and now it has been confirmed, thanks to your visit there. After they saw you, it all came out. So you have power to work my will, woman, and you shall work it."

"No!" she repeated despairingly, belief overcoming her.

"Yes!" Zotanas winced as that word was immediately followed by the sound of a blow and a falling body.

"Oh!" There was shock and pain and fear in the queen's

voice. It was obvious that she had never imagined such depravity, even in the King.

Hastily Zotanas stepped around the statue. Zanaan sat sprawled on the throne room rug, her red hair all about her beautiful face, her green eyes seeming to spark in their depths. Rowforth stood over her, fists clenched. He had one foot raised, ready to kick her. The king, for all his expressed confidence in his victory, was evidently badly frightened; he was reverting to childish force and cruelty.

"Because if you don't," the king was saying, "you will persuade them by suffering in a way they cannot abide. You will bring them great pleasure or great pain; I will settle for either. But my will shall be done!"

His head swiveled as Zotanas came into view. The king's eyes blazed almost as brightly as the queen's. "What do you want, Zotanas? To use your magic for me?"

"Yes." It was what he had long planned.

"Yes? It's a bit late, isn't it? With the enemy at the very palace gates?"

"It is, Your Majesty. But now that you have lost—"

"Lost? What are you talking about, you doddering old idiot?" Rowforth put his foot down without kicking. "Lost? I've won!"

"Have you, Your Majesty? I suggest you go out on the balcony, or up in my tower, where I have a view of the fighting."

Rowforth went pale to the edge of his grayish hairs. "My flopears, have they—"

"The strangers from another world have with them a weapon. A Mouvar weapon. Against that, the serpent's stare rebounds as a sword rebounds from a shield. Against that, the serpent people are helpless."

"No! No, you're lying! You're making that up!"

"Am I, Your Majesty? I suggest you go see for yourself."

"Yes, yes, I have to see. I—" Rowforth ran as hard as he could for the stairs.

"Father." His daughter spoke softly from the floor. "You said you'd help him? Use your magic for him?"

"Yes, my magic. I will use it to give him the help he needs—to surrender."

"Then—then you actually have magic?"

"For little things, daughter. For little things, as I have often said."

Smiling his most careful smile, Zotanas raised his palms to his eyes and brought them up close until all light was blocked out. Concentrating hard, he mumbled the words he had learned so long ago that aided in the transference. Unbidden and not completely welcome, a face intruded into his concentration: the face of Polzamp, who had saved him from a terrible fate as an infant and had bestowed immortality on him. Polzamp the Restless. Polzamp the Kindly and Just. Polzamp, the onetime ruler of his people before his change. Polzamp, born from the mating of a mortal sorcerer and a serpent person not unlike Gerta. Polzamp, his own most extraordinary father.

Concentrate: black, black, blank. *Cannot see, cannot see, cannot see. Blank, blank, black. As in deepest outer space, nothingness.*

He couldn't see. His eyes were shut tight. Now he could visualize Rowforth looking out from the familiar tower window. Staring down at the grounds, the swirling men and horses, the clouds of dust, the carnage at the gates and beyond.

From above their heads came a scream. "I can't see! I can't see!" The screaming was Rowforth's. In a moment it gave way to crashing sounds and a continuing series of thumps. "Oh, oh, oh!" screamed His Majesty, his pain-racked body at last reaching the foot of the unseen winding stairs. "I can't see, Zotanas! You are the official sorcerer of the realm—help!"

"Hud must surrender to the victor," Zotanas said, using the tone of wisdom. "Afterward your sight will be restored."

"NO!" Indignation supreme. "Never! Rowforth will battle forever! Rowforth will fight though he's blind!"

"Are you certain, Your Majesty? The magic here is very strong. It will be displeasing never again to see pain in a face or torment in a soul. Strike the flag now and you will see, even though it may be joy instead of suffering."

"It's you! You're doing this! I will never surrender! Never! GUARDS!"

Listening to running feet, Zotanas kept his eyes firmly closed and his hands in place. For as long as he could not see, neither could the king. He knew this; the king did not.

"Help! Help!" the king cried. "Broughtmar, is that you? I can't see, Broughtmar, old friend. It's magic—magic used against me."

Broughtmar? Naturally that thug had managed to escape being assigned to the hard battle outside! But Zotanas suspected that the man would not be much comfort to the king at this moment. Broughtmar was a bully who seemed to exist only to torment the helpless—and now the king was helpless.

"You can't see?" Broughtmar's voice came. "What a pity when there's so much for you to revel in. Outside a man looks at his own steaming innards and a flopear swings a great sword at another man and creates a fountain of blood. You'd enjoy those scenes, Your Highness." Obviously Broughtmar had not checked recently, but that hardly mattered.

"Ouch! You stepped on my hand! Find that doddering old fool who shares the palace! Make him stop whatever he's doing! Make him stop! Kill him *and* the queen!"

Oops—that would break up the magic fast enough, if the guard obeyed. "Hide us, daughter," Zotanas murmured. "This must be complete, before—"

He felt the queen's hands guiding him to a safer place. He kept his own hands locked in place, maintaining his blindness —and the king's. How quickly it was degenerating into a comedy of malice, as the king's empire fell apart before it could form. Now was the falling out of thieves. But he had to keep the king blind while it proceeded.

"You fool, you lost!" Broughtmar's voice came again.

"Those Freedom Fighters won the war. The mercenaries did it—the ones they bought with silver."

"No! No! No! Ouch! That hurt, Broughtmar! You're stepping on me deliberately!"

"How perceptive of you, blubber belly. Maybe a heavy tromp here—?" Broughtmar was certainly acting true to form!

"AHHHH! Stop, stop, stop! This is your king, Broughtmar! Your king! I thought you loved me! I thought we were friends!"

"You were wrong, Your Arrogance."

"NO! NO! NO! AHHHHH!"

It was exactly such sounds that had given the queen nightmares. Only now it was not some unfortunate prisoner or fancied enemy of the realm Broughtmar was methodically beating, it was the king himself. Zotanas recognized a bit of evil in himself as he hesitated to stop the torture. But perhaps it had proceeded far enough. Reluctantly he took his hands down and opened his eyes.

"I CAN SEE!" the king cried. "I can see, Broughtmar, I can see! Don't you realize what this means? I'm back in control, no thanks to that sorcerer! Find him, stop him!"

"Stop whom from doing what?" Broughtmar inquired nastily. He was evidently too far gone in his sadism to reverse course now. "Stop me from doing a little more of this to you?"

"AHHHHH! STOP!!"

Zotanas crossed the throne room and the dining hall and came to where Broughtmar was brutally beating the monarch. It was obvious that the moment it appeared the king lacked power, the guard's loyalty was forfeit.

Very softly Zotanas said: "It wouldn't be wise to kill him, Broughtmar. He needs to surrender us."

Rowforth raised a bruised and bloody face. He pointed a shaky finger. "KILL HIM! Kill him, Broughtmar! I order you. Kill!"

Broughtmar grinned, ignoring His Majesty. "You say he

should surrender? By lowering the flag from the tower?"

"Yes. That is the way surrendering is customarily done. Can you carry him back up the stairs? Place the flag-rope in his hand so that he can lower the flag himself?"

Broughtmar looked confused. "Why?"

"To live. Or at least not to be tortured. One who does this thing is certain to be rewarded."

"Rewarded?" Broughtmar sounded both suspicious and eager at the same time. He liked the notion of a reward, but wasn't quite getting Zotanas' drift.

"With life. Instead of execution."

"Oh." Now at last it dawned: his own life could be at stake.

"Well?"

Broughtmar leaned over the king to pick him up. The king promptly kicked him expertly in the mouth, sending blood and broken teeth spraying.

Zotanas sighed. He should have foreseen that, though Broughtmar hadn't. The king was like a wounded animal, dangerous even when seemingly helpless.

Broughtmar spat out more teeth and blood, looking surprised. In a moment the light of kill would be in his eyes. He was not the smartest man, but he made up for that in viciousness.

"This isn't going to do," Zotanas said aloud. He closed his own eyes again, cupped them with his hands, and concentrated. It was easier this time. Blackness, blackness, black blank. *Transfer.*

"I can't see! I can't see!" Rowforth cried. "Broughtmar, you must help me! You—what are you doing!"

"Take him up the stairs, Broughtmar, and see that he surrenders," Zotanas said. "For a man with your strength, it shouldn't be difficult."

"P-please," the queen added, sick at heart.

Even though concentrating heavily on the black, Zotanas heard Rowforth gasp as Broughtmar picked him up. Then

Broughtmar tromped heavily as he carried the king to the tower and beyond it to the roof.

Blars Blarsner, amateur wrestler and boxer in better times, was fighting with the confounded sword that seemed forever out of his control, and putting all his energies into staying alive. He finished off the Royalist with a sudden lucky stab and looked for an opening between thrashing horses and battling men. The back of the otherworlder known as Kelvin was toward him. As usual, the hero of another place was battling three Royalists with his shield and his sword, handling both brilliantly. He chopped off the hand of the Royalist in front of him, swung the sword back, and slashed the eyes of the man to his left. He seemed hardly to look; it was as if he knew exactly where his opponents were without having to use his eyes. In the meantime the swordsman on his right had stabbed him, not quite touching him but severing the leather thong that held the Mouvar weapon secure against Kelvin's leg.

The Mouvar weapon! It had fallen! It was down there in the dust!

While Blars was wiping sweat and dust from his eyes, Kelvin finished off the third of his three attackers with an expert stab. But ahead the way was clearing before the gates. There was a clanging noise and a billow of dust that hid even Kelvin from him. Something was happening!

There was no time to speculate. He had to get the Mouvar weapon while he could, and get it to Kelvin. Without it Kelvin couldn't continue to win, and none of them could win.

Unless, he suddenly thought, he could manage to use the weapon himself.

With sheer brute strength Blars reined his huge war-horse over to where Kelvin had been. One of the Royalists was still there, horrified as he stared at the spouting end of his arm. Reluctantly, Blars finished off the man and turned his attention to what was under the horse's hooves.

At first he didn't see it, and then he did, next to a dead Royalist and a riderless horse that was whinnying pitifully with its guts pouring out. He reached, grabbed, and had it.

He stared dazedly at what he held. He pulled his horse to one side of the fighting and examined the weapon closely for the first time. He had heard so much about it, yet had never seen it in action. It was a strange-looking device that resembled a crossbow only in the most superficial manner. It had a bell-shaped muzzle that would be pointed at whatever was to be attacked. The part that fitted the hand was like the handgrip on the smallest of crossbows—the kind used mainly for games, for children to train with. There was a strange dial set in it, with two odd marks and a little fin-shape pointed at the higher of the marks. Without thinking, Blars turned the fin-shape to the lower mark.

"Flopears! Flopears! Flop—" came the cry.

Realizing that things were happening and that he was wasting time, he urged his horse out into the dust. Now he could make out the figure of Kelvin sitting oddly still astride his war-horse. Riding hard down on him, standing upright in a small saddle on the back of a gigantic war-horse, was a small figure with upraised sword. A flopear! About to kill Kelvin!

Blars hardly knew that he pulled the trigger while pointing the weapon. All he knew was that it hissed and jumped slightly in his hand. Nothing seemed to come from the bell of the weapon except for a few too-bright sparks.

Had it failed? Yet it had seemed to do something. He had felt the slight recoil, seen the spark. But was that all?

But as he watched the flopear swing down, he saw Kelvin save himself and his horse with some amazing maneuvering. Freedom Fighters who had been stationary in the dust resumed their motions. All kinds of action were occurring where a moment ago there had been none except that of the flopears.

Blars looked at the weapon in his hand. It must have worked! He felt that he had accomplished something. He said a prayer of thanks to Mouvar. He had no idea how the

weapon had worked, but it seemed to have brought the
Freedom Army to life again.

The flopears were still fighting, but no longer against frozen
opponents. How a weapon could bring folk back to life
instead of making them dead, he hesitated to guess. Certainly
this was nothing for him to gamble with. Concentrating hard
on the deed at hand, he maneuvered his horse, bypassing
fights when he could and working steadily closer to Kelvin.
When he reached the hero, he would place the weapon in his
hands, where it belonged.

The movement of the gauntlet surprised Kelvin as it had
never done before. It shot up, grabbed the swiftly descending
blade, and wrested it from the flopear. The flopear lost his
balance, toppled from the saddle, and fell under the war-
horse's pounding hooves. There was a scream of agony from
below which should add spectacularly to Kelvin's future
nightmares.

He pulled his eyes away from the gory sight of the small
ruined face. In so doing, he turned his head.

He could move! The stasis spell was gone! He could move
hands, arms, feet, and legs. The horse was moving, too.
Everyone was moving—every man and every horse. All the
Freedom Fighters and the Royalists and their horses—
unparalyzed! All moving as they were supposed to, naturally
and right. What had happened? What magic had come to his
rescue and stopped the flopears' spell?

"Here, Captain, you lost this."

It was a large, swarthy Freedom Fighter who was holding
out the Mouvar weapon to him, using the rank Kelvin had
been given. Something about the man's face instantly bothered him. With supreme shock he realized that this was the
near duplicate of the pointy-eared guard at the notorious
Franklin Girl Mart who had forced himself on Heln. Kelvin
had seen the ravisher dead after one of his Knights, a brother
to one of the other girls there, had finished him. At the time
Kelvin had both thanked the gods that he hadn't been the one

to strike the fatal blow, and regretted deeply that he had *not* been the one. Now here the man was, or his counterpart in the frame, unbloodied and alive and round-eared. Holding out to him their one small hope of winning this fight. This man, nearly identical in appearance with the one who had raped Kelvin's wife.

"I . . . lost it, and you . . . used it?"

"I saw one of those three last men you fought cut your belt with his sword. Your horse did some jerking after that, and the gates fell and the flopears appeared. I got the weapon for you because I knew you'd want it, and had it in my hand and—you were frozen then, so I tried it—and now you're unfrozen, and I brought it to you. I don't know what I did with it, but I guess the thing worked, somehow. You're the hero, not me; you know how to use it. I—"

Kelvin took the weapon from the big man's hand. He had to say something, and he fought to get it right.

"You're the hero. You, not me. Thank you for saving me and for returning the weapon I should have guarded with my life." *You are the hero,* Kelvin repeated to himself. *You, who in another world, another time, raped my beloved. You, who in that other world, were a person who ruined and harmed without conscience. Only it was not you, but another who resembled you in all things but character. What a universe this is, that two who look so much alike could both so touch my life in opposite ways!*

"Captain," the man said, "the war's not over until they lower the flag on the palace."

"I know."

After a startled intermission the fighting continued. Nobody was frozen that Kelvin could see, either Freedom Fighter or Royalist. Mortal Freedom Fighters now fought immortal flopears hand to hand.

Yet the battle had seemed to be turning, just before the flopears appeared. Now, looking around, he could see more green-clad soldiers on their mounts than red-uniformed Royalists.

The battle was not over. The war was not over, until the flag was lowered. Would it come down? Kelvin did not yet know.

Zanaan looked up from the floor at her father as he covered his eyes. She listened to her husband screaming. Then, assuming a philosophical poise befitting a queen, she got to her feet, wiped her face, put her robe in order, picked up the ring of keys she had been carrying, and resumed her journey to the dungeon.

John and Kian were at the bars as she descended into their gloom. Both were thinner than they had been, worn by the days and the nights of harsh confinement. Dark half-moons were under their eyes, reminders of more than sleeplessness.

The neighboring cell was empty. After Smith had finally died, the result of his desperate banging of his head against the wall with all the strength of a madman, there had been a lingering and sullen silence. Broughtmar had complained about having to carry out the corpse; in the old days he would have let it ripen. But the king had remembered that prisoners subjected to bad air sometimes died. Rowforth had wanted the prisoners alive and helping him. How well she knew!

That reminded her of what the king had said: that John regarded her as resembling his mistress, and Kian, as resembling his mother. In the frame from which they came—

She shrugged that off. Certainly she had not misbehaved like that in this world! Nor would she. She was simply doing what was proper.

She also wondered whether her father had done something to deflect the king. She had never seen him use actual magic before this day, only minor illusions for show.

The young man looked at her with widened eyes, swallowed, and said, "You look so much like—"

"Hush, now," she chided him, oddly flattered. Her husband had sought to use her to corrupt these men; it would not have been an unpleasant task, were it not so reprehensible morally.

She inserted the big key in the lock and turned it, knowing

that they watched. "Your ordeal is over and your victory all but won. The Freedom Fighters are at the gates and winning back the land. Your brother, Kelvin, is in their very midst—a hero to base legends on. Soon, very soon, it will be over."

"Thank the Gods!" John Knight said, and his son echoed him.

Looking at the Mouvar weapon he held, Kelvin saw that the knob on the butt had been turned. Possibly when it fell, he thought. Could a different setting account for the fact that the flopears were not themselves the victims of their own stares? He had wanted to see them frozen into statues, as the serpent in the valley had been. If he moved the knob to its former place, would that cause it to happen?

It was worth a try. He twisted the knob, heard a click, and raised the weapon just as another flopear rode at them with suicidal fury. He pulled the trigger, wondering whether he should be raising his sword instead.

Bright light dazzled him. There was a WHOOMPTH noise that echoed on and on. Then silence.

The horse and the flopear were stopped, frozen as if by the staring paralysis. The mortals and their horses were not affected; the fight could continue with the flopears out of it. But would it?

Just then there was a shout. He saw the big man pointing. There was the silver-and-gold flag creeping down the pole on the palace roof. This meant that the king was surrendering—finally, totally, unconditionally.

As he looked toward the palace, past the gates, two men and a woman awaited him.

"Father! Kian!" he shouted. "We've won! We've won! We're going home again to those who love us. Home, home, at last!"

But Kian, though released from a dungeon, looked as if balanced on a precipice. His face, already pale from imprisonment, paled perceptibly more. When he spoke it was in a hoarse croak that seemed devoid of the joy it should have held.

"Home. That's very good. Really wonderful," he said without enthusiasm.

"Well, Cousin, it's over," Herzig said. "The good mortals won."

"Yes, won well," Gerta agreed. "As planned, though the Mouvar weapon cost us."

"Did it, Cousin? Good members of our band?"

"Your enemies, Herzig, though not acknowledged as such. Those who wanted to go with Rowforth and share his triumphs. Those who wanted to be rulers of mortals in this and other lands. Was it fair, Herzig, giving them what they wanted?"

"Fair is a mortal concept. Call it just. They wanted to fight for Rowforth, and they fought for Rowforth. Now, slain or not, they will never again be involved in a mortal's fight."

"True," Gerta said. "You are very old, Herzig, and very wise. You prove the wisdom of a saying mortals have."

"Yes, Cousin, and that is—?"

"Wily as a serpent," Gerta concluded.

Kian could not understand why he felt as he did. He was going home. Home to the girl he wanted and always had wanted. Why, then, did he feel that his execution was at hand?

"I'm going to miss you, Kian," said Lonny Burk. That made him realize why he felt so inappropriately bad. "We will all miss you, but I know that I will miss you most."

"I—" He swallowed a lump. "Know." And how he wished she was the girl who would be his bride. But the right girl had pointy ears and always had had. Not too long ago Lonny wouldn't even have looked desirable to him. No, the right girl had to be the one at home. It hurt, but somehow it had to be right. His mother had known what was right—hadn't she?

"Good-bye, Lonny, good-bye." Saying it, he felt his insides tormenting him as if from a sword wound. Dungeon food did not account for it. "If—if things were different—"

"I know." He felt her hand delicately touch his, and then, incredibly, her kiss. It was almost—in fact it was—too much for one weak man to bear. Tears filled his eyes.

They were waiting for him. He forced himself to turn away from her and to begin, step by step, what had to be his successful return.

But Kelvin and John Knight were with Queen Zanaan, and the older man looked just as uncomfortable as Kian felt. The queen turned, her great green eyes bearing on him, so familiar yet strange in their gentleness.

"I understand that in your frame my analogue was your mother," she said. "I have had no children, but had I done so, I would have been pleased to have one like you."

Kian found himself hugging her, just as if she were indeed his mother. If only things were different!

CHAPTER 30

Victory Home Front

THEY EMERGED FROM THE chamber to discover Jon and Heln waiting. Without a moment's delay all embraced.

"Oh, Kelvin," Heln said against his chest. "I had this dream! I think the dragonberries have caused me to dream what is actually happening! I saw all of you back here, so I persuaded Jon—"

"There was only the one boat here, and that too small for the four of you," Jon explained. "Mr. Yokes was kind enough to lend us another, particularly after I explained about the baby coming."

"Baby! Baby—you?"

"No, you idiot!" Jon managed to sound offended. "Your wife."

"Heln! Heln?" Kelvin's face paled, as though real danger was upon him. "You?"

She nodded, smiling prettily in the manner only a pregnant wife could. "You're going to be a daddy, Hero, like it or not."

Kelvin's whoop echoed and reechoed from the surrounding rock for a distance up and down the underground river. Kian pounded his back and shook his hand enthusiastically. But even so, there was a certain half-hidden reticence to his congratulations that registered with each of them.

St. Helens took a deep breath, trying to shut out of his consciousness the sounds of screaming men and terrified, suffering horses. She might take all their lives, he thought, but by the Gods, he'd get this witch! Burn a witch alive, he'd been told. By the heavens, if that was what it took, he'd do it!

Back in the pass, the avalanches went on and on, boulders dislodged by the quake bounding and rebounding and often striking flesh. Great cracks were opening like hungry mouths, swallowing men and horses unfortunate enough to be under.

Was she laughing, up there? If so, he'd stop it! He'd stop it for all time, whatever it took!

St. Helens drew the polished, razor-sharp sword the young king had given him and pressed its cool metal to his lips briefly. Now, he thought, and activated the levitation belt.

He floated soundless as a rising balloon. He cleared the overhang and the three ledges of Conjurer's Rock and disturbed some buzvuls brooding on their nests. In a moment they were after him, circling, crying out hoarsely, snapping their beaks, trying each and every one of them to snap out an eye. He swished the sword, downed two of them, and then another. The remaining buzvuls circled, coming in more cautiously. He wished that Melbah could have been one of those killed.

Stunted trees, twisted and gnarled, grew on the sides of Conjurer's Rock as he approached the top. At the crest the trees seemed all occupied by buzvuls—hundreds if not thousands of them. His sword made a continuous flash, but few of the ugly birds risked the blade. Silently he drifted above the trees and the buzvuls, ignoring the squawks. If she was preoccupied with her magic, maybe then he had a chance.

There she was! At the very edge of the rock. Her black cloak flapping, her arms stretched out toward the pass, her lips making sounds that were lost in the rumbling of the earth and the cries of brave and good men. She couldn't hear the buzvuls, he thought, and she couldn't hear him either. Now, now was his chance!

He drifted at slow speed toward her back. Not quite sporting, he thought, but then how sporting was she? Just end her life and he would end that of a killing germ. He visualized her head bouncing down the rock with her hair flowing. He raised the sword, prepared to sever her neck.

A buzvul screamed above him, and the witch vanished. "Fool!" the bird cried. "Fool, to seek to destroy me with nothing more potent than an ordinary sword!" She had fooled him again, the cunning crone!

He raised the blade but could not reach her with it. "Come! Come!" he cried.

Suddenly the air thickened between them. It was a wall of heavy air, pushing down like a wedge of water, forcing him down with his belt.

"Two can play at that game," he said, though he knew he was in trouble. He pushed the control to Accelerate, Maximum, Up. His body shook and he felt as though being pressed flat. Then the trees of Conjurer's Rock were nearer and he was in them. Buzvuls flew up in a cloud. Sharp branches like oversized thorns reached and grasped. Wind shook him. Tips of ugly gnarled branches entered his arms, his legs, his back. He screamed, loudly, and he thought finally. The wind took away his scream and left him impaled and mute: a crucified prisoner. He was stuck, probably forever. The penetrating branches burned with the fire of thistles deep in his flesh.

Finally, it seemed a year or two later, he gained some control. His flesh was tormented, but there appeared to be no vital injuries. He could still fight his way free, and—

A buzvul lit at the edge of the rock. Abruptly it was an old woman with a wrinkled face and a squat body wrapped in a cloak that flew like dark wings on either side. Her naked form was grossly distorted. Ugly? There were no words!

Her hands reached, claws extended, as if seeking to grasp the men and horses down in the broken and trembling pass. St. Helens had to see, and for once cursed the fact that he had eyes. Men and horses were fighting to get free of rocks heaped upon them; men and horses and parts of men and parts of horses, squashed, broken, ruined. Equipment sticking up through jagged wounds in the earth. It was a victory that would have seemed complete to any general, but the creature on the rock's edge was no human general. There was, he realized at last, little that was human about her.

Melbah, the witch triumphant, raised her hands, palms facing each other. Was that a chant? St. Helens shivered, despite the heat and the pain.

A small spark formed between Melbah's stubby fingers. It grew to the size of a grape, an apple, a watermelon. Suddenly there was a great roaring ball of fire floating just off the rock in front of her stark and disturbingly ugly form. The heat blasted back at him, suffocatingly. *Gods,* he thought, *she intends to hurl that at them! To burn them, each and every one! Gods!*

A loud, cackling laugh chilled him even through the heat. "Now, St. Helens, you pitiful excuse for an opponent, see what becomes of my enemies! See the folly of defying me! See the destruction you have wrought!"

St. Helens wanted desperately to stop her. He could not. Failing that, he wanted only to close his eyes—and could not. She had him captive, as audience as well as enemy.

Mor crouched beside a fallen boulder next to a horse's sightless head, the body of the animal buried in the solid earth. "Lester," he said, feeling the bump on his own forehead and the gash made by the rock. "Lester, where are you?"

Then he saw his son, half buried under his own dead horse. Lester's head and shoulders were visible, the rest of him under the horse's throat. It was hard to know whether he was crushed, or unconscious, or even dead.

Mor crawled to him, swearing softly, angrily, helplessly. So many dead around. So many hurt. So many screaming and moaning. Brave men in the prime of health but a short breath ago. Now—

A figure staggered over to him through the dust. With shock he recognized General Broughtner.

"Mor, we're done. We need to retreat, if we can scrape up the strength even for that. There's no going into Aratex. The witch beat us! I thought her magic was fake . . ."

Mor had to agree. Only something like the laser John Knight had used with his son Kelvin to slay dragons could accomplish anything now. But they didn't have any such weapon, and as far as he knew, none now existed.

"They were right about her," he gasped, hating the taste of his own bitter words. "She's more powerful than any army! Deadlier, even, than the sorcerer the Roundear destroyed."

"Stronger than the Roundear," the general said.

Mor winced to hear it, but he had to agree. Zatanas' deadliest magic never equaled an earthquake, and for all the prophecy, Kelvin would be as helpless as they were. How could anyone fight a witch who could make the very earth open up and swallow an army?

"He's alive," General Broughtner said, bending over Lester and looking under his eyelids. "Unconscious." With his strong hands the general lifted the dead horse's head. Despite his dizziness, Mor managed to pull his son free. He could see that Lester was alive, and might recover with proper care if they could get him home to Jon in time.

But that brought up another question. "Do we have the men and strength to get the wounded out?"

The general shook his head. "It will be tough. We'll need help just to retreat. If we surrender now, maybe she'll let us go."

"You think so?"

"No, but we have to hope. I'll get the surrender flag out of the supply wagon. If I can find it."

The general moved off, head down. Mor was alone with his son. He smoothed Lester's brow, wiping away some blood and sweat and dirt. He cursed for a while, then swore for a while, and finally prayed a little. They would never get away from here, he thought. None of them. The witch meant to destroy every vestige of their army. This, barring a miracle, was total defeat.

He tried looking at Conjurer's Rock and wishing St. Helens had gotten there. Yet he knew that even if the man had, Melbah would have smashed him as readily as a man swatted a fly. There was no defeating Melbah; the witch was just too strong.

As he looked toward the distant stubby shape, trying to discern her form, a great brightness like a rising sun formed between him and the rock. There was a fireball there—a great mass of flame. It was streaking toward them, like a monstrous flaming arrow. It was witch's fire, the stuff Mor had heard about. Coming to burn them all, to destroy every one of them.

Mor tried to grasp it. Not defeat; this was beyond that. Annihilation.

On the way out of the underground river to the remains of the old palace, Heln and Jon filled them in on St. Helens and the affairs of Aratex. Kelvin listened carefully, not revealing too much of what had happened after he had started out with St. Helens. His anger at his father-in-law had been burning like a white-hot coal ever since he stepped back into his home frame. Now, hearing what trouble the man was in, he could almost rejoice. *Let him stay there! Let old Melbah have him for a plaything! Good riddance to bad in-law!*

His father surprised him. "I think the three of us had best get to Aratex fast!"

Kelvin gave him as cold a stare as he could manage. There was just no way that his father was making sense.

"He saved your Heln, Kelvin. Surely that must move you, if the insult to your country and your countrymen does not."

"Not to mention the prophecy," Jon said.

But can we help? Kelvin wondered. *Can we do anything at all against a genuine witch?*

"You're right, Father," he said. "We have to try."

They deposited Heln back at her room in the Rud palace. King Rufurt was there to greet them and shake their hands. He made no objection to their leaving immediately for Aratex. Lines etched in his face told more deeply than words how seriously he was taking this.

"I'm coming, too!" Jon proclaimed.

"No, Brother Wart, definitely not this time."

She stuck her tongue out at him. "I've got better eyes than any of you! I can spot danger before you think about it! Who hit Zatanas with a rock?"

"Who nearly had all her blood drained?" Kelvin retorted. "You have to stay, Jon. It's not right that you—"

"Chauvinist! Whose man do you think may be in trouble? My man Lester, that's who!"

"Certainly you can come, Jon," Kelvin's father said, to Kelvin's disgust. "Glad to have you along. I don't think we could leave without you."

Thus were things settled as they usually were where Kelvin's point-eared sister was concerned. The four of them rode to the river without incident, found the new bridge, and crossed it into Aratex territory. The ride to Deadman's Pass was marked by numerous horse droppings and wagon ruts. Just as they reached the entrance to the pass, there was a roar ahead, and the ground shook under the hooves of their borrowed war-horses. The shaking continued, and clouds of dust billowed from the pass. A terrible roar developed, making it worse.

"Earthquake and avalanche!" John Knight proclaimed. "Lord, if they're caught in that—"

"It's her!" Jon shrieked. "It's Melbah, up on Conjurer's Rock! She's doing it! She's causing the ground to shake!"

"You're crazy, Brother Wart!" Kelvin said, in his usual patient way with her. He was trying to control his mount's nervous jerking.

"Crazy, am I? Look, just look! On top of Conjurer's Rock! Up above the dust cloud, up above the pass! Look!"

Kelvin strained his eyes, and so did his brother and his father. From here Conjurer's Rock looked like a foreshortened tree stump rising above the dust and the pass. Could there be a little ant on the top of that stump, with outstretched arms? Jon seemed to think so. He had known that his sister possessed almost unnaturally clear eyesight, but seeing Melbah on top of Conjurer's Rock from this distance seemed impossible.

"You've got to *do* something!" Jon insisted. "You've got to, Kel! She'll kill all of them! She'll kill Lester!"

Do? What could he do? From this distance he couldn't even see Melbah, let alone stop her if she was indeed there.

"The Mouvar weapon," his father said. "Use it, Kelvin! Try shooting it at her!"

"It won't do any good," Kelvin said. Then, recognizing the desperation in his father's voice and his sister's face, he reached for it. Immediately he was jolted, almost lost his balance, and had to grab suddenly for the horse's mane. Jon, in an unlikely maneuver, joined him on the back of his war-horse. She had almost dislodged him!

"Hurry! Hurry!" she said urgently.

He got out the weapon. What should he do, just point it at the rock and pretend he could see something there? Should the weapon be elevated, as an impossibly powerful crossbow would have to be? Just what should he—

A tiny spark shone brightly against the top of the stump. It did not dim and go out, but immediately started swelling, moving like a flaming arrow.

"It's a fireball!" Jon shouted in his ear. "Stop it! Stop it now!"

As if he could! Yet all he could do was try.

The Mouvar weapon was pointed in the right direction. *Do your stuff, Gauntlets!*

Jon's hand was over his and the gauntlet. Her finger was over the gauntlet finger. The trigger squeezed in a quick, sure motion.

Bright light flashed, filling his eyes and head. WHOOMPTH! echoed and reechoed as before. The horse reared, and Kelvin and Jon slid together down the sloping back and ignominiously off the rump.

Thump! Oof! And the world spun around and about for what seemed far too long a time.

St. Helens watched the fireball as it receded from the face of the cliff. It grew larger as it flew, streaked with terrible brightness and destructive potential. The men at the pass would be cooked along with their horses, and only their charred bones would remain. This was a victory for Melbah so complete, so overwhelming, that never again would Aratex be invaded.

"Damn you, witch!" St. Helens muttered. It was an insignificant thing to do, hardly even a decent oath. Yet a bit of defiance, however futile, was better than silence. His flesh hurt where the tree branches pierced it, but the pain of his crucified form was as nothing compared with the agony of witnessing this total defeat of his side. This was, of course, why Melbah had let him live: so he could suffer more.

Suddenly, almost as if the fireball were responding to his curse, the fireball slowed. In fact, it hesitated. Melbah, on the cliff's edge, screamed at it. She leveled her arms, fingers extended, but to no avail. *The fireball was reversing course!*

Now it came roaring back in all its fury. It loomed monstrously large, throwing off sparks, hissing loudly, its heat blistering even as far as St. Helens. The foliage of the trees shriveled and twisted, and the sky seemed ablaze.

Melbah did not wait to embrace her creation. She raised her arms and flapped them wildly. The arms became wings, and her body had feathers, and she was climbing desperately skyward as only a frightened buzvul could.

The fireball changed direction. *It was following her!*

Melbah climbed higher. She zigged and zagged in the evasive action of a bird. But the fireball caught her, engulfed her, and devoured her in its flames. There wasn't any shriek, only a loud pop as the fireball and its contents disappeared.

Then, seemingly from the open sky, came a fall of feathers, burning as they fell. As they landed where the witch had been, they became bits of flesh and bone. The fragments continued to burn, steaming and blackening, losing all semblance of human or animal nature. Not even a skeleton, not even bones remained, only simple ash, spread across the edge of the rock.

St. Helens found that the tree branches had loosened. They were only misshapen trees now, no longer the magical henchmen they had been while the witch lived. Wincing from the pain, he pulled himself out of his trap. He activated his belt and flew over to the rock edge.

Still it was only ash. Had his curse done this? Was there something magical in his makeup? He did not believe that for a moment! After all, he cursed all the time, and it didn't even generate a haze, let alone incinerating fire. But certainly the witch was dead; that he had to believe.

He lowered himself to the rock's edge. He scattered Melbah's ashes and watched them fly away in the wind. She wasn't coming back! There were no buzvuls bothering him. He had won, or someone had won, though he couldn't figure out how.

He had to get down there in the pass and see if there was a magician among them. Somehow this thing had happened, catching him completely by surprise, not to mention Melbah! Someone there had to know.

He reactivated his belt, flew from the rock, and lowered himself down into the pass, where the carnage appeared even worse than it had from above. The witch had just about finished this army before sending the fireball!

He spotted Mor, bent over his son, and suffered a stab of

remorse. Was the boy dead? He paused and called out to Mor, getting his attention.

Mor's face lighted as he looked up. "You did it, St. Helens! You stopped her! You destroyed her for all of us!"

St. Helens decided against enlightening the man at the moment. "Lester—is he—?"

"Unconscious. Not hurt bad, I think. He's a Crumb. We Crumbs have hard heads."

"General Broughtner—is he alive?"

"He's checking the damage done back there," Mor said, indicating the way with a wave. "There's a lot of it. At least up this way."

"Thanks, Mor. I'll be back." He flew up the pass, seeing more and worse destruction the farther he went. Men were squashed by great rocks, and horses were half buried.

Finally he spotted the general straining with other men to lift the huge supply wagon off the shattered leg of a mercifully unconscious man. When the job was accomplished, St. Helens landed silently beside them. The general had the aspect of a thoroughly defeated man.

"The witch is dead, General," St. Helens said. "She was the main obstacle."

"Dead?" The man seemed reluctant to believe this.

"She sent a fireball, and it turned on her and destroyed her. It burned her to ashes. She is gone, dead by her own magic. Didn't any of you see it happen?"

"I saw the fireball," a man agreed. "I saw it turn—and then it winked out."

"When it burned up its creator," St. Helens said. "What are your plans, General?"

"Plans?" Broughtner looked around at the dead and dying. "You think I've got plans?"

No, St. Helens thought. Of course he didn't. His army was in sad straits, even without further molestation by the witch. It was a shame, because with Melbah gone, King Phillip should be vulnerable. There was that prophecy for a Roundear that was supposed to apply to Kelvin: uniting two.

Yes, damn it, if Phillip would just abdicate! That would complete the job.

St. Helens made up his mind in that moment. His hands played at the controls on the levitation belt.

"Don't give up hope, General. I have a plan." With that he rose vertically with the belt, angled his body and flight path past Conjurer's Rock, and took himself down the darkening sky to the palace of the boy king of Aratex. Once there, he entered the window he had left with Heln a lifetime ago.

The room appeared much as it had before, and with his careful surveillance and good luck, he believed he had not been spotted. As he looked around the room a horrible apparition was suddenly facing him. He grabbed for his sword, and the other did likewise in perfect synchronization. With a shock he realized that it was he himself, reflected in a mirror: battered and bruised, hair and beard unkempt, blood and dirt on his clothing and hands and face, and bits of leaf and bark from the trees he had been in.

He shuddered, wishing he could clean up. He had never been a really handsome man, and he wasn't young anymore, but this was ridiculous!

He tried the door and found it unlocked. The guards had not bothered to lock it after the prisoner had escaped. He started down the stairs. If the king was inside today, as he was nearly every other day . . .

He had made up his mind that what young Phillip needed was a hiding. That was what his own daddy had administered to him on occasion, and eventually it must have worked. Today he was what he was, and if he hadn't had the hidings, there was little question that he could have been worse. Yes, indeed, young King Phillip was going to get the hiding he had long promised himself to deliver.

"Where do you think you're going?"

It was Bemode, standing at the foot of the stairs, sword drawn.

Well, I've done it before, St. Helens thought, and drew his sword. Only this time he was weaker, more tired, and older in all respects. So it would be more difficult. He started down the stairs cautiously, hoping he could last.

"Bemode!" a shrill voice called out. His Majesty Himself strode from the playroom and stopped, standing there with red, swollen eyes, but with more than a hint of command in his voice.

"But, Your Majesty—"

"Please go outside, Bemode. Leave us alone. There are things we have to discuss."

Bemode looked from St. Helens to his nominal boss and back again. His piggish eyes drifted in confusion and he seemed to be trying to decide.

"That's a command, Bemode!"

The man sheathed his sword. St. Helens sheathed his. The man left. St. Helens was disgusted. John Knight, back in the old days of their unit, had never given a command twice, knowing it would be obeyed with alacrity the first time, whatever it might be. John Knight had been a real leader then. These undisciplined palace guards nauseated him.

"Now, St. Helens, friend, come with me."

St. Helens followed, wondering why. The king was acting as if this return were routine. Inside the toy room was much as it had been; toys were on the shelves, and there was a table set with a chessboard and chessmen St. Helens himself had made.

"One last game, friend," Phillip said, gesturing at the board. "One last, and I won't throw a tantrum if I don't win."

St. Helens brushed some sweat out of his eyes, trying hard to understand what was in the young king's head. "You kept it set up, just as when we played every night!"

"Yes. Melbah was no good as a player. So please, one last game, and then you can kill me as you plan."

"Kill you!" St. Helens exclaimed, genuinely astonished. "Kill you? Why?"

The boy's stricken face rose from its contemplation of the chessboard and the chairs. "She's dead, isn't she, St. Helens? Isn't that why you came here? You couldn't have, otherwise. Not alone. She was watching for you; she had magic telltales set. She would have captured you, tormented you, and then brought you back."

"You really think that I—with this sword you gave me—?"

The king lowered his eyes. "It is all I deserve or ever have deserved."

"Gods!" St. Helens said. There was just no beating the kid after this. He had been in effect checkmated—by a pupil who had learned his lessons better than the teacher.

Mor blinked in astonishment, and Lester gaped, as St. Helens dropped from the air with the young king on his back. He started to reach for his sword, but then stayed his hand. This was the king, after all, and St. Helens obviously had brought him in for a purpose.

"Lester, Mor, the fighting's over and there's no more Aratex. My son-in-law's prophecy is going to be fulfilled, with him or without him." *And how I wish he were here, alive and in good health! How I wish I had not tricked him, betrayed him, with all the arrogance and forethought of a Phillip. Maybe I was bewitched at the time, or at least out of my head. But no, I know St. Helens better than any man, and I know the responsibility is mine. What would I say to him now if I had the chance? What would I say?*

"Hello, St. Helens. I'm glad you managed to redeem yourself."

It was St. Helens' turn to blink. Four horsemen were there behind the fallen rocks. He was certain they hadn't been there when he had left.

They were: Jon Crumb, Lester's wife. John Knight, his old commander and Kelvin's father. Kian Knight, Kelvin's half brother. And the fourth was none other than Kelvin Knight Hackleberry, who had just spoken.

"Kelvin, can you—can you forgive me for what I have done to you?"

"Maybe, Father-in-law. Maybe when your grandchild is old enough to ask. Maybe then I'll forgive you for helping me fulfill the two words of prophecy."

"Grandchild? Heln?" He had been told before, but it was almost as if he were hearing the words for the first time. Recent events had almost banished the matter from his mind. The world whirled, and somehow it seemed quite natural that he crash-landed on his face with the young king on top of him. He lay there, quite moved but unmoving, as King Blastmore proclaimed the words they had agreed he should:

"As the sovereign ruler of the kingdom of Aratex, I solemnly proclaim Aratex's complete and unconditional surrender to the kingdom of Rud. With this I abdicate Aratex's throne, relinquish all claims, and beg the mercy and forgiveness of King Rufurt of Rud!"

Sweeter words, St. Helens thought happily, he would never live to hear.

Heln dreamed, and knew that she dreamed.

In her dream a beautiful young woman with long blond hair and deep blue eyes was undressing. With her was a man, a former queen's guardsman she had seen at the palace petitioning for a pension. The man, too, was undressing, his every motion evincing eagerness. In back of them stood a waiting bed.

Must I see this! Oh, must I! Heln thought.

Instantly she was outdoors, outside the cottage her dream-self had been in. There, coming toward the cottage door, a smile on his face that she somehow recognized as forced, was Kian, her husband's brother.

Oh, poor Kian! Poor Kian! she thought. Then she was awake, a sob choking her and taking her breath.

"Oh, poor Kian!" she said aloud to the empty room. "Poor

man! I feel so sorry for you, Kian! But there isn't anything I can do." For though she had seen it in a dream, she knew it was not; it was another aftereffect of the astral separations she had done before. She had seen the ugly truth.

Her life was happy now, but that wasn't enough. Sadder than she had been for a long time, Heln broke down and wept.

Epilogue

THEY WERE FINALLY GATHERED together again in Kelvin's house. The wars were over for the time being, and they could relax and be family and friends.

"Apparently it's antimagic," Mor was saying, looking at the Mouvar weapon Kelvin was showing them. "The way it took the fire back to the witch, and the way you say it stopped the flopears and the serpents in that other world."

"Yes," John Knight said. "I figured out that it turns the magic energy back, whatever it is, on the sender. Thus in the other frame the hypnotic freezing stare was returned, while here it was the witch's fireball. When the control knob got moved, it merely blocked the magic without returning it in kind. Thus the flopears remained a danger but could not paralyze with a glance. But once the knob was at its original setting, it returned the magic and the flopears paralyzed themselves."

"Hooray for here!" Jon said, lifting her second glass of razzlefruit wine with bright enthusiasm. "Hooray for making Kel use that weapon!"

Kelvin glared at her, deciding that his little sister should never, ever be allowed to touch wine. It was obvious to him that all she had done was interfere in what he and the gauntlet would have handled.

"Well, at least you were saved," Lester said, coming to Kelvin's rescue and taking the glass from her hand.

"Except that you did fall on your butt," Kelvin added, referring to the time she slid off the rear of the horse and he fell on top of her.

Jon glared at all of them until Heln rescued her in turn.

Heln, now rapidly approaching parturition and all that it implied, began reciting without the help of wine:

> "A Roundear there Shall Surely be
> Born to be Strong, Raised to be Free
> Fighting Dragons in his Youth
> Leading Armies, Nothing Loth
> Ridding his Country of a Sore
> Joining Two, then uniting Four . . .

"You've joined two, Kelvin," she pointed out. "Now that the citizenry of Aratex has voted to unite its country with that of Rud!"

"That means," said St. Helens, now permanently reunited with the group, "that the next task you face is uniting four. I suggest—"

Kelvin gave him a hostile look and St. Helens subsided, doubtlessly remembering. They had almost been to blows after Kelvin's timely arrival in Aratex. The tongue-lashing Kelvin had delivered on the spot in front of Aratex's young king was more than St. Helens had stood for since his basic training. Now the two were friends, or at least relatives. But Kelvin suspected, and St. Helens knew, that St. Helens felt he should have been given a governing position. Kelvin didn't believe in nepotism, particularly extended to in-laws, and the voices of the people were now being heard in the first of the infant country's elections. The new name for Aratex annexed to Rud was going to be Kelvinia, not Helenland, as St. Helens had unblushingly suggested.

Kian still looked sad, an entire month after their triumph in Aratex. Everyone noticed it, particularly Heln.

"Why so sad, Kian?" she finally asked.

Kian was not long in answering. "Lenore. Lenore Barley. I don't want to marry her. I want Lonny back in the other frame."

"I could have told you that, son," John Knight said gently.

"You could? Why didn't you?"

"I felt you'd need to find out yourself. Didn't you notice that almost all the look-alikes had characters opposite to their counterparts? King Rufurt, for instance, is mostly kind and gentle, but his counterpart was cruel and delighted in inflicting pain. Cheeky Jack was a contemptible bandit who sold mere boys and girls into slavery. Jack's counterpart is a heroic person, a genuine patriot, and one of the finest men I've met. What does that say to your inherited intelligence, son?"

Kian thought for a moment. Then his expression lightened as he faced the notion that he had somehow resisted before. "Lonny—she's opposite!"

"Right!"

"When I called on Lenore she was—" He choked, his face now red. "With someone. A man. An ugly man who had served the queen. It wasn't like Heln imprisoned in the Girl Mart and unable to help herself. She—she wanted him. He challenged me to a fight. She laughed, clapping her hands as if delighted. I walked away, the first time I ever walked away from such a challenge. I didn't want to give her the satisfaction. I—"

"And what does this say about the nature of your mother?"

John Knight spoke with dignity and sadness. "Think back. Her counterpart was as different from her as Lonny is from Lenore."

Kian's face clouded. This was the source of his reluctance to accept the situation. "She's my mother. She's—"

"Probably dead," John said. He said it matter-of-factly, having come to terms with this in his own time. "Remember, I thought her everything the queen in the other frame is, and she wasn't."

Kian wiped at a tear. "I guess I have to accept."

"You'd better, Kian. There is no real choice. You loved what you felt should be there, just as I did."

"Lonny—"

"People have some choice whether to be good or bad," St. Helens said, breaking in. "Phillip had no choice, but if I had had his upbringing, I might have been as bad. Now he's got a chance to be good, and he's going to be, making chessmen and chessboards with me and having tournaments. You know, the boy has a real talent for chess. Right now, except for me, I'd say he's this world's champion."

"But only two of you play that silly game in this world!" Jon retorted. Everyone laughed.

"No, I know how to play, too," John Knight said, ignoring St. Helens. "You'll have to go back to get her or to stay with her. You haven't any choice. It's like Kelvin and the prophecy: no choice for either of you."

"No choice," Kian agreed. He stood up from the table, a determined and happy look on his face. "I'm going back! To live there or to bring her back!"

"And I'm going with you," John said, also rising. "There's no way I'll miss attending my older son's wedding."

Kian paused, looking at him. "You know, Queen Zanaan's a widow now, technically, and—"

"And it remains awkward for me in Rud, where I'm supposed to be dead. Charlain—"

"Is married to a good man," Kian agreed. "I don't think she'd mind if you—"

"That was my thought," John Knight agreed. "I think I need a wife as much as you do, and you need a mother again."

The two exchanged glances, understanding perfectly.

St. Helens, wineglass in hand, flush on nose, lurched to his feet and, unasked, led everyone in a rousing cheer. "And don't come back!" he bawled as the two departed. There had been a time when that would have been an insult.

Kelvin looked at Heln, and then at Lester and Jon. They nodded. It was the best way to lose a father or a brother.

It was a great, fine time in Kelvinia.